CHARLES ROSENBERG

DEATH
on a
High
Floor

A Legal Thriller

Sliding Hill Press

Credits:
Just a Girl, Lyrics by Gwen Stefani and Thomas Dumont. Copyright 1995.

ISBN: 0615492398
ISBN-13: 9780615492391

For my mother and father, Ruth and Joe, who taught me to write, and for my wife, Sally Anne, the true **über** editor of this work.

CHAPTER 1

—

Iam a lifer. Came here at twenty-four in seventy-four. So that's sixty years on the planet, thirty-six years here. Of course, it's not like being a lifer at, say, Wal-Mart. Last year I made six hundred fifty thousand dollars. Not a lot these days by some standards, I know. Not a million or more, like some of my more ambitious colleagues with a weekend place in Santa Barbara and two kids at Yale. But then again, I don't work all that hard. I billed maybe eighteen hundred hours last year. Nothing like what they make the kids do these days. Twenty-two hundred hours required, twenty-five hundred for a real shot at partner.

After thirty-six years, you know a place. You know who drinks too much. You know who screws too much. You know who hates too much. You even mostly know who it is they hate. So it didn't immediately strike me as surprising that someone had buried a knife between Simon Rafer's shoulder blades. There were a lot of people with motive enough. Simon, at forty-eight, is—well, was—the firm's biggest business getter, and he had been on the warpath, clearing out dead wood, as he called the poor schmucks. Guys who'd been here, some of them, twenty, even thirty years. Nice people, good lawyers, but not the kind of folks who could rope in a Fortune 500 company.

"Old Mules," he had labeled them at one Executive Committee meeting. Lowering our profits per partner. Not people who were going to move the firm ahead. Whatever that meant. Two thousand lawyers in twelve countries, instead of a mere thousand in six, like now?

A lot of associates with a motive, too. Simon was a screamer. I'd heard him screaming at them. Even at Jenna. Simon could make or break your shot at partner.

I wish I had not been the one to find him. God's punishment for getting in at 6:00 a.m. every day, I guess. Usually, no one else is on the eighty-fifth floor when I get in. Usually, it is dark. Usually, the big double doors into reception are locked. Usually, there are no bodies face down on the floor.

I shouldn't have touched him I know. Maybe I wanted to see if he was really dead. He was. Cold as ice. But then it had been a cold night, even for Los Angeles in December, and the firm's energy task force had decreed that the heat would go off at eleven each night, no matter what.

I called 911 on my cell phone and they came. First the cops, three of them. Then the coroner, four of them. Then two more cops. Then the crime scene guys, five of them. So by 7:00 a.m. there were fourteen of them, one of me, and Simon.

A few minutes after seven, the early bird lawyers started stepping smartly off the elevator, Starbucks in hand, ready for the day. Taken aback. Barred from entering by the yellow tape across the doors. Cops telling them to leave. Most staying.

Who wouldn't? Who wouldn't want to get on a Blackberry and tell the other nine hundred ninety-nine lawyers, scattered across four continents, that they had personally seen that consummate asshole Simon Rafer face down in his own blood with an ornate dagger buried to its hilt in his back? Not to mention the nice touch that all the blood had nearly obliterated the special weave that had—at a cost of God knew how much— emblazoned MARBURY MARFAN in a deep red across the width of the cream carpet. The whole thing would no doubt have to be replaced.

I didn't see Jenna get off the elevator, but suddenly she was beside me. Despite our almost thirty year age difference, we have a joshing relationship.

"Did you have to ruin the carpet, Jenna?"

"Robert, I had every good reason to off him, but I would have put the knife very precisely lower down."

"You're not sad he's dead, then?"

"Are you sure he's dead?"

"I touched him. He's ice cold."

"You found him?"

"Yeah."

"So you're a suspect."

"Guess so. Technically, anyway."

"Well, I'm not. And I'm out of here. I can work at home." With that, she turned crisply on her little black Mary Janes and was gone.

A guy in a baggy suit stepped up and flashed his badge at me. I had only seen that in the movies. Never been personally flashed before.

"Are you the guy who found him?"

"Yes, I am."

"You're Robert Tarza?"

"Yes."

"You're a partner here?"

"Yes."

"I'm Detective Spritz. Homicide. Is there somewhere we can talk?"

"My office would work. But we'd have to cross the yellow tape."

"Can't do that."

"Okay, let's use the conference room on eighty-four."

Spritz followed me down the elevator and into the main conference room on eighty-four. It used to be called 84-A, but the year before the firm had given all of its conference rooms names. There was even a naming contest and a formal Naming Committee. Big law firms have lots of mindless committees designed to make the people on them feel important. I submitted *Cochise* for this one, since so many of my fellow litigators like to think of themselves as members of the warrior class. But *Cochise* wasn't picked. 84-A is now called *da Vinci*.

Da Vinci was designed to impress. Its floor-to-ceiling windows look northwest into the hills, with the Pacific as distant backdrop. The decor is understated Italian contemporary, although what that look has to do with Leonardo is beyond me.

I sat down on the side of the table that faces away from the windows, so that Spritz would have to face the view. I did it on purpose.

Although I had of late come to feel much more like a tenant farmer at Marbury Marfan than a true partner-owner of the place, thirty-six years at the firm had not left me immune to the nuances of status. Making the other person face the view leaves them to admire the wealth and power that can afford to have the view. Particularly someone like Spritz. Perhaps I imagined it, but he seemed a tad ill at ease. I didn't think he was accustomed to investigating the murders of managing partners at elite international law firms.

Spritz took out a notebook. "Mind if I take some notes?"

"Not at all, Detective."

"I gather that the deceased was a rather big cheese around here."

"He was the managing partner of the firm."

"What does that mean, exactly, Mr. Tarza?"

"Hmm. Well, it means he was the biggest cheese. Sort of the CEO of the firm. But without the kind of power a CEO has. For the most part, a managing partner can't tell people what to do. He can only punish them if they don't do it."

"Punish them?"

"Yeah, like cut their compensation. Or redo the floor their office is on, so they have to go live in a temporary closet for a year. Or discover that they are the perfect candidate to open the firm's new office in Bangladesh. That kind of thing."

"Did Mr. Rafer have any enemies that you know of?"

"No." Now some might think that I lied about that. But after years of advising clients to answer questions asked in depositions literally, I can honestly say that Spritz asked the wrong question. Simon had no announced enemies that I knew of. Just a lot of people with a potential motive to kill him. I thought to myself that I could teach Spritz a thing or two about how to ask questions.

"Was there anyone with a potential motive to kill him?"

Shit. "Hundreds of people, really. Every lawyer whose compensation got cut last year. Every associate who didn't make partner last year because Simon dinged them. Every mail-room clerk he screamed at. The list is endless, Detective."

"Want to name the top five on the endless list?"

I hesitated. It was tempting. It was easy to think of five people whose day I would have liked to ruin.

"No."

"You paused, sir. Does your 'no' mean can't or won't?"

"Can't. I really don't have a clue who did it."

"Would you be in the top five yourself, Mr. Tarza?"

"You always suspect the one who found him?"

"Yes."

"I doubt I'm a candidate. You see, Detective, I got to Marbury Marfan before Simon Rafer. In fact, I hired him when I was a young partner. Just before his graduation from Stanford. But mean as this place is, there is a certain well, call it an ethic, that the young don't mess with those who brung 'em, even years later. So however unproductive I might be, Simon never messed with me. I have no motive."

"Unproductive?"

"Let's just say that I am not the picture of what everyone is looking for these days in a senior partner. I pay my way, but I don't make rain."

"What about Mr. Marbury and Mr. Marfan? Would they have a motive?"

I laughed out loud. I couldn't help it. "Marbury and Marfan have been dead for almost a hundred years."

"I knew that. It was a joke."

I didn't think it was a joke, but it didn't seem wise to press the matter. "Of course, Detective. I knew you knew. Who in this town doesn't? Anyway, is there more you need from me? I have some work I need to get done."

"There is something more. We'll need to take your suit jacket, tie and shirt. Just to make sure they don't have blood on them. We don't want to end up looking like those idiots in the O. J. Simpson investigation." He seemed to be staring at the right-hand sleeve of my suit jacket.

I followed his gaze. There, just at the cuff line, was a dark brownish-red spot, about the size of a postage stamp. It was easily visible against the blue fabric.

"I touched him," I said. "To see if he was dead."

"Uh huh." He said it in a short explosion of breath through the lips, somewhere between a grunt and sigh. I took it to mean he didn't believe me.

"No, really. It must have come from my touching him."

"Sure, sure," Spritz said.

"Okay," I said, trying to keep my aplomb from thudding to the floor. "You can have the shirt, tie and jacket. I've got spares in my office."

"I'm afraid we've got your office taped off. The criminalists have to swab it down. Same reason. You won't have access till tonight."

"So I have to go home in my undershirt?"

"No, we'll give you a windbreaker."

So much for the view and the power. Half an hour later, I was on my way down the elevator wearing sharply creased, pin-striped suit pants, black shoes and a pink windbreaker that said DUNKIN DONUTS on it. I made a mental note to ask Spritz someday if it was SOP or just getting even for, let's face it, my snotty non-cooperation.

On the way down the elevator, it really hit me. Simon Rafer was dead. Not by heart attack or car accident, or other things that sometimes befall forty-eight-year-old men. But by murder. By a dagger in his back.

It also hit me that I was a suspect. A serious one, maybe. After all, I found him, I had no alibi, and I apparently had blood on my sleeve. Although I couldn't fathom what anyone would think my motive might be. By the time the elevator reached bottom, the Starbucks in the lobby looked like a very good idea, even in my pink windbreaker outfit. The particular very good idea I had in mind was not just coffee, but a fat-filled muffin.

I hadn't really counted on the Jenna muffin being there. She was sitting on one of the high stools by the window, nice legs nicely crossed, adding sugar to her coffee. I had been calling her the Jenna muffin since I recruited her from Harvard six years earlier. Sometimes I even called her Jenna muffin to her face. It had become part of the banter of our friendship. A friendship that the difference in our ages had made easier. I had no designs on her, and she had none on me.

She hadn't seen me come in. I slipped onto the stool next to her and struggled to reacquire my usual cool demeanor, so thoroughly undone in da Vinci. "So, Miss Muffin, got a list of the top five suspects?" She didn't turn, but continued staring into her coffee cup. She registered no surprise that I was there. "Well, I hate to say it, Robert, but you'd be at the very top of my list."

I hadn't expected to be anywhere at all on anyone's list. "Me? Why?"

She looked up from her cup. "Do you remember what you told me that first day I interviewed at M&M, when you met me for breakfast to orient the day?"

"Not really."

"You told me I would have a great day, but to watch out for, as I recall your exact words, 'that asshole Simon Rafer, whose only interest in life is to become managing partner of this firm, and if he has to do it over your dead body, or anyone else's, he will.' So even then you thought he was a total jerk."

"That was right after I stopped liking him," I said.

"Yeah, I know you were friends before that," she said. She paused, as if thinking about what to say next, then continued. "After he became managing partner, as you've told me over way too many martinis, he hurt a lot of people you think of as your friends. And you're loyal, Robert. Despite your snotty aloofness, you're loyal to your friends, and I can imagine you killing Rafer for what he's done to some of them."

"Shit, Jenna, that stuff goes on in every mega firm on the planet. It's hardly a motive for murder."

She said nothing. I felt suddenly, sinkingly defensive. "I didn't do it," I said.

I paused and waited. Still, she said nothing.

"You do believe me, don't you, Jen?"

She looked up at me and tilted her head in that funny little way of hers. "Oh, I believe you. But remember all those people milling in reception, right before that guy in the baggy suit took you away?"

"His name is Spritz. Detective Spritz."

"Whatever. After he took you away, the buzz was that you did it."

"Cut it out, Jenna. This isn't funny."

"I'm just telling you what they were saying." She paused and stared again into her coffee cup. "Well, to be honest, they said more than that."

"Like what?"

"I heard a cop say, 'We've nailed him.'"

I had a feeling in the pit of my stomach I hadn't had since I stood up to say "ready" at my first trial. There is something gut-twisting about coming to work in the morning, ready for a bright, shiny productive day and ending up, a couple hours later, sitting on a stool in a Starbucks, discussing why people think you killed someone you didn't.

I tried to make light of it. "Well, Detective Spritz must share their suspicions about me, I guess. That's why I'm wearing this stupid pink thing. Spritz was nice enough to give it to me after he took my suit jacket and shirt to check them for more blood."

"More blood?"

"I got blood on my sleeve when I touched him."

"That's not a great fact."

"I guess not."

"Well, why didn't you just go back to your office and change out of that thing?"

"We were in da Vinci. My office was taped off."

There was a small silence. "Earth to Jenna."

"I'm thinking whether I should tell you something. Something to do with da Vinci."

"What?"

"Da Vinci is where I had my first tryst with Simon."

Now the small silence was on my side.

"Are you telling me you did it with Simon?"

"My generation would say *fucked him* Robert. But yes, I'm telling you I *did it* with Simon. If he weren't dead, I wouldn't have told you. Ever." She looked at me directly. "Are you shocked?"

Shocked wasn't exactly the word for it. Try bowled over. Sickened, really. An image conjured itself for me.

"Want me to be blunt, Jenna?"

"Yes. Friends can be blunt with friends."

"It's hard to picture that shit on top of you on that table."

"I was the one on top."

In some ways, discovering that Jenna had, to use her own word, fucked Simon Rafer, was more shocking than discovering Simon with a dagger in his back. Or maybe more upsetting. More something. I could not fathom why someone as classy as Jenna would have sex with a slime like Simon. She didn't need to do it to become a partner. She was already a star. I said the only thing I could think of. "Why?"

"Cause I *like* to be on top."

"Shit. You know what I meant. I meant why did you *do* it."

"I've thought about that a lot. I don't know exactly. I think I did it for the standard male reason—conquest. You're from a different generation, Robert. Girls have changed. Sometimes we just want to notch our belts. Like the boys in your coin club."

"That club is defunct."

"You know what I'm talking about."

"I don't, really, Jenna. In fact, I don't know why we're even talking about this. He's dead. What you did with him, on top or on the bottom or on the side, is your business. I'll keep it to myself."

"Maybe I shouldn't have told you."

"Maybe you shouldn't have."

"I needed to tell someone."

"I can see that," I said.

"Okay."

An intense need to get out of there washed over me.

"Jenna?"

"Yes?"

"I need to go." And with that I slipped off the stool and walked out.

CHAPTER 2

————

After I left Starbucks, I decided to do the only sensible thing for a man suspected of murder. Go home. I assured myself that once I got there, I'd sit down, regain my composure, make a few calls, and get the whole thing sorted out.

I did not drive home in my own car, however. When I took the elevator down to Level B, I found that the police had cordoned off my car with more yellow tape and posted a guard. A woman cop with a bright smile and a large gun on her hip. She didn't say anything, but she didn't need to.

Taking a cab was an option, but I've never taken a cab in L.A. Only tourists take cabs in L.A. I was saved from that fate by Stewart Broder, whose car was parked just down the row from mine.

"*Need* a lift, Bob?" he asked.

Stewart had persisted in calling me Bob for thirty-six years, ever since we entered the firm together as first-year associates. He knew I loathed it. I had never been a Bob, not even when I was in first grade. It didn't fit. But this didn't seem to be the right time to make objection.

"Can you take me home, Stewart?"

"Sure. Get *in*."

Stewart drove a red Ferrari. He looked stupid in it. He was overweight, bald, and had never been handsome, even in his thin, hirsute youth. He also had terrible skin—adult acne. In the last year or so he'd been making it even worse by trying to cover it up with heavy makeup, which looked even more gooped on than usual.

I doubted that even the Ferrari helped him pick up girls, which is, after all, why most sixty-year-old guys own cars like that. Not that any girl in her right mind would have stayed in the car with him for more than one turn around the block. He drove like shit. Crazy fast with no skill.

Which is exactly how we left the garage. Crazy fast up the ramps, screech of rubber on the final exit. I hunkered down in my seat and hoped we wouldn't be rubbed out by a passing truck. Then I waited for the questions to start.

"Is it true you *found* him?"

"Yeah."

"What'd he look *like*?"

"Like he was dead."

"Come on, Bob, *you* can trust me."

"Stop calling me Bob."

"Okay, okay. *Robert,* what'd he *look* like?"

"Dagger between the shoulder blades, lots of pooled blood."

"Just *like* in a murder mystery."

"I guess. But the angle of the blade was wrong."

"Meaning?"

"Meaning it looked plunged in sideways. In murder mysteries the blade is always straight up and down in the back."

There was a pause. "It is? Doesn't it depend on how *tall* the killer is or how the victim is *standing*, or something like that?"

"I don't know, Stewart. It just seemed odd to me."

"Okay. But what did you *see.*" Stewart has an odd and irritating habit of stressing random words. I remember noticing it the first day I met him, when he asked where I had *gone* to law school. I told him I had *gone* to law school at Harvard. Where had he *gone*? Yale he said. I remembered thinking that he looked like the kind of person who would go to Yale.

I was beginning to drift in my own head. I had not answered Stewart's question.

He tried again. "What did you *see*?"

"Stewart, I don't know. He was dead, all right? Dead in a pool of blood with a knife in his back. Is that why you were hanging around the garage, so you could ask me what I *saw*?" To my surprise, I was getting angry. Which I knew was unfair. Who wouldn't be curious to know the details of such a thing?

We drove on in silence.

The image of what I had seen had begun to beat around inside my skull. Ugly death. I was having difficulty with it. It was surprising. I am famous for calm and collected.

Stewart had turned on the radio. KFRG, the country station in San Bernardino. Hard core twang. I like country. I turned it off.

"Why did you *turn* it off?"

"I don't know. I need quiet, I guess."

"Okay."

We drove on in more silence. Almost forty-five minutes more, all the way from downtown to my house in the canyon.

When we pulled into my driveway, I just sat there without moving. Stewart came around and opened the door.

"You don't look *so* good. Do you want me to come in?"

"No."

"Are *you* sure?"

"I'll be okay. It's just beginning to hit me."

"Are you *sure?*"

"Yes!" I just wanted him gone, and I wanted inside. I managed the polite exit. "But thank you, Stewart. I really appreciate the ride."

"I figured you needed a *friend* today."

We hadn't truly been friends in many years. But it didn't seem the thing to say right then. "I know, Stewart. But I'll be fine, really."

I got out of the car and walked up the stone walkway to my front door, maybe fifty feet in all. My legs felt rubbery. I could feel Stewart watching me. I took out my keys and noticed my hand shaking. I managed to get the key in the lock, open the door, walk inside, and sit down in the big leather chair by the window. I heard him drive off.

I am not sure how long I sat in the chair. For a while I just looked at the profusion of trees through the big windows. Mock orange trees on my side of the canyon, tall eucalyptus on the steep slope across the way. I thought about the body. I thought about the fact that Detective Spritz must think I did it. I tried to imagine what they could possibly have found that nailed me. It couldn't be the blood on my sleeve. That was obviously there just from finding the body. Maybe Jenna didn't hear it right.

The ringing of the phone roused me. It was Jenna.

"Can I come over?"

"I thought you were still at Starbucks."

"No, I went home."

"Come over if you want."

"Be right there."

I stumbled to the bathroom and threw up. A long, wrenching, gagging throw-up that left that awful smell in my nose. I cleaned myself up as best I could and went back to my leather chair. Jenna arrived maybe ten minutes later. She walked in without knocking. Which was something she had never done before. I had apparently left the front door wide open.

"You don't look so good, Robert."

"I am having trouble with all of this."

"Trouble with the fact he's dead or the fact you're a suspect?"

"Both."

"I don't think I've ever seen you like this before."

"I never came upon someone murdered before."

"Do you want a drink?"

"I don't drink." That wasn't really true of course. My drinking had, over the last year or two, simply faded away. I only drank socially now, and then only a little. But there still was a lot of liquor around. It's the one food that doesn't rot.

Jenna went over to the cabinet where I kept the booze, an old wooden sideboard that had belonged to my great-grandmother. I think she brought it from Kansas in 1903. Or maybe she just bought it at a secondhand store. My mother never seemed sure. Anyway, I guess Jenna knew where the stuff was because she'd been there for six years of summer clerk parties. I'd had a lot of them. A big old country-style house in a canyon is a nice place to do that kind of thing, even if the house is really only faux old.

She handed me a rather large glass. "Here's some Jack Daniels. Bourbon will do you good."

"Jack Daniels isn't a bourbon, Jenna. It's a sour mash."

"Hey, that's more like your old self. Full of snotty information."

I drank the whole thing down in a swallow. "Leave me alone, Jenna."

"After you left Starbucks, the cops came in. I heard them talking some more."

"And?"

"They are *sure* you did it. Blood on your shirt cuff, like you said. For some reason, they don't buy that you got it from touching him. Plus they kept talking about "the other thing." The thing that nails you. But they never said what it is. I overheard one of them say something about a vator. But I don't know what a vator is. Some kind of test maybe? Do you know?"

The warm bourbon going down had been helping but suddenly it wasn't helping anymore. I wanted to answer her, but I couldn't. I had no clue what kind of test a vator was. More important, I couldn't really even think.

Jenna came over and sat on the arm of the chair. She put her hand on my shoulder. Yesterday, I would have thought it was a come-on. Today it just felt nice. And needed. "Robert, you need a lawyer."

"I am a lawyer."

"Very funny. You know what I mean. You need a criminal defense lawyer. You are not one of those." She paused. "You're shaking. I'm going to call your doctor."

"Doctors don't make house calls."

The rest is a blur for me. John Donald, M.D., actually came to my house, for the first time ever. I recall him injecting something into my arm, and I recall wondering if it would put me to sleep. That's it.

CHAPTER 3

———

When I woke up, it was morning, early. I was in my bed, under the white duvet, naked. The smell of bacon and coffee was coming from the kitchen. I felt good. A bit groggy, but good. Then I remembered. Simon was dead. I was a suspect. And, oh yeah, Jenna was Simon's lover. Maybe it was all a bad dream.

Jenna stuck her head in the bedroom door. She was wearing black jeans and a white T-shirt that said LAWYER in red letters. "Good morning. You look much better."

"Is it the next day?"

"It is. You slept more than eighteen hours. Some of it drug induced, I might add. Dr. Donald thought it would improve things. You know, 'Sleep that knits up the raveled sleeve of care' and all that."

I was feeling word-grounded again. "Shakespeare didn't have drugs in mind when he wrote that."

She laughed. "Only because he didn't know about drugs. Well, other than alcohol. Anyway, you taught me those lines."

"I did?"

"Yes. You don't remember?"

"No, I don't."

"It was when you interviewed me at Harvard. I had been up all night, studying. I must have looked sleep deprived. I said something about needing a good night's sleep. You quoted that to me."

"Jenna, you hadn't been up all night studying. You had been up all night fucking, to use your term for it."

"The morning seems to have brought your old self back. Which is good, Robert. You're going to need your old, snotty self to get through this."

"I didn't do it."

"I'm sure you didn't. There are dozens of people at M&M with better motives than you."

"I don't have any motive."

She just smiled. "Robert, some people might think you did. But we can talk about that after you formally ask me to be your lawyer in this."

"You?"

"Yes, me."

"You don't know shit about criminal law."

"I don't. But I'm a very fast study. And I do know a lot about you, sir. Maybe more than you realize. We've never been sexually intimate, but we've been intimate on a lot of other levels. I know you well enough to help you a lot. Help you to . . . what's that old phrase? Oh, yeah, 'Keep your head about you.' We can hire some crim-head to front the thing."

"Jenna, I don't think I need a lawyer. Once the cops really get into this, it will blow over. In the meantime, I can just lie low."

"Well, when you get out of bed and go look out your front door, you may feel differently about it."

"What's outside my front door?"

"A couple of reporters. But you should check it out for yourself."

"Okay, I will."

"Oh, and you might also want to know that Simon's murder is the right-hand lead in today's *L.A. Times*. You're mentioned."

"Mentioned how?"

"I think it would be better if you read it yourself."

I needed to see what Jenna was talking about. I started to swing my feet over the edge of the bed when I remembered I was naked. Jenna was still looking at me, with a smile on her face. I slid my feet back under the duvet.

"Jenna, how did I get to be naked?"

"Your doctor undressed you and put you in bed."

"Somehow, I don't believe you. But let's not go there." She continued to smile, but she hadn't budged. Was she planning to just stand there like that, while I got out of bed, buck naked? I tried to recapture my dignity.

"Jenna, please leave. I need to get dressed." As I listened to my voice echo inside my own head, it didn't sound all that authoritative really. But it seemed to work. Jenna flashed me one more smile that was somewhere between a dazzle and a smirk, turned and left.

I got out of bed, walked into the master bath, and turned on the shower. The newspaper could wait.

The shower stall was oversized, resplendent in turquoise tile with a motif of leaping dolphins. I'd had it built to mimic one I'd seen in some palazzo in Sicily. Stupid, really. I got in and the water flowed out on me in its usual thin, unsatisfying stream. I do hate low-flow showerheads. I've thought about sneaking in a real showerhead from some water-flush place like Ohio. Still, the hot water felt terrific. Showers invigorate you. Every man feels like a king in his shower.

As I soaped up, I began to think about the whole dumb thing. Why should I give a shit that some asshole detective thought I killed Simon? I didn't. Why did I give a shit that there were a couple reporters outside my door? Didn't. Why did I give a shit what the *L.A. Times* thought? Didn't care about that, either. Anyway, the *Times* was now owned by people in Chicago.

I emerged from the shower determined just to ignore the whole thing. It would blow over.

I dried off, padded over to the walk-in closet in the bedroom and stopped dead in my tracks. It was Tuesday. A business day. Every business day for the last thirty-six years, unless I was on vacation or sick, I had showered, walked to that closet, taken fresh underwear from the wooden drawers to the side, unhooked a nice blue pinstripe suit from the rack, picked out a crisp white shirt, selected whatever color tie was *de rigueur* that year, put it all on and gone off to work. It was a uniform that made me feel like I was officially part of a big important world, all governed from the tops of tall buildings.

Now it was a business Tuesday and I wasn't sure whether it was going to be a business day or something else. Screw it. I was going to make it a business day like any other. I was going to have some coffee and go to work. I got dressed. Maroon tie.

When I got to the kitchen, Jenna was sitting at the small round table in the breakfast nook, reading the newspaper. I stood in the doorway and looked at her. She seemed not to notice I was there. She was wearing a different T-shirt than an hour earlier. This one said MARBURY MARFAN SOFTBALL.

"You changed your T-shirt."

She still didn't look up. "Yeah. I went home while Dr. Donald was here last night. Brought some stuff back and moved it into one of the spare bedrooms. The one that looks out over the fishpond."

"You moved in? Just like that?"

"Yeah, just like that."

"For how long?"

"Just for a few days."

I was feeling jocular. "Will the Jenna-muffin cook and clean, too?"

"The Jenna-muffin's already cooked for you. Sit down and have some eggs. When you're done, we need to talk seriously. Because you are seriously in a lot of trouble."

I took up her invitation and sat down at the table, but I wasn't inclined to talk seriously about anything. The shower high was still with me. "Look, Jenna. I didn't kill him. I don't know who did kill him. And I hate to say it, but I don't really care who killed him. I'm going to finish these eggs, walk out that door, get in my car, and go to work. I thank you for making the eggs."

Jenna just looked at me for a moment and then went back to reading the paper, which she had folded to an inner page. We ate our respective eggs in silence. Part of me wanted to reach over, grab the paper from her, and see exactly what was in it. The other part of me desperately craved a perfectly normal Tuesday, and I had the sense that looking at the newspaper would not be helpful to that desire. So I just finished my eggs. It was going to be a perfectly normal Tuesday. I was going to insist on it.

I got up from the table and walked to the front door, ready to go to work. Then I opened the door. I have trouble even now describing what was out there. The word "blob" comes to mind. A large, pulsing blob of boom microphones, TV cameras and at least a dozen reporters screaming questions and leaping at me like I was prey.

I shut the door.

When I turned back around, Jenna was standing there, in the doorway between the kitchen and the living room, sipping a cup of coffee. "Still going to work?"

"Maybe not." Normal Tuesday had vanished.

"Just as well. Your car's still in the garage downtown, remember? Surrounded by yellow tape? And even if it were here, it would be in the garage, not out front."

I continued to stand there, facing her, my back to the front door, frozen in place. I felt like an idiot.

Finally, Jenna spoke. "So *now* do you want to see the *L.A. Times?*"

"I guess."

"It's in the kitchen."

CHAPTER 4

———

When I got back to the kitchen, the paper was lying in the middle of the table, headline up. I saw instantly what Jenna meant for me to see—the right-hand lead: *Prominent Lawyer Stabbed to Death*.

Below it was a color picture of Simon Rafer, dead on the carpet, with the dagger in his back.

"How did they get that picture?"

"Cell phone camera. One of the people who stepped off the elevator probably snapped it, sold it to the *Times*."

"Who?"

"No clue. Check it out below the fold, too."

I flipped the paper over. There was my own picture, pink windbreaker and all. I leaned closer and read the first few sentences of the article:

Police confirm that Robert Tarza is a person of interest in the stabbing death of Simon Rafer. Rafer was the socially prominent managing partner of powerhouse law firm Marbury Marfan and was honorary chairman of the Los Angeles Opera. Tarza is a senior partner in the same firm.

I collapsed into a chair. "Oh my God."

Jenna said nothing.

"I need coffee," I said.

Jenna walked over to the coffee pot, poured the coffee, and brought it back to me. I raised the cup toward my lips, but couldn't quite get it there.

"Robert, your hand is shaking."

"I'm sorry."

"Do you want me to call Dr. Donald?"

"No. I'll be okay. And I'm really sorry."

"Well don't be sorry. It's normal in this kind of situation."

"This kind of situation isn't normal for me."

"I know."

My hand started to shake even more violently. I tried to set the cup down without spilling. It didn't work, and a large amount of coffee slopped onto the table.

Jenna gazed at me across the table. A look that was somehow part caring and part cold appraisal. "Robert, do you get it now? The trouble you're in?"

"Yes. But I still think it will be straightened out."

She got up, took a sponge from the counter, and started to sop up the spilled coffee. "If they discover your possible motive, it's not going to straighten out."

"I don't have a motive."

My denial had come out in a croak, even though my brain had instructed my mouth to say it firmly.

"Why don't we go sit in the living room and talk this through?" Jenna said.

"Okay." Talking the whole thing through with her seemed like a good idea. She was, as I had told the Associate Evaluation Committee only a month ago, on her way to being a great lawyer, even though she'd been practicing for only seven years.

Jenna was already moving toward the conversation pit. A big design feature in the seventies, when my house was built, it's a semicircle of couches built-in over red tile, the whole thing a step down from the main floor, facing a white brick fireplace. Ugly and dated, but a good place to talk. Jenna sat down on one of the couches, and I placed myself carefully upright on the one across from her. I stuck my right hand under my thigh in hopes it would stop shaking.

Jenna looked more serious than I had ever seen her look.

"When I mentioned motive just now," she said, "I said *possible* motive."

"I don't have any kind of motive."

"I think you might."

"Like what?"

She scrunched her fingers into the pocket of her jeans, took out a tarnished silver coin about the size of a dime, and held it up between thumb and forefinger. "Like this one. Here, catch!" She tossed the coin to me. Overhand.

I managed, barely, to jerk my hand out in time to snatch it out of the air. It was a close call.

"Jesus, Jenna. I could have dropped it."

"Well, it's already lasted since before Jesus. I didn't think a quick three-foot toss would bother it all that much."

"They crystallize inside. It could have shattered if it had hit the floor."

I still couldn't believe that she had shown such . . . disrespect. I placed the coin ever-so-gently on top of a copy of *The New Yorker*, which was sitting on the table.

"Your hand has stopped shaking," she said.

I ignored the comment. "Where did you get it?"

"At Simon's condo, yesterday morning. After I left Starbucks."

"It's incredibly valuable. Precious, really. It should be stored in an archival coin envelope, not sitting out on a table, naked."

"Maybe so," she said. "But when I picked it up, that's where it was. Sitting out on a table. Simon's kitchen table, to be exact."

"You must be kidding."

"No."

"Simon left it out on a table?"

"I don't know who left it there," she said. "But that's where it was."

I shrugged. "Well, he bought it, so I guess he could do whatever he wanted with it."

"How much did he pay you for it?"

I hesitated. "Five hundred thousand dollars."

Her eyebrows went up. "Jeez, I had no idea." She seemed genuinely shocked.

I was staring at the coin. I couldn't stand to see it sitting there, unprotected. I pictured it somehow sliding off the *The New Yorker* and shattering on the floor.

"Excuse me a moment." I got up, went back to my study, and returned with a small, transparent vinyl coin flip. I picked the coin up off the table and placed it in the flip, which is about two inches square.

Jenna just watched.

"Jenna, do you understand what this coin is?"

"Sure," she said. "Simon was like a small kid when he first got it. Couldn't stop talking about it and showing it off. I must have heard its little history twenty times: 'The Ides denarius. Minted by Brutus in 42 B.C. to commemorate his assassination of Caesar. Double daggers and the Latin words Ides of March on the back. Most famous coin of the ancient world,' blah blah."

She smiled at the "blah blah." It was a phrase she had picked up from me.

"Why did you take it?" I asked.

"So you could say you were in the process of unwinding the deal."

"Why would I have wanted to unwind the deal?"

"To avoid having the police think that your motive for killing him was a fight over the coin."

"What fight?"

Jenna reached in her back pocket and extracted a piece of paper that had been folded in quarters. She handed it to me. "This fight."

I unfolded it. It was an e-mail Simon had sent me about ten days before he was killed.

Subject	Forged Coins
Date	11/25 4:03:37 PM Pacific Daylight Time
From	srafer@marmarflaw.com
To	rtarza@marmarflaw.com

Robert—

Quit pretending that your Ides is anything other than a clever Becker-like forgery. Take it back and return my money.

I'll be out of the office the rest of the day and the rest of this week and next. Your worthless fake will be in the top drawer of my desk. Pick it up while I'm gone. Don't bother to leave a check. Just wire the $500K to my off-shore bank account in Shanghai. Name on the account:

Simon S. Rafer. The bank name, routing number and my account number are on a sticky on top of the coin.

This is my final offer. Accept it and I'll forget the whole thing. Stall any longer and it's going to get very public and very ugly. I think that at the very least you knew all along that it was a fake and I'm going to say so. Maybe you won't go to jail. But no one is ever going to buy a coin from you again and it won't exactly be good for your legal career. Here or anywhere else. Assuming you can find a job somewhere else.

The only reason I'm not going to the police right now is in deference to our long professional relationship.

Do the right thing, Robert.

Simon

First I tried humor. "You have a lot of interesting stuff in your pockets, Jenna."

She just sat and looked at me.

"Okay," I said, "where did you get this e-mail?"

"Printed it out. Right after I read all of Simon's e-mail exchanges with you."

"Why were you reading his e-mails?"

"Let's come back to that. Right now I'd like to learn some more about your dispute. It's important."

It hit me that Jenna was starting to interview me as if I were a new client. Facts first. I also recognized a specific technique I'd taught her. Don't let the person you're questioning change the focus to you. The focus is on him, not you. Keep it there.

I gave in. "What else do you want to know, Jenna?"

"Who is Becker?"

"Was. Carl Wilhelm Becker. Perhaps the greatest counterfeiter of ancient coins who ever lived. Swiss. Died in 1830. As you saw, Simon claimed the coin was a Becker forgery."

"Is it?"

"Can't be. There are only fifty-eight of them in the world, and a new one showing up would have attracted too much attention, even back then. Becker enjoyed his quiet life in Geneva, peddling flawless counterfeits to coin rubes. Why would he have risked it all by forging such a famous coin?"

"Why did Simon think it was a fake?"

"He had it appraised."

"By whom?"

"I'm not sure. But it doesn't matter. This coin"—I leaned over and tapped the vinyl flip—"is real, damn it. I've owned it myself for more than fifty years. I know who owned it before me and where it came from before that."

"So you never went and picked up the coin from his office?"

"Shit, no."

"Well, now you've gotten it back in a different way. I brought it back to you. I suggest you keep it and send Simon's estate a check for five hundred thousand dollars. Pretend you agreed to undo the deal before Simon was killed."

Maybe I was still in shock. But what Jenna was saying made no sense to me.

"I'm sorry, Jenna. I'm not getting it."

"We don't want the police to think you killed Simon so you could keep the 500K."

"Why would anyone think that? I'm not a lowlife who would kill someone over money—not for that amount or any amount."

"If there's some other piece of evidence that links you to the crime, a lot of people are going to think that."

"It's ridiculous."

"Robert, do you remember what you told me right before we did our first jury trial together?"

"I told you a lot of things."

"One of the things you said was to keep in mind that the average juror in Los Angeles makes less than $50,000 per year.

"Yeah, I remember that."

"How much did you make last year, Robert?"

"Sixty hundred fifty thousand dollars."

"So five hundred thousand dollars is what? About seventy-five percent of what you pull down every year and ten times what they take home? A lot of jurors are going to think that's worth killing over, even for you."

"Okay, okay," I said. "I get it. I get it. But I still can't do what you're suggesting. You've tampered with evidence."

"If you didn't kill him, the coin isn't evidence of anything and, therefore, no evidence has been tampered with." She said it with a wry smile. We both knew it was an utterly horseshit argument.

She didn't wait for me to respond. She reached over, picked up the flip, and held it out to me. "Take the fucking coin, Robert."

When I didn't reach for it immediately, she continued to dangle it there in front of me, waiting.

Finally, I took it from her and dropped it into the right-hand pocket of my suit jacket. "I'll think on it," I said. "But I'll probably just give it back."

Jenna changed the subject.

"Ready to talk about lawyers now?"

"I guess we should. Who should I hire?"

"Me."

"We've been through this. You don't know enough."

"I've done seven long jury trials. Six of them with you."

"None was a criminal trial."

"Don't you remember? I also spent six months on loan to the Criminal Division of the U.S. Attorney's office. I tried four federal criminal cases to verdict. All convictions."

"They were misdemeanor drug trials. Pigeons on a fence."

"Maybe so, but I learned the ropes and the rules."

"Just help me find a good, *experienced* criminal defense lawyer, okay?"

"I want to do more than that. You're my mentor. I want to help you."

"I'm truly touched, Jenna. But I can't risk it. For the lead, I need somebody with deep experience. But if it's okay with whoever that turns out to be, you can be second chair."

She sighed. "Okay, I figured that's what you'd say. This morning, while you were still asleep, I called Oscar Quesana. He's agreed to join the team."

I cringed inwardly at the word *team*. Whenever I thought of criminal defense teams, I thought about defendants who were obviously guilty. Like O. J. Simpson.

"Quesana's always struck me as slow," I said.

"He is. But he's slow like the tortoise, you know?"

"I don't know, really."

"We have an appointment with him at two o'clock at your office."

"I'd rather he came here."

"He can't. The media will see him."

"Oh."

I sat for a moment, thinking. "Jenna, why are the media people out there so interested in this? Simon wasn't famous. Not even a little."

"He was prominent, Robert. He had been on a million mayoral commissions and like the *Times* said, he had just been elected honorary chair of the opera."

"Who in this town goes to opera?"

"Lots of people."

"Do you go?"

"That's not the point."

"All right, fine. I still don't understand it. But how am I supposed to get to my office? That thing outside is like a man-eating blob."

"You can escape in the trunk of my car."

"I'm not doing that!"

"Robert, I'm joking. I parked my car in your garage facing out. We're going to open the garage door and drive out slowly. The Blob, as you call it, will part. They'll take your picture in the car. Nothing to be done about that. Other than that, it will be fine. Trust me."

"Okay."

Suddenly, my brain returned from some kind of vacation-from-logic it had been on.

"Jenna, how do I know that you didn't kill him yourself?"

"Why would I want to kill him?"

"How should I know? Maybe you killed him because he was doing it with someone else."

"Probably was. That was his M.O."

"I don't know anything about his M.O.," I said.

"Do you really think I killed him?" she asked.

"I don't know what to think."

"Look, Robert, the reason you should believe me when I say I didn't kill him is the same reason I believe you. Faith in each other."

There was a small silence as I considered what she had said. It was true that there was no particular reason for her to believe me. No more than my reason for wanting to believe her.

I was starting to feel overwhelmed again.

"Maybe," I said, "we should see Oscar another day."

Jenna got up, came over, and sat down next to me. She put her arm around me. Rather gently, I thought. "Robert, after you get a grip, I think it will actually help you to meet with Oscar today. We need to get a strategy in place quickly, and that will make you feel better."

"What's the rush? Why don't we just wait and see what happens?"

"We can't wait. The police were already here asking to interview you again. I told them you were sick. So we have to get going on figuring out a strategy."

I looked down at my tie. "Okay, but before we go downtown I need to change my tie. There's a spot of coffee on it."

"I can't see a spot."

"It's there."

"Okay, okay. Change it and we'll go."

I got up and headed to the bedroom to get a clean tie. One without a damn spot on it.

CHAPTER 5

———

The drive to the office was not as bad as I had feared.

Jenna pulled her car slowly out of the garage, and the Blob parted, just as she had said it would. Jenna drives a Toyota Land Cruiser. Whatever its political and environmental correctness, it is big and high. High enough that the reporters moving alongside the car as we inched down the driveway had to peer across at me, instead of down at me. Jenna had instructed me to look straight ahead, and I did. The flashes were annoying, but at least they weren't in my eyes.

I had expected the Blob to follow us, but it didn't. I still had a lot to learn about blob behavior. Among other things, I hadn't yet learned that there was more than one blob. I would learn that later.

The first few minutes of the drive, neither of us said a thing. We just watched the trees go by as we wound our way down the canyon. It's not a road you can take at much more than thirty-five. Finally, as Jenna exited the canyon onto city streets and headed to the freeway, I broke the silence.

"May I ask you something?"

"Sure."

"Where'd you learn how to deal with the media? In the trials we've done together, the courtroom has always been empty. Zero press interest. They certainly didn't teach you that in law school."

"You've forgotten who my father was."

"Senator James. Democrat of Ohio."

"Right. Do you remember the scandal?"

"Not well."

"Accused by political enemies of taking bribes when he was on the Cleveland City Council. Accusations leaked two weeks before he stood for election to a second term in the Senate. I was twelve. When the media mob—and Blob really is a great name for it—materialized in front of our house, my mother was terrified by it. My father was enraged by it.

"And you?"

"For some reason I found it fascinating. So I became the family blob expert. I took coffee out to them. I chatted them up. As a twelve-year-old girl who hadn't yet reached puberty, I could go out and do that without becoming a camera target. Today, it might be different. But back then, news directors weren't about to put images of a guy's daughter on the news. It would have crossed the line. So I learned what you might call the Way of the Blob without being devoured by it."

"That's how you knew it wouldn't block our car?"

"Yes. I even learned when and how to feed it."

"Meaning exactly what?"

"Meaning that I learned exactly what the Blob lives for. Which is to be 'in the moment.' From the anchor all the way down to the guy who holds the boom mike, there's a craving to be where it's happening—to be where it's at."

Now I am a guy who, far from being in the moment, doesn't even watch the local news. To the extent that I had ever let the thought of journalists enter my mind, I pictured them scurrying around taking notes on those funny little rectangular pads featuring a tightly wound spiral binding at the top. From my perch on the eighty-fifth floor, they had seemed nobody I needed to care about. Let alone worry about becoming a snack in their food chain.

"What do you feed something that wants to be in the moment?"

"First, you feed them the feeling that you like them and respect them. Journalists crave approval almost as much as they crave the moment. Second, you help them create the very moment they're seeking. You hold press conferences. You slip them the names and addresses of people they can blob up. You feed them inside stuff."

We were approaching the freeway on-ramp. It's a place where a driver has to pay attention. A bad merge can kill you. As Jenna focused on executing a good merge, I reflected on what she had said. It made sense. But what the hell was I supposed to do while she fed the Blob its moment? Hide?

"Jenna, what does all that mean for me?"

"It means your lawyers might do a few careful interviews on talk shows—the ones where ground rules can be negotiated and followed. But it also means you're never ever going to talk directly about it to anyone, least of all to the Blob. Instead, you're going to learn to wave the jaunty wave of the innocent as you get in and out of cars."

"I am so thrilled."

"More questions?"

"Yeah. Why do you want to help represent me? Really?"

"Cause I like you a lot."

"You like a lot of people," I said.

"How about because you've protected me from the assholes in the firm and given me great advice?"

"I try to do that for all the associates."

"Put it this way, Robert. When I came here, I knew I was smart enough to do the work and do it well. I assumed I'd get to be a partner, no sweat. But you made me see that everybody here is smart, one way or another, and that it's a brutal competition. A hundred associates enter every year. Eight years later, only three or four get to wear the garlands. If I make it, it will be because of you, and I want to repay you. I never thought I'd actually get to do that."

I didn't know what to say in response to such an encomium, so I just asked one more curmudgeonly question. "Any other reasons?"

"Uh huh."

"Such as?"

"I want to be famous."

As Jenna said that, she accelerated suddenly and then swerved deftly to avoid a semi that had changed lanes without warning. Unlike Stewart, Jenna could drive. The maneuver shoved me back in my seat.

"Well, at least you're honest about it."

"Look, Robert, face it. Big deal civil litigation— the stuff we do—is intellectually interesting. But you can't dine out on it. I mean, sure, it's better than being a dentist. But guys at bars aren't exactly fascinated by what I do. It's not going to land me an up-and-coming movie producer."

"Do you want a movie producer?"

"I don't know. But I'm twenty-eight going on twenty-nine, and if I'm not careful I'm going to end up married to some other lawyer, for God's sake. But if the media stays focused on this and I help get you off,

I emerge seriously famous, and I get to do something both more lucrative and more interesting. So it's a twofer. I do good for you and good for myself at the same time."

I had always known Jenna to be ambitious. It was one of the things that attracted me to her. The "tiger, tiger burning bright" thing. But I'd never before seen the tiger glow with quite so many kilowatts.

"Maybe I shouldn't want a lawyer on my team who wants to be famous."

"Every criminal lawyer in this town wants to be famous."

"What about Oscar Quesana?"

"It's too late for him. He's achieved the enviable status of 'respected,' and that's as far as it's going to go for him. Ever. Besides, I'm more telegenic. A five-foot-five pert size six looks great on camera. So the guys in the press, and maybe even some of the girls, will find me very interesting indeed. Even more so when they discover I'm a natural blonde who dyes her hair black. And their interest in me will translate into a favorable interest in your story."

"My story? I don't have a story. Except that I'm not guilty and I didn't do it. What possible story do I have beyond that? That I was home alone Sunday night? That I watched a re-mastered DVD of *The Maltese Falcon*? Because that is God's truth."

"Well, we'll need a better story than that. Because the DA is going to be sitting in the courtroom weaving a scarf that says 'guilty' in both English and Spanish."

"Courtroom? Shit, I haven't even been arrested, let alone indicted." I was feeling agitated. "I mean they've got nothing. Nothing." If I were the kind of person who pounded things, I would have pounded the dashboard.

Jenna turned her head and gave me a quick, eyebrows-arched look before focusing again on the road ahead. "Robert, you don't read the newspapers you subscribe to, and you don't watch television. You don't surf the Net. You don't have a Facebook account, and you've probably never even heard of Twitter."

"I know about Twitter. I just don't use it."

"Whatever, you've mostly missed the brave new world of crime stories."

"I think I've even missed the brave old world of crime stories, Jenna."

She laughed. "I don't doubt it. But here's the scoop. These days, the police and the DA need to solve high-profile killings pronto. DA's don't get reelected if they don't solve them before the next election, and police chiefs don't get reappointed by the mayor if they're not solved. There's an election for DA in six months, and the Chief's first term is up in nine. He wants a second term. So right now you're what they call second-term security."

By now my agitation had dissolved into a petulant mutter. "They've got nothing."

"They think they've got a lot. They've got opportunity. They've got you tied physically into the crime by the blood on your suit coat. If you decide to return the coin to Simon's estate and then the police find the e-mails, they'll also have a plausible motive."

"I still think it's a dumb motive."

"Well, I don't think so. And my gut tells me that they *do* have something more. Or they wouldn't have leaked to the *Times* that you're a person of interest."

"Like what?"

"I don't know. We need to find out. Maybe it has to do with that 'vator' thing I heard them talking about."

We never finished the conversation, because a white news van suddenly pulled alongside us, a TV camera poking out its window. Jenna saw it, too.

"Don't turn your head!"

It was hard not to turn my head, but I obeyed. I was trying to be a good client. The van was still alongside. I could see it in my peripheral vision.

"Robert, grab my cell. In the glove compartment!"

I opened the glove compartment, rummaged for the phone, extracted it, and handed it to her. She punched in a number.

"Who are you calling?"

"The news director for KZDD. That's their goddamn van."

I heard a click as someone answered.

"Hey, Mike. Jenna James. . . Uh huh. Well, I'm representing him. . . Yeah, it *is* hard to believe. Fun stuff, huh? Hey, I have a small request . . ."

Then she laughed and said, quite sweetly, really, "Tell your fucking news van to get away from my car?"

I could not help but notice that she had used the vocal mannerism so common to her generation—an upward lilt at the end of the sentence, turning it from a statement into a question.

There followed more banter between Jenna and Mike. Then, to my amazement, the van dropped back and away.

"How do you know that guy?"

"He's Janet Bui's boyfriend."

Janet is a third year associate. I had a vague recollection of a bearded guy who sometimes hung around Janet's office late in the day and on weekends. Must be this Mike guy.

"So Mike did you a favor?"

"More like he backed off now in exchange for an implied promise of some tasty tidbit later."

"What difference would it have made if they'd filmed me this way?"

"Being filmed in a moving car makes you look like prey."

"Oh." This constant obsession with image was going to take getting used to.

We were exiting the freeway onto the streets of downtown and making our way toward our office building. That was when I learned that the Blob has a downtown cousin. Because a Blob that would have done the one in my driveway proud was milling about at the entrance to the building's parking garage. In fact, it was blocking the way.

"Okay, now what, Jenna? I can't not look. They're right in front of us."

"Look right at the cameras and give them a big thumbs up."

I did it. It seemed to work, because the Blob parted and let us through. But it felt truly and utterly stupid. I never learned if it looked truly and utterly stupid, because I resolved then and there that I was not going to watch myself on television.

CHAPTER 6

————

The garage was blessedly empty. No cops, no crime scene tape, no people. We parked on B-Level without incident, got in the elevator and rode up to eighty-five. As the elevator doors opened, I was seized by a slight panic. Was just walking past reception and then down the hall to my office going to be an ordeal?

I need not have worried. Our stolid, mannish, but extra-friendly receptionist, Christine Mulcahy, greeted me with a cheerful "Hi, Mr. Tarza!" Like a lot of Marbury Marfan staff, Christine is a fixture. She's not the first receptionist since I arrived at the firm, but she's been there at least fifteen years. Maybe twenty. And we like each other, to the extent you can like someone you never actually talk to other than to say "hi."

Some people, by the way, think that Christine is a cross-dresser whose real name is Christopher. But I've always just put that down to the rumor mill that runs its mouth in all law firms. A mill in which speculation about everyone's sexual proclivities seems to be a topic of intense interest. Maybe it's like that in all big organizations. But then again, I've never worked anywhere else.

I was apparently just standing there, running those disjointed thoughts through my head, because I suddenly noticed Christine staring at me. A little poke in the small of the back from Jenna got a "Hi, Christine!" out of me and a start down the hall toward my corner office, with Jenna following.

A corner office is, of course, what my seniority commands. One of the few perks it's hard for them to take away without causing the whole pecking order to tumble down. As we entered, the snowcapped San Gabriels were breathtakingly on display through the windows. They were not obscured by smog, like they are so many months of the year. Maybe, I thought to myself, the smog is good, because it keeps even more people from pouring into our city.

I was wandering again. And I was again just standing in one place, not moving anywhere.

"Robert, sit down, will you?"

I went behind my desk and sat down in the leather chair, as instructed. Jenna continued to stand, looking at me intently.

"Robert, you are, I think, still a bit out of it. Not surprising. First you find a dead body. Then your picture gets in the paper as a suspect. It would unnerve anybody. But you have to get a grip."

"I'm trying to get a grip," I said.

"Well, grip harder. Oscar Quesana will be here in less than an hour. In the meantime, ask Gwen to get you a cup of coffee, read through your mail, and just try to chill, man." She gave me a smile that I think was supposed to be reassuring, and left.

So, for the first time since Jenna had come over to my house the morning of the murder, I was alone. I looked around my office and felt comforted by the familiar. The furniture is light oak, well made and modern. There is only one painting on the wall. It's a large oil, maybe three feet by five, done by my college roommate, now dead almost twenty years. It depicts a field of wheat, wind-blown on a gently sloping hillside. Craig was no great artist. I suppose you could call him an early Wyeth imitator. But the painting works somehow, at least for me.

In the corner of the office, abutting the east-facing window, there is a short couch, covered in a subdued herringbone tweed fabric, and two small armchairs, all arranged around a glass coffee table. Two of my favorite coins—a gold aureus of Augustus with a crocodile on the reverse and a silver tetradrachm of Athens with its famous owl on the front—are on the table.

Neither coin is especially valuable, so I have had each of them slotted vertically into a Lucite cube. That way, if you want to, you can turn the cube upside down and dump the coin into your hand. There is no romance in a two-thousand-year-old coin you can't touch.

Gwen Romero, my secretary of twenty-five years, stuck her head in the door. It still surprises me that she's pushing fifty. She was only twenty-three when she started. But, then, I was only thirty-five. So we have kind of grown up together. Passed through the demise of the typewriter together. She still calls me Mr. Tarza. And she still respects my privacy, in the sense that she rarely asks directly about my personal life.

Even though she pretty much knows everything there is to know about it, since she pays my bills and screens my mail.

"Mr. Tarza, there is a Detective Spritz to see you." Gwen said.

It shocked me down to my toes, but I pretended indifference. "He doesn't have an appointment."

"I know, but he's very insistent." She paused. "He's the one I saw on the news last night. Talking about poor Mr. Rafer."

Gwen stood there, waiting. She is not one to push, and she knows that I hate people who show up without an appointment. I'm a lawyer, not a barber. But still, as the gatekeeper, she needed a decision.

"What the hell. Bring him in."

Decision made and communicated, I had expected Gwen simply to go and fetch him. Instead she continued to stand there, looking stricken. "Shouldn't I call Jenna and get her to join you?"

I think I may actually have rolled my eyes. "Are you part of some collective keeper they've installed to look after me?"

She stared back at me, even more stricken. "Robert . . . I'm not stupid you know. I read the papers. I know what's going on. When Jenna left here, she came by my desk and told me to make sure that nobody—*nobody*— connected with this whole thing got near you without her."

On one level, I was touched. I had been trying for twenty-five years to get Gwen to start calling me Robert instead of Mr. Tarza. But she calls only associates by their first names, and then only while they remain associates. She only calls me Robert when she wants to show me that she really cares about me on some personal level. It doesn't happen very often.

"Okay, you can call her. But please go and get Detective Spritz first. Then call Jenna."

She nodded and left. While I waited for her to return with Spritz, I considered how petulant, even stupid, I was being. Hadn't I myself told clients, hundreds of times, in the most direct of language, that they were absolutely not to talk to other people about their cases unless I was there to oversee the conversations? I had. Most had grudgingly obeyed. Now the shoe was on the other foot and it pinched.

Gwen returned with Spritz. I showed him to the corner seating area and offered him the couch while I took one of the chairs. Gwen offered him coffee or a soft drink, but he declined.

We looked at each other. Yesterday—was it only yesterday—I had not registered his looks. Today I did. Tall, gangly, very thin, almost bald. He reminded me of no one so much as Ichabod Crane.

We sat a moment, waiting to see who would speak first.

"It's good to see you again, Mr. Tarza."

"I wish I could say the same."

"Touchy, are we, huh?"

"No, pissed."

"What about?"

"Well, the picture in the paper, for one."

"I thought you looked kind of fetching in that windbreaker."

My reply stuck in my throat as Jenna charged into the office. And charged is exactly the right word. One moment she wasn't there, and the next moment she was standing directly behind my chair, glaring at Spritz. I swiveled my head to get a better look at her. She didn't actually have her hands on her hips, but she might as well have.

"Detective Spritz, I'm Jenna James. Mr. Tarza's attorney. I'm sure you didn't know that he is represented by counsel, but now that you do know, I'd appreciate your scheduling any interviews through me."

Spritz leaned back and actually guffawed. "Now that is a howler. Perhaps you didn't know it, Miss James, but you are a potential suspect in this case. But now that you know, I'm sure you'll want to withdraw and help Mr. Tarza find other counsel. While you're at it, you might want to find counsel for yourself, as well, huh?" He locked his hands behind his head and waited to see what would happen.

"Get out."

"As you wish. But you're passing up the opportunity to learn some things, you know. Far be it from me, though, to teach learned counsel how to do her job."

I said nothing. I was becoming more client-like every minute. Woof, woof.

Spritz got up from the couch and headed for the door. Jenna followed. After they had gone, I got up and wandered around my office, enjoying its familiarity. Then I saw it. A small patch of fabric, maybe two inches square, had been cut out of one arm of my couch. I was about to yell for Gwen, to ask her about it, when Spritz and Jenna reentered. Jenna spoke before I could say anything.

"Detective Spritz and I have had a little chat in the corridor and concluded that it's in both his interest and yours for all of us to talk a little more. But we've agreed that he's going to speak first, and you'll talk only if I say it's okay."

"Yes, ma'am." I tried to say it with panache, but I'm not sure it came across that way. In any case, we all repaired back to the sitting area. Jenna took the couch while Spritz and I took the chairs. Meanwhile, I couldn't take my eyes off the missing spot of fabric on the couch arm. But I couldn't figure out any way to bring it to Jenna's attention.

Gwen popped in and again offered coffee or soft drinks to all. Spritz asked for a Diet Coke. Maybe he was worried about gaining weight. Jenna ordered her usual Orange Crush. I said no, I didn't want anything, thanks. Truth is, what I really wanted was coffee. I didn't ask for it because I was afraid my hand would shake again.

Spritz picked up the Lucite cube with the Athenian tetradrachm in it and held it up. "You collect coins, huh?"

"Yes, I do."

"Any particular kind?" He rotated the cube so he could see the other side of the coin.

"Well, truth is, I just collect coins I like. As long as they were coined before 400 A.D."

"Huh," he said, and put the cube back on the table. "Do you also collect daggers, Mr. Tarza?"

I looked over at Jenna. She nodded, and I answered. Although I don't think she knew what was coming.

"Once upon a time, I did."

Spritz took a tiny notepad out of the inner pocket of his suit coat and jotted something down.

"Huh. Once upon how long a time ago, Mr. Tarza?"

"Well, until about ten years ago, when my whole collection was stolen from my house. I reported it to the police."

"Yes, I know. We have the police report."

Jenna made a note and looked up. "Detective, could we get a copy of that?"

"Sure." Spritz looked at me again. "Mr. Tarza, would it surprise you to learn that Simon Rafer was murdered with a Holbein dagger?"

"No."

"Why not?"

"Because there were hundreds of Holbein daggers made in the 1530's. They were the 'in' dagger in Switzerland at the time. There have since been thousands of copies. Maybe tens of thousands. So it's like asking if I'd be surprised to learn that someone had been shot with a Colt 45." I felt smug. Superior knowledge always makes me feel that way.

"Well, would it surprise you to learn that the murder weapon matched almost exactly a particular Holbein dagger stolen from your house some years ago? Or should I say supposedly stolen?"

Jenna put her hand on my arm. "Don't answer that." Then she turned on Spritz. "I thought that we agreed out in the hall that you weren't going to ask my client what he knows and doesn't know about this crime."

"Sorry, I forgot."

"Sorry, I think you should go."

Spritz put his hands out in front of him and turned them palms up. "As you wish, Counselor. But too bad, you might have learned even more, huh?"

"Maybe we can learn whatever it is later," she said.

"Yeah, maybe." Spritz unlimbered himself from the chair.

I knew I was off message, but I couldn't stand it any longer. "Detective, what do you know about that hole in the arm of my couch?" I pointed to it.

He turned slightly and looked casually down at the gap in the fabric. "Oh, there was maybe more blood there," he said. "One of the officers who checked the floor found it and the criminalists took it to the lab for analysis."

Neither Jenna nor I said anything.

"Good day, then," Spritz said. And he ambled out.

Jenna waited until he'd cleared the doorway. "Robert, why the fuck didn't you tell me you collected daggers?"

"I want to talk about the blood on the fabric."

"He's just pimping you. It was probably an old wine stain, left over from those dorky wine and cheese parties you used to have in your office on Fridays. I want to talk about your dagger collection. Why don't I know about it?"

"Jenna, do you know how old I was when you were born?"

"What does that have to do with the price of beans?"

"I was thirty-two. Which means I was forty-three when you graduated from grade school. During those forty-three years, I managed to do quite a few things that you don't know about. Then another ten years went by before I finally met you."

"Huh." We both laughed at her imitation of Spritz. "Alright, Robert, when we see Quesana at two, we can trace a little more of your collecting habits, maybe."

"Maybe."

She left too, followed by Gwen coming in.

"Mr. Tarza, we need to redo your schedule. I cancelled all of your appointments for today. They all understood."

"I bet."

She ignored my sarcasm. "To remind you, there's a Hiring Committee meeting tomorrow morning at ten."

"Oh, right."

"Will you be able to attend?"

"No. There's nothing critical happening tomorrow. The others can take care of it." She made a note on her ever-present notepad.

"Gwen," I asked, "do you know anything about the fabric that's been cut out on the arm of my couch?"

"Yes. There was yellow tape across your office doorway when I got here this morning. Then someone from the LAPD in a white coat came and cut out the fabric. I asked him why he was doing that, but he wouldn't say. When he left he took the yellow tape off and handed it to me. It's in the waste basket. Do you want to see it?"

"No."

"May I ask you something, Robert?"

"Sure."

"Did you kill him?"

"I did not."

"Good." She said it as if someone had just reassured her that the grocery store had not run out of bananas. Then she said something that really caught my attention.

"I'm not sorry he's dead," she said.

"You're not? Why not?"

"He was mean to people."

"Was he mean to you?"

"Yes."

"He was?" We both knew what we were talking about, and I realized as soon as it was out of my mouth that my surprise had offended her.

"I was a looker back then."

I ran my head back twenty-five years. Sometimes you have to do that quite consciously to remember how we all used to be. She was right. When she got to M&M, Gwen was, if not really well put together, at least very respectably put together. Simon arrived not all that many years after her. As a young associate he wouldn't have been powerful enough to sate himself farther up the food chain.

"Well, Gwen, did *you* kill him?"

"No."

"Thank God. That makes two of us who didn't, then."

"What about Jenna?"

"What about her?"

"She had plenty of motive."

"How do you know that?"

"Robert, the secretaries are an in-house spy network. We know everything."

"I suppose so." Then I had a thought. "Do the secretaries know who did do it?"

"We have our theories."

"Want to share them?"

"It wouldn't be right. I mean, it's just gossip."

Over the years, Gwen has always, in the end, been willing to tell me everything the secretarial spy network knows. At least most of the time. About ten years ago, I'd had the temerity to doubt a secretarial finding that two of my married partners were having an affair. In fact, I had uproariously derided the information. So when the two partners eventually divorced their respective spouses and got married to each other, the secretarial network, offended at my derision, cut me off. I didn't get another crumb of gossip for more than four years.

They had restored my security clearance about five years ago. As a thank you for leaking to Gwen, a week in advance of the announcement, that Simon was going to be the next managing partner. And for revealing the vote of the Nominating Committee.

I decided not to press her for the moment. In due course I'd find out who the secretaries thought had done it.

Gwen didn't budge from her position in the doorway. "Mr. Tarza, you had a lot of phone calls today. Would you like the list?"

"Any that were important?"

"Your daughter called, for one. From Prague."

"And said?"

"She said she loved you and was coming home to help."

"Bullshit. She's coming home to see her boyfriend."

"She didn't say that." Gwen is a great secretary, but she is something of a literalist who is unable, or refuses, to read between the lines. You could say she doesn't get sarcasm.

"Did she say anything else?"

"That she needed the airfare."

"I'll think about it. Who else called?"

"Mr. Penosco. He wants you to call him."

Peter Penosco is the CEO of Bright Bulb Productions. Bright Bulb, or BBP, as we call it, was my largest remaining client. It used to produce feature films, but had shifted to mostly made-for-television movies and direct-to-video stuff. I did all of its contracting work, which was pretty interesting. But mainly I did BBP's litigation. Peter had a habit of breaking the deals he'd made, so people often sued him. Call it his way of renegotiating the deals, which is not exactly unheard of in the movie business. Peter usually netted out a profit when the litigation was over. Whether that was due to his business acumen or my lawyering skills is something we'd been known to argue about.

"Okay. Would you let him know that I'll call him back tomorrow?"

"I already did. I explained you were out this afternoon." She smiled. Gwen knows that I make it a fetish to get back to clients promptly and don't like them left in doubt about when I'm going to call back.

"Thanks. If you don't mind, let's go over the rest of the calls tomorrow."

"Okay," she said, and left.

Once again, I was alone. And exhausted. I was in no shape to meet with Oscar Quesana or anyone else. I picked up the phone and called Jenna. She answered on the first ring. "James here." I had always thought that an odd way to answer the phone. Maybe it sprang from her father's career as a general before he became, later in life, a Senator.

"Listen, James Here, I'm toast. Can we put the meeting with Quesana off until tomorrow?"

"Sure. It can wait."

"Good, I'm going home."

"You don't have a car."

"Right. I forgot. Will you drive me home?"

"Be right there."

The drive home was not much different from the drive in, except no TV truck shadowed us on the freeway. I gave the thumbs up sign to the Blob as we left the building, and, later, stared straight ahead as we inched through its companion Blob in the driveway of my house.

Jenna drove away as soon as she dropped me off, and went I knew not where. Once inside, I cleaned up the breakfast dishes, puttered around the house, and watched two old movies on Turner Classic Movies. Blissfully, TCM carries no news. I was in bed by ten. I slept neither fitfully nor well. But I did sleep.

CHAPTER 7

———

I was awakened by the thin December light filtering through the trees. It must have been about seven. I thought about my situation, then just pulled the blanket up over my head and lay there for a few minutes, savoring the warmth of my bed. I would have lain there forever if I could have.

But I couldn't. So I tossed the blanket off, got up, and vowed to myself that today was going to be different. For the last two days, I'd been a victim—reacting to events, letting others lead me around by the nose. Which was in stark contrast to the last thirty-six years of my life. I'd always been the take-charge person. An investigator of complexity. A solver of disputes. I could solve this one, too, if I just went about it methodically.

The way I figured it, Simon must have been party to a major dispute with someone. I needed to learn who that someone was. Because that someone probably killed him. To figure it out, I first needed to learn a great deal more about what Simon had been up to lately. Who he had spent time with. Where he had been.

I'd paid Simon scant attention of late, even though I had remained on the M&M Executive Committee, over which he presided monthly. I remarked sheepishly to myself that I hadn't even clued into him and Jenna. I had a big task ahead of me.

After breakfast by myself—Jenna was nowhere to be seen—and with the goal of starting to find out more about Simon, I went out and climbed into my car. Someone, Jenna maybe, had thoughtfully had it returned to my garage. Apparently, the police had decided not to impound it.

I drove out of the garage, bulled my way through the driveway Blob, and headed down the 405 to pay a visit to Horace Crestway Marfan III. "Harry" to his friends, "Three" to his true intimates.

Harry's grandfather founded the firm back in 1880. A few years ago Harry, by then in his eighties, had sold his Bel Air mansion and retired to Manhattan Beach, a small seaside town just a few miles south of LAX.

It's a picturesque place, with several streets of beach houses and sidewalk cafes that spill down a steep hill to the inevitable bike path, boardwalk, and white strip of sand. Harry lives in a contemporary townhouse two streets up from the beach. Considering his substantial fortune, it's a rather modest place. He has no phone. He says its absence encourages people to drop by.

Five years ago, when the Nominating Committee had initially deadlocked on the choice of a managing partner to succeed me—I had termed out—Harry was the force that propelled Simon to the forefront. Harry had argued forcefully that the two leading candidates were "too old, too set in their ways and too damn stuffy" to lead the firm into the new century. Coming as it did from Mr. Stuffy himself, the argument persuaded four of the five of us. But I had already begun to have a glimmer of what an asshole Simon would become, and voted no. Simon, whose mentor I had once been, had never forgiven me.

After Simon became managing partner, Harry had taken him quietly under his wing. I had seen them huddled together in many a corner, talking earnestly, and once or twice noticed them drinking together at the DownUnder, a bar still frequented by what was left of the pinstripe crowd. If anyone knew about Simon's recent activities, Harry did.

I didn't think Harry would mind my asking. If nothing else, it could be justified by the many intertwined threads that connected the three of us. Thirty years ago, Harry had stirred my interest in ancient coins—beyond my idle curiosity about the one coin, the Ides, that I had owned since boyhood. I, in turn, had opened that world up to Simon. An interest in collecting old chunks of metal is something of an addiction, and addicts tend to gravitate to one another. And to help each other out. The three of us, as well as some others, had even met monthly at the DownUnder in what we called the Coin Club—a club that had died promptly upon Simon's ascension to the throne.

When I knocked on Harry's door, he swung it open almost immediately. He was dressed in what had become his new uniform since shedding his suit—topsiders, beige Dockers, and a blue work shirt. Harry, at 86, still towered over me, a good eight inches taller than my five-foot-ten. And he still resembled a big sheep dog, except that the shaggy thatch of hair has thinned some over the years. Still as black as the day we first met, though.

"Robert, Robert, do come in. I've been half expecting you." He ushered me through the door and into the big square of a main room, lit from the front by floor-to-ceiling windows that faced the sea and from above by clerestory windows that hugged the tops of the other three walls. Through the tall windows, I could see the surf rolling in on long swells.

I plunked myself down on one of the beige couches that faced the ocean. Harry pulled up a weathered maple chair with a cane seat and sat himself down a few feet in front of me, but slightly to the side. The better not to block the windows. I ignored the view. I wanted to get down to business, and Harry apparently sensed that.

"So, my friend, what can I do for you?" he asked.

"I need to figure out who killed Simon."

"Ah, yes. I've been reading the papers. They think you did it, do they not?"

"Apparently so."

"Did you?"

"No."

"Well, didn't think so, didn't think so. You're not the killer type, really." He paused and peered at me. "But what makes you think I might be able to help you? I've been away from the firm some time now. Can hardly be said to have my ear to the ground anymore."

"You knew Simon well. Had a lot of mutual interests. I know the two of you continued to talk even after you left," I said.

"You were always a good observer, Robert. Did you observe who he was dating?"

"No, but if you mean Jenna, I'm aware of it now."

"Yes, Miss James. She'd be *my* prime suspect. Simon wanted to end it, you know."

"I didn't know that," I said.

"Be that as it may, she was resistant—even threatened him with some sexual harassment law suit or other—and he was upset about it. Came down here on Friday night and used language that was unkind. Called her a conniving, manipulative little bitch." He paused. "In fact, he used a much cruder word. One I do not wish to repeat."

"She's representing me, you know."

Harry just looked at me and raised his eyebrows. Then he got up, walked over to the windows and stood with his hands behind his back, gazing out at the ocean. "Robert, you are, if I might be so bold, being blinded by a skirt. Sorry for the mixed metaphor, but you need to fire her and get yourself a real lawyer. One who isn't a bigger suspect than you are."

"She's not the lead. She's just backing up Oscar Quesana," I said.

He turned to face me again. "Oscar Quesana? For God's sake, Oscar does murders!"

"That's what I'm suspected of, Harry. Remember?"

"Right. Of course. Nevertheless, you need an entirely different class of lawyer. But surely you already know that." He fixed his gaze on me. "Or perhaps the stress has addled your brain."

My goal in going there had been to learn more about Simon. Not to discuss my choice of lawyers.

"Harry, you may be right, and pardon me, but I don't want to talk about that right now. I came to talk about Simon and who had a motive to kill him. Besides Jenna."

"Well, I suppose it could have been somebody from the nether world which he had been—how shall I put it—exploring?"

"What are you talking about?"

"Simon had developed an interest in high stakes gambling. The kind where you wear a tux, play with silver chips in an elegant private room, and are served champagne by women who look like they just stepped out of a James Bond movie. Unfortunately, gambling turned out not to be Simon's forte."

"He owed them money?"

"In the vicinity of five million dollars."

"To whom, exactly, did he owe it?"

"He declined to tell me. All I know is that he didn't have the sum and that it was woefully overdue." Harry had begun to pace up and down in front of the windows with his hands behind his back. He had always been a guy who couldn't stay put.

"Who else knows about it?"

"Well, the policeman who came to visit me last night, for one. Spitz I think his name was. He asked about it."

"Spritz."

"Yes, that's right. Spritz."

"Did he tell you how he knew about it?" I asked.

"No, Robert, he didn't. But as I think you know, when the police interview you, they generally ask the questions."

"What else did he want to know?"

"In addition to asking about the gambling debts—about which I knew and know almost nothing—he inquired about Simon's interest in ancient coins."

"What did you tell him?"

Harry walked over to a low cabinet and bent down to open it. He lowered himself slowly, in a way that betrayed the age of his joints. I had known him since he was in his early fifties, and it pained me to watch.

He pulled from the cabinet a thin, white, folio-sized book, not yet bound, and brought it over to me. "I told Spritz that Simon had been a collector for more than twenty years and showed him this."

"What is it?"

"It's the printer's proof copy of Simon's private catalog. For his coin collection."

I was taken aback. Normally, *museums* make catalogs of their coin collections. I opened it. It was arranged chronologically, coin by coin. I paged to the section that covered the 50 years before Christ. There, exactly where I had expected them, were thumbnail pictures of both sides of the Ides denarius of Brutus. Brutus' portrait on one side, double daggers and the words "Eid Mar"—Ides of March—on the other.

"This is a picture of the one I sold him?"

"Yes. Although he was planning to strike it from the final, bound edition."

"What did you tell Spritz about it?"

"Not much."

"Meaning?"

"I'm afraid I volunteered that you and Simon were having a tiff about the authenticity of the Ides."

"So you know about our dispute, then?"

"Sure. Did you ever take the coin back, as Simon asked, and return his money?"

I hesitated. I do not make a habit of lying. Little white lies in social situations, maybe.

"I did," I said. "At his request, I picked it up from his office last Saturday morning when I was in for a few hours. I'll need to send his estate a check."

Harry gave me what I interpreted as an odd look.

"So you came to agree the Ides was a fake?" he asked.

"No, no. I just got tired of arguing about it. I'll sell it to someone else. You were bidding on it, too, Harry. Maybe you'll want to buy it."

"Not now. It's got a cloud over it."

"It's not a fake, goddamn it."

Earlier that morning, I had picked up the coin flip and put it in my suit coat pocket. I stuck my hand in my pocket to assure myself that it was still there. It was. I had a decision to make. Once I showed it to him, there would be no going back on my lie.

I pulled the vinyl flip out of my pocket. "Here it is. Look for yourself." I held it out to him.

Harry came over, took it from me, and sat down again in the wooden chair. He opened the flip and took the coin out, holding it up to the light between his fingers. Even in the bright light from the windows, it did not glimmer. Coins that old can often appear dull, with no sheen.

"It looks real enough to me," he said. "Good patina, correct heft. Feels pretty much the same as it did the few times you let the rest of us touch it."

He put it back in the flip and handed it back to me. "But I'm hardly an expert."

I dropped it back into my pocket. "What else did Spritz ask you about, Harry?"

"He wanted to know about someone named Susan Apacha. I told him I did not know who that was."

"I do."

"Well, please do not tell me. I want to be nothing more than a distant witness to this whole sordid thing."

"Did he ask you anything about the frosty nature of my relationship with Simon in the five years since I voted no?"

"No."

"Thank God. They would probably drag that out as another motive."

"You know, Robert, I wouldn't, if I were you, count on this Spritz fellow's ignorance. He seemed quite thorough. Indeed, he had with him a very thick notebook that he had mostly filled with notes. He was writing on the last page when he was interviewing me."

"Harry," I said, "I'm not counting on anything except the fact that I didn't kill Simon and don't know who did. But I aim to find out."

Harry got up, in what was clearly a signal that our talk was over. "Well, I wish you good luck and Godspeed in doing it." He smiled. "With emphasis on the speed part, because I think Spritz is in a hurry."

I knew that I should have pressed to stay. To question him in more detail about what Spritz had said and what else he had wanted to know. But I was discombobulated. Lying did not agree with me.

Harry saw me to the door, and we parted with the usual pleasantries, including a mutual promise to have dinner sometime soon. We both knew it wouldn't happen, but it's the kind of thing people in L.A. say to one another. Let's have lunch. Let's have dinner. Let's have whatever. No one ever really means it. It's just a more elaborate form of goodbye.

I headed back to L.A., to my office.

CHAPTER 8

———

In early afternoon there is *relatively* little traffic in L.A., even on the freeways. Unless it's raining of course. People in L.A. can't drive in the rain. The exact reason is a mystery, because it rains every winter. But since it wasn't raining that December day, I covered the twenty miles between Manhattan Beach and downtown in just under twenty-five minutes.

I spent most of those twenty-five minutes justifying my lie—to myself. I wasn't very persuasive. Then I imagined trying to repair the damage. Calling Harry up and telling him that I had lied. Explaining why. I rehearsed the call in my head. Several times. It always came out sounding like an admission of guilt.

When I arrived back at our office building, the Blob, somewhat thinner than the day before, as if it hadn't eaten, was still hunkered down at the entrance into the garage. It seemed, however, to be uninterested in photographing my cheery thumbs up and parted quickly. Perhaps they already had too much tape of my up-thumbing them.

I drove into the garage, then took the elevator to eighty-five. Still thinking. By the time I got off on our floor, I had pretty much persuaded myself that the lie had been inconsequential and necessary to prevent an injustice. I felt a lot better.

When I got to my office, Gwen was sitting glumly at her desk, hands folded in front of her, doing nothing. As I went past, she didn't even look up. But she was clearly aware I was passing by. "Mr. Tarza, there is a letter on your chair." She said it in a flat voice, kind of the way you'd announce to someone that his dog had just died.

"Who's it from?"

"The Executive Committee."

I suddenly understood Gwen's tone of voice. She was probably thinking that, for all intents and purposes, *I* had just died. Because I am *on* the Executive Committee. So getting a letter from them is a rather ominous event. Also, Gwen had no doubt come to understand, as we all had in the last few years, that nothing much moved anymore via paper in envelopes.

Especially not internal communications among lawyers. Everything of importance came by e-mail. Except notices of termination. For some reason, no doubt at one with the reason that some documents still have red wax seals, termination notices at M&M still come on paper.

But there it was, sitting on my chair. A business-size white envelope, sealed and with my full name neatly typed on it: *Robert Winthrop Tarza*.

I opened it. The letter had two sentences and was signed by Caroline Thorpe, "Interim Managing Partner." So, sometime this morning the Executive Committee had apparently gotten together without me and appointed an interim managing partner. Perhaps they thought I was too busy talking to Spritz to attend.

The first sentence of the letter asked me to join the committee for a meeting at 2:00 p.m. in da Vinci. The second sentence alerted me that the topic of discussion would be "the advisability of my taking a temporary leave of absence from the firm." The word temporary was italicized. *Temporary*, I was to understand.

I looked at my watch. It was 1:55 p.m. Just enough time to take the internal stairway down one floor and arrive punctually for what was no doubt being contemplated as my "temporary" professional execution.

The letter actually made me feel upbeat. Perhaps it is because I have always enjoyed confrontation, particularly with the bozos on the Executive Committee. Gwen, I noticed as I passed by her desk, did not look upbeat. She still had the same hangdog look she had had when I came in. Maybe she knew something I didn't.

As I opened the door to da Vinci, I wondered why it had been chosen as the venue for the meeting. It will easily hold forty people. The Executive Committee, counting the now-deceased Simon Rafer and me, consisted of only nine people: The managing partner, three partners from L.A., one each from our largest domestic offices in Seattle, Chicago and Washington, and two "floaters" from whichever two of the other nine offices get the nod in any particular year. This year they were from Hong Kong and Boston. Usually, only the Los Angeles-based partners attend in person, with the others there by speaker phone. Usually, the monthly meeting is in *Yeats*, which is a cozy little room that seats six.

This time though, all the still-living members of the committee were there, even Charlie Wing from Hong Kong. So they had picked da Vinci for the same reason I had picked it for my interrogation by Spritz. For effect. Except this time the desired effect was the formality that they no doubt thought should accompany the execution of a beloved partner. Or perhaps they just thought that I would protest less vehemently with the hills and the Pacific Ocean as backdrop. That the view would calm me.

The seven of them were clustered toward one end of the long mahogany table. They had left a seat for me at table's end. Perhaps as a courtesy due me by dint of being the most senior among them, but more likely just to make me feel isolated from the group. It may not even have been conscious.

Caroline spoke. "Robert, please join us." She gestured toward the chair. I sat down, folded my hands in front of me, and waited for her to continue. I didn't bother to greet anyone. I had long ago concluded that in certain situations, it went better if you just dropped the pleasantries and got right to the ugly business at hand.

Caroline squirmed, which is what I had intended.

"Robert, as you can imagine," she said, "we've done a lot of talking since Simon's murder."

"And saying?"

"Saying that we all need to think of the common good. This firm employs more than two thousand people around the world. No matter how much we value you as a colleague—love you really—we can't allow this scandal to overwhelm M&M. Can't allow a hundred thirty years of work to be destroyed by a scandal."

The amazing thing was that the other six of them, normally so prone to chatter, were stone silent. They just sat there looking at me like crows on a fence. I looked back. I decided on the spot not to make it easy for them by following Caroline's comments to their natural destination. Which was to my execution ground.

Instead, I just looked at Caroline and said, "And so?"

"And so we have decided to place you on temporary administrative leave—with full salary of course, plus your year-end profit share. We will issue a statement saying the firm has full confidence in your innocence, but that *you* have asked, for the good of the firm, to take a brief leave while the situation works itself out. Of course, we know you will need a place to work with your, um, defense counsel."

I picked up immediately on the "um." Caroline is one of those people who always speak in perfect sentences, nested in perfect essay-like paragraphs, with nary a pause, let alone an um. So the um meant that she wasn't sure she wanted to say what she was about to say. But after a slight pause she conquered the um.

"So," she said, "we have arranged for you to have an unofficial office in the Annex, and Gwen will move there with you."

I stifled a laugh. The Annex is a nondescript seven-story building in the Mid-Wilshire area to which we have moved many of our lower-level administrative functions and staff. Like night word-processing and our internal archival storage. If M&M were a farm, the Annex would be the equivalent of the tool shed on the back forty.

"I'm sorry, Caroline, but I'm not taking a leave," I said. "I'm not going anywhere." In truth, I was surprised at my own decisiveness. It appeared that self-confidence had flown back into me on my drive up the freeway from Manhattan Beach. "To do that would be like admitting guilt. Haven't you ever read the jury instruction that says that the jury may consider evidence of flight from the crime scene as evidence of guilt?" The question was meaningless to her, I knew. Caroline is a tax lawyer.

Caroline didn't respond to the jury remark. She just sat there and looked at me. I don't know whether I'd call her look perplexed or stunned. Apparently, she and her friends had really expected I'd just roll over and leave, thirty-six years with the firm be damned.

Finally, after the silence had grown awkward, she spoke. "But, um, we have decided."

I let the silence reign again for a moment, and then spoke myself. "You don't have the power to decide, Caroline. You want to fire me? You'll have to put it to a vote. Go read the fucking partnership agreement."

With that I pushed my chair back, very carefully standing up as I did so, turned and walked out. So far as I could hear, there wasn't even a rustle as I left. I would have liked to have looked back to see if their mouths were agape, but it would have broken *Old Man Mather's Rules*.

John Cotton Mather, or Old Man Mather, as we called him with affection, had been eighty-something, white-haired, crotchety, bent-over, and decidedly witty. A partner in a hoary old Boston firm, he had crossed over the *Charles* to the Law School every year to teach trial practice, although most of what he had to say had little to do with trials.

My favorite Mather lecture was called "How to Stomp Out of a Room Without Looking Like an Ass."

As Mather put it, "Gentlemen,"—he never did acknowledge the three women in our class—"by the time you get to be my age, you will have had but one or two really choice opportunities to leave a room in anger. Three if you are lucky. But unless you do it properly, you will simply have had several opportunities to make yourself look like a horse's ass. Leaving a room in anger is an art, gentlemen, an *art*." He then offered his "Five Rules for Leaving a Room in Anger":

One: *Do not* pick up your books or papers. Leave them there. They will serve as a perfect reminder that you are gone.

Two: *Do not* shove your chair back from the table while you are still sitting in it. Push back *as* you are standing up.

Three: *Do not* try to put your jacket on as you leave. Don't even fling it over your shoulder. You'll never be Jack Kennedy. Leave it on the chair back.

Four: *Do not* announce that you are departing. Say nothing. Just go.

Five: Never . . . *ever* look back.

I recall now, with some amusement, that he then actually had us *practice* stomping out of a room.

I once had the temerity to ask, "Well, wouldn't it be risky to just leave your stuff there?" To which he replied, pushing his reading glasses down on his nose and fixing me with a withering stare, "Mr. Tarza, if the people you are dealing with are well-bred, they will return your briefcase unopened, your papers unrifled, and your suit jacket with its pockets unprobed." I dared not suggest that one might someday have to walk out on the ill-bred.

John Cotton Mather has been dead now for more than twenty-five years. But I think he would have smiled on my leave-taking of Caroline and her crew. I never ever looked back.

CHAPTER 9

———

As I took the stairs back up to eighty-five, I reflected that my victory over Caroline and her crew was likely to be but temporary. If they really wanted me gone, they weren't going to forget about it just because I had walked out on them, however elegantly. Not one of them had risen to power in the snake pit that Marbury Marfan had become by giving up after a first defeat. I needed to watch my back.

More immediately, I needed to keep my appointment with Jenna and Oscar Quesana. We had agreed to meet in my office at two-fifteen, and I like to be on time. I had to get a move on. As I hurried past Gwen's desk on the way into my office, she thrust an e-mail at me, still printer-hot. I shoved it in my pocket, to be looked at later.

Jenna and Oscar were already there, sitting side by side on the couch. I hadn't seen Oscar in maybe ten years, but he hadn't changed. Same small, lithe, wiry body. Same unlined face. Same bow tie. Same not-quite-the-right-fit gray suit. Probably bought at *Suits Way Below Cost*.

"Sorry guys," I said. "Unexpected meeting."

Oscar sprang off the couch and came toward me, hand extended. "Robert, good to see you again after all these years. Wish the circumstances could be better."

Then he gripped my proffered right hand with both of his, using that clasping double handshake that is supposed to communicate "so *very* sorry," or "I like you *so* much" or some other patently false sentiment. A device known to the unctuous and to undertakers everywhere. But then, a criminal defense lawyer is an undertaker of sorts if you think about it.

"Good to see you, too, Oscar." Out of the corner of my eye, I caught Jenna smiling at me, still on the couch, making no move to get up. She was wearing a white silk blouse and tailored black pantsuit, with a small cloisonné dragon perched on the lapel. Emerald green and spouting a bright red flame from its mouth.

Oscar dropped our handshake, and I moved quickly behind my desk.

Early in my career, I favored sitting next to a client or a guest on a couch. But I had long ago dropped that egalitarian hangover from the seventies. If you put yourself behind the desk and leave the client "out there," it immediately establishes an implicit and important hierarchy. One that works especially well if the client is some powerful captain of industry accustomed to being in charge.

Facing Oscar and Jenna, I needed every inch of hierarchy I could muster. For the very first time in my life I was the client, not the lawyer. I sat down in what I hoped was an authoritative, take-charge sit.

"Okay, Oscar. Let's get down to business."

But Oscar was himself apparently not unskilled in the dominance ritual that takes place on first meeting. He did not make the fatal mistake of sitting back down on the couch. That would have acknowledged my trump and my triumph. Instead, he put his hands behind his back and began to pace in front of my desk, at first saying nothing. It was a move that said, "Sit where you will, I own the room."

Then he double-trumped me by sitting smack on the corner of my desk, left foot planted on the floor, butt firmly on the corner, body-weight on his right hand, leaning in toward me. I actually shrank back.

"Robert, I'm not gonna give you VIP treatment. I'm not gonna treat you with kid gloves. That's the way VIPs get hosed in this business. I'm just going to ask you the same first question I've asked every murder suspect I've ever represented."

"Which is?" I wasn't sure I really wanted to hear it.

"Did you kill him?"

I did not expect that question. For one thing, I had always heard that criminal defense lawyers prefer not to know whether or not you are guilty. For another, it was too direct a question on such short acquaintance. There's something enormously intimate about being asked if you have killed another human being. Maybe it would have seemed an okay question later, after Oscar and I had gotten reacquainted some. After all, it hadn't bothered me when Gwen asked. Or Harry. But Oscar was still almost a complete stranger.

I looked over at Jenna for guidance. She remained stock-still on the couch. Despite the snappy outfit, she did not look at all well. She was not going to be of help.

"I'm innocent," I said.

"If only," Oscar said, "that were an answer to the question I asked. Look, you could be innocent even if you killed him. Not all killings are crimes."

He was still sitting on my desk. "So why don't you just answer the question I actually asked you?"

I was apparently on trial with my own lawyer. He was going to listen to what I said and judge me. How, I wondered, are you supposed to declare your innocence? With anger? Calmly? Slowly, each word distinctly separated from the other for effect? I chose calmly.

"I didn't kill him," I said.

"Good," Oscar said. "Now, ask me why I want to know."

"Is this a game?"

"Not at all. Ask me the question."

"Okay, why do you want to know?" Physically, I was still behind my desk. Mentally, I had begun to float somewhere out in the room. Was I really having a conversation about whether I killed Simon Rafer?

"Let me try it with a hypothetical," he said. He slid off my desk, walked over to the window, and stood looking at the view, hands behind his back.

"Suppose," he said, still facing the window, "you were to change your mind and tell me, 'yes, I killed that schmuck.' What do you think we'd need to do then?" He turned to hear my answer.

"But I didn't kill him," I said.

"Well, my friend, as our now mostly departed profs used to say to us in law school, oh so long ago, 'It's my hypo.' And since it's my hypo right now, you have to play along and say, 'I killed him.'"

"Okay," I said, "let's suppose I killed him." Like every lawyer, I am easy prey for an absurd hypothetical.

Oscar put his hands in his pockets and lounged back against one of the windows. "So," he went on, "if you were to tell me that, yes, you did kill him, we would proceed to have a nice talk about it."

"Like what?"

"About how and why you did it. What you need to know about the temporary insanity defense. How not to cave too early in a plea deal."

I wasn't liking being guilty, even in a hypothetical. So I interrupted it. Or tried to. "Oscar, could you stop leaning against the window? It's making me nervous."

"I'm okay," he said. "The window isn't going anywhere."

I tried again. "Wouldn't that be unethical? To coach me like that?"

"Could be," he said, then went right on, as if there had been no interruptions.

"After we finished our little chat, Robert, you would have to fire me and get yourself a brand new lawyer. We'd put it out to the press as a 'difference of opinion' maybe. Or that you insist on pleading innocent just because you are." Then he laughed with a kind of explosive "hah!" A laugh that seemed to imply that very few people protesting their innocence really are.

I finally got it. This whole thing was Oscar's *shtick*, no doubt perfected over years, to give me an opportunity to change my statement with a minimum of embarrassment. This time, he didn't have to tell me what question to ask.

"Why would I have to fire you, Oscar?"

"Because knowing you killed him, I wouldn't be comfortable insisting to the press that you're an innocent man being hounded by a vote-hungry DA. Or bargain very effectively for a great plea deal. Or put you on the witness stand and let you lie your little heart out. I wouldn't even be able to argue to a jury that you didn't kill him—only that the state didn't prove that you did."

I was beginning to feel like I was back in first-year Legal Ethics. "Okay, Professor Quesana," I said. "What's the bottom, bottom line?"

"Just what I said. You'd need a new lawyer."

"And what would I tell this new lawyer?"

"That you're as pure as a new fallen snow."

"What about Jenna?"

"She will leave the case with me." I noticed that he had dropped the conditional "would" and switched to the immediate future tense, "will."

Jenna sat up straight. "I'm not going anywhere," she said.

Oscar unleaned himself from the window and went to sit beside Jenna on the couch. He turned slightly to face her. "Robert can think it over. If he tells us he killed him, then, toots, when the strategizing's done, the party will be over and we'll both be going."

Jenna's voice was no stronger, but still firm. "Like I said. I'm not going anywhere. And don't call me toots."

"Fine, I will call you Miss James then . . . Miss James, this is not a civil case. This is a criminal case. About murder. About Robert going to jail for twenty-five years. The rules are different here. I know them, you don't."

Jenna looked straight at him and said it again. "I'm not leaving him, no matter what."

"Yes you are," Oscar said. "If Robert comes clean and tells us he killed Rafer, then when we're done with the strategy part, you're leaving with me, even if I have to drag you out of here by your pretty hair."

"You are not a nice person, Oscar." She said it, not so much as an accusation, but in sadness, as something she was resigned to.

"Once upon a time, Miss James, I was. Criminal defense is a blood sport. It takes away the nice in you."

I was taking this in as if from afar. Like watching a bad play from the last row. I wanted to put an end to it.

"Both of you, please shut up," I said. "Let me say it again." This time I *did* string the words out, one by one. "I . . . did . . . not . . . kill . . . Simon . . . Rafer."

I paused for what I hoped would be the impact of brief silence. Neither one of them said a word in response. Then I continued. "Get it guys? And I have no clue who did kill him. Is that definitive enough for you, Oscar? Can we now get on with it?"

"Yes, now we can get on with it," he said. "I'm well on the way to being persuaded."

I felt better.

"Subject, of course," he added, "to looking at all the evidence."

There it was. He was qualifying it. All lawyers do that, of course. I do it myself. But this was the first time I had been personally qualified to.

Oscar must have seen the sudden look of discomfort on my face, because he went on to qualify his qualification.

"At the very least, Robert, I'm persuaded enough to start talking about how we can prove that you're innocent."

"I thought I was innocent till proven guilty."

"In high school civics books maybe. Here in the real world, the jury looks over at you and thinks, 'Well, damn! If he weren't guilty, he wouldn't be here, would he?' So, practically speaking, we'll need to prove you *didn't* do it. Unless, of course, you're famous and the jury can imagine that they already know you and trust you." He grinned. "Are you famous, Robert?"

"No."

"I didn't think so. Unfortunately, the victim, while not really famous, was locally prominent. So the jury will feel more anxious to avenge him than it would a homeless, nearly nameless drunk."

"Wait a minute," Jenna said. "Okay, Robert found the body. And sure, he was stupid enough to touch it and get blood on his sleeve. But aren't those pathetically small facts to lead Spritz to suspect him of murdering Simon?" That seemed to drain her. She slumped again into the couch.

"Do you know what spatter is, Jenna?" Oscar asked.

"Only from TV shows."

"TV shows get it mostly right. It's a pattern in the way blood hits a surface that suggests the blood flew through the air and landed on the surface with a splat. Not what you'd expect from a glancing touch."

I never watched TV, but I got it. "Like," I said, "blood flying through the air when a dagger strikes flesh."

"Exactly."

"Well, since the blood on my sleeve didn't get there by flying through the air, that test will exonerate me. Bring it on."

"Unfortunately, Robert, spatter analysis is like reading tea leaves. You see what you want to see. A junior criminalist at the LAPD crime lab took a look at the stain and saw spatter."

"That can't be."

"They're sending the blood stain to an outside expert. You may turn out to be right. Let's hope so."

"How do you know what the criminalist said?" Jenna asked.

"A former wife's cousin runs the LAPD crime lab. Twenty years ago, I helped him land his first job there. So I called, and asked him what he knew."

"Corruption," I said. To no one in particular, for no particular reason.

"That's one way to look at it," Oscar said. "Or you can look at it as business as usual that's helpful to my clients. Like you."

"I guess," I said.

"Oscar, are we done for today?" Jenna asked.

"For today, yes. Except for a nicety. Robert hasn't said whether he actually wants to hire me."

"I do want to hire you," I said.

I got up from behind my desk and walked over to offer my hand. It was a ritual I had picked up from my father. Always seal a deal with a handshake.

Oscar rose from the couch, took my proffered hand and shook it. "Great. My initial retainer is $50,000."

I should have said, "That's a lot of money," or "Perhaps we could start with a lower amount since this case isn't going anywhere," or any number of other things.

Instead, I just said, "Okay. I'll have Gwen messenger a check over to you."

"Thanks," he said. "I'll set up another meeting in a couple of days. We'll go over the evidence. The detailed facts, your relationship with the victim, possible motives, stuff like that. In the meantime, here's my first piece of paid-for advice. Stay home and watch TV, even though you don't watch TV."

"I'm not going to do that," I said.

Oscar stared at me. Much, I thought, like a father might stare at a sixteen-year-old who has just announced that he's taking his girlfriend to Las Vegas for the weekend. But instead of taking my keys, he just said, "No, I don't suppose you will. Clients like you are so smart they're stupid."

He gathered up his coat and left.

I looked at Jenna, still sprawled on the couch.

"I'm not accustomed to being talked to that way."

"Maybe not," she said. "But, on the other hand, are you accustomed to being suspected of murder?"

"Fair point. But it's only been two days. I need some time to clothe myself in the rags of my lowered status. Which status is undeserved, by the way. This is all a bunch of bunk. The cops don't really have anything on me."

"You didn't tell Oscar about the dagger or the piece of cloth they removed from your couch," she said.

"I forgot. I'll tell him at our next meeting."

Jenna didn't respond, but instead reached over to the table between the couch and the chairs and picked up the cube with the Athenian tetradrachm in it. She turned it in her hands, studying the coin inside. "It's pretty," she said.

I knew what she was doing, of course. Distracting me from my embarrassment at being treated like a child by Oscar, not to mention my defensive reaction to it. Jenna is talented at distraction. At times it has annoyed me. This time, I relished it.

"Take the coin out of the cube if you like," I said.

"Really?"

"Sure. I always let people do that."

"I didn't know that. Thank you." She turned the cube over and dumped the coin into the palm of her left hand, then held it up to the light.

"I've always loved the owl," she said.

"I love it, too," I said, "but the really nice thing about that wonderful piece of art is that it only cost me three hundred bucks."

"I always assumed it was rare. It's not?"

"No. The Greeks minted hundreds of thousands of them."

"But the Ides is rare, right?"

"Very. At most Brutus probably struck only a few thousand of them. Only fifty-eight are known to have survived. No one has dug up a new one in over a hundred years."

"Maybe we should put together an expedition to Rome and try to dig more of them up ourselves, Robert."

Jenna had moved from distraction to implementing our mutual joint stress reduction strategy—fantasizing about getting out of Dodge and doing something entirely unrelated to law. During some dark moments in the Media Sausage trademark trial, the last trial we'd done together, we'd developed a plan to start a Ferrari dealership in Costa Rica. Using my money, of course.

"Actually, Jenna, we'd be better off going to Northern Italy or Macedonia. That's where Brutus's army was when he minted the Ides. Fighting Anthony."

"Perfect. We'll dig there, then. I've never been to Macedonia."

"Well, you don't usually dig specifically for coins. People hid coins in clay pots beneath the floor stones of houses and shops—hoards, they're called. Sometimes, when you dig up a building, the hoards are still there."

"People buried their coins? That's interesting. Why?"

"For safekeeping. There weren't any banks."

"What about ATMs and credit cards?" she said, grinning.

"Nope."

"Then how did they shop?" She laughed out loud.

"The same way I did the year I came here. With cash."

"Oh, geezer money," she said.

"You don't really call it that, do you?"

"Sometimes."

We were bantering again. It felt good. Maybe it really was going to be all right.

"We've got some other things we need to talk about," I said. "But first I'm going to get myself some coffee. Want some?"

"No, I think I'll just sit here and admire your partner-level view. We can finish talking when you get back."

"Okay." I walked out the door. Gwen was at her desk.

"Mr. Tarza," she said, "you have a lot of phone calls."

"I'll deal with them a little later. Right now I want to get myself some much needed coffee."

"I can get it for you." Unlike a lot of the more modern secretaries, Gwen doesn't mind getting my coffee.

"Thanks, but I feel like getting it myself today," I said.

I didn't wait for her response, but turned left into the hallway and headed for the small kitchen on the other side of the floor. The long walk felt good.

Once in the kitchen, I pulled a mug off the shelf and started to pour myself some coffee. I watched it spill into the mug and told myself that all the cops had on me was opportunity and a bloodstain subject to expert interpretation. By the time I had poured in a small bit of milk and stirred in the sugar, I had dismissed the dagger thing as too far-fetched for anyone to believe and had also persuaded myself that the stain on the couch would turn out to be an old red wine spill. I felt great. I picked up the mug. My hand did not shake.

On the way back to my office, I stopped along the way to say hi to a couple of people. They seemed a bit reserved, but that was understandable. I mean, who wants to chat up a killer? Soon, the true facts would come out and everyone would crowd around me, hanging on my stories of what it had been like to be wrongly suspected. Maybe I'd even speak about it on a few bar association panels.

Gwen didn't say a word as I walked past her desk on my way back to my office. She just gave me her patented "you need to deal with these phone calls" look.

"I know, I know," I said. "As soon I get done talking to Jenna."

And speaking of talking to Jenna, it seemed to me like an excellent time to wrap up an unresolved issue. Whether Simon really had been about to dump Jenna, as Harry claimed. It was time to find out.

I walked into my office, intending to learn the answer. And there was Oscar, sitting casually in one of the chairs, chatting with Jenna.

CHAPTER 10

———

"**O**scar, what the hell are you doing here?"

He turned his head toward me without getting up. "I'm your lawyer," he said. "I'm here because it turns out we need to talk some more."

"About what?"

"Well," he said, "I have some new information. But why don't you sit down?"

It was unbelievable. He was inviting me to take a seat in my own office. I gave in and took the other chair.

"Okay, what is it? I've got a lot of phone calls to return."

"On my way out, I ran into my old buddy Spritz in the lobby."

"You know him?"

"Sure. Ever since we were both rookies in the DA's office back in the late sixties. He was a rookie investigator and I was a rookie Assistant DA."

I was not thrilled to learn that Oscar had known Spritz for many years. I should have been, but I wasn't.

"What did he want?" I asked.

"I'll tell you. But let me ask you a few questions first, so I don't pollute your recollection with what Spritz told me."

Oscar's approach was, of course, a standard technique for good lawyers. Get your client's first recollections pure, unsullied by what someone else has said.

"Okay," I said.

"What did you tell the cops when they arrived the morning of the murder?"

"Very little."

"Tell me what you remember."

I shrugged. "I told them that I had arrived and found Simon's body face down with a knife in his back. That I had called 911 and then just waited there for them to show up."

"Anything else?"

"The only other thing I can think of is that they wanted to know if there was anybody else on the floor. I told them I hadn't seen anyone else. That was pretty much it."

"Did they ask what time you arrived?"

"Come to think of it, they did. I told them I had arrived exactly at six. I knew that because the elevator unlocks automatically from its security mode at 5:59 a.m. I remembered looking at my watch, right before I got into the elevator, to see if I needed to pull out my key card to get up here. It read exactly 6:00 a.m., so I didn't need to get it out."

"When I ran into Spritz," Oscar said, "he was just coming out of the building Security Office, right off the lobby."

"I've never been in it."

"I have," Jenna said.

Oscar seemed not to care that Jenna had been in it. He reached into his inner suit coat pocket and took out a folded piece of paper. "Spritz gave me this," he said. He unfolded it and handed it to me.

It was a four-columned list of numbers on an 8 1/2 by 11 page.

CenterCityBldg 12:05 12:06
18:00-5:59 PA90834, PT7251210

20:02	235627	1209	3
20:04	234523	1209	1
20:21	236173	1209	2
20:43	232947	1209	2
20:45	234521	1209	3
20:49	444988	1209	2
20:50	443682	1209	1
20:55	442210	1209	1
20:57	443188	1209	3
23:45	526428	1209	2
00:04	443271	1209	3
00:10	527744	1209	3
00:13	525454	1209	3
00:18	522891	1209	3
04:30	239738	1210	3

"What is it?" I asked.

"A printout of the computerized elevator records for this building's M&M floors for late Sunday night and early Monday morning before Simon's murder, stating at 8:00 p.m. on Sunday."

"And the numbers mean what?"

"Left-most column is the time on a twenty-four hour clock. Next one is the number of the key card used to unlock the elevator if it was in after-hours security mode. Next after that is the date. Right-most is which of the three elevators that serve the eighty-fifth floor on weekends came up when. The printout shows only trips up."

"And?"

"Well, why don't you compare the number on your elevator key card with the last entry on the list?"

I pulled out my wallet and took out my key card. There was no number on the front. I flipped it over and examined the back. There, right above the magnetic strip, was a small, printed number—239738. I had never noticed it before. I looked down at the list again. My number matched the last entry—the one for the elevator that came up at 4:30 a.m. on the morning Simon was murdered. I felt an icy tingle run up my spine.

"I think this is a problem," Oscar said.

"This is bullshit. You said you got this from Spritz?"

"Indeed I did."

"Well you tell that asshole I was *not* on the elevator that morning at 4:30 a.m.," I said. "I didn't get here till 6:00 a.m. Period."

"There's more."

"Like what?"

"The coroner's estimate for the time of death is between 4:00 and 5:00 a.m. So the cops think you came up early, killed him, left, and then came back later to 'discover' the body. If you ever left at all."

"That's nonsense."

"And they also think," Oscar said, "that they've caught you in one of those incriminating lies they like to tell juries about."

"It's utter bullshit."

"May I see the card?" Jenna asked. Oscar handed it to her, then turned back to me.

"I believe you, Robert," Oscar said. "But it seems no one else does. So we need to find out how your key card came to be riding up the elevator at 4:30 a.m. without you. If we don't, they'll need only one more piece of evidence to feel comfortable charging you."

He turned toward Jenna. "You see, Miss James, if you add this sad little fact to the other sad little facts we were talking about right before I left, you're a long way toward an indictment and a conviction."

"Don't condescend to me, Oscar," she said.

"I'm not condescending to you. But despite your snotty credentials, you appear to know zero about criminal defense. The only reason I'm not tossing you off the case right now is because you called me and got me hired."

"I'm not totally ignorant about it," Jenna said. "I'm sick today. I'm not myself."

"Okay. I'm sorry," he said.

I didn't think he was sorry.

"Back to Robert's key card," Oscar said. "Robert, could someone have taken your card, copied the magnetic strip, then returned the real card without your knowing about it?"

"I don't see how," I said. "When I'm not using the card, it's usually in my wallet. Once in a while I leave it in my suit coat pocket. When it's hung up on the back of the door."

I glanced over at Jenna. She was, of course, the only person who would have had access to my office before the murder as well as access to my wallet *after* the murder. While I was in a drugged sleep that first night. I thought I saw a slight twitch in her face. Maybe I just imagined it.

"Then perhaps," Oscar said, "someone borrowed it out of your coat pocket."

"They didn't have to copy his physical card," Jenna said. "The encoding on the magnetic strip on the back of each card"—she held the card up—"is on record somewhere. Someone could have copied the data from the source and made a duplicate card without borrowing this one."

Oscar looked at her. "Smart girl."

"I'm not a girl."

"Smart *lady*."

The whole Jenna-Oscar thing was beginning to tire me out. "Would you two cut it out?" I said. "It's not helpful to have my two defense lawyers behaving like children." It felt good to say it. Like I was in control again.

Neither of them responded, but they did stop bickering.

"Jenna," I asked, "what else do you know about key cards?"

"I know," she said, "that copies have been made before. By associates who . . . Well, there were some sexual liaisons that people wanted to cover up. Wouldn't do to have a record of who was up here with whom in the middle of the night."

Oscar looked intrigued. "Do you know someone who did it?"

"Well, yes," she said.

"Who?"

"Simon did."

"He did?" Oscar seemed genuinely surprised. As a guy who had been a sole practitioner most of his life, he probably had no inkling of what a managing partner could bring to pass if he put his mind to it.

"Yes," Jenna said. "He created one for me and another one for him. So that when I met him up here late at night, it would look like two male associates working late. He duped the cards of two guys who always left by six each night. Then each of us came up separately, fifteen or twenty minutes apart." She smiled wanly. "Those two guys are gone now, of course. Not enough billable hours."

I looked over at Oscar looking at Jenna. His eyebrows were arched. Like he couldn't quite believe what he was hearing. Then he pulled his head back a bit, in what I took as mock surprise, and just asked her outright. "You were sleeping with Simon?"

"Yes."

I could almost see Oscar's brain running, mulling it over. "Do the cops know?

"Not so far as I know. We were very careful."

"Who does know?"

"Nobody." She paused. "Well, there is someone who might be able to put it together if she tried."

"Who?"

"Susan Apacha."

"Who is that?"

"The security chief for the building," she said. "She was a former, well, flame of Simon's. They were over but still friends. She helped him make the fake key cards for us. Although I don't think she knew who his female partner was. Unless he told her about me. Which I doubt. He was very discreet."

Oscar looked thoughtful. Hopeful even. "So the cops don't know about her yet?"

I piped up. "I think they do. They were asking Harry Marfan about her last night. And I'm guessing that's why Spritz was in the security office."

"Yeah," Jenna said. "That's where she works."

Oscar took a tiny notebook out of his jacket pocket. I saw him writing down Susan Apacha's name. "Maybe," he said, "they also wanted to talk to this Apacha woman about something else. The something else being that someone disabled the security camera in elevator 3 right around the time it was being used by whoever killed Simon. If they hadn't, we'd have a picture of whoever it was."

I hadn't thought about the security camera in the elevator. Dumb not to have thought of it. There was one in each elevator. "How did they do that?" I asked.

"They aimed a laser pointer at the camera lens. Like the one in that pencil holder over there." He gestured in the general direction of my desk.

"I use that when I teach."

"No doubt. But that is what they used, and not many people around here have them."

"Did Spritz . . . ?"

"Yes, he made careful note of it when you two imbeciles let him in here."

Jenna just glowered at him, and I could tell she wanted to hit him. But he was right. We had been imbeciles.

"What about the security cameras in the lobby?" I asked.

"According to Spritz they were reported 'out-of-order' sometime late on Thursday. Supposedly. They were to be repaired on Monday morning."

Oscar got up, clearly getting ready to leave. "I think I need to talk to this Apacha woman. Have you got her home number, Jenna?"

"Yeah. Somewhere they gave everybody a list of how to reach the security people day and night. I'll have to find it."

"Why don't you call me with it?"

"Can I just e-mail it to you?"

"I don't have a computer."

"What's your cell number, then?"

"I don't have one of those, either."

"Okay," she said. "I've got your regular number. I'll call you with it."

"Good." He stood up and left.

I got up, too, and said, "Jenna, I think it's time to go home. Maybe we can even do it without hearing more bad news on our way out."

"Yeah, let's go," she said.

She got up and started to head for the door. And almost fell over. Fortunately, I was right next to her and managed to catch her before she went down.

"I'm sorry," she said, and collapsed back into the couch.

"Are you okay?" I asked.

"Not really. I threw up right before our meeting with Oscar. I still don't feel very good."

"Do you have the flu?"

"Uh, yes, I guess so."

I eyed her. I could have sworn that she had hesitated before answering me. I hoped to God she wasn't hiding something awful. The year before, a young associate had died of brain cancer. It had all started with his throwing up. But I didn't press her.

"Okay, Jenna. Why don't you sit for a few more minutes. I'll check with Gwen about my phone calls, and then we can try again. Do you want us to get you something? A Coke, maybe? That can calm your stomach."

"No, I'll be okay. I just need to gather myself."

"Okay."

I walked out to Gwen's desk. She got up and came around to me, holding a small pad on which she had obviously written a list of names.

"Mr. Tarza, you've gotten seventeen phone calls. Do you want all of them?"

"No. Just tell me the important ones."

"Okay. Your former wife keeps calling. She says she's being hounded by the *National Enquirer*. Says she doesn't want to talk to them. But it sounds like she's going to if you don't call her back." She paused. "I never did like her."

"I'll call her. I promise. Who else who's important?"

"Your daughter. She called again about needing airfare."

"Call her and tell her my lawyer doesn't want her to come back right now." It's always great to blame things on your lawyer.

"Anyone else?"

"Peter Penosco. He seems annoyed, too. Complained you didn't return his call of yesterday. And someone named Serappo Prodiglia. He called four times. Says he knows you." She hesitated. "Is there really someone with that name?"

"Yes."

Gwen said nothing. She was clearly waiting for me to tell her who Serappo Prodiglia was.

"He's a rare coin dealer."

"I've never heard of him before," she said.

It was a reproach of sorts. Why hadn't I ever mentioned him to her? That was the unspoken question. Gwen had once explained to me that having a top secretary was like being married. She had to know everyone you knew and where you were going and what you did when you got there. Otherwise, she had explained, it would be embarrassing for her.

"I haven't talked to him in more than ten years."

"I was here ten years ago." She paused. "He refused to give me his contact information. I'll just get it from you later, I guess." She huffed back behind her desk.

I went to call Peter Penosco. Jenna was still sitting on the couch, although she looked a bit less pale.

The direct line on my desk rang before I could pick up the phone to dial. It was Stewart Broder.

"Hi, Robert, how *are* you?"

"I've been *better*." It was so hard not to mimic his speech pattern.

"Yeah, well, that *makes* sense. Listen, I know who *did* it."

"You do?" A lead. The first one maybe. Of course, one had to consider the source. "Well, tell me." I could feel my heart racing.

"I don't want to do it in the *office*."

"Call me at home, then?"

"Not on the *phone*, either."

"Okay. Just name a place."

"Meet me at the DownUnder at 7:30 tomorrow *morning*."

"I'll be there," I said.

"They've got that great breakfast with *beer,* you know."

I refrained from saying yuck. "I remember, Stewart. I'll see you there."

After I hung up, I thought about whether I should actually go. What the hell. I'd go, but I wouldn't put too much stock in it. I also realized that I had become way too tired to return Peter Penosco's call. Tomorrow morning would have to do.

Then I remembered the e-mail I'd shoved in my pocket earlier. I took it out and read it. It was from Stewart, confirming our meeting at the DownUnder. Which was odd, because he had sent it before we talked. But then Stewart was an odd fellow.

I had almost forgotten that Jenna was still there, until she spoke up.

"Who was that?" she asked. "On the phone."

"Stewart Broder."

"There's a weird man. What did he want?"

"He says he knows who did it."

"Yeah, right."

"You never know. Maybe he does. I'm going to see him tomorrow morning and find out."

"Well, good luck," she said. "Maybe when your meeting is over you can go out to his house and visit his talking parrot—the one who quotes Macbeth. Anyway, I'm feeling better. But I'm not up to driving. Will you take me home?"

"Sure. Where are you . . ." Then I remembered.

"I'm living at your house, remember?"

"Right. Do you think it's a good idea for the Blob to see us together as we leave?"

"They've already seen us together. I just want to get out of here. But I'm in no shape to drive."

"You could always take the bus."

"Oh, Robert." She smiled that very nice smile of hers. The smile and the "Oh Robert" seemed somehow to sum it up. We were going to be in this together. For better or for worse.

On the way down to B-Level in the elevator, I again thought about confronting Jenna with what Harry had told me about Simon wanting to dump her, but decided it wasn't a good time. After all, she was sick. And, perhaps even more importantly, I didn't think I could take any more news right then, good or bad.

When we drove out of the garage, the Blob was still there, hovering by the exit. But we varied our routine. This time *Jenna* gave them the thumbs up sign. We both laughed uproariously. Odd what tension will make funny.

CHAPTER 11

———

When I went to bed that night, I set my alarm for 6:00 a.m. I needn't have bothered. I was wide awake by 5:30 a.m. When I drove out of my garage an hour later, the sun had not yet risen. During the night the Blob had shrunk to a boom mike lying on the ground, a camera, its attendant camera guy, and a reporter in a red parka. I think the two humans were asleep until the sound of the garage door woke them. I waved as I went by. I don't think they managed to get any footage.

The DownUnder has a sign that says SINCE 1975. In other words, since the year *after* I got to M&M. I recall going to the Grand Opening on New Year's Eve that year. Even then it had seemed grotty. The place is down a rather dank set of steps, set below ground in what must once have been a basement. The decor is a grain-mismatched knotty pine, of the type found in suburban rec rooms built in the fifties. The booths are emerald green leather of a particularly bright hue. The bar looks rescued from the set of an old gangster movie.

Stewart was sitting in one of the booths. He didn't look good, even for Stewart. He looked fatter than ever, and his skin seemed to have a sickly pallor, or at least the patches of facial skin I could see through his ever-present hide-the-acne makeup. I thought to myself that I ought to stop disliking Stewart. After all, he was trying to help me. Maybe when this was all over, I'd see if I could find him a better dermatologist.

Stewart already had the house breakfast special in front of him—Huevos Pancho Villa. Eggs under huge dollops of salsa, topped off with red and green peppers shaped to resemble a sombrero. All accompanied by a large stein of beer. I have never known whether the special had been given that name because Pancho liked an overabundance of salsa, because he wore a sombrero or because he drank a lot early in the morning. Whatever the answer, it has become a local culinary classic and there are lawyers and judges in town who make almost a cult of ordering it. I am not among them.

I sat down across from him. I restrained myself from making a snide comment about the beer. He was already half done with his salsa and eggs and the beer was well below the mid-line on the stein, which was marked by the barrel of a six-shooter engraved into the glass. He didn't look up. "Drugs were involved," was all he said.

"What kind of drugs?"

"I'm not sure. Maybe heroin."

Stewart was still looking down, still eating.

"And Harry Marfan did it," he added, almost as an afterthought.

"Yeah, sure."

"I'm pretty sure it was him." He hadn't yet looked up.

"Why would he do it? He loved Simon like a son."

He looked up. "It had to do with drugs. I heard them talking about drugs."

"Who? When?"

"I came into the *office* on Sunday afternoon. To work on a year-end *tax* deal. I stayed till around 2:00 a.m. that night. My office is right *next* to reception on eighty-five. But you *already* know that. Just before I got up to leave, the two of them walked through. Simon and Harry."

"Saying?"

"I couldn't hear it all. Something about a drug deal and something about 'Hello.'"

"Hello like on the telephone?"

"Yeah. What you say on the telephone when you answer," he said. "Except it sounded like they were talking about the name of a place."

"What else did they say?"

"I couldn't hear most of it. But Harry sounded really angry. Almost screaming. He kept telling Simon the drugs were late."

"So all that was when, exactly?" I asked.

"Like I said, about 2:00. I left just a couple minutes later."

"Down the elevator?"

"Yes."

"Did they see you?" I asked.

"I don't think so."

"So what's your theory?"

"Simon was involved in a drug deal, he got into an argument with Harry about it, and Harry killed him. Later that night."

The whole story was so absurd that I seriously considered getting up and leaving. But then I thought to myself that if I was going to be my own detective, I needed to pursue all leads, both the landish and the outlandish.

It still didn't make any sense, though.

"Why would Simon and Harry be involved in drugs?" I asked. "Neither one of them needs the money. Simon was pulling down well over a million bucks from the firm and was independently wealthy to boot. Harry has more money than Croesus."

Stewart shrugged. "Simon actually made one million eight *last* year. And as for why, Harry told me you *talked* to him and he *told* you about Simon's gambling problem."

"He did, but I find it hard to believe."

"Well, believe it. Simon told several of his friends about it."

"Including you?"

"Yes."

"Well," I said, "I hadn't been on his friends list for quite a while."

"Yeah, he pretty *much* hated you," Stewart said. "I *couldn't* understand why you sold him the Ides."

"He outbid everyone else. So fair was fair. Friend or no friend."

Stewart made no response to that. He just went on eating his eggs.

I needed to move the conversation away from firm politics and back to what happened the morning of the murder.

"Stewart, just because Simon and Harry were there together doesn't mean that Harry killed him."

He put down his fork and looked at me. "You remember Professor *Neery*?"

"Dreary Neery? Crim Law?"

"Yeah."

"Remember he was always *talking* about Occam's razor? Pick the *simplest* explanation?"

"That's not exactly the way Occam put it," I said. "But in any case, Neery taught about it at Harvard, not Yale."

"Visited *at* Yale."

"Oh."

"Anyway," Stewart went on, "Neery would have analyzed it this way: if Harry was screaming at Simon at 2:00 a.m. in the office, and Simon was found dead in the office maybe four hours later, the simplest explanation would be that Harry killed him. Instead of a complicated explanation? Like, you know, someone we don't know about was kicking around the office late at night and killed Harry for some reason we don't know?"

I noticed that Stewart's odd inflection had come and gone during our conversation. It was hard to figure out what drove it. I was thinking about that, trying to puzzle it out, when I realized Stewart was waiting for a response from me.

"I take your point," I finally said.

"You gonna *eat* something?" he asked.

"Just a quick cup of coffee." I looked around for the waitress, but didn't see her.

Stewart took a big swig from his beer stein, then started in on his eggs again.

"Stewart, wouldn't Occam's razor, if it were especially sharp, suggest that you did it?"

He put his fork down, with a bang this time, and looked up. He had egg on his lip. "Because I was there until 2:00?"

"Yes."

"Well, first, I left at 2:00. And the razor only works, Robert, if there's *some* other fact to *go* with my being there. *Which* there isn't."

"I think there is." The egg on his lip was driving me crazy. The impulse for primate grooming arises at the oddest times. I picked up my open napkin, reached across the table, and brushed the egg off his lip. He did not protest and waited to respond to my statement until I had finished.

When I was done, he said, "Like *what?*"

"Like the fact that you were about to be fired. By Simon."

"That's *not* true."

"Stewart, you haven't billed squat since you lost Physical Science Concepts as a client. Four years ago."

"I didn't lose *them*. They *went* bankrupt. Because their CEO was a nut *case*."

"Whatever the reason, you lost them and your billings went to hell. You've become a financial drain on the firm. We talked about you in the last executive committee meeting. You were on the list."

"Simon *would* never have me fired. I *came* here before he did. We were friends. *And* anyway, I wouldn't care if I were fired. I have plenty of money."

"I don't believe you. I think you knew your head was on the chopping block, and you killed him. And now you're making up the drug thing."

"I'm not."

Stewart pushed his plate aside, looked at me rather directly, and said, "If anybody *has* a motive, it's you, Robert."

"And what would my motive be?"

"Your argument with Simon about the Ides. He wanted you to take it back. And give him his money back. It was a lot of money, even for you."

The opportunity to lie had presented itself to me once again. It seems that once you tell a lie, the lie has to be nurtured, protected, and repeated or it will rupture and let the truth inside it spill out. I could have withdrawn the lie right then, of course.

"You've got it wrong, Stewart. I took the Ides back from him the day before he died," I said. "On Saturday morning. I was about to write him a check. I guess I'll send it to his estate now."

Stewart smiled. I could tell that it was not the kind of smile you get when someone thinks you've said something amusing that doesn't quite merit a laugh but needs an acknowledgement of some kind. It was a "gotcha" kind of smile.

"If you picked it up on Saturday," he asked, "why *was* it still on his kitchen table on Sunday then?"

"What are you talking about?"

"Harry and I were at Simon's *place* on Sunday for brunch. He had the coin out on the *kitchen* table so we could look at it. We had heard about *the* dispute, and we wanted to see if we could tell if the coin was a *fake*."

I retreated into the thing people always say when they are caught in a lie. "I can't explain that, Stewart. I only know what I know. I got it back on Saturday."

"If you *say* so."

"Anyway," I said, "if you're so sure it was a drug deal gone bad, why don't *you* tell the cops about it."

"You can tell the cops if you *want* to. I don't *want* to be involved."

"If I tell them you were the one who overheard the argument, they'll just come talk to you anyway."

"I know. But I don't *want* to be the one to call them up right now."

"Okay," I said. "I'll ask my lawyer to tell them."

"You know what you should do, Robert, don't you?"

"No, what?"

"Go see Harry again. Ask *him* if he was there that night."

"I'll think about it," I said.

"Okay, but aren't you *going* to have some coffee?" he asked. He asked it in a way that made clear that the important part of our conversation was over.

"Sure."

I ordered the coffee, then sat and talked to Stewart for another fifteen minutes. About nothing at all really. It's odd how you can share important information with someone and then proceed directly to banal chitchat, as if the first exchange never happened. So Simon was involved in drugs and Harry killed him, and, by the way, how's your golf game?

CHAPTER 12

——

I was back at my house by 8:45. Jenna was in the kitchen eating, with five or six tabloids spread out in front of her.

"Where did you get those?" I asked.

"The guys out front."

"You talked to them?"

"Sure. I took them some coffee."

"Oh," I said.

"The tabs have a name for you now," she said.

"What?"

She flipped the *National Enquirer* around so I could see it right-side up. There I was on the front page, suited up, looking directly at the camera. The headline above my picture said: "Coin Killer?" And under that: "Dagger in Back over Coin?"

Next to my picture was a fuzzy picture of an 1804 silver dollar.

I laughed. "Wrong coin. But if it's an original and not a re-strike, I'd love to own it. I don't collect that stuff, but I bet I could cover the costs of hiring Oscar by selling it to somebody who does. Anyway, who the hell told them anything at all about a coin?"

Jenna stretched her arms above her head. She was wearing flannel pajamas. The stretch bared her very thin waist. It was not unattractive. I tried not to look. "Well," she said, yawning and continuing the stretch, "the police probably leaked it to them. The first of many leaks to come. When they tortured my dad, they leaked two or three things each week. Takes its toll because you never know what's coming next. Or exactly how wrong or twisted it will be."

"And our strategy is?"

"Counter leaks. Oscar's job." She picked up the remote, pointed it at my small kitchen TV, and clicked it on. To my amazement, there was Oscar on the morning news, standing on the steps of some nondescript courthouse, condemning the police for the leak, saying none of it was true, proclaiming my innocence, and asserting there would be no indict-ment, all without pausing for breath.

I was incredulous. "Did you know he'd be on?"

"No. Just blind luck." She grinned. "But it is the top of the hour, and there's not much else going on. Too close to Christmas. So I took a shot." She clicked it back off.

"Jenna, how does Oscar even know about the coin?"

"I told him about it."

"Oh."

I looked again at my picture in the *Enquirer*. "Where do you think they got that picture? I don't even recognize it."

She shrugged. "Someone from the firm probably sold it to them. Or maybe your ex-wife. There'll be a ready market for pictures of you from now on. Are there any nudes of you?" She grinned again.

"No. How about of you?"

"None that I know of."

"Speaking of which, would you mind getting dressed, Jenna? It makes me uncomfortable. You sitting around in your pajamas. It doesn't seem right, even though you're living here for the moment."

"Simon rather liked me in pajamas." She grinned for the third time. "But, okay." She got up and left the kitchen. I could swear she twitched her butt at me as she went through the doorway, but, then, maybe not. Jenna was certainly in a different mood this morning than she had been at the end of the day yesterday. Almost giddy.

Truth is, my complaint about the pajamas, while based in fact, was mostly an excuse to get her out of the kitchen while I considered whether to tell her what Stewart had told me. It was odd that I, of all people, was thinking of withholding it. I have always hated it when clients keep things from me.

Sometimes clients hide things to avoid revealing a case-losing bad fact. Like a ten-year-old who doesn't tell his parents that he's just put a baseball through an upstairs window, in the hopes they won't notice. Sometimes clients hide things just to try to keep control. If information is power, then telling even your own lawyer everything offers you up to the heartless ministrations of expertise. You have nothing left to give.

Jenna reappeared in a black turtleneck sweater, black jeans, and black tennis shoes. With a flash of white sock. She posed in the doorway, one hand behind her head, the other at her waist. "More appropriate, Mr. Uptight?"

"You look like a nun in a Vatican-approved tennis outfit."

She smiled and did a small curtsy. "Did you know you can date nuns now?"

"No. Really?"

"Yes, as long as you don't get into the habit." She giggled. "My seventh grade lesbian gym teacher told us that joke." She came over, sat back down at the table and paused for a moment.

"You know, Robert, I seem to be in the giddy phase of sad."

"So I noticed. Let me tell you something that will sober you up."

"What?"

"I had breakfast this morning with Stewart Broder at the DownUnder."

"Now there's a boys' club."

"Maybe so. Anyway, Stewart told me that he thinks Harry killed Simon."

"Really?"

"Yes, really."

I told her what Stewart had told me, word for word, including the whole weird thing about "hello."

Jenna was instantly suspicious. "Well, if *Stewart* was there at 2:00 a.m., he's as much of a suspect as you. More so. He admits he was there. You don't. Shit. I think Stewart did it!"

"And his motive?"

"How would I know? Motive is just the icing on the cake of opportunity. Stewart is really weird. Who knows what his motive was? Who cares? He was there."

I was about to enlighten her about what *I* thought Stewart's motive might have been when Jenna cocked her head to the side, looked thoughtful and said, "Oh shit. Wait. 'Hello!'"

"What?"

Jenna looked startled. Almost as if she had let slip something she hadn't intended. "Hmm. To tell you, I guess I have to go into a part of my life you don't really know about."

"What can there be that I don't know about? Are you about to tell me you're really a secret agent?" I said it about as unseriously as you can say anything. I thought I knew the general outlines of Jenna's life almost as well as I knew my own. After working together for seven years and sharing a rather large number of martinis, we had few secrets between us. Or so I thought.

"Do you know about my time in Hawaii?"

I shrugged. "I guess not."

"I graduated from high school when I was fifteen. My parents thought I was too young to go to college. So they sent me off to spend a year in Hawaii with my Uncle Freddie. My father's half-brother. On the Big Island. I don't think they knew a lot about Uncle Freddie and his friends. It was like my own, private version of *Almost Famous*. I got quite an education."

"About what in particular?"

"Drugs, among other things."

"Using them?"

"Uh uh. Selling them."

I sat there and didn't know quite what to say. People walk around with the damnedest pasts hidden inside them, and for the most part you can't tell. Drugs? Jenna?

I chose to say something well-modulated. "Well, reprehensible as that was, I still don't see what is has to do with Stewart and Simon."

"Uncle Freddie lived in Hilo. We used to call it Hell-lo. To describe what a pit it is. A lot of the drug dealers there call it that. It was full of fine art galleries. Could just as easily have been rare coin galleries. So rare coins and 'hello' spell a drug deal gone bad."

"Lay it out for me. It's beyond my world."

"Assume you're a drug dealer. You arrange for heroin to be brought into Kona by boat." She tapped the bowl of sugar cubes. I guess the bowl was the boat and the cubes the drugs that I'd delivered.

"Then suppose," she said, "that the local dealers pay you in cash. One million dollars in hundreds." She handed me her napkin, which was apparently the one million in cash. "So now you've got a problem."

"Which is?"

"You have to do something with the money. You can't deposit it in a bank, because any cash transaction with a bank over $10,000 has to be reported to the feds."

"I could put it in many banks," I said.

"You'd have to put it in at least a hundred and one banks. Won't be easy and will itself arouse suspicion. It will also make it very difficult to buy big things." She smiled. "You'd have to write fifty checks for your new Maserati."

"You seem to know a lot about this."

"Yes and no. Much of it is theory to me. Some of it isn't. Anyway, one solution is to buy something valuable from someone and pay cash for it. Like a nice Picasso."

She took the million-dollar napkin back and handed me the box of Cheerios. Which I guess was the Picasso I'd just acquired. "Maybe you overpay for it a bit, Robert, so the art dealer doesn't become too interested in why you have a million dollars in hundreds."

"Okay, but now all I've got is a nice Picasso." I waved the Cheerios box.

"No, what you've got is a medium of exchange with a relatively fixed value, which is all money is anyway. One that's lightweight and not reportable, to boot. So you take the Picasso out of its frame, roll it up, and stick in your suitcase. It won't arouse suspicion. Most people will think it's just bad art."

I looked at the Cheerios box. Trying to think of it as a Picasso I could roll up.

"Then," Jenna said, "you go to an art dealer in a different state and sell the Picasso. Let's say I'm the art dealer."

She reached out and took the Cheerios box from me. "In exchange, I give you a check, maybe for somewhat less than a million. Made out to some small business you've opened." She handed me another napkin, which was apparently the almost-million-dollar check. I took it and put it in my pocket.

"In recognition of the discount I got on the price," she said, "I don't ask you why you happen to have the Picasso in the first place, or what your company does. The check you just received is from a legitimate business. Your own 'business' then deposits it in your bank. Or maybe you ask for the amount to be split into a couple of checks and you deposit them in a couple of different banks. No reportable cash transactions."

She sat back, looking pleased with her explanation. Then she added a further lesson in laundering. "Or, maybe you find an art dealer who's really in the know, and you just trade the art. He takes the Picasso and maybe deeds you a house in exchange. It's not a cash transaction that is a reportable transaction. It's not even a check that will show up as a deposit in your bank account. Either way, you've laundered the money."

"You think rare coins could be used in the same way?" I asked.

"Well, let's put it this way," she said. "There are an unusual number of fine art galleries in the backwoods around Hilo. A rare coin business would hardly be noticed, and a coin is even more easily transported than art."

She took a quarter out of her pocket, snapped it down on the table in front of her, and then tossed the Cheerios box into the nearby sink. It landed with a thud. "Out with art, in with coins."

"Seems a stretch," I said. "Someone supposedly said 'hello' while shouting at Simon. So from just that you've concluded that they were importing drugs and laundering the money by buying and selling ancient coins in Hilo? Occam's razor says that's hardly the likely explanation. Simpler and requiring fewer additional assumptions would be to assume they were arguing about the coin and that the 'someone' used 'hello' in its original, old fashioned way. You know. '*Hello! Wake up and smell the coffee, Simon. The coin is fake! I've been cheated.*'"

"Oh, right, old William of Occam," she said.

"You know his first name?"

"Cambridge. Mathematics degree," she said. "Remember?"

"Sorry, I forgot."

"Well, there are some things you and Bill Occam don't know," she said.

"Such as?"

"Simon owned a house on the Big Island."

"He never mentioned it to me," I said.

"Owned through a blind trust. Not many people know about it."

"Anything else?"

"Yeah. Simon did coke. Maybe not in a big deal way, but he always had it around."

For some reason, that seemed utterly unlikely to me. "Jenna, did you ever actually see Simon use cocaine?"

"A few times."

"When?"

"You're uncomfortable just seeing me in flannel pajamas."

"Oh. That kind of use," I said.

"Well, yes."

"You aren't really much of a nun, are you?"

"If you only knew."

"I don't think I want to," I said. "But now that I know all this, aren't you really the prime suspect? You had a key to Simon's condo. So you had access to the coin. You could have taken the real Ides denarius, swapped it out with a cheap if effective fake, and then used the real one to launder drug money. Yourself. In Hilo. With your Uncle Freddie."

"Trust me," Jenna said. "I didn't kill him and I don't launder drug money. And Uncle Freddie never personally ran a laundry."

"Huh," I said.

"You're talking like Detective Spritz again. Are you bonding with him?"

I realized that my head was in my hands. In what you might call morning despair.

"Listen, Jenna," I said. "I say, 'I didn't do it. *Trust me.*' You say, 'I didn't do it. *Trust me.*' And every other possible suspect will no doubt say, 'I didn't do it. *Trust me.*' Including Stewart. He's already said that, in effect. So how will we find out who to trust for real? By drawing straws? By taking lie detector tests? By examining the entrails of chickens?"

"The entrails of chickens aren't admissible in evidence."

"This isn't funny."

"Why don't we just go and see Harry?" Jenna asked.

"Why do we want to see him?"

"To confront him about being there that night."

"Okay, let's go see him. But Oscar won't approve," I said.

"Screw him," she said. "Call Harry and tell him we're coming."

"He doesn't have a phone."

"Well, that nails it, then," she said. "He must be a drug dealer, too. Drug dealers never have personal phones."

"Come off it."

"I'm deadly serious. Dealers only use cell phones these days. And they use disposables, which they change every couple of days."

"But," I said, "Harry doesn't even have a cell phone."

"So he claims," Jenna said. "Let's go right now."

At Jenna's insistence, we drove down to see Harry, still another person who claimed not to own a cell phone.

CHAPTER 13

———

Jenna insisted on driving. As I climbed into her Land Cruiser once again, which now had a seemingly permanent slot in my garage, I thought about the fact that when Jenna bought the thing, maybe three years ago, I had thought it an odd choice for her. L.A. is the kind of town in which you are your car, and Jenna seemed like the kind of girl who'd want to be a sports car. Or at least a convertible. But glancing in the back seat as I got in—something I'd not bothered to do the day she drove through the howling Blob to take me to the office—I began to understand why she bought it.

The front of the car, with bucket seats of black leather and red trim—custom made she told me—was pristine, except for the tiny white rabbit on the dashboard. The back seat was filled with the debris of daily living. Clothes, file boxes, a couple dozen scattered CDs, and two or three old copies of *The New York Times*, still unopened in their blue home-delivery wrappers. So the thing was clearly like a second home for Jenna. No tiny sports car could have filled the role.

We drove slowly down my driveway, and the Blob parted for us once again. It seemed thicker and somehow more restless than usual. I felt like shouting out, "Why are you so damned interested in me?" But I didn't.

We drove down the canyon and then took Sunset Boulevard to the San Diego Freeway and headed south. The traffic on the freeway was heavy, but moving. Jenna moved into the left-hand lane and took the car up to about 70 m.p.h. Usually in L.A., the cops won't ticket you at that speed.

I started in on Jenna not long after we got into the left-hand lane.

"Is it true that Simon tried to dump you?"

"Who told you that?"

"Harry."

"That's bullshit," she said.

"Then why did he think that?"

"How should I know."

We drove on for a while in a thickening silence.

"Harry had no reason to just make it up, Jenna."

She twisted the steering wheel sharply to the right, careened the car across two lanes of traffic, and braked to an abrupt stop on the narrow shoulder.

"Jenna, what the hell are you doing?"

"If you're going to take my deposition, Robert, I don't want to be driving while you do it. Go ahead, ask what you fucking want."

A large truck roared by, only inches away on the left. The car shook from the air blast.

"Jesus, we could be killed here."

She hit the flasher button. "Ask away, ask what you want to know. We're not leaving till you're done."

"Have you gone nuts?"

"Like I said, ask what you want. Now's your big chance."

I seriously wanted to ask her a lot of things. On the other hand, I seriously wanted to live.

"If you're not gonna ask, why don't I just tell you what you want to know, huh? The volunteering witness. What could be better?"

"Could we get back in the lanes, please?"

"First of all," she said, "Simon and I had an arrangement, not a love affair. Second of all, if anyone was unhappy it was me. I was the one who threatened to end it, not him."

It had become clear we weren't going anywhere until we got done with this, so I followed up.

"Why?"

"Maybe I wanted a love affair. I don't know. We had been screwing around for quite a while, and it wasn't going anywhere. But the last time I brought up leaving was at least a month ago. So it wasn't a current issue between us." She paused. "And I certainly didn't need to kill him to leave him. Girls don't have to do that anymore. Happy now? Anything else you want to know?"

Another passing truck rocked the car. "Not right now," I said. "Can we get back on the road, please?"

Jenna glanced at the outside mirror, then gunned the car back onto the road. She found the left-hand lane and quickly brought the speed back up to 70. I relaxed. We drove along without talking.

"It's a pretty day, isn't it, Robert?"

"I guess."

She reached over and switched on the radio. "Just a Girl," sung by the group No Doubt, came on. I knew it well. My daughter had played it incessantly when she was home from college one summer. I listened for a while, then turned it off, right after the line, "I'm just a girl in the world," began.

"I love that song, Robert. It reminds me of myself sometimes. Why did you turn it off before it ended?"

"It's a very good song, but I'm not really into music right now. I have another question, though. If I ask it, do you promise to stay on the road?"

"Yeah, I'm sorry about that back there. Hit me with it."

"I'm wondering why the police haven't been around to question you. Your fingerprints had to be all over Simon's condo. The police could easily match them. Your fingerprints are on file from when you became a member of the State Bar."

"I wiped them off. It only took a couple of minutes. And I don't think there were all that many. They would mainly have been in the bedroom and the bathroom. Anyway, that's not where Simon and I spent most of our time together."

"You wiped the place down for your prints?"

"Yeah."

"I'd be surprised if you got them all."

"As long as I got the ones in the bedroom, the police will just think they've found the prints of one more lawyer from the firm who was visiting Simon. Lots of lawyers from the firm went over there, and you can't date fingerprints."

"If you say so. But it brings up another question, Jenna. The question of why the police weren't there before you."

"Simon's apartment is like two minutes from the office. The cops had plenty to do at the crime scene first, and I had a secret way in. So I took a risk and it worked out, okay?"

"Secret way in?"

"You don't really need to know about that."

"You know, as I think about it, I think I need to know pretty much everything there is to know about your relationship with Simon."

"Look, I've already said too much, okay? The less you know at this point, the better. You're the client, not the lawyer. I'll tell it all to Oscar."

"I can't agree with that logic."

"Then fire me. And find Oscar another second chair. Seriously."

I sat there for a few seconds and considered doing just that. It was the rational thing to do. But I was having trouble hanging on to the rationality that had, until two days before, been my pole star. I didn't want Jenna gone from my life. She seemed like my one link back to my real life. I could press for more later. Sometimes later *is* more.

"I don't want to fire you."

"Okay."

The silence resumed. Jenna reached over and turned the radio back on, but lowered the volume.

We were by then well past the airport, with maybe twenty minutes still to go. I didn't feel like sitting there, alone in my own head. And I didn't feel like making small talk. I turned to my cell phone for solace and companionship. Sure, Oscar had warned me not to use it, but I was oblivious or foolhardy or stupid or all of those things, and so I used it anyway. The first call I made was to Peter Penosco. Peter was one of those rare entertainment executives who still answered his own phone. Maybe only because no assistant ever lasted with him more than about two weeks. I reached him on the first ring.

"Robert, it took you two fucking days to return my call."

I tried humor. "Being suspected of murder is time consuming."

"Tell me about it," he said.

This was, I knew, a not-so-subtle reference to the time five years before, when Peter had himself been investigated for allegedly bribing the key development guy at a network. To get Bright Bulb a production deal for a TV movie about Joan of Arc. One that painted her as a schizophrenic with overtones of manic depressive disorder. It bombed. Peter claimed it was because people didn't want to know the truth about their saints. In the end, he wasn't indicted. Perhaps the DA just took pity on him. Or had a script he wanted Peter to look at.

"Peter, I'm really sorry. My life has been totally screwed over the last few days. But I'm back in the saddle now." What a lie. I tried to get the call back on a business track. "What can I do for you?"

"I called to volunteer to do whatever I could for *you*, pal," he said.

"That's very kind of you, Peter. It really is. At the moment, I don't know what you can do. Unless you can tell me who killed Simon." I laughed. Rather inappropriately maybe.

"Well, I don't know who did it or I would tell you for sure. But, listen, you need to watch your back."

"Why?"

"Because Caroline Thorpe called me yesterday to tell me you were taking a leave of absence. Until, as she put it, 'This all blows over for poor Bobby.'"

"She actually called me Bobby?"

"Yeah. But I didn't think it was in a spirit of cuddly friendship, you know? Then she called back later and said that, well, you weren't taking that leave of absence. But that you might not be able to devote full attention to Bright Bulb's matters. And . . . get this. She invited me to come in and meet with another partner who'd be 'helping you out.'"

So the second strike was already under way. "Did she say who it would be?"

"She never got a chance. I told her that if it wasn't you, I was taking my business to the competition."

"To Phineas & Crouch?" *P&C* was our archenemy in the entertainment space.

"Yeah. That shut her totally up," he said.

"Peter, I genuinely appreciate your doing that. I really do."

"It's nothing, Robert. You've been a hell of a good lawyer for us all these years. Even if you sometimes do have a too-conservative stick up your ass about some of the things we need to do. I'm not throwing that kind of good advice away just because some dick-head cops have got it all wrong and because your cunt-head tax partner is worried your high-and-mighty firm will be sullied." He paused. "Which reminds me that there's something else you should know."

"What?"

"A couple weeks ago, Simon Rafer called me and tried to set up a lunch. Without you. Very specifically without you. I had the impression he was interested in taking our business away from you."

"And?"

"I told him no way."

"Well, again, I need to thank you."

"Well, you're welcome. Again. But do watch your back, man. This is serious shit."

"I will."

"I mean it. If there is anything at all that we can do for you, just pick up the phone."

"Okay, Peter, I will. And thank you." After he hung up, I thought about what Caroline was trying to do. Bright Bulb brought in about a million and a half a year in fees. Although a lot of other lawyers in the firm worked on their deals, they were still my client, and I got the origination on the billings plus all of my own hours on their stuff, which were still substantial, albeit not huge. Without Bright Bulb, my days at M&M, at least as a full partner, would be numbered. I wondered what Caroline and her friends were going to try next. I also wondered what Simon had been up to. Had he really been trying to get rid of *me*? Stewart, sure. That made sense. But, like Stewart, I had thought I was immune. Naively, apparently.

Jenna had not said a word during the conversation. She just held on to the wheel with both hands and looked straight ahead. But she had clearly heard both sides of the conversation. Cell phones can be like that in small spaces, even with music going.

"Peter has a foul mouth," she said.

"You were listening?"

"Hard not to. He's started using the c-word a lot, I've noticed. Probably because the f-word no longer shocks anyone."

"Could be. Why do you think Simon was trying to have lunch with Peter?" I asked.

"I don't know," she said. "He never wanted to talk to me about firm business. In fact, he actively hid it from me. When he had to talk business on the phone from home, he always went into a little private office he had and shut the door. When he went out, he always locked it."

"You were never in it?"

"No. I tried to respect his privacy."

"Okay."

I turned back to the cell phone and called Serappo Prodiglia. Another person who'd been waiting almost two days to get his call returned. He was not in. I left a message.

No sooner had I hung up than the phone rang. It was Oscar.

"Are you with Jenna?" he asked.

"Yes, I am."

"Well, call me back when you're not." He hung up.

Jenna continued to drive. "I heard that."

"I would have told him to go ahead and talk, but he hung up before I could say anything. I have no secrets from you, Jenna."

"Was that a sly way of saying I may have secrets from you?"

"You already admitted that you do," I said.

"They're for your own good."

"So you say. But Jenna, I think we are going to have to resolve all of this, and soon."

"How about not today?" she said.

"Okay."

We drove on in relative silence, but without frost.

Harry was not exactly thrilled to see us. In fact, he initially refused to open the door when we knocked. Jenna used a direct approach to pry it open.

"Listen, Harry, Stewart Broder told us that *you* killed Simon."

It worked. The door opened a crack, and Harry peered out at us.

"That's ridiculous," he said.

"Well if it's ridiculous, let us in," Jenna said.

Harry opened the door all the way and waved us in. He was wearing his usual outfit, but he looked somehow disheveled. His Dockers were smudged, his blue work shirt wasn't very well tucked in to his pants, and he was barefoot. He pointed us over to the couches that faced the ocean, but the bonhomie of my visit two days earlier was distinctly missing. He didn't offer us anything to drink, and he skipped the pleasantries.

"Who sent you here?" he asked.

"No one sent us," Jenna said. "Stewart told Robert that *you* killed Simon, and that it involved a drug deal gone bad. So we just came down to ask if it's true." She smiled a tight little smile.

Harry was still standing, leaning against the wall. For a while he said nothing. He just stared at Jenna. She stared back. Jenna is a world-class starer. I noticed that Harry's fists were clenched. Finally, Jenna won, and he spoke.

"Listen," he said. "I didn't kill anyone. Stewart is a nutcase. And not a very good lawyer. We should never have made him an offer. It was close, you know. A 4-3 vote in the Hiring Committee, and if I had wanted to block him, I could have, but I figured, 'what the hell' and let it go forward."

I had to stifle a laugh. "Harry," I said, "that was more than thirty years ago."

"I have a long memory."

Jenna jumped on it. "How's your memory of last Sunday, Harry? Stewart says the two of you were at Simon's for brunch, looking at the coin."

"Yeah, I was there. What of it?"

"Got an alibi for the morning of the murder?" she asked.

"Are you Detective Spritz now, Jenna?"

"Do you?"

"Yes. I've even told it to the police. But unless you've got a badge now, it's none of your business."

"You still haven't said whether you and Simon were involved in drugs," she said.

Harry actually rolled his eyes. "I wasn't. He wasn't. Like I told Robert yesterday, Simon was in debt for gambling. But if he was trying to cover it by selling drugs, I'm unaware of it. Now, if you don't have any more impertinent questions, I'm rather busy."

"I think we do have more questions," she said.

"Well, I fear they will have to wait, Jenna. If you do want to discuss it further, I suggest you make an appointment."

"You don't have a phone," Jenna said.

"Well you're a smart young woman. I'm sure you'll find a way."

Then he showed us the door.

CHAPTER 14

————

We climbed back in the Land Cruiser and headed up the 405, back to L.A.

"This whole trip was a waste of time, Jenna."

"Maybe not," she said.

"We didn't learn a thing. We weren't with him two minutes before he threw us out. And you scared him off by flat-out asking him if he killed Simon. Now he's not going to help us out at all."

"My gut tells me he's involved in this somehow," Jenna said. "If he weren't, he would have talked to us more. Maybe he *did* kill him."

"Got any evidence?"

"No."

"Okay, so like I said, the visit was a waste of time and probably counterproductive."

"No, our visit is going to roust him out."

"Meaning what?" I asked.

"Well, he doesn't have a phone, and you say he has no cell phone. So if he was involved, he's going to need to tell someone that we were there, asking questions. He'll have to go out to do it."

"Wherever do you get this stuff?"

"In truth, I read detective novels," she said.

"Oh, great. I feel heartened. But we won't be there to watch where he goes if he goes out."

"Remember my friends at KZDD? The guys who followed us with their news van on the freeway the other day?"

"What about them?"

"Well, I promised the news director something in trade if they backed away. I just paid off."

"I'm utterly confused," I said.

"I gave them Harry. I called them up, told them Harry knew something about this case, told them I'd lead them to him, and asked them to stake him out and follow him if he left his place."

"When did you do that?"

"When you were in the bathroom, right before we left to come down here."

"You bear watching, Jenna."

"Maybe so. But you bear paying more attention to your surroundings. The KZDD car followed us all the way down, and you never even noticed. They parked just down the block from us at Harry's."

It was true. I had been oblivious to it. And in contemplating my oblivion—oblivion not being my normal state of being—I suddenly realized I was starving.

"How about something to eat on the way back?" I said.

"There's some food somewhere on the back seat."

I turned around and looked, but couldn't see much. "All I see is a dead pizza box."

"I'm sure there's something there. Protein bars I think, under that big file box maybe."

I didn't want to eat old protein bars. "How about fast food instead?"

"Sure."

We chose an In-N-Out Burger. The lines can be longer there than at the other chains, but the burgers are better enough to make the wait worthwhile. I have even learned to ignore the citations to Bible verses on the burger wrappers and on the inside bottom rim of the cups.

I told Jenna I'd take a cheeseburger and a vanilla shake. When the voice on the speaker asked for our order, I heard Jenna give my order and then say, "And an Animal Burger and a Coke." I raised an eyebrow.

"What's an Animal Burger? It's not on the menu."

"It's from their secret menu."

"Their *secret* menu?"

"Right. There's a lot of stuff not on their printed menu. You just have to know. Or, just check it out on their website. But you don't surf the web, remember?" She shot me a sly smile. Like the ones I used to get from her before this all began. "You, Robert, should be ordering the Protein Burger. Wrapped in lettuce. No bun." She reached over and patted my stomach. "You've put on a few pounds lately, eh?" Another smile.

I ignored that. "What exactly is in an Animal Burger?"

"Lot of extra stuff on it. Mainly, the mustard's fried into the patty."

While we waited, I considered the dire implications of my ignorance of the existence of a secret menu at the area's most popular burger chain. Now that the dot-coms are gone, the entertainment industry is the only business in the world where age discrimination begins at twenty-five and is held at bay only if you can continue to show a certain cool knowledge of pop culture without seeming like a geek. At sixty, it's a serious challenge. I am ever on the alert for the first signs of my own pop decrepitude, and this was not a good sign.

Ten minutes later, we had our food. The guy who handed us the bags was staring at me. I looked away.

We decided to park and eat rather than drive and eat. We found a place around the corner on a residential street. Neither of us said much. Mostly because trying to eat a dripping burger, wrapped only in paper, without spilling it all over yourself requires a certain amount of attention. It doesn't interrupt thinking, though. When I had finished the burger and was struggling to suck up the overly thick milkshake through the too narrow straw, I decided to tell Jenna what I had concluded somewhere in the middle of my attack on the burger.

"Jenna, we need to have what my grandfather used to call a come-to-Jesus meeting."

She laughed. "What? Have you been reading the bible references on the bottom of your cup?"

"No."

She reached over and took the almost depleted milkshake out of my hand, held it up high , and read from the inside rim on the bottom. "Proverbs 3:5."

"Don't know it," I said. "Memorizing Bible verses has never been my thing."

"Trust in the Lord with all thine heart, and lean not unto thine own understanding."

"Jenna, I'm always amazed at your vast store of knowledge. But I'm trying to get serious."

"I thought we were back to having fun again, Robert, like in the old days."

"In the old days I wasn't suspected of murder. So we're not having fun. We're having serious. I seriously don't like your withholding facts from me."

The old days were, of course, only a week ago. Time flies when you're a person of interest.

She switched her mode. "I told you on the way down. As your lawyer I think it's best."

"And I think that's horseshit," I said. "Not to mention unethical. Lawyers can try to put the best light on bad facts. Buck their clients up, and all that. But when the client asks flat out what the lawyer knows, he has to tell them. Period."

"*She*. And not if it will harm the client."

"Horseshit! You have a conflict, Jenna. Maybe the facts that you're keeping to yourself prove *you* killed him. And you're utterly wrong on the ethics."

"Didn't we just have this same conversation about an hour ago?"

"That was about trust between friends. This one is about my rights as a client." I was finally ready to say what I had been thinking. "Tell me what you know or you're fired. And I'll just tell Oscar to go out and find himself a new second chair."

By this time, Jenna had her head on the steering wheel. I could hardly hear her response. It was more whispered than spoken. "Really?"

"Yes, really."

Unlike the frost that had earlier filled the car, it now seemed filled with a kind of sadness. The kind that comes from a friendship about to splinter. Or an uncomfortable truth about to be told. I felt oddly compelled to explain myself, even though, in truth, she should have been the one doing the explaining.

"Jenna, I don't want to go to jail, okay? I know there are clients who don't want to know too much—who want their lawyers to tell them only what they need to know. I'm not one of them. So please tell me what you know or please get off the team."

Jenna started the car and headed back toward the freeway on-ramp. Once there, she floored it up the ramp. It seemed an indicator of her mood. Aggressive. But I misread her. The acceleration was somehow tied to resignation.

"What do you want to know, Robert?"

"When did you start going out with Simon?"

"A year ago. At the firm Christmas party."

"An entire year." I said it slowly.

"You're wondering how you could have failed to notice for so long?"

"Yes."

"We kept it very quiet. Very underground. On purpose."

"Why?"

"Simon said that if it got around, my elevation to the partnership would be cheapened. He said a lot of people would think I got there on my back."

"I thought you liked to be on top."

"You know what I mean. Anyway, he used a more vulgar term."

"I won't ask," I said.

We drove for a few minutes without talking.

"How close were you and Simon?" I asked.

"Close and not close. We spent a lot of time together, mostly out of town. Places like Riverside."

Riverside is a rather nice town about forty miles east of downtown L.A. It's got a lovely river, a historic inn, and about three hundred thousand people, but it's the kind of place people from the Westside never go. It might as well not exist, which is no doubt why Simon had picked it.

"And in town?"

"In his condo on Bunker Hill. I always came late at night and left early in the morning. We never went out."

I was quite familiar with Simon's condo. In the old days, we had had a regular Friday night poker game there. Simon also had a big, classy place on the Westside—an old movie star's house in Brentwood—but holed up downtown during the week. He told everyone it shortened his commute and gave him more time to work. More time for a lot of things, apparently.

"How many people knew about you and Simon?"

"Just Harry."

"Why did he get to be in the know?" I asked. That question of course, contained within it the unspoken statement that if Jenna needed to confide it to someone, that someone should have been me.

Jenna ignored the implication.

"Simon told him," she said. "It was the night I threatened to break it off. Simon said he needed to confide in someone. I was pissed, frankly."

During this entire conversation, Jenna had been looking straight ahead, weaving amidst the traffic, exceeding the speed limit in whichever lane she happened to be in. When she's driving and talking, Jenna usually glances frequently at her passenger. So frequently it had made me nervous in the past. Now I wondered if her road stare meant she was lying. Or leaving something out. Once distrust begins, it quietly twines its little vines around everything.

I finally asked the thing that had been bothering me the most.

"Why aren't you upset that he's dead?"

"What makes you think I'm not upset?"

"You haven't shed a single tear."

"That you've seen."

We drove on for a while in silence again. It had been tacky of me to question her grief. She turned the radio back on. No Doubt's "Just a Girl" had moved on to Chris Isaak's "San Francisco Days." I turned it back off.

"Are you really grieving for him, Jenna?"

She shrugged. "In my own way. I grew up in the home of a politician who had once been a general. Emotions were to be kept in your bedroom or saved for a studied moment in front of the cameras."

"So you're gonna cry for the Blob?"

"That was cheap."

"It was. I'm sorry."

"Robert, I've cried a lot. It's just that you've been so caught up in your own troubles that you couldn't see my grief."

"What do you mean?"

"Why do you think I looked so awful in your office yesterday?"

"I thought maybe you were pregnant."

She ignored that and went on. "Earlier, I had been looking at mementos. Ones of me and Simon. A couple pictures I took, a few small gifts he gave me. I lost it. Spent an hour crying and then another half hour throwing up. So don't talk to me about grief."

"I feel like a shit."

"Well, you don't need to. You do have a few problems that other people don't." She smiled.

"I really am sorry, Jenna. I guess I thought what I thought because it seemed like you plunged into defending me without a backward look."

"Maybe defending you will help avenge him. I know you didn't do it. Maybe I'll be able to help nail the asshole who did do it."

"How can you be so sure I didn't do it?"

"You're not a killer, Robert. And besides, you couldn't have killed Simon with a knife even if you had wanted to."

I felt oddly offended at that. I was still strong and agile. I go to the gym three times a week. Most weeks, anyway.

"Why not?"

"He had a black belt in Tae Kwon Do. You wouldn't have gotten close."

"He did that stuff a long time ago."

"He still had a hard body." She said it in a very soft voice. Almost a whisper. Then a tear rolled down her face.

I reached into the In-N-Out bag, the one that had had the fries in it, pulled out a napkin and handed it to her.

She took it from me without looking at it and dabbed at her eye.

"Ugh! It has ketchup on it!"

She began to giggle. I followed. Soon both of us had dissolved into gales of laughter. I fumbled around in the bag again and located a ketchup-free napkin. I reached over and wiped the smear of ketchup from under her eye.

"There you go, Jenna. Ketchup off."

"You are such a dork, Robert."

"Sometimes, I guess."

"Can we change the topic?"

"Sure. What do you want to talk about?"

"I've been thinking that a key to all this might be what is in Simon's secret room. The one I never went in."

"You may be right. Maybe we could ask Spritz what he found in there. Or maybe your friends at KZDD could ask him." I laughed.

"Maybe we should just go find out ourselves."

"Yeah, right."

"Seriously. We could go over there. And I think I know how to get into that room."

"Even if you do, there will be cops everywhere."

"I doubt it. It's been four days. There's probably one cop at the front door of his apartment. But I bet not inside the apartment itself. They'd be afraid of messing up the crime scene. Hand me my cell phone, will you?" I gave it to her and she dialed a one-button, preprogrammed number. "Hey, Mike," she said, "What's the scoop over at the Rafer condo?" She pressed the phone close to her ear and I couldn't hear what was said on the other end. "Thanks. *Que pasa* with Harry? . . . Okay. *Ciao, amigo.*"

"Well, Roberto, there's only one cop, at the front door of the apartment. No one out front of the building."

"What's with the *amigo, que pasa* stuff?"

"I dunno. Just silly I guess."

"So there's only one cop at the front door," I said. "Isn't *he* going to see us go in?"

"Only if we go in through the front door."

"That condo only has a front door. The backdoor would be a window that drops down about 200 feet."

"There's another way. You'll think it clever," she said.

"I'll wait to see, I guess. Anyway, what did he say about Harry?"

"That Harry left his place about fifteen minutes after we did. They followed him to LAX. He's going somewhere. Mike promised to call me back and tell me where."

We were beginning to approach the clot of traffic that always surrounds downtown's freeways. It's there day or night. I've never understood it. Maybe it's because four freeways converge there. Maybe it's because motorists slow to look at the road-hugging Convention Center and wonder how anything so ugly could have been built in the capital of glitz. We slowed our way through the traffic, until Jenna took the 1st Street off-ramp. She parked a couple of blocks away from the glitzy building in which Simon had his condo.

As we got out of the car, Jenna reached into the back seat and grabbed a small leather purse from amidst the debris. Jenna doesn't usually carry a purse. She once described them as a male plot.

"Are we really, seriously going to do this?" I asked.

"Yes, we very seriously really are."

CHAPTER 15

———

I walked with Jenna to the building, through the lobby, and then into an elevator. She punched the button for twenty-four.

"Isn't his condo on twenty-three?"

"It is. But it's a two-story penthouse, and the second floor of the condo is on twenty-four."

"Okay," I said. "But there's no door into his condo from twenty-four."

"Right. But there's a door into 2402. Which is a small, detached maid's room and kitchen that's been empty for a couple of years."

"So?"

"Just watch."

We got off the elevator, and she produced a key to 2402. We went in.

"Now what?" I asked.

"You'll see." Jenna walked across the single room to a dormer window, which looked out on a small, roofed deck. She pushed open the bottom half of the window and skinnied herself through onto the deck. Then she walked across to a set of tall, floor-to- ceiling glass doors that looked into the second floor of Simon's condo. She rattled one of the glass doors, and it opened.

"Come on over, Robert. Loose latch. My secret way in."

I managed, just, to push myself through the narrow window, although I felt ridiculous. Then I followed her through the open door into the second floor bedroom of Simon's condo. It was a large, perfectly square room furnished in a spare Japanese style. Tatami mats and no western furniture. Just padded cushions around the walls, with four low, lacquered tables pushed together in the middle of the room, each set with a small black vase. Three were empty. One held red blossoms that were well beyond wilt.

"Is this how you always arrived?"

"Sometimes. We used to play . . . games. You know, naked girl arrives in your bed in the middle of the night?" She giggled. "Haven't you ever played games like that, Robert?"

"No." I changed the subject. "Won't the cop outside the front door hear us if we go downstairs?"

"Not if we're quiet. Take off your shoes and leave them here."

I did, and we tiptoed down the stairs in our stocking feet. The decor on the main floor had been changed since the last time I had been there, maybe five years before. Back then, it was done in classic bachelor pad. Mostly stuff bought at Cost Plus. Since then, a decorator who learned her craft in the nineties had clearly gotten her hands on it. Big stuffed couches done in nubby white fabric, red-and-black Navajo-style rugs on top of beige Berber carpet, a large coffee table of speckled granite. Art on the walls that matched all that. Primary colors. No depictions of humans.

Off to one side of the main room was a closed door. Jenna walked over to it.

"This is the secret room," she said.

"If you touch the knob," I said, "you'll get prints on it."

"Not a problem."

She unbuttoned the right-hand sleeve of her blouse, pulled the cloth down over her hand and, using it as a kind of glove, tried to turn the knob. "It's locked."

"So we're stymied."

"Not necessarily."

She rummaged in her purse and took out a small leather kit, about the size of a wallet, but with a single flap. She extracted a very thin, flexible metal strip from it and bent over to inspect the lock on the doorknob.

"What is that?"

"A pick kit."

"You're joking."

She turned and looked at me over her shoulder. With a look that the French would call *un regard méchant*. Slightly wicked in a charming way. "Don't all the girls you know have pick kits?"

"Let me guess. A gift from Uncle Freddie."

"Uh huh. A sweet sixteen present."

She bent back to the doorknob and, holding the thin blade between thumb and forefinger, worked it delicately into the lock.

"This lock is a piece of cake."

I heard a click, and the door popped open. Jenna went in and I followed.

It was a small room, with an old wooden table shoved up against the wall. There were no drawers or file cabinets. On the table were the to-be-expected computer monitor and printer. But there was no computer. Just some marks on the carpet where it had clearly sat until recently. There was nothing much else in the room.

"Well," I said, "it may be a secret room, but it doesn't look like it contains a lot of secrets."

"I guess the cops took the computer," she said, and pointed at the marks on the rug.

"Where was the computer on which you read Simon's e-mails?"

"It was a notebook computer in the kitchen."

She turned away from the wooden table and looked around the room. "What are those books over there?" She pointed to the back wall, which held a small bookshelf, with about half a dozen books on it.

I walked over to the shelf and glanced at them.

"They're just standard books for someone who collects Roman Republican coins. Syndenham's *The Coinage of the Roman Republic*, Hill's *Historical Roman Coins*, Crawford's *Roman Republican Coinage*, and, of course Grueber's *Coins of the Roman Republic in the British Museum*—the magnum opus. Usually it's three volumes, but only two are there." I peered more closely at them. "Volume III is missing."

"None of them would be my bedtime reading."

"I suppose not, Jenna. But if you love these coins, they make great reading."

"If you say so."

"I do."

"Which volume of the magnum opus would the Ides be listed in?"

"It would be described in Volume II, and there might be a plate—a picture of it—in Volume III. But I don't recall if it's in there or not."

Jenna walked over to the shelf. "There's a dust outline of a book on the shelf," she said. "It must be where Volume III used to be."

I looked more closely. She was right. Then I noticed Jenna staring at the painting above the bookcase. It was a copy of an old Dutch master. She reached up, grabbed the bottom corner, and pulled it toward her. The painting moved away to reveal a small green safe sunk into the wall, with a combination dial in the middle.

"There's the secret," she said.

"Can you open it?"

"It's probably beyond me," she said.

I was about to make some wry comment about the educational limitations of Uncle Freddie's School for Girls when I heard a muffled voice outside the front door, talking to another voice. And then the scratch of a key being fitted into a lock.

"Shit," Jenna said.

We bolted from the room almost as one, sprinted through the living room, and took the steps to the master bedroom two at a time. Jenna scooped up her shoes and hurtled through the door, out onto the deck. I went through right behind her, shoes in hand, exiting just in time to hear a voice on the floor below say, "Hey, wasn't the door to that small room closed the last time we checked?"

We raced across the deck, and I watched as Jenna skinnied herself back through the window into the maid's room. I willed myself not to look over my shoulder while I waited. When I finally squeezed myself through it seemed an even tighter fit than it had been going the other way. Or at least a more urgent fit. I pictured being arrested while stuck in the window frame.

I finally made it through. Jenna closed the window behind me, then dropped to all fours and made a beeline for a wall that was out of the sight-line of the windows. I followed. We sat on the floor and leaned up against the wall. I was breathing hard. Jenna was sweating.

"We should get out of here," I said.

"No, we should stay put. If we stand up, and they're out on the deck, they might see us."

"They could look through the window."

"They still won't see us."

"Alright," I said. "We'll stay here for a while."

We put our shoes back on and then just sat there, saying nothing. My breathing slowed. The emptiness of the room came to seem soothing. Then the silence came to seem awkward.

Jenna broke it, speaking softly, just above a whisper.

"Robert, where did you get the Ides?"

"From my grandfather."

"You've never mentioned him. Who was he? Where did he get it?"

"Roberto Istarza. I don't know exactly where he got it. From some Loyalist officer he killed during the Spanish Civil War. Or at least that's what he said."

"Istarza?"

"It was the family name before my father changed it. Dropped the 'Is.' He thought it made it more American, less Basque. All it did for me as a kid was to bring on all the Tarzan jokes."

She giggled, but so quietly that it came out as more like a suppressed sneeze. "Yeah, I remember thinking that when I saw your name on the interview list at Harvard. Thought about starting the interview by saying, 'Me Jenna, you Tarza.' But thought better of it."

"Good thing."

Sitting there next to Jenna in the empty room, it was almost like being a kid in a secret place, where you could talk to other kids about things you didn't normally talk about. I had not talked to anyone about my grandfather in many years.

My thoughts about my grandfather were interrupted by the sound of footsteps on the deck outside. Jenna pointed to the window and put her finger to her lips. We sat there, unmoving, hardly breathing, for what seemed like forever. The sound of footsteps faded.

Jenna looked at me and shrugged. Then she resumed the conversation, almost as if there had been no interruption. The sign of a good lawyer. Never lose the thread.

"When did you get the coin from him?"

"When I was eleven. He gave it to me right before he died. Said I should treasure it always. That's why it took me so long to sell it."

"Why did you?"

I hesitated. I knew that what I was about to say would sound very strange. "I concluded that it was cursed."

"That's odd."

"Well, I lent it out twice. Each time to a respected museum. And each time, the curator of that museum died in some violent way. I'm sure it was all a coincidence, but it was beginning to creep me out."

"Did you tell Simon that?"

"Uh huh. He tried to wheedle a discount out of me because of it. Said a cursed coin should be worth less. I told him it should be worth more."

"That is *really* creepy."

"I know. It's probably just coincidence. The loans were ten years apart."

"Who did you lend it to?"

I never got to answer. Jenna got up in mid-conversation and moved to the door of the apartment. She put her ear up against it and listened.

"Someone was just out there. I heard the elevator door open and then close again," she said.

I guess her hearing was more acute than mine because I had heard nothing. She opened the door a tiny crack and peered out.

"There's no one out there now. But I think now's the time to get out of here," she said.

And we did. Furtively. Jenna kept looking over her shoulder as we crossed the street, on the way back to where her car was parked. I glanced back once. The windows of Simon's condo faced the street and, looking up, I thought I saw Spritz standing in the window. It was probably just my imagination.

The drive back to M&M's office building was short.

"We didn't learn anything," I said, "and we took a huge risk. Plus now our fingerprints are all over that empty maid's apartment."

"Even if they do go over there, I don't think they'll wipe it down for prints. And we did learn something. We learned the police took Simon's computer, we learned there's a safe in the secret room, and we learned that volume III of whatever that big book is called is missing."

"*Coins of the Roman Republic in the British Museum*," I said. "And maybe it's not missing. Maybe Simon just put it somewhere else for a while. Anyway, so what if it's missing?"

"I don't know. But somehow, it's important," she said.

I changed the topic. "Jenna, when did you first learn about Simon buying the Ides?"

"Right when you were selling it to him. He was like a little kid. So excited. I remember the day he brought it home. He even let me touch it. I was excited too. More than two thousand years old. Thinking how many hands it had passed through."

I looked over at her and detected the little gleam in her eye that people who collect old things get when they talk about them. But I had never known Jenna to collect anything. She had once told me that she had an aversion to owning things. Except clothes.

"What did he do with it when he got it?" I asked.

"He put it in a plastic envelope and then put it in his little red coin box, and then put the box away somewhere. I don't know where."

That rang true. Coin collectors are an odd lot. Usually, they don't display their coins. They just put them in an oblong box, and look at them every once in a while. Many coin collectors would consider the coffee table display in my office somewhat outré.

"And then?" I said.

"Harry came over the next day. He took it out of the box, and they looked at it together. Then he put it away again. Maybe two weeks later, I don't know why, they decided to have it appraised."

"Who appraised it?"

"They sent it to someone in Chicago. It came back with a report that said it was a forgery. Then they sent it somewhere else. It had just come back from wherever that was last Saturday."

"Do you know who they sent it to in Chicago?" I asked.

"Somebody with a weird name."

The somebody had to be Serappo. Whose call I had not yet returned.

"Was it a guy named Serappo Prodiglia?"

"Something like that."

We had reached our building, but the Blob was not there. At all. Jenna did not seem concerned and told me not to worry about it, that it was probably off feeding somewhere else. I never did learn where it had gone that day.

CHAPTER 16

W hen I got up to my office, Gwen was sitting at her desk. It was bare. So was my office. No books, no furniture. Gwen was almost in tears. "Oh, Mr. Tarza, a window panel is loose in your office. They say it's too dangerous for you to stay in there until they figure out what the problem is. But they don't have any spare partner offices."

In the old days, a week earlier, I would have been taken aback. But after five days of a murder investigation, a possible blood stain on my office couch and faked elevator records, not to mention secret menus, this was nothing. Far from being nonplussed, you might say I was totally 'plussed.' "So where are we going then?"

"They gave you an associate office on eighty-two." She looked stricken.

Eighty-two is fondly known as FYG. First-Year Ghetto. Several years before, the HR people at the firm had persuaded the Executive Committee to house all first-year associates on the same floor. The better to create a "cohesive cohort" amongst each year's incoming class of about thirty associates in the L.A. office. Or so they claimed.

Maybe it works, but God knows partners never venture near. Even senior associates stay away. Half college dorm, half fraternity, it features offices filled with video games, old pizza boxes, half-empty water bottles, dead bras, and the general detritus left by new lawyers pulling all-nighters to try to unearth those twenty-five hundred billable hours the firm insists on sucking out of them.

I doubted seriously that there was any real problem with a window panel in my office. Caroline and her court were just trying to humiliate me. If they couldn't move me to the Annex, they would send me down amidst the unwashed. My attitude was: to hell with them. I'd go and make the best of it.

"Gwen, if you don't want to go down there with me, you can ask to be transferred, and I'll just use the pool."

"It's okay," she said. "I went down and checked it out. I want to go with you." She looked up at me. "But could we have your new office there steam cleaned first?" We both laughed. Then I took the elevator down to eighty-two to check it out myself.

My new office was the absolute farthest you could get from the elevator bank. On the trek there, I passed a few associates, who just stared at me. I heard later that some of them thought my arrival was the first step in a nefarious plot to break up FYG.

Coming down the hall, I could see through the doorway that my desk and desk chair had been moved into the office, but not my couch and coffee table. No room. There was only one guest chair. And sitting in it was Oscar, casually reading my *New York Times,* with his suit jacket draped over the chair back.

I loathed seeing him there. It reminded me of things. Like the fact that the afternoon's activities with Jenna had not been a game. Or the fact that Oscar now felt no compunction about just waltzing into my office, plopping himself down and appropriating my newspaper. Like he was waiting for a shoeshine.

I went in and tried to act cheerful about it. "Hi, Oscar."

Oscar dropped the paper on the floor, folded his arms across his chest and glared at me. "You didn't call me back."

"You said to call back when I wasn't with Jenna. We just now left each other's company."

I sat down in the chair behind my desk.

Oscar seemed not to be interested in my excuse. "Listen, my friend, I had a chat this morning with Susan Apacha. The key card queen."

"And?"

"Jenna's key card came up the elevator late Sunday night, not long before midnight."

"Oh." It was the kind of "oh" you utter upon feeling pole axed.

"Oh, indeed. And even more indeedly, it turns out that Miss James reported her key card stolen two days earlier."

"You're telling me Jenna did it?"

"Either did it or helped frame you. Or both."

"Maybe her key card really was stolen," I said.

He ignored my thought that Jenna might be innocent and plowed straight ahead. "Right now," he said, "I'm leaning toward the 'both' theory. The police, meanwhile, are leaning toward the theory that you stole her card and used it as part of your plot, probably to bring up a co-conspirator. Somebody strong and good with a knife, according to them."

"Mr. Tarza and his friend in the foyer with a knife?"

"What?"

Oscar apparently hadn't played endless games of Clue as a child.

"Never mind. Why don't we just call Jenna and ask her about it?" I said.

The phone, no doubt meant to rest on a desk when the office was fully put together, was still on the floor, next to Oscar's chair. He reached down and picked up the hand piece.

"What's her extension?"

"8502."

He punched it in. "Hi, Jenna. It's your warm and loving co-counsel, Oscar. Could you come and join me and Robert for a few minutes? We're in his office. He's on eighty-two now." He hung up. "She's on her way."

When Jenna arrived, Oscar didn't waste any time. "Susan Apacha says the building computer shows that it was *your* key card—number 526428—that came up the elevator at 11:45 p.m. Sunday evening."

Since the only guest chair was occupied, Jenna had had to stand in the doorway. On hearing what Oscar had to say, she slumped against the door jam. "Oh, stupid me."

"Meaning what?" Oscar asked.

"I leave my key card in my desk drawer. I never use it. You only need it if you get here super early or leave after seven and come back after dinner, and I never do either. Someone must have stolen it."

"According to Susan Apacha, *you* reported it stolen last week."

"No I didn't." Then, apparently detecting the look of disbelief in Oscar's eyes, she repeated it more distinctly and more slowly, holding his gaze. "I . . . did . . . not."

I decided I needed to say something. Something really powerful.

"Are you sure?" I asked.

"Utterly sure. I haven't reported anything missing. In fact, I don't even know if my key card really *is* missing. But I'm going to go and find out. Right now."

With that, she turned and left. I had the impression that she would have slammed the door if she could have. That was when I first noticed that the door was gone. The hinges were there, but no door.

Oscar had not unfolded his arms. "You should get rid of her."

"I'm loyal, Oscar."

"Benedict Arnold was loyal."

"To the wrong side."

"Precisely my point," he said. He finally unfolded his arms, put his hands above his head and stretched. "Look, my friend, this is nuts. You've asked me to take on as my co-counsel—my second-in-command—the prime suspect besides you. By doing that you're protecting her. When we should be out investigating whether *she* did it. Or even insisting to the police that she did it."

"Oscar, you don't understand. I'm divorced, my only contact with my ex-wife is to send her checks. I'm estranged from my daughter. My only contact with her is to say 'no' to her requests for checks. I don't have a lot of friends. So the law firm is my family, and it's trying to kick me out."

"So?"

"Emotionally, I *need* Jenna. She's a friend."

"I see," he said, sounding very much as if he didn't see.

"Anyway, she didn't do it," I added. "I'm sure she didn't."

"Sure you're sure. How the hell do you know that?"

"I just do," I said. "She's even shared some things with me that might help us catch who really did do it."

Oscar smiled a big smile. Then he laughed, not quite uproariously, but close. "Oh, right. I forgot. You're out looking for the true killer. Have you figured out who it is yet? Someone from the world of Faye Resnick perhaps?"

I had forgotten that Oscar had had a small, hidden role in the O. J. Trial. Faye Resnick had been a friend of Nicole Simpson's, and the defense had floated a totally bogus theory that maybe someone Faye was acquainted with did it.

I ignored the sarcasm. "Actually, Oscar, we've made progress."

"Yeah, like what?"

"Harry Marfan may have done it."

"Harry Marfan? The guy who was a senior partner here for years?"

"Yes, him."

"What makes you think he did it?"

"Stewart Broder heard Harry and Simon arguing here in the office. Arguing about drugs. Around 2:00 a.m.—just hours before I found Simon's body."

"Who is Stewart Broder?"

"He's a tax partner in the firm."

"How well do you know him?"

"Not all that well. He came here the same year I did. We were friends at first, but in recent years, we've lived in different worlds. He's single. He has some interest in coins, but his real passion is collecting butterflies. Minds his own business. That's about it."

"What was Harry Marfan's motive?"

"Drug deal gone bad maybe? I don't really know."

"Great. Do you at least know if he has an alibi?"

"He says so, but he wouldn't tell us what it is."

Oscar looked suddenly ashen. I realized we must have violated the rules.

"You actually went and asked him about it?"

"We did."

"Both of you?"

"Yes. Was that a mistake?"

"Oh my God." Oscar got up, got down on the floor, and began to do super rapid push-ups. "One, two, three, four . . ."

"What the hell are you doing?"

"Deflecting . . . five, six seven . . . tension . . . eight, nine, ten, eleven . . . So I won't . . . twelve . . . yell at you . . . thirteen . . ."

"So we screwed up?"

". . . fourteen . . . Big time."

He was slowing down.

"Why?"

"If he did do it . . . you tipped him off, so now . . . fifteen . . ."

He was puffing a bit.

". . . he'll try harder to . . . sixteen . . . cover his tracks."

He strained to make the next one.

"... seventeen ... And the two of you are now ... witnesses to what ... he said when ... he was first accused ..."

He was starting to turn red, but then seemed to find a burst of energy. "Eighteen ...... nineteen. ...... twenty!"

Oscar stopped, got up and sat back down in the chair, breathing hard.

"That is why lawyers in the real world don't interview suspects, Robert. They let investigators do it. They let the damn investigators do it!"

It seemed to me that Oscar had written off our efforts too easily. "Harry seems like a pretty good suspect to me."

He rolled his eyes. "Listen, I got a look at *all* of Susan Apacha's key card records for Sunday evening and Monday morning. The ones that match names with numbers. Aside from Jenna, thirteen people rode the elevator up to the eighty-fifth Floor between 8:00 p.m. Sunday night and 4:29 a.m. Monday morning. Apacha says the cops have interviewed all of them, and each and every one has a legitimate excuse—coming back from a late dinner, working late or whatever. So even if Harry was in the office and yelled at Simon, so what? Lots of other people were probably still here, pulling all-nighters. And anyway, Harry's name is not one of the names on the list."

"If the cops interviewed everyone whose key card came up, why haven't they interviewed Jenna?"

"Maybe they did interview her and she forgot to tell you."

"She would have told me."

"Uh huh. Well, then, maybe they haven't interviewed her because she's your goddamn lawyer." He paused, got up, came over to my desk, put both hands on it, and, leaning across it, got as close to my face as he could. "Don't you understand, Robert? She is *hiding* behind you!"

Just then, I noticed that Jenna had returned. From the look on her face, she had heard everything Oscar said.

"I'm not hiding behind anyone," she said. "You want the cops to interview me, Oscar? Give them my cell number. I'm happy to chat."

Oscar began to pace back and forth, hands behind his back.

"Robert, let me explain something to you," he said. "You are going to be arrested. Soon. Spritz thinks he's got everything he needs now. They probed the hard drive on Simon's home computer and found deleted e-mails between the two of you. E-mails where Simon accuses you of defrauding him in a coin sale and demands his 500K back. Rather vehemently. E-mails where you refuse to give the money back. Vehemently. So there's a motive."

"But, I said . . ."

Oscar ignored me and continued. "And Simon's blood on your suit cuff, and maybe his blood in your office, so there's physical evidence. And your elevator key card coming up to eighty-five—with you in tow—at 4:30 in the morning. According to Spritz, you came up at 4:30 a.m. to kill him and then again at 6:00 a.m.—if you ever left at all—to call 911 and make it seem like you had just stumbled on the body. So there's opportunity. Which we could also call the nail in your coffin."

Oscar stopped pacing, turned and swept his right hand toward me, index finger outstretched and jabbing at me.

"But even in the face of all that, Robert, you're just going to go out and do exactly what you damn well please. Well, I'm too old for that. I need to have clients who are not nuts. Clients who follow my advice. I quit."

Then he aimed his finger at Jenna. "You can be his lawyer all by your-self, sweetie. If you're not indicted as a co-conspirator."

He lowered his hand. "I wish you both the best of luck."

With that, he simply walked out. Since he was already standing up, he didn't need to worry about how to push back from a table. He didn't try to retrieve his jacket from the back of the chair, and he didn't look back. It was a perfect exit.

I didn't blame him for leaving. There's nothing worse than a client who simply ignores his lawyer's advice. And nothing *twice as worse* as a client who insists on doing his own investigations, unbidden and unsu-pervised. The legal profession requires that clients submit. I had refused to submit to Oscar. Truth is, had I been my lawyer, I would have dumped me as a client in a heartbeat.

I realized that Jenna was still standing there, looking at me. She was holding an envelope in her left hand.

"What's in the envelope?"

"My key card. It was still in my desk drawer, right where I always keep it."

"How do you know it's really yours?"

"Years ago, I pasted some tiny fake jewels on the back. So I could tell it apart from my parking card, which looks just like it. The little jewels are still there. It's mine, for sure."

"Why the envelope?"

"To keep from smudging any fingerprints on it."

"You going to send it to Uncle Freddie to dust for prints?" As soon as I said it, I knew that I was being a jerk.

Jenna gave me a disgusted look. "No. I've hired an investigator. He'll take care of it. Probably, it's got only *my* prints on it. But if somebody else's prints are on it, the somebody else will have some explaining to do."

"Do you suspect someone?"

"Uh huh. Stewart."

"Stewart?" I wrinkled my nose. "You still think he did it?" It did not seem even remotely possible to me, even though I'd accused him of it at the DownUnder.

"He could have," she said. "He admitted to being here."

"And his motive?"

"I don't know. Maybe we should burgle his office and find out."

"When?"

"Well, soon if I'm going to be the lead burglar. I've been told that Monday is my last day. So after that, I'm going to lose my access here. Maybe we could do it late tonight."

"What do you mean Monday's your last day?"

"Caroline came to see me when we got back today. She told me that representing you is a conflict of interest. She told me to get off your case or get out of the firm."

"That's crazy. The firm isn't even a party in my case."

"Not according to her. She called it a *business* conflict. Something about too much attention on the firm already. Something about your taking a leave of absence. Something about keeping a low profile."

"I'm not taking a leave of absence."

"Neither am I. I'm staying on your case, and I'm quitting the firm."

"No, you're not. You have a great future here. You'll probably be a partner next year. You shouldn't throw that away on my case. I'll find someone to replace Oscar. You and I can always chat informally about the case."

"Get real, Robert. This murder is already stuck to you like tar. Even if you avoid indictment, you'll always be the 'lawyer suspected of killing Simon Rafer.' It will follow you all your days. It will stick to me, too. The newspapers are already calling me one of your Dream Team. And when the Blob finds out about me and Simon . . ."

"Maybe it won't."

"Oh, it will. It will. There are already fifty reporters in town looking at every inch of his life. They'll find it. Once they do, I'll be front page fodder for the tabs. Right beside alien babies. So I'm toast here. They'll never make me a partner."

"Of course they'll make you a partner. Your work is first rate, and clients love you."

"No, they'll just trump up ways to say I'm no longer any good and fire me. You know how they do that to associates they don't like. Used to be fabulous. Flamed out at the last minute. So surprising. So too bad. It's all subjective. If I stay I'll be gone in a year. I know it. I might as well go now and try to have some fun." She paused. "I'm sorry. I don't mean fun. It's just that . . ." She burst into tears.

I have never been very good at trying to comfort people who are crying. Maybe I lack the gene for it. Usually, I just sit there and wait for it to stop. But I felt I ought to do something, so I got up and stood beside her and hugged her to me. She sobbed into my shirt. If I'd followed my father's lead and carried a handkerchief, I could have taken it out of my pocket and offered it to her. It's what they always do in old movies. But I had never even owned a handkerchief.

Eventually, the crying stopped, and she pulled back from me. "I'm just so ineffably sad, Robert. So sad."

I tried to make light of it. "Ineffably? Is that one of those twelve-dollar words you learned at Oxford?"

"Cambridge, you big shit. I went to Cambridge. And you know it." We were back to joshing. It seemed to help both of us.

"Jenna, I don't think you should leave the firm."

"I've made up my mind."

"Will you at least sleep on it?"

"Yes. But it won't change anything."

"All right," I said. "On other fronts, I assume you were joking about burgling Stewart's office."

"Yes, of course. But it wouldn't be beyond me to call Spritz and suggest he take a closer look in that office himself."

"Good idea," I said.

"Maybe I'll go call him right now," she said. "Which reminds me, speaking of calls. The news director at KZDD called me back. They watched Harry check his baggage at the ticket counter at American Airlines and then go through security."

"Where was he going?"

"They don't know, exactly. They couldn't follow him through security to his gate. Could have been any one of American's destinations. We'll need to figure it out, somehow," she said.

"Yeah, and we'll need to figure out how to replace Oscar."

"You still think I can't do it alone."

"Right."

"Okay, I'll think about who might be good while I start to pack up my office."

"Need help?"

"No, but maybe when I'm done I could give you my door." She laughed. "I won't be needing it anymore." And then she left.

CHAPTER 17

——

Ipicked up the phone and dialed Caroline Thorpe. Her voice mail answered. I left an exceedingly rude message, the gist of which was that giving me a dumpy office was not going to push me out the door, and, speaking of doors, they should find my damn door and bring it back. Only seconds after I dropped the phone back into its cradle, it rang. I picked it up.

"Robert Tarza here."

"Good evening, Robert."

It was Serappo.

"Good evening Serappo. Sorry I wasn't able to call you back." Then I got right to the point. "So what do you want?"

"I would be delighted if you were to come and see me."

"This isn't exactly the greatest time to travel to Chicago."

"The weather here has not been too inclement as yet. No snow. Reasonable temperatures."

"I wasn't referring to the weather."

"Ah, well, yes. Perhaps I might be able to help mend your personal weather as well. One never knows."

I didn't want to travel to Chicago. I didn't want to see Serappo. I had never liked him, and he tended to be a bullshitter. "Maybe, Serappo, you could mend my weather, as you put it, right over the phone, right now."

"Telephones are so uncivilized. I would strongly prefer to interact with you in person, Robert. Come to Chicago."

"I will think on it," I said. "But don't hold your breath."

"At my age, holding my breath might not be the wisest thing to do. But will you seriously think on paying me a visit?"

"I will."

"Good. Well, then, my young friend, I will wish you a pleasant evening."

I hung up the phone. I had to smile at having been referred to as his young friend. It's all relative, I guess.

I sat there and thought about his invitation to go to Chicago. On the one hand, Serappo might actually know something useful, since he'd apparently appraised the Ides for Simon. On the other hand, leaving town right now to pursue another will-o'-the wisp lead didn't seem like the most prudent thing to do. I could just have Jenna call him and try to wheedle out of him what he knew and what he wanted. She'd probably even enjoy talking to the old geezer.

I plucked my suit jacket off the back of my chair, walked to the elevator bank and headed down. When I got to the ground floor, I walked through the lobby and out the big glass doors that lead to the street. I expected to see the Blob outside, but it was still gone. Oddly, I kind of missed it.

Then I hoofed it the few blocks over to the *Yorkshire Grill*. I had eaten my first dinner in Los Angeles there back in 1973. I had been in town to interview for a possible first-year associate's job at M&M, starting the next year. Crusty old John Jordan, who didn't believe in fancy recruiting dinners, had taken me there, saying, "There'll be time for fancy later if you turn out to be more than a flash in the pan, sonny."

Since I first set eyes on the place in 1973, the management of the *Yorkshire* has changed it hardly at all. At max, they've replaced the vinyl in the booths a few times, refurbished the sit-at counter a bit, maybe even hired a new cook or two or three. But that's about it. It's still a small, classic deli with very good, but hardly gourmet, food. Ambience? If a guy from 1952 were somehow parachuted into the twenty-first century and plunked down in the *Yorkshire*, he might not notice that almost sixty years had gone by. He might even be able, still, to understand the menu. No free-range chicken. No arugula. No organic non-fat soy milk.

I ordered a Coke and a grilled cheese sandwich. American cheese. On white. A *real* grilled cheese sandwich. I knew that it was bad for me, but I was happy that it didn't have a secret name or a secret menu companion, or come wrapped in lettuce with no bread. It was extraordinarily tasty.

When I finished dinner, I walked back to the office. As I swiped my card to activate the elevator I was acutely conscious that I had just made a record of my entry. Something I didn't used to think about. Or even be aware of.

I went up to eighty-five, then walked down three floors of internal stairways to my new office on eighty-two. There was now a door leaning against one of the office walls. Waiting to be installed, I hoped. My message to Caroline had apparently paid off. At least temporarily.

Looking around, I saw that someone had put my inbox in the middle of my desk. It was piled high with almost a week's worth of mail. I sat down and went through it. The most interesting things in the stack were half a dozen notes from friends trying to buck me up in my time of trouble.

There are apparently no "So Sorry You're a Person of Interest" cards in the stores, so people had had to make do with short, hand-written messages penned inside those blank no-message cards. Most people had written, "Hang in there," or something equivalent. One, from an old girlfriend, said, "Kick 'em in the balls." I visualized doing just that to Detective Spritz and found the thought almost as satisfying as the grilled cheese sandwich.

Less than an hour after I began, the box was empty. I felt oddly at peace. There is something quite soothing about doing a familiar, repetitive task that takes no effort. Meanwhile, it had gotten dark out, and very quiet, even on the dorm floor. The Christmas season had depleted the ranks. They were probably off spending their overly munificent salaries on the latest consumer electronics. Or on Blackberries that would fit inside your decoder ring. Or whatever. My thoughts were wandering. I had nothing left to do except sit and think.

Normally, I am not very contemplative. Or, as Gwen once put it to me in a moment of unusual candor and intimacy, I am not "in touch with my inner feelings." That has always seemed to me a good thing. Most of the people I know who are in regular touch with their inner feelings are seriously miserable.

Every few years, though, my inner feelings start yelling at me. Usually late. Suddenly, it was one of those nights. As best I could tell, what my inner feelings really wanted was simply to have me go away somewhere so they could go back to sleep for another few years.

I fantasized, maybe seriously, about going to Mexico. With enough money, of which I had an ample supply, no one in Mexico would want to find me, let alone return me. I could just get in my car and drive across the border. Then I emerged from my reverie. I didn't want to live out my life as a fugitive in Mexico. I'd spend my whole life washing everything I ate in bottled Evian.

Then I started to think about Jenna. Why *weren't* they after her? I thought about the Ides, which I stupidly still had in my pocket. Was it a fake? Did the police even know I had it? Should I give in and go see Serappo? I wondered what he really wanted. I doubted it was to wish me a Merry Christmas in person.

My state of grilled cheese-induced serenity was beginning to fade, so I did what I always do when I need to try to master the universe. I took out a pad of yellow legal paper and sketched out a little chart. Four columns along the top for suspects. Four rows down the side for the evidence on each. I love charts. So orderly. So informative:

	Jenna	Stewart	Harry	Me
Opportunity				
Phys. Evidence				
Motive				
Alibi				

I started to fill it in.

Jenna had opportunity, if you believed the key card records, and maybe a motive. But why would she want to murder Simon just because, at least according to Harry, Simon had wanted to dump her? Which she denied in any case. And Jenna attracted men like flies. It wouldn't have been hard for her to find a replacement. I put a question mark in the Motive box. Next, I looked at the Alibi box. I realized that I had never really queried Jenna about her alibi. I put a question mark there, too.

Then there was Stewart. By his own account, he had opportunity. But I had no idea what his motive could have been. It was true that I had confronted him at the DownUnder about the possibility of his being fired, but, so far as I knew, he hadn't known about that. Who knew about his alibi? Everyone seemed to have one but me.

What about Harry? If Stewart were to be believed, Harry had opportunity and was angry at Simon about something, maybe about drugs. But Harry had told us he had an alibi. I'd believe him for now.

Finally, I filled in my own column. Just looking at it made me queasy. It was little wonder Spritz was after me.

	Jenna	Stewart	Harry	Me
Opportunity	Yes (key card)	Yes	Yes	Yes (key card)
Phys. Evidence	?	?	?	Blood
Motive	Angry at S? S at her?	?	Angry at S? Drugs?	$500,000
Alibi	?	?	Claimed	No

No wonder Oscar had wanted to focus first on simply defending me—on getting some of that stuff out of my column, instead of trying to blame the murder on someone else. There was little hard evidence on which to lay blame on anyone else.

Two days ago, I had set out to learn enough to find the killer myself. But the only useful thing I had learned had been volunteered by Stewart. Which was that I should put a "yes" in the Opportunity box for both him and Harry. Other than that, I hadn't learned shit.

I suddenly wondered: Had the police searched Stewart's office? I bet not. Why would they? And what *was* in that office? Sometimes, despite my patina of control, I get uncontrollable impulses.

I got up, grabbed my suit jacket, walked to the lobby, and took the elevator down to the parking garage. I went over to my car, popped the trunk, and found the brown leather gloves I'd left there after my ski trip to Mammoth, plus the flashlight I keep in the trunk for emergencies. Then I went back up the elevator.

When the elevator doors opened, I peeked out and looked furtively around the eighty-fifth floor lobby. There was no one in sight, and it was dark. I held the elevator doors open with my shoulders while I put on the gloves. My heart was beating fast.

Stewart's office is right next to reception. I actually sprinted over to it. The door to the office was closed. I tried the knob, and the door opened. I went in and closed it behind me, but not all the way. I wanted to be able to hear anyone who came onto the floor. Then I switched on the flashlight.

Even by flashlight, Stewart's office was nondescript. Smallish, with only two windows. I had always wondered why he kept it when his seniority entitled him to a much nicer one.

Under the windows there was a couch covered in a bright green chintz with a motif of overlapping ferns. An old oak desk sat in the middle of the room, with a tall bookcase on the wall to its left. On the wall to my right there was a large, bright-green abstract oil no doubt bought because it matched the green couch. Beneath it there was the required potted plant. Also green, of course.

I sat down behind the desk and thought about where I would hide something. Under papers in a drawer maybe. I opened each of the desk drawers in turn. The first two were mostly empty. A few pencils and pens, a few pads of Post-its, some of the stray paper clips that seem to inhabit the bottom of all desk drawers. In the third drawer, there was a large pile of papers. Old tax returns of some corporate client. I lifted them up and looked underneath. Nothing. My hands were sweating profusely inside my gloves.

I remembered reading somewhere that people sometimes hide things in false bottoms in potted plants. I got up, walked over to the plant, and started to feel around the bottom of the pot, looking for a secret door of some sort. My hands were trembling.

"Hi!"

I almost jumped out of my skin. It was Jenna, standing in the doorway, outlined by the faint light from the hallway. I had not heard her push open the door.

"Jesus, Jenna. You scared the shit out of me."

"Why Mr. Tarza, whatever are you doing in here?"

"Um . . ." That was all I could think of to say. I couldn't even manage an "oh".

"Are you going to answer?" she asked.

I didn't respond.

She shut the door behind her and turned on the overhead lights. "Well, you look really stupid in those gloves. Brown. Utterly wrong for that suit."

I blinked as I tried to adjust to the bright lights. "I'm looking for some kind of evidence that Stewart did it."

"Find anything?"

"No. But I haven't been in here very long. I was looking for a secret compartment in the pot." I pointed at it.

Jenna stood there for a moment and then looked slowly around the room. You can always tell when a professional is looking at something. They examine whatever it is differently from the rest of us.

"Give me your gloves, Robert."

I took them off and handed them to her. She put them on, went over to the bookcase, and inspected it closely. After a while she bent down and ran the flat of her hand slowly along the molding on the left side of the bookcase, at the very bottom. She paused for a second and then pushed gently. I heard a very faint click on the other side of the bookcase.

Jenna got up, moved to the right side of the bookcase, bent down, and pulled at the side molding at the bottom with the tips of her gloved fingers. A small door opened. She looked up at me with a distinct expression of triumph.

"There's a cable that runs from a pressure point on the other side to a hidden latch over here," she said. "The idea is that if someone accidentally pushes the trigger plate on the left side, they won't necessarily realize they've opened a latch on the right. Give me your flashlight."

I gave it to her. Jenna aimed the beam into the secret compartment and peered inside. Then she reached in and pulled out a small coin and a thick book.

"That's all there is," she said. "This coin looks like the Ides to me. But I'm guessing it's a copy." She pulled off her right-hand glove, handed the glove to me to put on, and then passed me the coin with her still-gloved left hand.

I hefted it, brought it up to my eye, and studied it more carefully. "It looks real enough."

"How can you tell?"

"Experience," I said. "I'd have to examine it more carefully with a loupe, but it looks just like the one you picked up at Simon's and gave to me."

"There are two of them?" She raised one eyebrow.

"So it seems."

"And what is this book, Robert?" She held it up. It had dust clinging to the bottom.

"It's volume III of Grueber's *Coins of the Roman Republic in the British Museum*. From the look of the dust, it's the one that was on Simon's bookshelf." I started to reach for it with my ungloved left hand.

Jenna pulled it back. "Don't touch it with that hand. Use the one with the glove."

Using only my gloved right hand, I took the book and opened it, awkwardly. "Yeah, it's got his name written on the flyleaf, 'S. Rafer.'"

Jenna looked at me. "Really. Well, the plot thickens."

I managed a small joke. "Congeals even."

"Is the Ides pictured in that book?" she asked.

"I'm not sure." I turned to the pages in the back with pictures of coins, which are called the plates. I couldn't immediately spot the Ides among the photos.

Jenna peered over my shoulder at it. "Is the whole volume just coin photos?"

"No. A lot of it is lists of coin hoards. Where they were found, what they were found in."

"Were there hoards of Ides?"

"I've never looked that up in this book, but not so far as I know."

"Maybe we should look it up," she said.

"Maybe." I was starting to feel nervous about being there. It didn't seem the time or place to conduct research on the hoard history of the Ides. "What should we do with this stuff, do you think?" I asked.

"How about we put the stuff back and get out of here before we get caught?"

"No, I think I want to keep both the coin and the book."

"That's risky, Robert."

"Probably. But I want them anyway."

The coin Jenna had nicked from Simon's kitchen was in my left suit coat pocket. So I dropped the coin we had just found into my right pocket, brushed the dust off the bottom of the book, and tucked it under my arm. Jenna closed the secret compartment. It made a smart click as she pushed it shut. We turned off the lights, closed the door behind us, and went to Jenna's office, which was just down the hall. It was full of packed boxes. We chatted about this and that, while Jenna packed some more, almost as if nothing had happened. Then we drove our respective cars back to my place.

Jenna got there first. Let's face it, she just drives faster than I do.

When I walked into the house, she was standing in the living room, stock still.

"What's wrong?"

"Things are out of place."

I looked around. She was right. Stacks of paper had been moved. A vase here and there was out of place. The sofa had been nudged closer to the wall.

"Burglars?" I asked.

"More likely cops. With a search warrant."

"Oh. Well, they won't have found anything of interest. There's nothing to find."

"I hope you're right."

"I am. And I'm wiped. I'm going to bed. Goodnight, Jenna."

As I left the room, she was still standing there, looking around. With her hands on her hips, muttering about the perfidy of Detective Spritz.

CHAPTER 18

——

I got up at 5:00 a.m. and showered. I picked out my usual suit and put it on. I felt refreshed. I had not, however, forgotten that there was now a deepening coin mystery to be solved. Exactly the kind of mystery I liked to sink my teeth into, and one for which, finally, I actually had some competent teeth. Not like investigating murders.

I took the original Ides, the one Jenna had taken from Simon's kitchen table, and placed it obverse-side-up—the side with Brutus's portrait up—on my nightstand. I put the second Ides, the one I had borrowed from the secret compartment in Stewart's office, next to it. I looked at them carefully. To my naked eye, they looked identical. I turned them both over. The reverse sides—the side with the daggers—looked identical, too.

I needed to see if their small flaws, too hard to see with the naked eye, were also identical.

I went to the closet where I keep my coin supplies and pulled out a high magnification jeweler's loupe and a small, bright Maglite. I picked up the original coin, bathed it in light and peered through the loupe at the reverse side. Then I did the same with the reverse of Stewart's coin. I noticed that each had the same tiny, circular pit right next to the left-hand dagger. I recognized those pits as die flaws, possibly left there by a protruding rough spot on the die when each coin was struck.

I turned the coins over and began to examine their obverse sides with the loupe. There, on the original, to the left of the first letter of his name—"B"—above Brutus' portrait, I could see a small, incuse—indented—triangular die flaw. I looked at the obverse of Stewart's coin. It had exactly the same flaw.

Which troubled me. What were the odds that I had accidentally stumbled upon two, two-thousand year old coins struck from exactly the same reverse *and* obverse dies?

I could not for the life of me recall exactly how many obverse and reverse dies had been identified for the Ides issue, and the books that

143

would have told me the answer were in my office. I did recall that, over-all, the numbers had been relatively small. Which made sense to me because the Ides coins had, after all, been minted by Brutus to pay his sol-diers, using a mobile military mint while he was fighting in Macedonia, falling back from Anthony. So it was likely a small issue, not equivalent in numbers to a huge issue of standard coinage minted in Rome.

I also seemed to recall that fewer obverse dies had been identified than reverse dies. Which also made sense because the obverse die, containing the image of Brutus's head, would have been on the bottom of the stack, fitted into the anvil. The reverse die, holding the image of the daggers, would have been on top of the stack, fitted into the trussel, and would have received the force of the hammer more directly, which would have caused it to wear more quickly. But I couldn't remember those details for sure, either.

Whatever the true number of dies, though, it seemed to me that the odds of finding two coins that were die duplicates, drawn at random from history, were quite small.

Was there a way to make those odds better? Only if I were to assume that each of the Ides had been drawn from a hoard buried by a single sol-ider, which had survived as a hoard for over two thousand years. But how likely was that? The coins were a soldier's daily wage and were usually spent. Plus Brutus's troops were constantly on the move and would have had little reason to bury a hoard since they could not have expected to be able to return to retrieve it.

What really nailed it for me, though, was that Stewart's coin appeared to be in Very Fine condition, bumping up against Extra Fine. Had a new Ides of that high quality been discovered, it would have made news in all the ancient coin publications. But there hadn't been a peep about it.

"Shit." I said it out loud. The coin was very likely a forgery. Because a forger of rare coins, who would need to strike only a few coins, wouldn't have to make more than one set of reverse and obverse dies. So all of the forger's Ides would be die matched.

I put the first coin, the one that supposedly came from Simon's kitchen, back in its transparent coin flip. But I needed to make sure that I didn't confuse the two. So I went and found a flip I had that was tinted slightly red, and put the second coin, the one from Stewart's office, in that flip.

Then I walked over to my bed, sat on the edge, and began to ask myself some questions. Was the coin Jenna had taken from Simon's kitchen table my grandfather's original and the other a fake copied from it? Or were they both fakes? I searched my memory to try to recall whether my grandfather's coin—which I still thought of as the true original—had had those die marks. I could not recall.

More questions began to carom around inside my head. If both of the coins were fakes, what had happened to my original, and who had it now? If one of these two coins was indeed my original, who had copied it and why? Were there even more copies somewhere? Was my original actually just an old counterfeit and this one its counterfeit twin?

Sitting there on the edge of my bed, I was now fully in touch with my inner feelings. They were afraid. They were telling me—screaming at me really—that if I didn't find the answers to those questions, my feelings and I were going to be sharing a very small room in a big building surrounded by barbed wire.

Serappo was a logical place to start looking for answers. After all, if Jenna was to be believed, he had supposedly declared my original—if it really was my original he looked at—to be a fake. But to pull the answer out of Serappo, I was going to have to reverse course and do what he wanted: go to Chicago to meet with him in person.

I decided to do it.

First, though, I had to get there, and I for sure did not want to get there on a commercial airliner. Then I remembered that Peter Penosco had said to call him if I needed help. Now I did need help, and Peter had exactly the variety of help I needed. A very nice *Citation*. I'd flown on it dozens of times. If it didn't have the range for Chicago, we could refuel somewhere.

I got up off my bed and went into the kitchen to call him. It was still dark out, and there was as yet no sign of Jenna. The dim glow on the wall clock said it was not yet 6:00 a.m. The phone has a lighted keypad, so I didn't bother to turn on the kitchen light. Over the years Peter had called me at home before six God knows how many times, so I simply returned the favor.

He answered on the first ring. When I identified myself, there was a distinct lack of enthusiasm in Peter's responding "hi." From a sixth sense developed over a lifetime of business phone calls, I knew in an instant that he would rather be hearing from his dentist. But I plunged ahead.

"Peter, you said if I needed anything, just call."

There was a slight pause. "Um, yes."

"Now I do need something."

I expected him to say something along the lines of "Just name it." Instead, I got something more curt.

"What is it?"

"I need to get to Chicago. Right away. I'd like to borrow the Citation. There and back in one long day. I'll pay for crew and fuel."

There was an even longer pause.

"Roberto, I'd love to do that. Love to. But I can't. As you know from the papers, this thing's getting out of hand."

"I don't read the papers," I said.

"Well, you should. You should. The *Times* says you're about to be arrested. I have to think about the company. Can't take a publicity hit like that."

"Like what?" I genuinely didn't get it.

"Lending a plane to a killer."

Now the long pause was on my side. I was getting it. I had become a pariah.

"I'd probably do the same thing in your place, Peter. Thanks, anyway."

"Actually, Robert, I'm real glad you called. Was gonna call you."

I should have seen it coming. "Why?"

"Well, under the circumstances, we can't use you anymore. As our lawyer. At least right now. You know how this business is. Pure image." He plunged right on, in a rush to get it all out. "But the good news is, we'll still be able to use the firm! I've been talking to Caroline about who to go with while you're on leave."

"I'm not on leave."

"Right, right. But you know what I mean. It will be hard for you to negotiate our deals from jail." He tried a small chuckle, as if it were a little joke between us.

"I'm not going to jail."

"Okay, okay. *If* you go to jail."

I realized it was hopeless. "Peter, I hope Caroline arranges someone top notch for you."

"She will. I'm sure she will. She says there are some good young guys there who can do it even better than you." He must have realized how cruel that sounded. "Well, you know, not as good as you." There was the forced little chuckle again. "But, you know, guys who can climb the old learning curve really fast."

"No doubt. Hope it works out."

"Thanks. And, hey, Roberto. Good luck to you, pal."

"Thanks." I hung up.

Just then, Jenna flipped on the lights. I blinked. It seemed as if that was our M.O. now. I'd be in a dark room, and Jenna would blind me by turning on the light.

She must have had the same thought. "So, Mr. Tarza, sneaking around in the dark again?"

"Just making a call."

She stifled a yawn. She was still in her bathrobe. "At six in the morning?"

"I was trying to get a ride."

"Where to?"

"Chicago."

"You're going to Chicago?"

"Yeah. To find out what Serappo knows about all this."

"About all what?"

"I looked at the two coins under a loupe this morning. They came from identical dies."

"So?"

"It means that at least one of them is almost surely a fake. Maybe both."

"Want to enlighten me as to why you concluded that?"

"Not right now. I'll explain it when I get back from Chicago. I'll even show you."

"Okay, fine. But it's dumb to go there."

"Why?"

"When they arrest you, they'll use your having left town to try to deny you bail. Flight risk."

"That's stupid," I said. "I'd be just as much a flight risk if I'd never gone anywhere."

"A lot of legal rules are stupid."

"Do you really think I'm going to be arrested?"

"Yeah. And if you go to Chicago, it will be sooner rather than later." She paused. "When I got back to the office last night, there was a call on my voice mail from Spritz. Asking if we'd surrender your passport."

"What did you say?"

"I haven't called him back yet. Maybe you better give it to me before you go to Chicago."

"In the top drawer of my dresser," I said.

"I'll get it later. Want some breakfast?"

"You're what, the full service lawyer? Cook and defend?"

I thought it was funny, but Jenna didn't, I guess, since her only response was to ask, "Eggs over easy or scrambled?"

"I'm going to skip breakfast this morning, but thanks."

Then I went to my study to make some reservations online. Something I'd only recently started doing. Except my computer wasn't there. I went back to the kitchen.

"Where's my computer, Jenna?"

"I assume the police took it when they searched the house yesterday."

I felt outraged. "They just took it? The whole thing? You can't do that with a subpoena."

"They didn't use a subpoena. They had a search warrant—to uncover evidence of a crime. You remember—like a civil subpoena on steroids?"

"Okay, fine," I said. "But now I don't have a computer." I was sounding whiney. I knew that. But I couldn't help it.

"My law firm has one," she said.

"Where's your law firm?"

"In the back bedroom. I kind of figured even before my meeting with Caroline that my days at M&M were numbered. So a couple of days ago I printed out "JAMES AND ASSOCIATES, ATTORNEYS" on a piece of paper and taped it to my door. I think the police were hesitant to go in there, even with a warrant for the house. Which reminds me."

"What?"

"They slipped a copy of the search warrant under my office door."

"Would you stop calling it your office?"

"Okay. They left a copy of the search warrant under my bedroom door."

"And?"

"It included the garden. Do you have any idea why they wanted to look in the garden?"

"No." As I said it, we both moved, as if by agreement, to the kitchen window, which overlooked the garden. It was still dark out, so I flipped on the outside floods.

"Wow," Jenna said.

A large but shallow hole had been dug in the northeast corner of the garden. The dirt from the dig was piled beside the hole.

"I wonder what they found," she said.

"I don't know," I said. "Lots of dirt and some old pottery shards would be my guess. Anyway, I need to make my airline reservations. You can inspect the garden later if you want."

"Shall I bring out my computer?"

"No. I'll just use the phone."

Which is what I did.

United and American were booked solid. I finally called Southwest and discovered that they had a 10:30 a.m. flight that got into Chicago Midway at about seven in the evening. It stopped in Kansas City, but that wasn't a big deal. Then I called and made a reservation at Swissôtel, down by the River on East Wacker. Not the most elegant hotel in Chicago, but it's got a terrific view, and it's only about a ten-minute drive from Hyde Park. That's where Serappo has his office. If you can call it an office.

It didn't take long to pack my small roll-aboard. I was planning to stay only one night, so I figured I could get away with wearing the same suit a second day, much as I hated that. All I needed was a clean shirt, some underwear, and my travel kit. I picked up Volume III of Grueber's *Coins of the Roman Republic in the British Museum* and tossed it on top of the clothes. Maybe when I had a little spare time I could take a look at the list of hoard finds in the front of the book and see if there were any for the Ides. Then I thought better of it and took it back out. It would make the roll-aboard too heavy. It was still a little early to leave for the flight, but I decided I might as well go early and miss the traffic. I could grab a bite at the airport and spend the extra time there instead of gridlocked on the 405.

When I came out of the bedroom, heading for the door to the garage, Jenna was standing there, still in her bathrobe, sipping a cup of coffee.

"Hey, can I say something before you go?" she said.

"Sure."

"I need to apologize to you."

"For what?"

"I've been kind of snotty to you the last couple of days."

"Not really."

"Well, yes, really. I've been behaving like I know it all, and you know nothing. Maybe it's because I'm nervous about all this responsibility. Extra nervous now that Oscar has quit. Anyway, I just want you to know that I really care about you, and I'm going to try to do a really great job."

All of a sudden, I was brought back to the reality that my lead counsel had departed and that Jenna was now my only lawyer—a seventh-year associate with very little criminal law experience. Even if she did know the difference between a subpoena and a search warrant. But I no longer cared. In the last couple of days, I had come to think of Jenna as the adult. We had reversed roles. Now she was giving me a chance to bail out if I wanted to. I didn't want to. I had a premonition about Jenna. A good one.

"Jenna, I know you'll do a great job," I said. "I have a lot of faith in you to first-chair this. When it's all over, we'll go out again and drink martinis. Just like the old days."

She came over and gave me a big hug. "Thank you, Robert. Be careful in Chicago, and remember the rule."

"What rule?"

"The one you taught me about interviewing: Ask lots of questions. Don't answer any."

"Yes ma'am," I said.

I went out and got in my car. I clicked the garage door open, turned the key in the ignition, and started to put the car in gear. Then I took it out of gear again, sat there for a moment, and thought carefully about what I had just said to Jenna. I turned the car back off, clicked the garage door shut, and went back into the house. Jenna was again at the kitchen table. She looked up.

"I forgot something," I said.

"What?"

"Something about your new law firm."

"You think we need trendier offices to attract good clients?" She grinned.

"No, I think you need to add something to continue to attract this client."

Her look turned serious. "Like what?"

"Like a senior lawyer to partner with James and Associates. In particular, a replacement for Oscar as lead counsel."

"You thought I was good enough to be first chair two minutes ago, but now you've changed your mind?"

"Yes. I came to my senses in the garage. For the next guy, you will be good enough. But let's face it, you're still too inexperienced in criminal law."

She looked crestfallen. In the past, Jenna had often gotten her way with me by using that look. Not this time.

"Don't take it so hard," I said. "Just make a list of candidates. We'll go over it when I get back."

I didn't wait for her response. I went back out, got back in my car, reopened the garage door, and drove out. At normal speed for a change, because the Blob was still missing.

CHAPTER 19

————

S ome days at six forty-five in the morning, the 405 is jammed. Other days, at exactly the same time, it's nearly empty. It's utterly unpredictable. This was one of those utterly unpredictable nearly empty days. So I was at the airport and parked in what seemed like no time.

I walked into Terminal 1 and glanced behind me to see if I was being followed. No one seemed to be paying me any heed. I got my boarding pass from the automatic ticket machine and looked around again. Nothing. I passed through the security check point and scanned the crowd for a third time. Still nothing, although I must have looked rather furtive if anyone was paying attention. Apparently, no one was. Somehow, my anonymity had been at least temporarily restored.

The only place to have a hot food breakfast in Terminal 1 is at McDonald's. I'm not normally a big patron of McDonald's, but an Egg McMuffin seemed somehow the perfect meal to match my mood. That and a hot cup of coffee, even if it was in a paper cup. I have always believed that the decline of American civilization is made manifest by the ubiquity of coffee served in paper cups.

With more than an hour to spare, I screwed up my courage and bought an *L.A. Times*. Except for the one Jenna had thrust upon me, it was the first newspaper I'd really looked at in nearly a week. I paged quickly through it to see if there was any reference to me in the first section. There wasn't. Nor in the second section. Maybe the whole thing had been a bad dream, and it would all just go away. Spritz would arrest the real killer, I'd go on the *Today* show, talk about how dreadful it feels to be a "person of interest" in connection with a murder, and then just blend back into my real life.

So I relaxed for the first time in many days and read the paper front to back. It felt great.

I was in the group that boarded first. Since there are no assigned seats on Southwest, I moved to the very back of the plane and took a window seat. The number of people waiting suggested to me that the plane was going to be only moderately full, and that a lot of middle seats might stay empty. Eventually, a very tall gentleman wearing a bright red shirt came and took the aisle seat in my row. No one sat down between us.

We'd been in the air maybe five minutes when he turned to me and said, "Aren't you Robert Tarza?"

I stiffened and considered denying it. But I didn't.

"Yes, I suppose I am. Why?"

"Edwin Larson. *National Enquirer*." He stuck out his hand. I didn't take it.

"Shit."

"Hey, don't be so negative."

"How did you know I was here?"

"We have sources, as they say. Your face has been all over the papers and TV. When you buy an Egg McMuffin in a public airport, someone is likely to notice you and give us a call. We've got a toll-free tip number. Somebody maybe got some bucks for phoning you in."

"I'm so very happy for them."

"Yeah, well, we'd like to interview you. An exclusive for a week. We'll make it well worth your while."

"I'm not interested," I said.

"Money always comes in handy in a situation like yours."

"Like I said, I'm not interested."

"There are advantages besides the money."

I should just have turned away and pulled out the in-flight magazine or something. But one of the problems with being a lawyer all your life is that you develop a built-in tendency to respond to statements like his with follow-up questions. Like a dog barking when the doorbell rings. "What advantages, exactly?"

"You get to tell your side of the story. For the first time."

"And what? Have it run next to some story about alien babies?"

He looked genuinely offended. "We do *not* do alien baby stories. That was the *Weekly World News* when it was still around in print form. We're a serious paper. We broke a lot of the O. J. stuff. Those fat fucks at the *L.A. Times* actually had to read our paper to find out what was happening.

So giving us an exclusive is a fast track to real people. The kind of people who'll be on your jury."

I had had a few dealings with the press before all this. I thought I knew the score with at least the print guys. I could probably get something out of this. Even as my responding words took shape in my brain, I could hear Jenna screaming at me: "Don't even think about it!"

"It would have to be off the record," I said.

"No problem."

"Okay, then, call it a maybe. But first I want to ask *you* something, Mr. Larson."

"Shoot."

"Why is everybody so interested? Simon Rafer wasn't a celebrity. No one had even heard of him before he was killed."

Before he could answer, the flight attendant came by, asked if we wanted coffee or soft drinks, and handed us the inevitable packets of peanuts. I couldn't help but think of the nice plate of bacon and eggs that would have been served aboard Peter's Citation. I ordered an orange juice. My seatmate ordered a double vodka on the rocks.

The flight attendant departed up the aisle, and Larson answered my question as if there had been no interruption. "They'd heard of him for sure," he said. "He was a man about town. Honorary chair of the opera. Big charitable donor. Frequently photographed at society fund raisers. And the *pièce de résistance*—as we say over at the *Enquirer*—he used to date a big movie star. Deanna Cuvtin."

"She hasn't been in a film in ten years," I said.

"Big movie stars are forever. It's not like she did TV."

"They broke up five years ago."

"Maybe so," he said. "But we've got a zillion pictures of the two of them doing the club scene."

"You're telling me the media's after me because I supposedly killed a guy who used to go out with a washed-up movie star, and you've all got great five-year-old pictures?"

"Life's a bitch, isn't it?" He paused a second to wait for my response, which wasn't forthcoming. "So how about that interview?"

"Explain to me again what's in it for me."

"Like I said, you get to tell your story. And I'll trade you some information."

"What have you got?" I asked.

"Tell me you'll do the interview, and I'll tell you. You won't be disappointed."

"That's a sucker deal."

"No, it's not. I've been covering this thing full time for four days. I've talked to a lot of people. If you think what I tell you isn't valuable, you can back out. Of course, I'll think you're a shit, and I'll be out to get you, but I won't be able to make you talk."

I thought about it. The logic of mutual obligation in our culture is a topic unto itself. He had me hooked. "Okay," I said. "Let's do it this way. Tell me this great piece of information, and we'll see."

We were interrupted by the orange juice and the double vodka being plopped down on our trays. I sipped at my orange juice. Larson looked at me and said, "The police searched your garden."

"I already know that."

"Well, they found something."

"I know that, too." Of course, that was a bit of fudge. I had no idea what they had found in the hole they dug, if anything.

"I'm betting you don't know what they found."

"That would be correct."

"They found an old metal box with a counterfeit Canadian passport in it." He paused. "In your name."

I wished I'd ordered the vodka instead of the orange juice. But I tried to maintain my aplomb. I think I succeeded. "Was there anything else in the box?"

"Why don't I save that till later."

I just sat there. After a while, Larson said, "You're very quiet Robert. You don't mind if I call you Robert, do you?"

"That's fine."

"How about that interview? When we're done, I might know a few more things, too."

I caved. "What do you want to know?"

It was odd to me, but what Larson mainly wanted to know about was what I knew about Simon's affair with Deanna Cuvtin. Which wasn't much, really. Although I did recount to him the time we had a New Year's Eve toga party at my place, and Deanna was thrown into the hot tub wearing only a thin sheet. Larson wanted to know if I had any pictures of the event. I told him I didn't.

It was only toward the end of the interview that he began to ask me about myself and Simon. I recognized the technique. Ask the person you're interviewing a lot of easy stuff first, gain their confidence, and then get to what you really want to know.

So I ended up telling Larson that Simon and I were friends, that I had recruited him and supported him for partner, that I had no reason to kill him, and that I had, indeed, just stumbled on the body. I explained how I was usually an early bird. I told him everything I thought a juror would want to hear. It wasn't until the very, very end, when I thought he had finished, that he got around to asking what he truly wanted to know.

"By the way, Robert, did you sell Simon Rafer some rare coin?" He asked it casually, as if he expected the answer to be no.

"I did," I said.

"What was it?"

"An Ides denarius of Brutus."

"Never heard of it. What is it?"

"The coin Brutus minted to commemorate his assassination of Julius Caesar. On the Ides of March."

Mostly, Larson had been listening, without making notes. Now he made a note. "So it wasn't some American silver dollar, like they said in the *Times*?"

"No. The *Times* got that wrong," I said.

"Wow," he said. "Assassination. That's something we can do something with." Then he muttered, almost to himself, "I wonder if our readers will know that he wasn't a salad."

The interview ended with my shaving the truth by a few millimeters. Larson's very last question was whether Simon was dissatisfied with the coin I had sold him. I said no. I justified my answer, in my own head, by assuring myself that the coin I sold Simon had been genuine. So if Simon was dissatisfied with the coin, it wasn't with the coin I sold him. It wasn't with me. It was with whoever switched the coin. If anybody did.

I figured I had told him enough to gain the next piece of information. "So what else was in the box?"

"Ancient coins of some sort, with some guy pictured on the front. We're trying to find out more."

"Really." I couldn't think of anything else to say.

"Do you know who put the box there?" he asked.

"No."

To my surprise, Larson didn't press me about the box or its contents. Not that I would have been able to enlighten him.

Instead, he asked, "Is it true you're going to take a plea deal?"

"No!"

"There have been rumors in the papers that your lawyers are discussing it."

"They're not."

He apparently had no more questions burning a hole in his notepad, because he thanked me for the interview and assured me it would be attributed to "well-placed sources" or something like that. He gave me his card and said, "Call me if you learn anything else you're willing to share with us. Or have one of your lawyers call. We can trade information."

"Thanks," I said.

He took a long sip of his vodka, pursed his lips, and seemed to hesitate. Then he said, "One last piece of information for you. When the police searched Rafer's condo the day after he was killed, they didn't find any coin. My sources tell me they didn't know to look for it. The cops only figured out yesterday that a coin was involved. Something they found on a computer tipped them off. Now they're wondering where the coin is."

I thought about saying, "Well, obviously, dummkopf, it's in the metal box." Instead I said, "Did they ever go back and find it?"

"Well, they went back yesterday and really tore the place up looking for it, but came up with nothing. But . . . and here's the big news. . . they think someone else broke in yesterday afternoon and took the coin out of a safe, right before they got there."

"Interesting." That was all I said.

Larson went back to sipping his vodka. I put my orange juice aside and ordered a vodka on the rocks, to which I added the orange juice. Then I did the crossword puzzle in *Spirit*, the Southwest in-flight magazine. It was neither hard nor easy, but it passed the time. Larson got off in Kansas City. He told me he was taking the next plane back to L.A. I flew on to Chicago. On the way, I ordered another vodka, straight up.

CHAPTER 20

———

As soon as I got off the plane at Midway and turned my cell phone back on, it rang. It was Jenna. "Don't say anything. Just listen."

"Okay."

"Spritz called to ask where you were. I think he wanted to arrange for you to surrender."

"Surrender?" I felt momentarily light-headed.

"Just shut up and listen. We'll worry about surrendering later. I told Spritz that you were on your way to Chicago. He's pissed as hell. I told him I had your passport, but he didn't seem mollified. You left your flight number on the notepad by the phone, so I gave it to him, just to prove you weren't going to Mexico. I'm betting he's going to have you followed. For some reason, he thinks you're going to Canada. So you need to lose whoever it is they put on your tail there. It will be bad if they follow you to you-know-who."

"What? . . . But how—"

"Bye." She hung up.

I had not a clue how to lose a tail. Let alone figure out who it was. In movies, you can always spot them. There's a clue of some sort. I looked around and saw no clues. Just a crowd of about a hundred people getting off the plane, another hundred or so waiting to get on, and maybe fifty assorted others. I gave up and went out to the cabstand.

There were at least twenty people waiting in the line. None of them looked suspicious. Most were men, most were wearing suits and over-coats. Most looked a lot warmer than I was. It was maybe 40 degrees out, and I had not bothered to bring an overcoat, even though it was Decem-ber. There's something about living in Southern California that puts you in denial about the fact that it might be cold somewhere else.

I stood in line for about fifteen minutes. When my cab finally pulled forward, I opened the door, tossed my suitcase on the backseat, and got in. "Swissôtel, please."

Just then I saw a gentleman in a suit, who had very definitely not been in the cab line, cut to the front of the line and flash his open wallet at the guy in charge. He got into the cab immediately behind mine. Obviously, he was a cop. Obviously, he was going to follow me.

My cab had already started forward and was about to pull out into the moving lane of traffic. I'm not sure where I got the psychological wherewithal to do it, but I told the cabbie, "Listen, I forgot something, and it may take awhile to find it. Please let me out. Sorry for the inconvenience."

We had moved only about twenty yards at that point. The driver put his foot on the brake, and the cab stopped with a jerk. I handed the guy a twenty, grabbed my suitcase, and scrambled out. I glanced back to see if the cop had managed to get out and follow me, but didn't see him.

I headed back into the airport and was thankful for the milling crowd inside. I spotted a CTA sign that said TRAIN TO CITY It was the way to the "El"—the Chicago elevated rapid transit. I remembered that you could now get from Midway into the city that way. I followed the signs. First up a ramp, then through a parking garage past the rental cars, then down two levels of escalators into the station, still not looking behind me. I bought a ticket from one of the automated machines.

I was in luck, because a train was at the platform, ready to leave. I made it on board just as the doors closed and saw four people enter the same car through the other door. Two were wearing parkas and carrying backpacks. They looked like high school students. The other two were in suits and overcoats. One of them looked like he might be the cop from the cab, but I couldn't be sure because I hadn't gotten a good look at the guy.

The car was crowded. I sat down on the hard plastic seat next to a woman with a huge red suitcase on wheels. One of the students—a guy lugging a black backpack—plunked himself down on the seat in front of me. I folded my hands in my lap and tried to look inconspicuous. As the car began to move and sway, I considered my situation and hatched a plan.

I had been headed for Swissôtel, but it's small, and its lobby wouldn't likely be crowded enough for what I was thinking about doing. I needed someplace much bigger.

The *Drake* sprang to mind. It's one of those oversized, early twentieth century hotels that was once elegant, then fell on hard and tattered times—when it had sometimes been called the 'Dreck.' It was finally restored to elegance in the 1980's, and then restored again a few years ago. Its lobby was likely, even in early-evening, to be crowded with the bustle-creating tourists and convention goers who had become its stock in trade.

I asked the girl with the huge red suitcase, who was to my right, which stop I should use for the Drake. She mumbled that she didn't know where it was and moved toward the window, despite the narrow seat. Apparently, my suit did not put her at ease as to my intentions. The student with the big black backpack, who had apparently overheard my question, turned his head around and said, "You're on the Orange Line. Change at Roosevelt to the Red Line, then get off at the Chicago stop, go over to Michigan, turn left, and walk up to Walton." I thanked him.

When I got off at Roosevelt, I noticed that the student also got off and transferred to the Red Line. I didn't give it much thought at the time since Roosevelt was a major stop.

The entire trip, including the transfer, took only about thirty minutes. Once there, I got off, took the escalator up, and went out onto the street. The temperature had dropped further. I walked briskly towards Michigan and then turned left toward the Drake, trying not to be cold.

As I passed Marshall Fields at Water Tower Place—now unfortunately renamed Macy's—I decided to go in and buy a coat. I wasn't particular, and I picked out a long wool overcoat for about $300. I paid for it with my M&M American Express card. For years, I had put all my expenses on it. When the monthly bill came in, Gwen went through it, added up what was personal, and wrote out a reimbursement check to the firm.

The clerk looked up at me with some distress on her face. "I'm sorry, sir, but the card is coming up as cancelled."

"That can't be," I said. "I used it this morning to buy airline tickets."

Clearly, she had gone through this drill before. The look on her face left distress behind and went entirely neutral. I might be telling the truth, I might not be.

"Sir," she said, "I'm sure there is some terrible error. But as you can understand, we can't charge against a card that comes up as cancelled. Might you have another card that we could try?"

I looked in my wallet. Once upon a time, I had had a Visa card. And there it was. I gave it to her. She looked at it and said, "I'm sorry, sir, this card expired last year." She handed it back and waited patiently for me to say something.

I had only one hundred dollars in cash in my pocket. God knew if my ATM card still worked. "Well, looks like a series of errors, eh?" I said.

I gave the coat back to her and walked away. I felt mortified. That was when I noticed that the student with the black backpack was also shopping in Marshall Fields, casually looking at men's dress socks, which were in the next aisle. That seemed odd. He didn't seem like the kind of person who would need dress socks. He was at that very moment wearing white athletic socks and old tennis shoes.

I left the store and hurried toward the Drake, colder than ever. I kept glancing over my shoulder to see if there was any sign of the student. There wasn't. When I got to the Drake, I realized that I had a major problem that was going to interfere with my plan. I had planned to check in before implementing the rest of the plan, hoping that they would have a room even though I didn't have a reservation. But now I had no credit card that worked. I was going to have to improvise.

As I was pondering my problem, I saw the "student" come through the revolving door into the lobby. He was clearly looking for me.

I went over to the valet desk and addressed the man behind the counter. "Excuse me, sir," I said. "I'm going to be checking in later, but I need to meet a business colleague in the lounge first. Could I leave my bag with you in the meantime?"

"Of course, sir." He took the suitcase and gave me a small yellow claim check. I tipped him a couple of ones.

"Can you tell me where the restrooms are?" I asked. He pointed to his left. "Just down the hall there." I walked in the direction he pointed and then looked behind me. The student was still searching the large lobby for me.

At the end of the corridor that I had entered there was a set of revolving doors, clearly giving out onto the side street. I pushed quickly through them, looked around for a cab, saw one, and sprinted toward it. It slowed and stopped, and I jumped in.

"Hyde Park, corner of South Hyde Park Boulevard and 47th please." As the cab started to move, I looked through the rear window and caught the student bursting out of the revolving doors, looking around. He had focused on my cab. I hoped we were far enough away that he couldn't read the license plate or the cab number.

Since cabbies keep track of where they pick up and drop off fares, I knew that sooner or later the cops would trace the records and figure out where I had gone. But I was getting smarter maybe. I had asked the cabbie to drop me a good ten blocks away from Serappo's office.

As we drove down Lake Shore Drive, I kept looking behind us to see if we were being followed. I didn't think so, although it had become painfully obvious that I wasn't very good at detecting exactly who was following me. At least not right away.

The cab ride down to Hyde Park took only fifteen minutes. The cabbie dropped me off at the requested corner. I paid him and got out. Getting out reminded me of at least one problem with my plan. It was the wind, which was blowing steadily off the lake. Whatever the actual air temperature, the wind chill made it feel at least fifteen degrees colder. By the time I had walked the ten blocks to Serappo's office, I was shivering badly, despite having my hands jammed in my pockets and my shoulders hunched up against the wind.

Serappo's office had always been above the Medici, a bustling little restaurant on 57th Street that's been a University of Chicago student hangout since the beginning of time, and a favorite of President Obama's, too. Serappo both worked and lived in the building, so it seemed likely he'd be in, even at nine o'clock in the evening. His office was up a stairway just to the right of the restaurant, accessed through a battered wooden door that was marked NO SOLICITORS in small, stenciled red letters.

The door was unlocked, and I took the rickety steps two at a time to the second floor, where there were three doors off the landing. Two were unmarked. The third was labeled ACME MEET BROKER. I knocked on that one, figuring it was Serappo's current disguise for his coin business, although I doubted anyone intent on robbing him would have been fooled. The last time I'd been there, ten years before, the same door had said ACME KITCHEN REMODELING.

I stood there waiting, but got no answer. I knocked again, louder. As I was about to give up, a gruff female voice asked, "What asshole is calling this time of night?"

I identified myself and was answered with a grunt that might have been an acknowledgement. After a brief delay, I heard the sound of three chains coming off, and then two deadbolts being turned. The door opened a crack, and Smirna Prodiglia peered out at me.

Smirna is Serappo's daughter. The first time I'd met her, ten years ago, she'd been about forty. The passage of a decade had not improved her. Her long brown hair, which I remembered as lustrous, was now matted and snarled. Her only makeup was vivid red lipstick, most of which had missed the mark. I couldn't really see her body, but the puffiness in her face suggested that she had consumed far too many donuts since I'd last seen her.

"Can I help you?" she asked. Although the question was reasonably neutral in tone, I sensed that she hoped the answer would be no, so that she could slam the door and go back to whatever she had been doing.

"I'm Robert Tarza."

"Yeah, that's what you just said a minute ago."

"Smirna, surely you remember me."

She frowned. "Now that you mention it, I do. So what?"

"I'd like to see your father."

"About what?"

"It's a private matter," I said.

"There are no private matters between Dad and me."

"Okay. I want to talk to him about the Ides."

She seemed to consider that. "The Ides denarius of Brutus?"

"Yes."

"Really. It must be National Ides Month, and it isn't even March," she said. "All right, come in. I'll ask him if he wants to see you."

She opened the door fully. I walked in and looked around the small reception area. It had not changed since the last time I'd been there. The only furniture was a government-issue steel desk, a metal-framed, office-style swivel chair with a green cloth seat, plus a faded red couch. There was no art on the walls. The desk was piled high with magazines. The top one on the pile was entitled *Render,* which appeared to be the national publication of the fat rendering industry.

Two doors led out of the reception area. One was wood, and I recalled that it led to the living quarters, where Serappo had entertained me the last time I'd been there. The other was steel and looked like the entry to a vault, except that it had no visible combination lock. I'd never seen what was behind that door.

Smirna walked behind the desk and stabbed at a small black button on the desktop. I heard a buzz in the next room. Then a voice I recognized as Serappo's came through a scratchy speaker, in a rather peevish tone. "What is it? I asked not to be disturbed tonight."

"Robert Tarza is here to see you."

There was no immediate response. Serappo was apparently considering whether to be disturbed.

"Send him in," the voice said. "You don't need to search him."

I looked at her. "You search people? What a nice professional touch."

"We've had some problems," she said.

"You do the search yourself?"

"Don't worry, you're not my type." She reached under the desk again and pushed something. I heard the pop of an electric lock unlatching and watched the door to Serappo's office swing open.

CHAPTER 21

———

When I walked in, Serappo was sitting behind a steel desk like the one in the reception area. The only other furniture in the room was a single bucket-style guest chair, in yellow plastic. The kind you find in a library's public function room. Serappo himself was impeccably dressed amidst the shabby surroundings. He was wearing a bespoke pinstripe suit—you could tell by the hand-stitched button holes on the cuffs and the way the soft gray fabric draped so nicely on his shoulders—a white-on-white Turnbull & Asser shirt and a maroon tie, probably Georgio Armani.

"Mr. Tarza," he said. "What a surprise. And here I thought you had declined my invitation. Please sit down."

I eased myself into the low-slung chair. So low that I had to look up at Serappo, the more so because both his desk and his chair rested on a platform raised several inches above the floor. I waited. Serappo, I knew, had a fetish of not speaking immediately at the outset of a meeting—and a desire that you also remain silent. He had once told me that it was a tradition inherited from his Tibetan mother.

Somehow, I had always doubted that. He didn't look the least bit Tibetan. He looked like a gaunt Caucasian of uncertain ethnicity. His olive skin suggested that he could be Italian or Greek, or maybe even something more exotic. His most arresting feature had always been his vivid green eyes. So unusual in color that his mother could well have been a cat.

I first met Serappo when I was fifteen. Back then, he had wavy black hair. Now, at the age of eighty-something, his hair had migrated to gray and wispy. But the eyes were, if anything, even more intense, and he was staring at me, his hands steepled in front of him, finger to finger.

After what seemed like an eternity, he spoke.

"So, Robert, do you still like the Cubs?"

"I suppose. I'm not really much of a sports fan."

"Do you recall when I took you to that Cubs game?"

I squinted my eyes in memory. "Yes, I do. It was when I was a first-year at U of C. It was the second time you tried to buy the Ides from me."

"I do not recall that part," he said, "although I do recall the score. It was a game the Cubs won one-to-nothing in the bottom of the twelfth."

"I don't recall that."

"It was a cold day in the fall. You were very cold. I recall that. In fact, you look a bit cold now. May we offer you a hot drink?"

"No thank you," I said. "I want to get down to business."

"You mean you didn't come to discuss baseball?"

"No."

"That is too bad. You know, I've been to over a thousand games."

I considered briefly whether Serappo was losing his mind.

"What are you thinking, Robert? That I have lost it?"

"The thought crossed my mind," I said.

"You are such an American, Robert. Despite your European background."

"I don't have a European background."

"Your grandfather was Spanish."

"Basque," I said.

"All right, Basque, if you wish. But still, a European."

"Your point is?"

"A European would be pleased to talk about nothing in particular for an hour or so before getting down to business."

"What is the business you think we will eventually be getting down to, Serappo?"

"I assume, Robert, that you came to sell me the Ides . . . finally, after all these years."

"I don't have the Ides. I have only this." I reached into my left-hand jacket pocket and pulled out the transparent coin flip—the one that contained the coin Jenna had taken from Simon's kitchen. I removed the coin from the flip and held it up, trophy-like.

"You keep it in your pocket," he said. "How quaint."

"I'm told it's a fake," I said.

"Let me see it."

I got up and put it on the desk. Serappo picked it up, hefted it briefly in his hand as if to feel its weight and then held it up between thumb and forefinger, turning it slowly. Then he took a loupe from his desk drawer and examined both sides again. Finally, he removed a tiny, sharply pointed rubber mallet from the drawer, held the coin up next to his ear and tapped the coin gently with the point.

"Yes, it is a fake," he said. "But a terrifically good one. Everything is perfect except the sound, and even it is quite close. They probably used some kind of laser technology to make it."

"Are you certain it's a fake?" I asked.

"Yes, I am. And speaking of inquiries about fake coins, Harry Marfan was here not long ago asking about the Ides."

"Oh? What was he asking about it?" I tried to make my question sound nonchalant.

"He assumed I had the real Ides, and he wanted it back."

"Because they sent it to you for appraisal?"

"Yes. He accused me of swapping it and returning a fake."

"Maybe it's always been a fake," I said. "Maybe the coin my grandfather gave me was this very fake."

He looked at me steadily with his green eyes. "Oh no. It was not. I assure you it was not. I held the coin your grandfather gave you in my own hands more than forty years ago, and it was the real thing."

"When you visited me and my mother in Los Angeles? When I was eleven?"

"Yes."

"Well, coming back to the present, what did you tell Harry about the coin you just appraised?" I asked.

"I told him what I just told you, my friend. That the coin they sent me to appraise was a fake."

"Was it this very fake?" I pointed to the coin, which was now resting on the desk in front of Serappo.

He shrugged. "Maybe. But I can't be sure. Perhaps there are two such fakes. Perhaps there are a hundred. There are a lot of collectors who have wealth but no sense of discernment, and they would be easy marks for this coin."

"So you don't think this is an imitation made for tourists?" I asked.

"No. As you well know, legitimate makers of tourist fakes put some mark on those to show that they're copies. This is designed to deceive. Nor was it cheap to make."

Then he fixed me again with his eyes. I waited.

"Robert, I have a proposition for you."

"What is it?"

"I believe I have learned some things that might be of use to you in your, what should I call it, predicament?"

"I'd be delighted to learn them," I said.

"I'm sure you would. But I want to trade you for the information."

First the *Enquirer* guy and now Serappo. Bartering information seemed to have become a regular part of my life.

"What do you want to trade for it?"

"If the true coin is ever found, I want you to agree that you will sell it to me."

"I don't own it anymore, Serappo. I sold it to Simon." I suddenly realized that I had just abandoned the fiction that I had already bought it back from Simon. "He paid," I continued, "much more than I thought it worth, but he offered the price, so I took it."

"So I have heard," Serappo responded. "But I have a feeling you will, eventually, find it again in your hands. So do we have a deal?"

"Sure." The truth is, having already gone through the wrenching decision to part with it when I sold it to Simon, deciding to sell it again to Serappo—if I ever did get it back—was not all that difficult. Even though I had sworn to myself, years before, that Serappo was the last person on earth I would sell it to.

"Good." He pushed a button and spoke. "Smirna, please bring that document in."

A few seconds later, Smirna walked in and placed a document in front of him. "Thank you, my dear," he said. "You do not need to wait." Smirna left.

Serappo picked up the document, got up from his chair, and brought it over to me. He walked slowly, and it was clear to me that, in the ten years since I had last seen him, he had become frail. As he handed me the document, his hand shook.

I took it from him and glanced at it. It was a contract, clearly prepared in the expectation that I would show up. It specified that in exchange for certain information, I agreed, "irrevocably," to sell him the Ides should I currently have or come into ownership of it.

"Is that contract enforceable, Robert?" He was standing beside my chair.

I thought about it for a second. "Candidly," I said, "I can immediately think of several good defenses I'd have to your action for breach if I refused to sell the Ides to you. They might not win, but they'd be formidable defenses."

"But you are a man of honor, are you not? Despite no longer being a Cubs fan?"

"Yes."

"So if you sign it, you will honor it?"

"Yes."

He pulled an elegant fountain pen from his suit coat pocket, uncapped it, and handed it to me.

I took the pen and said, "I'll sign, but why is having that coin so important to you, Serappo?"

"I have been collecting ancient coins for more than sixty years. The Ides is the most famous of them all. The Ides your grandfather gave to you is the only one I have ever touched, that one time when you and your mother permitted it. The others are all in museums or in the collections of the unduly rich. I want to own it and touch it again before I die. Precisely because I know that I will not be the last person to own that coin. Dozens who came before us have owned it and dozens more, yet unborn, will own it after you and I are gone. I want to be a link in that chain."

It would be fair to say that, romantic as that all sounded, I did not believe him. I assumed he wanted to own the coin so he could sell it to one of the unduly rich and pocket a profit. I briefly considered asking him if he had some premonition that he was going to be unlinked soon. But I thought it might be misinterpreted, so I simply took the pen from him, put the contract on my knee, and signed. "Will you give me a copy before I leave?"

"I will," he said.

"Now tell me what you know," I said.

"First, I think we should celebrate our deal, don't you think?"

I thought no such thing. But it was inevitable that we were going to do so. I sighed inwardly.

"Sure, let's celebrate."

"Do you enjoy peach schnapps?"

"It's okay."

"Good, I'm glad you like it." He pressed a button on the speakerphone and spoke into it. "Two peach schnapps, *meine kleine.*"

Smirna didn't strike me as anyone's little one, and I had no idea why Serappo had chosen German as his language of affection. But Smirna did promptly bring us two shot glasses of Schnapps.

Serappo raised his glass. "To coins."

I raised mine. "To coins and information."

I tossed it down in one gulp. In the hope that I might finally end the European part of the conversation and move on to strictly business.

CHAPTER 22

"You drank it down in one swallow," Serappo said. "Would you like another?"

"No thank you. But I would like to know what you know."

"Of course. Let me begin at the beginning."

"I would like that."

"About two months ago, Simon called and said you had sold him the Ides. He wanted to send it to me to authenticate and appraise. He wanted me to issue a certificate of authenticity. We agreed on a fee for me to do that."

"How much?"

"Twenty thousand dollars."

"And then?"

"About a week later, a courier brought the coin to me."

"Who was it?"

"A young woman I did not know. In her late twenties or early thirties I would guess."

"Did she tell you her name?" I asked.

"No. In fact, she was evasive about that. I asked her several times and never received an answer."

"What did she look like?"

"Neither short nor tall. Slim. Dark hair. Good looking."

"Did she say much?"

"Hardly anything at all. Just presented the coin, asked for a receipt, and left."

I suddenly had a very bad feeling. But I pushed on.

"Then what happened?" I asked.

"I evaluated the coin, using a variety of means, and determined it to be a very clever forgery. I called Simon and told him that. He was not very professional about it. He asserted that I must be wrong. I asserted that I was quite right. Then I sent it back."

"By courier?"

"No. By Federal Express. There seemed little point in using a courier to return a fake."

"Do you think the courier swapped it?"

"That is a possibility. One I mentioned to Simon. He said he knew her, and she would *never* do that. He called her an 'intimate.'"

I asked the lawyerly question. "What happened next?"

"Well, earlier this week," he said, "I read in the newspapers that Simon had been murdered. I called you the very next day. But you did not return my call."

"I was busy," I said.

"Yes, I think I understand that now."

"Then what happened?"

"Nothing happened. Until about ten days ago, when Harry Marfan showed up here. Just like you did. No appointment." Serappo smiled a small smile, as if to say 'you are all so impolite, where you come from.'

"What did he want?" I asked.

"He said he had joint-ventured the purchase of the Ides from you. At first, he demanded that I give him the real Ides, because he thought I still had it. Eventually, I persuaded him that I did not. Then I suggested he sue you to get the money back."

"Sounds reasonable," I said.

"Yes, but then the truth came out. The reason they wanted to get the real coin and not the money."

"Which is what?" I asked.

"He and Simon had concluded that your Ides is the Ides of Trajan."

"The what?" I thought that I knew a great deal about my grandfather's gift, and I had never heard of the Ides of Trajan.

"Do you know your Roman history?"

"In general terms," I said. "Trajan was an early Roman emperor."

"Do you know where he was born, Robert?"

"No, of course not."

"In Spain."

The mystery of it all, whatever it was, was not exactly enthralling to me. It was just irritating. I wanted Serappo to tell me what he knew and skip the history lesson.

"So?" I said.

Serappo pushed a button under his desk, and the wall to his left, peeling paint and all, slid back to reveal a row of shelves, some filled with books, others with the small, red cardboard boxes that coin collectors use to house their treasures. I have to admit it. I was boggled.

He got up, walked unsteadily over to the shelves, and pulled a slim paper-bound volume from the highest shelf. He leaned against the bookcase and opened the book, which was well thumbed.

"Here, let me read you this passage," he said. "It's called "The 59th Ides":

> The emperor Trajan, who ruled Rome for almost twenty years, between AD 98 and 117, was born in Italica, in the Andalusian region of Spain. He was known as an avid coin collector and was reliably reported to own a superb specimen of the Ides denarius of Brutus. Shortly before his death, he gave his collection, including the Ides, to the imperator of the Roman legion then headquartered in Italica. The path of the Trajan Ides can then be traced through almost 1,800 years to the Abbey of Roncevaux in the Basque country of Spain, from whence it was either lost or stolen during the Spanish Civil War. The provenance and location of the other fifty-eight silver coins of this type are well known. Should the Trajan Ides ever be located, it will be the 59th such specimen, with a rare and storied history!

"Who knew?" That was all I could think of to say.

"No one knew," Serappo said. "The whole thing is horseshit."

"Who wrote that?" I asked.

"A guy from Leeds named Harris Caruthers. He was an amateur coin nut. Used to hang out at the British Museum coin cabinet and drive the curators crazy with his theories. That thing I just read to you came from his self-published book, *One Hundred Mystery Coins*."

"And someone thinks my grandfather's coin is the 'Trajan Ides?'"

"Yes, Harry Marfan thinks it, and the late Simon Rafer thought it. Well, I don't know if either one of them really believed that, but they were prepared to persuade someone else of it and sell the coin for a pretty sum. Many times what they paid you for it . . . however much that was." He looked at me with something of a twinkle in his eyes. "How much did they pay you, if I might ask?"

"It was only Simon who paid me. The price was five hundred thousand dollars."

"Though it's in Very Fine condition, maybe even better than that, he vastly overpaid. But even at that price they were going to make a tidy profit," he said.

"How much were they planning to sell it for?"

"Harry hinted at something like two million dollars."

"Really."

"Yes, really."

"Do you know who the buyer was?" I asked.

"Not by name. Some sucker in Hawaii. Harry didn't use the word sucker of course. But someone they persuaded that this preposterous story is true."

"Do you think there's any chance it is true?" As soon as it was out of my mouth, I realized I had said the wrong thing.

Serappo smiled a crooked smile. "It's amazing."

"What is?"

"Romantic stories cling to objects like gum to shoes. Even your shoes."

"Maybe it actually happened," I said.

"Listen, young man. There is no evidence Trajan ever owned an Ides. There is no evidence he was even a coin collector. Nor, if he was, is there any evidence he gave a coin collection of any kind—his or anyone else's—to anyone. Indeed, even if you could somehow prove that he did give an Ides to someone, there are no records that trace who kept, owned, and treasured that object for one thousand nine hundred years. Ninety-five generations."

I was appropriately chastened. "So why would anyone find it plausible?"

"Because," he said, "the provenance of every one of the other fifty-eight Ides is well known, at least for the last hundred years or so. And that is particularly so for those in Very Fine or Extremely Fine condition. Your grandfather's coin popped up more or less out of nowhere. Since it has no provenance, anyone who wants to can make one up for it. The better the story, the better the price."

"Did this Harris Caruthers guy know about my grandfather's Ides?" I asked.

"Not so far as I know. He was just making up a good tale about the Roman world's most famous coin. Something to spice up his book. Since he died in 1992, we can't, alas, ask him."

Serappo put the book back and closed the fake wall.

"I hope," he said, "that that information is helpful to you."

"Yes, it is."

"Good, I knew you would want to know all of that."

The tone of his voice said, in effect, "That's all I have for you." But I was not about to make a newbie lawyer's mistake and assume that what he had just told me was all he knew. I asked the follow-up.

"Do you know anything else you think I would like to know, Serappo?"

"Yes, I do. You would like to know, I assume, that Harry insinuated that you were in a drug ring."

"What?"

"Yes. He didn't quite come out and say it, but he kept asking if I knew about your contacts in the drug world."

"What did you say?"

"I told him I knew nothing about it, and that I'd be shocked if you had anything to do with such things."

"Is there more?"

He seemed thoughtful. "Normally, I do not share mere suspicions. But under these circumstances, yes, there is something else that you perhaps should know. Given your situation. But I want you to understand that it is based on a feeling, nothing more."

"All right," I said. "I'd be pleased to hear it."

Serappo didn't speak immediately. He still seemed to be considering whether he wanted to say whatever it was he was going to say. I have never been sure exactly what it means to wait with bated breath, but I must have been waiting with it.

Finally, he spoke. "Harry seemed . . . how should I put it . . . overly interested in the exact reasons I had appraised the coin as a fake."

"That's hardly surprising," I said. "Harry's always been detail-oriented. When he was our managing partner, he once spent an entire hour at an Executive Committee meeting grilling the office manager about the reasoning behind her decision to buy a new brand of paper clip."

"Perhaps you are right. And I must say that he carefully disguised his intent by asking his questions as a challenge to my conclusion that the Ides was a fake. Yet the detail he sought was somehow more than that. He even wanted to learn the numerical details of the technical tests I had performed, which included some non-invasive metallurgical tests."

"Did you tell him?"

"No, I told him they were trade secrets developed during a lifetime of effort. But the truth is, my friend, that, in the end, I declined to share the intimate details with him because I had the distinct sense that he was trying to learn how to make a better fake."

I reached into my right-hand pocket and took out the red-tinted flip—the one that contained the coin I had taken from Stewart's office. I walked over to Serappo's desk and handed it to him. "Do you think this one is a better fake?"

He took it from me, removed the coin from the flip, held it up to the light, and looked at it through his loupe. He didn't bother with the pointed hammer.

"It looks and feels like an identical fake," he said. "Are there only two?"

I thought about the ancient coins Larson had said were in the metal box in the garden. "There could be more."

"If there are more, you might think about the Black Sea Hoard."

The Black Sea Hoard contained more than a thousand ancient Greek coins—diobols—supposedly discovered more than twenty-five years ago near the Black Sea. The find had caused enormous excitement, and the coins had sold for high sums. In the end, after the exchange of much scholarly vitriol, most of the hoard was proved to consist of clever forgeries copied from an original, legitimate hoard of about one hundred fifty coins. "If you're suggesting," I said, "that someone might be planning to create a fake hoard of Ides, it seems far-fetched. The coins are too famous, and too rare."

"Perhaps so, although . . ."

His thought was cut off by the ringing phone. He picked it up, listened, and said, "Put him through." Then he listened some more. "Robert Tarza? He was here earlier, but he left some time ago." There was another pause. "Let me find out if we know that."

He pushed the receiver against his pant leg, so that the caller could not overhear, and said, "It's a Detective Spritz of the Los Angeles Police Department. He's looking for you. I told him you had already left. Do you want me to tell him where you're staying?"

"No."

He picked the phone back up and said, "I'm sorry, but we don't know where he's staying. Yes, if I hear from him again, I'll certainly let you know. Let me take your number." He wrote it down, then hung up.

"Thank you," I said.

"You're welcome. You seem to need a break, and I'm happy to help, even in a small way. Not to mention that I have no fondness for *les gendarmes*. But perhaps you'd better go. I'm not sure the good detective believed me, and I have the sense someone will be here soon to check it out. We can talk more about fake hoards later. And in any case, two counterfeit coins do not a fake hoard make."

He got up from his desk and shook my hand. I said a quick goodbye and started to head for the door.

"Wait," he said. "You'll want this." He put the second coin back in the red-tinted flip and handed it back to me.

"Thanks."

I exited the way I had come in.

CHAPTER 23

———

When I got down to the street, it was already past eleven. The temperature had dropped ten degrees or more since I had arrived, and the wind was blowing even harder.

I had planned to borrow a coat and some cash from Serappo, but in my haste to depart, I had forgotten. So now I faced the challenge of finding a place to stay with no coat, no suitcase, no working credit cards, and what was left of my one hundred dollars in cash.

I was beginning to shiver.

Finding a coat was job number one, because without a coat I was going to freeze to death. Once upon a time there had been a Walgreens, not too many blocks from the Medici, that stayed open till midnight. I took off in that direction and found to my shivering delight that it was still there and still open late.

I needed more cash to buy a decent coat. I crossed the almost empty parking lot to a cash machine that was right outside the main door into Walgreens. I put in my ATM card and punched in my password. A little message came up: *Account Is Temporarily Unavailable*. Somehow, I was not surprised.

I went into Walgreens anyway. Maybe they had something really cheap. As I went up and down the aisles, searching for the right section, I got a few odd looks. Maybe guys in pinstripe suits aren't all that common in Walgreens. I found the right section and examined some seriously ugly leatherette coats for sixty bucks. Complete with fake fur lining. But even they seemed suddenly and remarkably out of my price range. Then I spotted a close-out on cheap ski jackets—twenty-five dollars each—hanging on four long racks.

The colors weren't ideal. The best was a kind of puke green. I went through the racks and discovered that no matter the color, the largest size was a medium. I tried on one of the green ones. It was super tight under the arms, and the sleeves were way too short. When I zipped it up, it was so snug below my waist that I looked like a green sausage.

But I had no other options, so I took the jacket up to the checkout counter. With tax, it came to $26.75. The cab ride down to Hyde Park had cost me $15.00, so that left me with $58.25. I had not watched my money so carefully since college.

The checkout clerk was a slim young woman who looked like a college student. She stuffed the jacket into a large shopping bag and tried to engage me in small talk.

"Buying this for one of your kids?"

"Yes. My son," I said.

"How old is he?"

"Uh, twelve."

"Well, enjoy."

I thanked her—after deciding not to remind her that "enjoy" is a transitive verb requiring an object—and went back out into the parking lot. As soon as I got outside, I swapped my suit jacket for the ski jacket, bunched up the suit jacket, and stuffed it into the shopping bag. I may have looked like a trussed-up sausage, but at least I was a warm trussed-up sausage.

With the funds I had left, I needed to find both a place to stay for the night and transportation to Midway in the morning. Going back to the Drake was out of the question. It was too expensive, and, in any case, didn't seem like a good idea.

I considered going to the airport and sleeping on a bench, but I didn't want to draw the attention of the authorities. I suddenly realized that I was shedding my self-image as a senior partner in a large law firm and adopting the mindset of a common criminal.

The motels in that area of Hyde Park, near the University, were going to be too expensive. So I walked west, into the poorer neighborhoods. I figured that sooner or later I'd find a cheap motel. Either that or I'd be mugged and put out of my misery, and the mugger would get himself a nice new ski jacket. After about ten blocks, I came to a half-decent looking place called The Sleepaway. Its sign read ROOMS $30.

I went in and rented one. When I unzipped my ski jacket to get my wallet, the desk clerk gave me an odd look. I couldn't tell if it was because I was wearing a puke-green ski jacket with pin-striped pants and wing tips or because I was a guy wearing a Turnbull & Asser shirt who didn't have a credit card. Since I didn't have one of those, he asked me to pay in advance. He also reminded me that I would not be able to make long-distance phone calls from the room without a fifty dollar deposit.

The room, with lodgers' tax, came to $33.00. That left me with $25.25. Just enough for a cab to the airport maybe, but nothing much beyond that.

"Is there a bus I could take to the airport in the morning?" I asked.

"Yeah, right out front. Can't miss it. Says 'Midway' on it. Takes about twenty minutes. Runs every ten minutes starting at 4:30 a.m." He paused. "Costs two bucks." Clearly, the clerk had recognized that I was not a big spender.

"Thanks."

The room was plain, but clean. I was just getting into bed when my cell phone rang. It was Jenna.

"Hi."

"Hi."

"Don't tell me where you are."

"Okay."

"I doubt they'd tape me talking to you, but you never know," she said.

"Where are *you*?" I asked.

"At my law firm."

"Meaning at my house."

"Well, yes."

"How are you?" she asked.

"I'm okay. But I have almost no money. Somebody cancelled my credit card and my ATM card."

"Spritz got the bank to kill your ATM card. Maybe he got the credit card cancelled, too."

"Why?"

"Like I said before, he thinks you're heading for Canada. He's trying to make it harder for you."

"I'm coming home tomorrow. That should show him I'm not."

"He'll just think he succeeded in blocking your plans."

"Whatever. Why are you calling, Jenna?"

"Don't be testy, Robert. I'm trying to help."

"Okay. Sorry."

"I have a piece of information for you."

"What?"

"You remember that little hiding place?"

"Hiding place?"

"Where the item was."

"Oh, right."

"The hiding place used to belong to Harry."

"Really?" I said.

"Yes, really."

"That's interesting. Maybe . . . well, we should discuss that later."

"Yes, we should."

"Jenna, do you really think we're being taped?"

"If Spritz managed to cancel your ATM card, you never know."

"You're right. Will you pick me up at the airport tomorrow?"

"Sure. What time?"

"The flight number's on the little scratch pad next to the phone in my study."

"I'll see you there," she said. She hung up.

I fell into bed, and, surprisingly, slept the sleep of the dead. Maybe because I had actually learned at least a little something from Serappo. Or maybe because I finally realized my whole life was now firmly in the hands of others, and I had come to accept it.

I got up at six, showered, and dressed. I put on my suit pants, my shoes, and my increasingly smelly white shirt, then reached for the parka. But I couldn't bear to put it on again. So I pulled my suit jacket out of the plastic bag and put the parka in its place. When I was done I contemplated my image in the mirror. My suit looked a little rumpled, especially the jacket, but nothing that was likely to be noticed on the bus. I hoped I wouldn't freeze my ass off before it came.

I checked out and, in the process, bought an envelope and a stamp from the front desk. Fifty cents for the envelope and forty-four cents for the stamp, which left me with $24.31. Once out of sight of the desk clerk, I dropped my Drake claim check in the envelope and addressed it to Law Offices of Jenna James at my home address. Then I marked it <u>ATTORNEY-CLIENT PRIVILEGE</u> in large, underlined letters even though, of course, the claim check itself wasn't privileged in the least because it wasn't a lawyer-client communication or even attorney work product, being a pre-existing document. But maybe it would keep the envelope from being opened. It's not that there was anything suspicious in my suitcase, but I was tired of other people going through my stuff, and I figured I could retrieve it when this was all over.

I got out front to the bus stop a little after six-thirty. There were about a dozen people waiting. There was no wind, and the bus came right away, so I didn't even get cold.

To my surprise, the bus was crowded, and I had to stand, gripping one of the overhead straps as we bounced along toward the airport. I looked around, but it didn't seem likely any of the passengers were tailing me. Most were clearly heading to blue collar jobs. A couple looked seedy enough, in tweed and ratty overcoats, to be U of C professors. There were, thank God, no student types with backpacks. No one seemed to notice that my suit was wrinkled.

It took about thirty-five minutes to get to Midway. I got off and walked over to the Southwest gates, still carrying the plastic bag. I wanted in the worst way to dump it. Then I wondered if I would look suspicious going through security with not a shred of carry-on baggage. So I hung on to it.

The bus had actually cost $2.25, not the two bucks the clerk had said, but it still left me with more than $20.00, plenty for a real breakfast. Assuming Jenna really made it to the airport to pick me up, and I didn't have to bus it back to town in L.A.

I bought a *New York Times* and then sat down for breakfast at a little cafe just shy of the metal detectors. I ordered coffee, orange juice and scrambled eggs. It tasted damn good. As I finished, I realized I hadn't eaten since yesterday morning. I ordered again—two bagels and cream cheese—and ate those, too.

After paying for the paper and the breakfast, I was down to just under $4.00. The last time I had had that little money in my pocket was when

I came back broke from Europe after the mandatory college graduation trip.

I went through security without incident, then looked for a trash can to dump the parka. As I was about to toss it, a paranoid thought intruded. It might look suspicious to dump something that big in a trash can after I'd already passed through security. The parka was going home with me. Maybe I could leave it on the plane. I looked behind me. So far as I could see, no one was following me.

No one bothered me at the gate. I just sat and read my *New York Times*. I boarded without incident, and the plane took off on time. The flight back to L.A. was routine, including the usual packages of peanuts, pretzels, and tiny Ritz cheese crackers. Somewhere over Colorado, I managed to cadge three extra of each—for a total of nine—plus two full cans of orange juice.

The college kid who was sitting next to me gave me an odd look when I asked for the extras, and I took the opportunity to strike up a conversation. Despite my penury, I was suddenly having an almost euphoric mission-accomplished kind of feeling and in a friendly mood.

"These snack packs are really surprisingly good," I said.

The kid looked at me like I was seriously out of my mind.

"If you say so," he said.

"So you a student?" I asked.

"Yeah."

"What school?"

"University of Chicago."

"I went to the U of C myself for a couple of years," I said.

"Then what happened?" he asked.

"Dropped out. Too intense and intellectual for me at the time. Finished somewhere else."

"Cool."

I tried again. "Going home for Christmas?"

"Yeah."

"Well, Christmas is a nice time."

"Um, yeah, sure."

I don't know exactly what came over me, since I almost never introduce myself to people on airplanes unless I have to because the other person's gone first, but I stuck my hand out toward him. "Hi, I'm Robert Tarza."

The kid looked at my hand, as if considering whether he could just ignore it, like one might step around a dead rat on the sidewalk. He apparently decided he had no choice and reached out to shake, mumbling his name in the process. "Clay Fierley."

"Fiercely?"

"No. Fierley. F-I-E-R-L-E-Y."

"Okay, got it this time."

Then Clay seemed to study my face. "You look familiar."

"I do?"

"Yeah, like a guy in the newspaper." He bent over and took a newspaper out of his backpack, which was under the seat in front of him. I could see that it was a *Chicago Tribune*. He thumbed it to an inner page of the second section.

"Yeah!" he said. "Here's your picture. Says you're wanted." He grinned and handed me the paper. There was a picture of me, over a short blurb saying the LAPD had asked the Chicago police to find me because I was fleeing a murder warrant.

Clay looked excited. "Did you do it?"

"No!"

"Yeah, you look too corporate to be a killer," he said. He had clearly not seen me in my parka.

"Thanks, I think."

"Can I get your autograph?" Clay handed me a pen and gestured at the article.

I was stunned. I sat there, pen in hand, and thought about the fact that whether I was acquitted or convicted, for the rest of my life people on airplanes would probably want to talk to me. I suppose I should have seen it coming with the Blob. But this was more up close and personal. I thought about the fact that if I got convicted, this might be my last airplane trip ever. I had a sudden image of myself sitting in one of those buses they use to transport convicts, dressed in an orange jumpsuit.

"Mr. Tarza?" Clay was looking at me. I had drifted off.

"Oh, sorry. Sure." I wrote my name across the "wanted" article and handed it back to him.

"Um, could you write something more personal?" he asked.

"Like what?" I was unskilled in this kind of thing, clearly.

"How about, 'To Clay, who didn't turn me in.'" He smiled.

I laughed, took the article back, and amended my autograph as he had asked.

"So you're not going to turn me in?" I said.

"Nah. But I do want to see them come on board and arrest you. It will be the coolest thing that's happened to me all year. I've been buried in Aristotle. Talk about dry."

"Aristotle had nothing to say about avoiding arrest?" I asked.

"No."

"Well, I'm sure they'll let me surrender. My lawyer's meeting me at the airport."

"Yeah, I guess so." He looked awkward. "Well, good luck, Mr. Tarza."

"Thanks." Then I realized I had one more question. "What are you going to do with the autograph?"

"Sell it on eBay."

"Oh."

CHAPTER 24

———

We both spent the rest of the flight reading, as if there were nothing unusual about anything. Just a suspected felon and a college student, heading home to Los Angeles.

The plane landed thirty minutes early and taxied to the gate. As soon as the little ping sounded, announcing that the plane had stopped, the flight attendant came on the PA and said, "Ladies and gentlemen, we have a special circumstance involving a request from airport security, and I ask all of you to remain in your seats for just a few moments. This won't take long." Several people who had gotten up sat back down.

Clay looked like he had just become the proud father of a new baby boy. "I knew it. They're going to nail you here."

"What?"

As I said it, three burly LAPD cops were suddenly beside me. Along with Detective Spritz.

"Are you Robert Tarza?" he asked.

"You know damn well I'm Robert Tarza."

"There's no need to be hostile."

"You could have let me surrender."

"You were fleeing."

"Coming back to L.A. to flee?"

I noticed passengers in the other rows craning toward us. No one looked the least bit irritated that they were being delayed. It was as if time had stopped.

Spritz ignored me. "Please put your hands on top of your head and get up, slowly."

I put my hands on my head and started to get up. It was hard, because I had to stoop slightly to keep my hands, now on my head, from bumping the overhead bin as I rose.

"Awesome," Clay said. Then he pointed his cell phone in my direction, casually, as if he were about to put it to his ear to make a call. Another damn picture. Spritz either didn't notice or didn't care.

"Now," Spritz said, "please walk slowly to the back of the plane."

I walked. One of the big guys had gone ahead and opened the door to the small restroom. When I got there, Spritz pushed me inside, not so gently.

"Lean over the sink and put your hands behind your back," Spritz said.

I leaned, and he clicked a pair of handcuffs on me. It was the first time in my life my hands had been irretrievably pinned behind my back. I felt, well, *sullied*. Two of the big guys patted me down as they continued pressing on my shoulders, shoving my head toward the sink.

Then Spritz Mirandized me in a rhythmic voice, as if he were reciting Homer:

You are under arrest
For the murder of Simon Rafer.
You have the right to remain silent . . .

Each time he recited one of the Miranda verses, the two big guys on my shoulders gave me another push, like I was a drumstick they were using to beat time.

Anything you do or say
May be used against you
In a court of law.
You have the right to consult an attorney
Before speaking to the police.

By now my nose was bumping the sink with the recitation of every line.

And to have an attorney present
During questioning.
If you cannot afford an attorney
One will be appointed for you . . .
If you wish.

He finished the last verse on a rising inflection.

"I already have an attorney," I managed to say from deep in the sink.

"Yeah, I've met her," Spritz said. "What can I say? You ought to plead guilty right away."

"I'm not guilty."

"I'll mark it down."

"I'm not."

"All right, let's take him out."

The two big guys pulled my shoulders up, so that I was standing again, half-in and half-out of the lavatory.

Spritz put his face up to mine. "Fritz and Fernando here are going to walk in front of you, and Sergeant Drady and I are going to walk behind. One bit of trouble and we'll have to let you use the front lavatory."

"I won't give you any trouble, Detective."

"Good."

With that, they frog-marched me down the aisle of the plane. Taking their good time about it, it seemed to me. Most of the passengers simply gaped, although I noticed that several of them were already on their cell phones, talking animatedly, and there were a few more flashes. I was news.

As we reached the door of the plane, I made an inquiry of Spritz, but without turning my head around, which seemed like it might be interpreted as giving trouble.

"Are you going to march me through the terminal?" I asked.

"Shit no."

It soon became obvious that I was to be taken out the little side door in the telescoping jetway that was hooked to the plane. The door the ground crews use to go in and out. I had the odd thought that this was a breach of airport security. None of us had security cards.

CHAPTER 25

There was a car waiting on the tarmac, next to the plane. It was an old LAPD black and white. Spritz put his hand on my head to keep me from hitting the door jamb as I got into the back seat, just like they do on TV. After Spritz buckled my seat belt, both he and Sergeant Drady climbed into the back seat through the other door, with Spritz in the middle. The two big guys got in front, and the car took off.

We drove in silence for five or ten minutes, as the car threaded its way out of the runway complex and onto city streets. I knew Spritz was just waiting for me to say something, but I counseled myself to remain silent. An attempt at self-Mirandizing.

In order to avoid talking, I spent some time examining the inside of the car. It was filthy. The windows were greasy, and it smelled of cigarette smoke. In the end, I failed Miranda.

"Where are we going?" I asked.

"Downtown, to book you," Spritz said.

"Parker Center?"

"No, the old Parker Center's closed, and the new one doesn't have its jail built yet. You'll be going to a temporary jail nearby." He looked over at me. "We thought about booking you at the airport station, but decided to give you a break and take you downtown."

"Why is that a break?"

"Fewer media around."

"Oh."

We rode on in silence again. No one said anything for maybe ten minutes. By then we were on the San Diego Freeway. There was a lot of traffic, and I tried to keep myself from opening my mouth again by watching the cars go by. Other motorists were staring at me. They would glance away only if I managed to catch their eye. It created in me an increasing sense of capture, and, frankly, a rising panic. Spritz must have sensed that.

"Do you want to talk about it, sir?" he asked.

"Talk about what?"

"The deep shit you're in."

"I have a lawyer. I'm not supposed to talk to you."

"You can talk to me if you *want* to. Who knows, you might even learn something, huh? Anyway, you're a lawyer yourself. How long have you been at it?"

"Thirty six years."

"Litigation, you told me, right?"

"Mostly." Although I didn't actually recall telling him that. But I took the point. He was reminding me of our first meeting. Of the contrast between then and now. Then, high above the city, looking out at the hills and the ocean, lord of all I surveyed. Being snotty. Now, handcuffed in the back of a beat-up old black and white, looking at the fly stains on the seatback, lord of nothing. Trying to be nice.

Spritz went right on. "So as a litigator, you can protect yourself, huh?"

"I don't know much about criminal law," I said.

"Neither does your lawyer."

"Don't dump on Jenna."

"Okay. But how about I tell you something to show my good faith in this conversation? Something your crackerjack lawyer hasn't found out."

"Sure."

Just then, the car came to a sudden, slamming halt. Despite the fact that I was wearing a seat belt, I tried instinctively to bring my hands around to keep from hitting the seat in front of me. Which simply caused the handcuffs to bite painfully into my wrists. Initially, at least, it's hard to remember you're wearing cuffs.

Spritz spoke to the driver. "What the hell was that?"

The driver turned his head around. "Accident. Just happened. We should be by it in a few minutes."

I had not really gotten a good look at the driver before. My view of him had been mostly from the sink. Now I concentrated on his face. It was beefy and flushed, like an Irish cop of old. Except Spritz had called him Fernando. Then again, we were in Los Angeles. For all I knew, his name was Fernando O'Shaughnessy.

Studying Fernando took my mind off my stomach, which was feeling queasy from the abrupt stop. I've never been a good back seat passenger. I used to beg to sit in the front seat when I was a kid. My parents never gave in to that request, but at least they didn't handcuff me.

The car started to move again. Somehow, with that momentary disruption of Spritz's smooth arrest machine, I had begun to feel in control again.

I heard myself saying, "So, Detective, you were about to tell me something I don't know."

"We know where the coin is," he said.

Now that was something I *did* want to know. I assumed that he was talking about the original, which I had concluded was missing. But if I said, "Where is it?" I'd be admitting that the coin was involved in all of this. On the other hand, they seemed already to know that the coin figured in this. So I wouldn't be telling them much.

And I *had* made progress with Serappo. I was now certain that there was a counterfeiting ring out there. The only questions were who and why. The more information I got, the sooner I could nail it all down and get the hell out of this.

Sergeant Drady spoke for the first time. "Don't you want to know where the coin is, Robert?"

Drady had apparently mistaken my non-answer, driven as it was by my internal ping pong match, as a lack of interest. But he had called me Robert. I smiled. "So you're Mr. Nice Cop?"

"Nope," Drady said. "More Mr. Bunco Cop. Bunco, computer fraud, forensics, forgery, that kind of stuff."

"Mr. Bunco cop, huh?" I said, in my most Spritzian manner.

Spritz shot me a look. Apparently, he was not unaware of his own verbal tic, but didn't like having it called to his attention.

Drady ignored all that and continued. "Detective Spritz and I talked it over, and kinda thought you might wanna know where the coin is, you know? If you're not interested, no biggie."

"Well, he sure as hell doesn't seem interested," Spritz said.

I was interested all right. I seized upon a cautious, middle-way to approach it.

"What coin are you referring to?" I asked.

"The one," Spritz said, "that you sold Simon Rafer, the Ides."

I tried to sound not all that interested.

"Oh, where is it?"

Sergeant Drady answered. "In Shanghai."

I don't know if my eyebrows shot up or not. They might have. Shanghai is world counterfeiting headquarters. Rembrandts, Sumerian cylinder seals, Homeric vases. Whatever you want. Not only that, Simon had asked me to wire his $500,000 to an account in China.

Spritz picked it up again. "In fact, the coin was overnighted to a Mr. Chen care of a tea store in Shanghai. Who is Mr. Chen?"

I did indeed know who Mr. Chen was. Or I thought I did. Sam Chen. A coin appraiser in San Francisco who was always willing to give a high appraisal to a needy seller. Popularly known in the trade as Mr. What Do You Need? I knew he also spent time in Shanghai.

Something told me, though, that it wouldn't be a great idea to cop to being acquainted with Mr. Chen.

"What makes you think I would know who he is?" I asked.

"How about because you're the one who overnighted the coin to him in Shanghai?" Spritz said.

"I did no such thing."

"Sure you did," Drady said.

"I didn't," I said, as if repetition would win the day.

"You want proof, Mr. Lawyer? We have your law firm's overnight mail log with your name on it as the sender."

"Anybody could have sent that."

"Just like anybody could have stumbled on Mr. Rafer's body."

"Sergeant, I absolutely did not send anything to any Mr. Chen. But since you are persuaded I did, and there seems no way to change your mind, I think now I'm just going to assert my Miranda rights and keep silent, okay?"

I pretended to look out the window again. We had passed the accident and were speeding up. Soon, we'd be downtown. I'd be out of the filthy car, and Jenna would make them stop talking to me. Did Jenna even know I'd been arrested? I didn't really know. I didn't know anything. This time, I really was going to keep my mouth shut.

"I don't know how staying silent helps you," Spritz said. "You're already pretty incriminated."

I continued to look out the window.

Spritz continued to talk. "One of the incriminating things," he said, "is what we found in the box in your garden. But I guess you already know what was in the box we dug up there, huh?"

I hadn't even known there was a box buried in my garden until Larson, the guy from the *National Enquirer*, told me about it. Knowing more about that box and exactly what kind of ancient coins were in it might prove very useful in unraveling the mystery.

"What box, Detective?"

Sergeant Drady leaned forward, over and across Spritz, and put his face next to mine. "Don't fuck with us, asshole."

"I'm not fucking with you, sir. I don't know anything about a box in my garden."

Drady backed away, settled into his seat again, and sighed. When he spoke, he seemed to be talking to Spritz.

"Here we are, trying to help him out. And all he does is fuck with us. Maybe we should just tell the DA to go ahead and charge it as a capital crime. Like he wants to."

I was stunned into silence. It had never occurred to me that what I was being accused of was a capital crime. No one had ever even hinted at it.

Finally, after many minutes went by, during which no one uttered a single sound, I managed to say something. "How do you figure it's a capital crime, Sergeant?"

"Whoever killed him was lying in wait. It's a special circumstance that gets you the big D."

"I didn't kill him, so I didn't lie anywhere."

"Somebody did," he said.

Spritz broke in. "There's no point in telling him anything more, huh. He hasn't told *us* anything we didn't already know. He won't even tell us who Chen is."

It seemed like it was time to bargain. I'm a world class bargainer. It's what I do for a living.

"Sergeant, suppose I tell you something you *do* want to know," I said. "And then you tell me something I want to know."

"Sure."

"Okay, I think Simon was counterfeiting the Ides. There are at least two high-quality fakes floating around."

"You mean," Spritz asked, "like the two we found when we searched your suit jacket after we took you off the plane? The one in the clear envelope and the one in the red envelope? Those two?"

"Those aren't mine."

"Sure, sure. They were just visiting your pockets. Somebody else counterfeited them. Not you."

I felt like an idiot.

It was Drady's turn again.

"Now we'll keep our end of the bargain," he said. "Here's what you wanna know, I bet. Right next to where Mr. Rafer was killed, there was a depression in the thick carpet. Shape of a stretched out body. Like somebody lied there. Waiting for him."

I decided to skip telling him the proper past tense of "to lie." And to just shut up again. Finally and completely. No exceptions. And I wouldn't need to keep quiet much longer. Fernando had been weaving erratically in and out of traffic, and we weren't very far from downtown.

Drady addressed Spritz. "Detective, what say we just tell him the other tidbit? Maybe he'll plead guilty after he hears it."

"Sure, go ahead, Sergeant," Spritz said. "You tell him."

"Well, Mr. Fancy Lawyer Who Doesn't Know Anything About Anything," Drady said, "you remember that pinstripe suit jacket of yours, the one Detective Spritz here took from you the morning of the murder? Well lucky you, the nice blue fibers from your jacket match the nice blue fibers found in that depression in the rug. Where whoever killed him was waiting. Which was you, of course. That's why you're gonna fry."

"They don't fry them anymore," Spritz said. "Never did in this state."

"Well, whatever they do."

I felt like throwing up. And then I did. In a great heave. Half-digested pieces of the bagel from breakfast, plus peanuts, pretzels and whatever else I had gobbled down on the plane. I don't really know whether it was the erratic driving, or the fear, or some combination, but whatever it was, it was all over Spritz, a lot on Drady and the seat back, and only a little on me. Although it was running down my nose.

"Fuck!" Spritz said. He had pulled a handkerchief from his pocket and was trying to clean himself off, without much success. Drady was staring at his hand, which was dripping vomit.

"Looks like this car will have to go to the carwash," I said.

CHAPTER 26

A s soon as they hustled me out of the smelly car and got me inside the building, Spritz disappeared. Maybe he went to clean up. Once inside, I heard someone ask if I needed medical attention.

"Nope, he's fine," Drady said.

They led me up to a set of cages that looked like the teller windows in a bank. Then Drady went through my pockets and handed my wallet, keys, money, and whatever else he found there to a man who sat behind one of the cages. Kind of like a bank teller who took deposits of objects instead of cash. Finally, he took off my watch and handed that to the teller, too, who put all of it in a plastic bag and labeled it. When that was over, I was frisked again and told to sit in a plastic chair, still handcuffed. I was there for maybe half an hour, after which Drady and another guy took me into the room next door, removed my handcuffs, and promptly stripped me.

There is nothing quite like being stripped naked in front of strangers to remove any feeling that you might still be important.

"Is this really necessary?" I asked.

"Standard procedure for felony arrests," Drady said.

After they went carefully through my clothing and conducted a body search I'd rather not describe—while wearing plastic gloves—they let me get dressed again, minus underwear, belt, and tie, and re-handcuffed me. Another cop, whose name tag identified him as Cronch, came in. He led me back to what I took to be a booking room. There was a second cop there, sitting at a desk, reading the sports section of the *L.A. Times*. He didn't identify himself, and I couldn't see his name tag. He didn't look up.

I looked at Cronch. "Could you loosen my handcuffs a bit, Sergeant?"

"I'm not a sergeant, Mr. Tarza. Just a jailer. No special title." He walked over to me, took a key out of his pocket, and made some adjustments to the cuffs. It helped; they chafed less.

"Thank you."

"No worry. Would you just stand over there?" He pointed to a mark on the floor, between a camera on a tripod and a height chart on the wall. I went and stood there, facing him and the camera.

He looked at me appraisingly, the way I imagined a portrait photographer might. Then he pulled a piece of Kleenex out of a box on the desk and walked up to me.

"I'm going to wipe your nose," he said. "Whatever dripped out of it isn't going to look so great in your booking photo."

I thanked him as he wiped. There wasn't actually a lot of drip. It was amazing how little had gotten on me.

"Aren't you," I asked, "going to hang a number around my neck?" When had I become so damn helpful?

"No, new process," he said. "It's generated digitally by the computer."

"Oh."

Cronch fiddled with the camera. I had a thought. "Could I have my tie back for the picture?"

"Sorry, can't do that. SOP is no tie or belt."

"Why?"

"So you won't hurt yourself. Or us."

He made some adjustments to the tripod, and then cranked it up a few notches. The last guy had evidently been shorter.

"Okay, Mr. Tarza, please look directly at the camera," he said.

I did, but immediately thought about something that had always bothered me when I saw booking photos in the newspaper. Almost no one ever smiled. I had long ago remarked to myself that if I were ever booked—not that that had seemed even remotely a possibility—I'd try to smile.

But I couldn't. I don't know whether it was because I couldn't summon a smile in the circumstance or because I was subconsciously worried that a smile might send the wrong message. In any case, I heard the shutter click and ended up with the same dour look on my face as every other suspect who'd ever had his mug shot taken.

Cronch glanced over at a computer screen on the desktop. "Looks good," he said. "Officer Grady will print you now." He motioned me toward the desk.

The guy who had now been identified as Grady put down his paper and produced two fingerprint cards and an ink pad. I could see that my name and some other data had already been put on the cards. Without a word, he took my right hand, inked the tip of each finger and, one by one, carefully rolled the finger's print onto the paper. I tried to make small talk.

"Hey," I said, "I'm shocked you guys still use ink instead of a computer scanner."

Grady didn't respond, but simply proceeded to do my left hand. When he was done, he handed the cards to Cronch and went back to reading the paper. It was odd, but I felt offended. The actual feeling I had was that I had been accused of an important crime, and that Grady should pay more attention.

A small color printer was whirring, spitting out the picture. Cronch picked it up and looked at it. "Good enough." He put it in a manila folder, together with the fingerprint cards.

"May I see the picture?" I asked.

"Sorry, that's against regs," Cronch said.

"I can't see my own picture?"

"You'll get to see it in the papers, I'd bet." He gave me a slight smile.

I found myself thinking that I liked Cronch. At least compared to Grady. Which was odd, trying to figure which one of them I liked. Three weeks ago, I wouldn't have thought twice about either one of them. Perhaps it was the beginning of the Stockholm syndrome.

"Officer Cronch, may I ask what happens next?" I said.

"You're free to go."

"What?"

"Somebody bailed you out."

"Who?"

"I have no idea."

With that, he led me back to the reception room, where the desk officer handed me the plastic bag into which he had put my things less than an hour before. "Please go through them, and if everything is in order, sign on that line there at the bottom," he said.

I rummaged through the bag.

"What about my tie and my belt?" I asked.

He shrugged. "If you want to wait around, I'll see if we can find them."

I wanted out of there before someone changed their mind. I would skip the tie and belt. "No, don't bother. I have others."

The desk clerk handed me a sheet of paper. "This is your arraignment date." I read the date. "It's more than a month from now."

He looked at me like I was some kind of moron. "Are you in a hurry to be formally accused of murder?"

"No."

"Well, then go thank the fairy godmother who bailed you out." He jerked his thumb toward a door to my left.

I opened the door, which opened onto a kind of waiting room, larger than the room I was exiting. I froze with surprise in the doorway. Oscar Quesana was standing there.

"What are you doing here, Oscar?"

"I bailed you out."

"Why?"

"Jenna asked me to."

"How'd she know I was here?"

"As soon as they took you off the plane, it was on the news. Anyway, let's get out of here."

I followed him through the front door, out into a large parking lot filled with dozens of cars.

"Where's your car?" I asked.

"Well, my friend, normally, they'd do me the courtesy of letting me park inside here to pick you up. But Spritz is apparently pissed at you about something, so they made me park out on the street."

"Okay, I could use the walk," I said.

"Right. But we'll have to walk through the media gauntlet that's right outside the front gate."

I looked out across the parking lot and could see that it was surrounded by a high wall, pierced by a large, filigreed iron gate. We started walking toward it.

As we walked, I could see the masts of microwave trucks poking above the wall, rotating, searching for something in the sky. The Blob itself was still mostly hidden from view. For the moment, it appeared as nothing more than a solid black mass that blocked the light from coming through the grillwork on the gate.

"How many of them are out there, Oscar?" I felt genuine horror. As if Spritz had arranged to have me fed to wild animals.

"A few dozen maybe. Fewer than there'd be if the mayor had just been booked."

"That's not funny," I said. "How far is your car?"

"About a block."

"That's not so far."

"No, but it's three o'clock," he said.

"So?"

"Feeding time for the four o'clock news, Robert. They'll be in a frenzy."

We had by then gotten up to the gate, and it slid back, retracting into the wall. I could see, just on the other side, the Blob manifest—a surging tide of boom mikes, bodies, and cameras. Then I could hear it. So many staccato shouts that it was hard to make out the individual words. One shout seemed to rise above all the others: "Mr. Tarza! Afraid of the needle?" I felt my stomach tighten, even as we penetrated the first wave of bodies.

The Blob jostled and pushed and grew still louder. A lot of flashes dazzled my eyes. Oscar was in the lead, blocking for me. We were managing to move, but not very fast. I kept ducking to avoid the boom mikes, which danced just in front of my face. The shouting had become a continuous din.

Suddenly, a woman's high-pitched voice was right in my ear. "We can take you live right now on *News Now*! Live! Right now!" I was tempted, if only for a second, to take them up on their offer. Maybe *News Now!* would protect me from the rest of them while it got its scoop.

Then I realized that my pants were about to come down. I've always had narrow hips, and without the belt, together with the weight I'd lost in the prior ten days from not eating very much—nerves I guess—my pants were going to be on the ground. I grabbed my waistband with my left hand, which prevented the disaster, just. But it left me with only one arm to block.

After what seemed an eternity, we finally made it to Oscar's car. Despite the sea of bodies and equipment that surrounded the car like the tentacles of a huge squid about to engulf its prey, Oscar managed to open the passenger door for me.

I got in, still holding up my pants, and shut the door. Oscar got in on the other side and started the car. We began to move ever so slowly through the crowd. Dozens of flashes were still going off.

"Why don't you just step on it and kill them," I said.

"Not a good idea right now," Oscar said.

We made it out of the Blob and began to accelerate.

I relaxed a bit. "How did you manage to bail me out?"

"What do you mean?" he said.

"I thought you couldn't bail out capital crimes."

"Who told you you've been charged with a capital crime?" Oscar seemed genuinely surprised.

"Spritz told me," I said. "He claimed I was lying in wait or something."

"Lying in wait? That is a special circumstance that can bring the death penalty, but it's rarely used and can be hard to prove."

"They kept harping on that in the car when they brought me in, and that reporter just shouted it out at me."

"Don't know anything about it in your case. They booked you on straight murder one. One killing, no special circumstance. At least for now."

"Oh. Who set the bail amount?"

"Nobody. They have a bail schedule. You look down the left-hand column. It lists the crime. You look across to the right, it shows the amount. Like a price list. Murder one is the priciest."

I was almost afraid to ask. "What's the price of murder one?"

"One million."

"A million dollars? Jesus."

"Jesus wasn't able to make bail," he said.

I ignored the comment.

"Where did Jenna get a million dollars?"

"She didn't. I posted it. In cash. Well, actually in short term CD's."

A million dollars is a good chunk of my net worth. After what must have seemed to him an awkward pause on my part, Oscar spoke again.

"Jenna said you were good for it and would pay me back?" He said it the way a teenager would, with the rising inflection at the end. It was the first time I'd ever heard Oscar unsure about anything.

"I am, and I will," I said.

"Good . . . Damn it! Behind us!"

I turned. "Shit! It's a news van."

"We need to lose it," Oscar said.

"Jenna got rid of a news van with a cell phone call," I said.

Oscar glanced behind us. "Well, good for her. I haven't fucked anybody in the media lately, so I've got no one to call."

"That's unkind."

"Whatever. I have an idea," he said.

Oscar made a screeching U-turn and accelerated back up the street, moving past the news van, which was still going the other way. I could see the driver's face as we passed, looking startled. I looked behind me and watched the truck, starting to turn. But he was big, so he had to do a three-point turn instead of an easy U. We were by then almost two blocks ahead of him.

"He'll catch up," I said.

"Yeah, but I know downtown like the back of my hand," Oscar said. "And there's one place he's gonna have a problem following."

Oscar turned onto the next cross street and then almost immediately turned again into a narrow alley. I looked behind us again. The truck was about to follow us into the alley. Ahead was an overhanging walkway that spanned the alley from one building to the other. A sign in large letters read, LOW CLEARANCE. NO TRUCKS OR VANS.

"Looks too low," I said.

"We'll make it," Oscar said. "But the truck won't. Especially with that microwave array on top."

Oscar stepped on it, and I instinctively ducked. We cleared the overhang by an inch or two. I raised my head back up as we accelerated even faster down the alley.

I looked behind us again. The truck had come to a dead stop at the overhanging walkway. Oscar sped through the first cross street, then into the next alley, and then through two more blocks of alleyways. He was going really fast. Finally, he screeched through a left turn at the third cross street, slowed abruptly and headed at normal speed for a freeway on-ramp.

"They'll never figure out where we went," Oscar said.

"You know, Oscar, I used to live a pretty calm life."

"Yeah, you were sure up there on a high floor," he said.

"Not anymore. Where are we going?"

"To my office," he said.

"I don't even know where your office is."

"I work out of an old place in Venice. The address isn't listed any-where."

"Your law office has no listed address?"

"I use a P.O. box. That way no one can bother me at work if I don't want to be bothered. Call me eccentric."

"Is that why you were so intent on losing the van?" I asked.

"In part."

"And the other part?"

"I just hate those fuckers."

We were by then moving on the Santa Monica Freeway, heading toward the ocean at seventy miles per hour, with no traffic. Which was surprising at that time of day. Another mystery of the L.A. freeways.

I kept glancing around, looking for more news vans. I had begun to feel like a hunted animal. Then I thought about how much trouble I was in and who my legal team was. I had one lawyer who worked out of my *own* house and another who had a secret office. Actually, I didn't even know if Oscar *was* one of my lawyers again.

"Oscar, are you back on my case?"

"It seems I came out at the top of some list again."

"Oh." I had utterly forgotten about the list I'd told Jenna to make when I left to go to Chicago. It seemed like months ago.

"So, yes, I am back on the team." He paused. "If you want me."

"Sure I want you. But didn't you quit?" I was tired and befuddled.

"I did. But Jenna called me yesterday morning and asked if I'd come back. I said I'd see. Then I spent all day with her. Was impressed, so I said yes. Smart cookie. Doesn't know a lot yet but learns like Sherlock Holmes."

"Was he a fast learner?"

"Don't know. Really meant she has a good strategic gut," he said.

"Okay," I said. "Welcome back."

"Mind if I put on some music?"

"No, go ahead."

He put a CD in the player. It was one of the Bach cello suites. Who'd have thought Oscar liked Bach. I began to think about Oscar and his musical tastes. That's the last thing I recall.

CHAPTER 27

———

The next thing I knew I was jerked awake as the car stopped in front of the gated garage door of an apartment building. The Bach was no longer playing. Oscar had switched to a Beethoven piano concerto. I had been asleep for at least twenty minutes. Amazingly, I actually felt refreshed.

As I climbed out of my slumber, I watched Oscar use the remote to retract the garage door.

"Where are we?" I asked.

"My office."

"It's in an apartment building?"

"Yep."

We pulled into a small underground garage—the type that collapsed on and crushed hundreds of cars in dozens of buildings in the '94 quake—and got out of the car. I noticed that it was an old Crown Victoria. I hadn't had a chance to note the model back when we were clambering in.

"Isn't this the car they make into cop cars a lot, Oscar?"

"Yeah. In fact, it *was* an old cop car," he said.

"Should I ask?"

"Bought it at an auction. Tipped off by a friend that this one was a really good buy. Low mileage. Off-loaded because somebody died in it in a bad way."

We were heading for the small elevator in the corner of the garage.

"That didn't bother you? The dying part?"

"Nah. A good detailing and the blood was gone. Pretty much anyway."

"How'd the guy die?"

"Did you ever see *Pulp Fiction?*"

"Yes."

"Like that."

"Oh."

We got into the elevator, and Oscar hit 4. The elevator began to grind its way upward, in the way that old apartment building elevators in Los Angeles always do. Life was slower in the sixties.

"Who tipped you to the car?" I asked.

"Spritz."

"Should I be worried?"

"No, you should be thrilled. He tells me things. Like he already did about the elevator access records."

The elevator doors finally opened, and we exited into a narrow hallway. Oscar fished out a key and opened the door to apartment 403, which revealed itself as a single, large, square room with a badly scuffed hardwood floor. Casement windows on the far wall looked out over rooftops and satellite dishes to the beach a block away. There was a large kitchen off to the left.

A narrow Formica counter-desk wrapped around three sides of the room, including beneath the casement windows. The Formica had once upon a time been red. Now it was only reddish. One corner of the counter held an old manual typewriter. A Royal. Stacks of paper covered every other inch of the surface. In the middle of the room stood a square conference table, fashioned from some indifferent oak. Four threadbare cloth swivel chairs, one to a side, completed the conference set. The only thing missing was anything made after about 1965.

"No computer?" I asked.

"Nope."

"No fax machine?"

"Negative."

"Cell phone?"

"Never."

"Multi-line phone?"

Oscar lifted a pile of paper and pointed to the black telephone beneath. It had a rotary dial. "My only concession to the modern world," he said.

"Don't you worry you're behind the times?"

Oscar was on his way into the kitchen. He answered me over his shoulder, in a near-shout. "Jury verdicts are delivered the old fashioned way. By voice!"

I took his point and sat facing the kitchen across the table. I heard the clink of glassware. "You want a drink, Robert?"

"A Coke, please?

"My friend, you need something stronger!"

"You're right," I said. "A very dry vodka martini, then. With an olive if you've got it."

"Coming up!"

CHAPTER 28

——

I should have thought about the fact that I had eaten hardly anything since breakfast. With the exception of what I snacked down on the plane, most of which I had deposited on Spritz and Drady. But I didn't think about that at all. At the very least, I should have asked Oscar for some cheese and crackers or something. But I didn't do that either. I just sat there and waited for the martini.

I heard Oscar shaking the ice in the kitchen. The martini was going to be gloriously cold.

The doorbell rang. I got up to open it. It was Jenna. She was wearing tattered jeans and a baggy, grey sweatshirt, and she was carrying a lumpy shopping bag.

"Hi, Robert. Welcome back!" she said.

All I could manage to get out was, "You look like a bag lady. I have a bag lady and a Luddite for lawyers."

Someone watching all this might have thought I was just being flip. But I was in fact suddenly teetering on the brink of despair.

She laughed. "Chill, man. You have *the* best combo. Young and smart, plus old and savvy." She dropped the shopping bag by the front door and headed for the chair that faced me across the table.

Oscar emerged, carrying two martinis in classic glasses. Each with the required olive. "I heard that," he said, "and I don't like to think of myself as old." He put both glasses down on the table. "One's for you, Jenna." Then he headed back to the kitchen.

Jenna swiveled her chair toward the kitchen. "Are you drinking, Oscar?"

"I'll be right back with what I drink," he said.

"Which is what?" she asked.

"A Manhattan. I keep a pitcher in the fridge, just in case."

Jenna laughed. "Talk about the fifties."

Oscar was by then at the far end of the kitchen. He had to shout to be heard. "You should learn to drink them, Jenna! They'll make you savvy!"

Jenna ignored him and swiveled back toward the table. I looked across at her. I was beginning to have second thoughts about my choice of libation.

"Maybe it isn't such a savvy idea for me to drink this," I said. "I may fall over."

"You need it for old time's sake, Robert." She paused. "Not to mention new times."

Oscar returned, Manhattan in hand, and took the chair at the end of the table, the one with its back to the windows. "Let's have a toast then," he said.

I didn't see a lot to toast. "What are we toasting?" I asked. "My arrest? My feeling that this can't be real?"

Oscar raised his glass. "To the acquittal of the innocent!"

We clicked glasses, and I watched Oscar down half of his. Jenna followed his lead. I took an even larger gulp of mine. The icy cold felt fantastic as it slid down my throat. It even revived once again, if only momentarily, my sense of control.

"Oscar, does your toast mean you now think that I'm really innocent?" I asked.

"Yes."

"What changed?"

"Nothing," he said. "I told you a couple days ago that I believed you when you said you were innocent. Remember?"

"Yes," I said, "but I had the sense that that was a professional courtesy kind of belief. What any lawyer will do for a paying client. Different from being really persuaded. Are you *persuaded*, Oscar?"

"I am," he said.

"I still have the same question, then. What changed?"

"Jenna told me about Stewart's office."

"About the counterfeit Ides and the book?"

"About the fact that they were hidden."

"That doesn't seem to exculpate me."

"It does," he said, "if you add to it the fact that the secret compartment used to belong to Harry. And then when you add another rather curious fact."

"Which fact is that?" I asked.

He motioned to Jenna, palm up, inviting her to speak. She beamed like the proverbial cat who had just made a gourmet meal of the canary.

"Betty Menino took me out for a delayed goodbye lunch," Jenna said. Betty was the long-time M&M office manager. She had been there for almost forty years and was rumored to know everything about everybody. "I wormed the history of the secret compartment out of her."

I took another swig of my dwindling martini and waited.

"She told me that ten years ago Harry asked her to get the book-case specially modified. Back when he was the managing partner. But he asked her to keep it strictly to herself. He told her that he needed a place to keep certain sensitive things where no one would sneak a look at them. He didn't trust the safes, he said, because someone else always had a key or the combination."

"Wow," I said. Which is not a word that normally plays a major role in my vocabulary.

Jenna continued. "Betty told me that when Harry retired, he didn't want to take the bookcase. So Betty put it up for grabs in the usual way. Partners got first shot by seniority, then associates. Stewart ended up with it."

Suddenly, despite the importance of what Jenna was saying, I was rapidly leaving wow behind. The martini had overtaken wow and passed it on the right. I was left staring into my drink, having trouble holding my head up. I heard Oscar following up, since I couldn't.

"Now tell our fast-fading client the really important thing," he said.

"Betty told me," Jenna said, "that starting about a month ago Harry became *very* interested to know who had ended up with the bookcase. He even called her to inquire. But he tried to make it seem like a "by the way" kind of thing in a conversation about something else. She told him that Stewart had it."

"But then," Jenna added, "she told me one other thing that was kind of odd."

"I don't think I've heard this part," Oscar said. "What was the odd part?"

"She told me that Harry knew damn well who had the bookcase. Because right after he left the firm, he had asked her who ended up with it, and she told him."

"Maybe," Oscar said, "old Harry's getting a touch of Alzheimer's."

I had been only half listening, focusing on the inch of liquid left in my martini glass. I figured what the hell and drank it down, head back. It was still chilled, and that last little shot of cold vodka gave me what I needed to ask the big question. The one I'd been pondering since my visit to Serappo.

I put my empty glass ever so carefully back on the table and looked directly across at Jenna.

"I suppose that's all very incriminating for Harry," I said. "But here's what I really want to know. Jenna, were you the courier who took the Ides to Serappo?"

Jenna had long ago finished her own martini. It showed in her eyes, which radiated a kind of defiant sparkle.

"In a word, yes," she said.

I held her look. She knew exactly what I was thinking. Many seconds of silence passed.

Oscar looked from one of us to the other and then back again, like someone who had been watching a tennis match and suddenly found both players frozen in place.

Jenna, eyes still locked on mine, broke the silence. "After you sold the Ides to Simon, Simon wanted Serappo Prodiglia to authenticate and appraise it. But he didn't want to ship it. So about two months ago, he asked me to take it to Chicago. And I did."

Oscar did a double take.

"But you didn't tell either of us this little fact before?"

"No."

"Why the *fuck* not?"

"I didn't think it was relevant."

"Don't you think that would be for us to decide?" he asked.

"Maybe."

"Maybe?"

"Okay. Yes," she said. "But I never saw the coin, and I never talked to Serappo about it. I was just the post office."

"Fuck," Oscar said again.

"Stop saying fuck," she said.

"Double fuck!"

"I'm sorry," she said. "I really am."

Now *I* felt like someone at a tennis match. A match in which the ball was going back and forth with increasing vigor.

"You lied to us!" Oscar said.

"It wasn't a lie!"

"Don't lawyer me, Jenna," he said. "Covering it up is no better than a lie."

Jenna didn't respond.

"Admit it!"

"Fuck both of you," she said.

As she said it, she swept up her martini glass, raised it above her head, and hurled it against the wall immediately behind me. I heard it shatter, then watched the ricocheting olive bounce neatly into the shopping bag.

Without another word, Jenna rose from the table, moved to the door, opened it, and walked out. She didn't close it behind her, and she certainly didn't look back. Even in my near-dead state, I knew it was the best exit I'd ever seen. Better even than Oscar's had been.

Oscar looked at me. "We need to talk about this, Robert." He was right. But I was too tired and too drunk right then. All I managed was, "Can't now."

He took me at my word. "Okay. We need to get you to bed then. Can't take you back to your house. Gonna be too much press there. I'll take you to my place."

"Apartment?" I mumbled.

"House," he said. He helped me get up and guided me out the door and down the elevator to the Crown Victoria. I vaguely noticed that he had grabbed Jenna's shopping bag from beside the door as we left. I don't remember much about the trip to his house, except climbing into a bed when we got there and falling instantly sleep.

It had been a very long day.

CHAPTER 29

———

When I woke up, it was pitch black. For a few seconds, I didn't know where I was. Then I remembered. I turned my head and looked at the bedside clock. The red digits said it was 5:15 a.m. When I'd climbed into bed, the sun had not yet set. I'd slept for more than twelve hours.

I switched on a bedside lamp and saw that I was lying in a four-poster bed beneath a puffy blue quilt. The bed was in the middle of a square room. Oscar seemed to have a thing for square rooms. A round, hooked rug in many colors partially covered the floor, which was crafted from wide wooden planks. A rocking chair sat in one corner, with an antimacassar hung on its back. HOME SWEET HOME, it said. Several prints inspired by Grandma Moses hung on the walls.

I got out of bed. I was naked, and it was cold. Oscar apparently didn't believe in leaving the heat on, even on a cold December night, when the temperature in L.A. can occasionally get down into the low thirties. I noticed a cedar chest at the foot of the bed, on which a white terry cloth bathrobe had been laid out. I assumed it was meant for me and put it on. At the foot of the cedar chest there was a pair of red felt slippers. I put those on, too.

A copy of *Southern Living* was lying on the bedside table, right next to the clock. Since there was not a sound in the house, and I didn't want to explore a strange house in the dark, I picked up the magazine and sat down in the rocker to read it. The first thing I read was an article on how to make bouquets from dried flowers. Then I read one on how to make paperweights out of old cream bottles by filling them with gravel and sealing in the gravel with colorful, hot wax.

Then I realized I was starving.

I opened the drawer on the bedside table, in the forlorn and pathetic hope that someone had left a package of crackers or maybe even a candy bar in it. It was empty.

I went to the door and opened it. It gave onto a narrow hallway, dimly lit by a couple of LED nightlights. I turned right and followed the hallway, which made a sharp turn and then emerged into a kind of dining area, where I could see the outline of a big table. I picked my way through the dining room to the kitchen, found a light switch, and flipped it on.

The kitchen was full-bore country. It had a small wood-burning stove in one corner and a big iron oven in the middle of the room. Pots and pans hung above it. The walls were made of pine boards that were either very old or made to look that way. If there was a refrigerator, it was well hidden.

The feature to which my eye was drawn, though, was the huge stone fireplace. In its hearth, three large pieces of wood sat on an iron grate, with twigs and paper kindling stuffed below. An extra-long match stuck out from between the logs, inviting someone to pick it up.

Accepting the invitation, I picked it up, struck it on a stone, and put the flame to the kindling. The fire sprang to life so quickly I had to jump back to keep from getting my nice white robe singed.

With the fire crackling, I went in search of the refrigerator. I finally located it disguised as a set of rustic kitchen drawers. Inside, I found some sweet rolls. I didn't think Oscar would mind if I ate a couple. I took a plate out of a cupboard, put two sweet rolls on it and began to eat. I tried very hard not to wolf them down, even though no one was watching. It took a big effort not to wolf.

"Stealing my fire and my sweet rolls?"

It was Oscar. I hadn't heard him come into the kitchen. He came over to the table and sat down.

"We could warm those sweet rolls up if you like, Robert."

"No, it's okay."

"Want some real breakfast? I make a mean stack of pancakes."

"Sounds fabulous, actually."

"I'm on it."

He got up and began pulling out what he needed—iron griddle, mixing bowl, flour, and any number of other ingredients.

I finished the sweet rolls and watched his preparations. "You make them from scratch?"

"Yep."

"I haven't had homemade pancakes in years."

"Not the sort of thing they serve up on those high floors?" he asked.

"No."

"Figures."

"Oscar, do you have something against people who work on high floors?"

"Not really. It's just that when I got out of law school, no one in law firms like yours would even give me an interview."

"Where did you go?"

"Southwestern," he said.

"Good school these days," I said.

"I thought it was a good school in *those* days too."

"I take your point," I said.

"Here." He handed me a wooden spoon and a red mixing bowl filled with batter. "This needs some work . . . these days." He laughed.

I stirred the batter. It felt therapeutic. Maybe I could work in the prison kitchen.

"Oscar, are you bitter about not getting interviews with firms like M&M?"

"No. Besides, I've been in them by osmosis, you might say."

"Meaning?"

"Turns out lawyers like you sometimes have problems that need the attentions of a discreet criminal defense attorney. Not murder, usually. But other stuff. Wife beating, embezzlement, tax evasion. That kind of thing. So I've developed something of a reputation on the high floors."

"Is that why Jenna called you?" I asked.

"I suppose."

"Have you ever represented *her*?"

"Not exactly," he said.

"Should I ask what that means?"

Oscar came over, took the bowl from me, and looked into it.

"Pretty good job of mixing," he said. "And no, you shouldn't ask, because I won't tell you. One of the things I am is discreet, like I said. Anyway, my prior relationship with the case Jenna referred is *truly* irrelevant to your case."

"Unlike her being the courier?"

"Yes, unlike that."

Oscar had heated the cast iron griddle on the stove. He put something that looked like butter on it, waited for it to melt, then poured on several dollops of batter. The sizzle of cooking pancakes joined the sound of the fire, which was by now roaring.

Oscar came back to the table and sat down. "Speaking of the courier, we need to chat about her."

I wasn't all that anxious to talk about Jenna. "Oscar, shouldn't you be watching the pancakes?" I asked.

"Nope. A watched pancake never cooks. Anyway, I know exactly when they'll be done."

"All right," I said. "What about her? She told both of us to fuck off, as I recall."

"Yeah, she did. She even broke an expensive martini glass. But I had just called her a liar. Which was maybe an overreaction. And you were only semi-conscious. Which didn't help."

"So?" I was still not feeling all that friendly toward Jenna.

"She called yesterday evening while you were sleeping," he said.

"About what?"

"Rejoining the team." Oscar got up and walked over to the stove. "They're done."

"Aren't you going to flip them?"

"No," he said. "Only fancy people flip them. It's totally unnecessary."

He took two plain white plates out of a cabinet and moved three pancakes onto each plate. "Syrup?"

"Sure."

Oscar took a tin of syrup off a shelf, went through an elaborate warming procedure, and poured the syrup onto the pancakes.

Then he grabbed two forks and plunked them and the plates down on the table. The pancake and syrup ritual was clearly intended to give me time to think about Jenna's desire to return.

"Why should I want her back, Oscar? You're back on board now, and you've got the experience. Plus you didn't sleep with the victim. And, so far as I know, you haven't hidden things from me."

"True enough," he said.

For a while, we just sat there in silence, eating our respective pancakes.

Eventually, Oscar asked, "So what do you think of my pancakes?"

In truth, I thought they were kind of underdone on top, and that the fancy people might have the right idea about needing to flip them. But it didn't seem like the time to say so.

"They're great, Oscar. With incredible syrup. Where do you get it?"

"My mother sends it to me from Vermont."

"Your mother lives in Vermont?"

"Yeah. You think there are no people named Quesana in Vermont, Tarza?"

"No. I just . . . never mind."

"Consider it never minded."

"The butter tastes kinda different," I said.

"Bad different?"

"No, just different."

"It's soy butter. And the pancakes are made with soy milk."

"Oh."

"So," he said, "moving on from what you think of my pancakes, do you want to know what I think about having Jenna back on the team?"

"You're my lawyer. Advise me."

"It has some things to recommend it."

"Like what?"

He got up, grabbed our now empty plates, and took them to the sink. "First, the two of you work well together, or at least you used to. So, like you said before, you trust her. That can be valuable on a legal team, especially in the kind of stew these cases cook up."

"Okay."

"Second, it always looks good to have a girl on the defense team."

"There are other women lawyers out there, last time I checked," I said.

Oscar had turned and was leaning back against the sink edge, looking oh-so-relaxed. "Third, there's that reason Lyndon Johnson used to talk about."

"What reason is that?" I asked.

"Better to have a guy inside the tent, pissing out, than outside the tent, pissing in."

"The metaphor doesn't work very well when it's a woman," I said.

"Maybe not. But you get the point," he said, not looking at me, because he had turned back around and begun to wash the plates.

"Your point is what?" I asked. "That she already knows a lot about a lot of things? So let's not have her bumping around, where the DA'd be more likely to call her as a witness?"

"Right," he said. "Or haul her in front of a grand jury. Plus, she's clearly brilliant, and her rep in town is she doesn't crack under pressure, even when there's incoming."

"And the argument against taking her back?" I asked.

"She's a little off her rocker about this case somehow. And it's more than just that she slept with the dead guy. I can't quite put my finger on it."

"Well, maybe she's the one who swapped the original Ides—the one I'm certain I gave Simon six weeks ago—for the counterfeit one I showed Serappo two days ago. She could have done it when she couriered it."

"To what end? You think Jenna was running a coin counterfeiting business out of her associate office at M&M?"

"You're right, I guess. It's hard for me to believe that Jenna was doing that right under my nose without my noticing. I mean I was in her office a lot." I paused. "On the other hand, she was doing some other things I didn't notice."

Oscar was by now drying the dishes. He didn't say anything for a while. Neither did I.

Finally, he asked, "Can I see the coin you showed Serappo, the one he says is a fake?"

"No, because the cops have it. They took it from my jacket pocket when they arrested me, along with the other counterfeit Ides. The one that Jenna and I picked up in Stewart's secret compartment.

"Oy," he said.

"I didn't know you were Jewish."

"I'm not, but there's no English equivalent that fits."

I laughed. "True."

"Actually the oys are even bigger than you know, Robert."

"Why?"

"The cops dug up a box in your garden. The box was full of dirt. In the dirt, they found five more Ides."

"Doesn't surprise me that much. Larson, the guy from the National Enquirer, already told me there were ancient coins in the box."

"And?"

"Anyone could have put that box there."

"Including you."

"Yes, except it wasn't me."

"I believe you. But now that they've found two fakes on you, the 'someone else must have done it' argument is gonna be a much harder sell."

"I'm being framed."

"Welcome to the Round-Up-the-Usual-Defenses Club."

"But I *am* being framed."

"The problem, my friend, is proving it."

He began to put the dishes away in the cupboard.

"Robert, do you recall what we were talking about before this?" he asked.

"Whether Jenna can come back."

"Right. And the decision still needs to be made."

"Let's invite her back," I said. "I think we should keep her inside the garden."

The line fell flat. Oscar didn't even smile.

"I'll call her and tell her," he said. "You go take a shower while I do it. The bathroom's down the hall from your room."

"I don't have any clean clothes."

"Ah, but you do. That's what was in the shopping bag last night. Jenna brought you a clean shirt, suit, socks, underwear, shoes . . . the works."

"The suit will be wrinkled," I said. As soon as it was out of my mouth, I knew I sounded like an asshole. Or someone from a high floor.

Oscar ignored my burst of attitude. "My friend, I ironed the suit last night while you slept."

"You cook *and* iron?"

"Yep. For a lot of years, I couldn't afford to pay someone to do that stuff. Low floor salary, you know."

I smiled at the metaphor. "Okay, I'll go quietly."

The shower felt good, and, true to Oscar's word, everything I needed was laid out in a little dressing area in the bathroom. I toweled off and started to dress. And tried to stop thinking about who had planted the box of coins in my garden.

But even putting on clean underwear was fraught with dark thoughts. It reminded me of what I had once been told by a CEO who had gone to prison for embezzlement—in prison they make you wear prison-issue underwear. You get different underwear back from the prison laundry every day. Never your own.

At the time I had thought it amusing.

CHAPTER 30

———

I wandered back to the kitchen, where I was greeted by the smell of fresh coffee. Oscar was sitting at the table, reading the *L.A. Times*.

"Who took this damn picture of you on the plane?" he asked, and handed me the front page. It featured a picture of me standing beside my seat on the plane, hands on the top of my head. Looking thunderstruck.

"Clay," I said.

"Who the hell is Clay?"

"The college kid who was sitting next to me on the plane. He used his cell phone camera."

"The little shit."

"He probably sold it to them to help pay his way through college," I said. "I autographed something for him, and he told me he was going to sell it on eBay."

Oscar looked at me with raised eyebrows. "You autographed something for him?"

"Just an article from the *Tribune* about how they were looking for me in Chicago."

Oscar shook his head. "Well, try to avoid that kind of thing in future, will you?"

"Yes, sir. I will."

"You want coffee?"

"You bet."

Oscar got up and poured coffee into an old chipped mug, with a faded Niagara Falls logo on the side. He handed it to me.

"Why Niagara Falls?" I asked.

"It's where I went on my honeymoon."

"I didn't know you were married, Oscar."

"It didn't last long. I was only eighteen."

"Oh."

"Jenna will be here shortly," he said. "I called her and told her she was back on the team. She was excited to be coming back. She even apologized for her outburst last night."

"Did you apologize for yours?"

"In a way. I told her I still thought it was untoward of her not to tell us she had been the courier, but, in the end, I understood it wasn't all that important."

"Untoward?"

"Yeah, I know," he said. "One of them high-floor words. But, uh, the fancier the word, the less emotion's in it, you know?"

"Not like saying she lied."

"Right."

There was a knock on the door. Oscar opened it. It was Jenna. It was only 7:00 a.m., but she was dressed in full business regalia. Dark suit, salmon-colored silk blouse. Gold lapel pin. Two-inch heels.

She stood in the doorway. "I'm ready to get to work."

I held her gaze a moment. I liked that she was back. We'd been a team for almost seven years. It was the right thing to do. "Okay, let's do it," I said.

Jenna came over to the table and sat down. She pulled out a white legal pad and flipped to a page on which she had made some notes. Seeing the white legal pad reminded me how much I regretted the demise of yellow legal pads. Yellow pads had gone away because yellow paper doesn't recycle. I still had a secret stash of the yellow ones in my desk drawer, but it was dwindling. I thought to myself that if I ever got back to my office, I'd have to look for a new supply. Maybe I could buy more on eBay or something.

"Robert?" Jenna was looking at me.

"Oh, sorry, I was daydreaming," I said.

Oscar the consummate host spoke up. "Jenna, would you like some breakfast?"

"Oh, no thanks. I ate before I came."

"Then how about coffee?" he said.

"Sure."

Oscar got up to get it. Jenna didn't wait for him to come back.

"We have some key decisions to make," she said.

That's what I had specialized in all my life, really. Decisions. Not detective work. Maybe, I thought, applying my real skills would turn out to be more useful.

"Okay, Jenna," I said, "what decisions do we need to make?"

She took out three identical typewritten sheets that she had tucked into the inner pages of the tablet. She handed one to me, put one at Oscar's place, and kept one for herself. "Here's a list," she said. "I tried to prioritize them."

Oscar came back with the coffee pot. He put a mug in front of Jenna. The logo on this one said *QE2*. I arched an eyebrow at him. He laughed. "Second honeymoon. I was more prosperous by then."

Jenna ignored the banter. I could see that she had returned to Ms. Efficient, someone I had not really seen around much since her first year at the firm, when she had been strictly business in all settings. So much so that some of her associate colleagues had dubbed her "Senator James."

"Let's look at the first decision," she said.

Oscar glanced at the list. "Number one. Preliminary hearing next week?"

"Yes," Jenna said.

Oscar guffawed. "Now there's a howler. Even assuming the DA doesn't just convene a grand jury so he can skip the preliminary hearing, he'll be lucky to get a prelim in ninety days. And since Robert's not even in custody, the prelim could be in September or even later next year—if it happens at all. I'm betting they just use a grand jury."

"Hey," I said. "Let's start at the beginning. It's been a long time since I took criminal procedure."

"My deepest apologies," Oscar said. "I'll explain. After they arrest you and arraign you, the DA has to persuade some judge that there's reasonable evidence you committed the crime. In short, the DA only has to show "probable cause" that you're guilty. Which is a lot lower standard than "beyond a reasonable doubt." And he can show probable cause in one of two ways."

"Which are what?" I asked.

"First way," Oscar said, "the DA just convenes a grand jury and asks them to indict you. He still has to present evidence—witnesses and documents—that show there's sufficient evidence you probably committed the murder, of course. But he gets to prove up his probable cause case in total secret. If the grand jury finds there's probable cause, the DA just presents their indictment to a judge, who rubber stamps it, and that's the end of it."

"And the second way?"

"Second way is through a preliminary hearing, where the DA puts on his witnesses and other evidence in front of a judge. Then tries to persuade *the judge* that there's probable cause you murdered Simon. Unlike a grand jury proceeding, a prelim is an open, public hearing."

"It's a naïve question, I guess, but which should we prefer?"

"The public prelim," Oscar said. "We can get free discovery by cross-examining the DA's key witnesses."

"Why can't we do that in a grand jury?" I asked.

"Because we don't even get to attend. The whole thing's done in secret. Sometimes we don't even learn a grand jury's looking into it. We just wake up one morning and discover you've been indicted. Or maybe we read it in the newspaper at breakfast."

"Okay," I said, "so if I were the DA, I'd pick the grand jury route."

"Yeah, and that's precisely what most DA's do these days," Oscar said. "Not that it really matters to the outcome. DA's almost never lose preliminary hearings in front of a judge when it's a big case, and grand juries indict anyone the DA tells them to indict."

"I know that drill," Jenna said. "My dad bitched about it when those assholes in Cleveland indicted him for a bribe he never took. He was always quoting Sol Wachtler, the former Chief Judge of the New York Court of Appeals, who said a grand jury would indict a ham sandwich if the DA asked them to."

"Probably," Oscar said, "a grand jury'd indict the leftover crust."

Jenna took a big gulp of coffee. "Okay," she said, "now that Robert's crim procedure refresher is over, back to why there's a decision to be made. Yesterday evening, I got a call from Charles Benitez."

"Who's Charles Benitez?" I asked.

"Sorry again," Oscar said. "Did you ever watch *The Godfather*?"

"Sure," I said.

"Well, call Charles Benitez the DA's *consigliari*," Oscar said. "The brains of the office. Mostly he stays behind the scenes. But when it gets politically important, he actually goes to court so it won't get screwed up."

He turned to Jenna, whose coffee cup was now completely empty. "So what did Charlie have to say, Jenna?"

"He said the DA has a deal to propose."

Oscar and I spoke almost as one: "What's the deal?"

"They want to do a preliminary hearing, but they want it to start next week. If we agree to that, they'll agree not to press for a trial before June, or move it even later in the year if we need it. Plus they'll give us the murder book right now."

"What's the murder book?" I asked. I was truly beginning to feel like a first-year law student all over again.

"All the investigation stuff that they're required by law to give us," Oscar said. "Witness interviews, expert reports, exculpatory evidence, blood tests, whatever. Usually they drag their feet on handing it over. It won't be complete yet, but it would be nice to get what they've already got right away. On the other hand, we need a lot more time to prep for a really great job on the prelim. So we'd give up a lot and not get much in exchange."

Jenna was staring, forlornly I thought, at her empty coffee cup. "There was more," she said. "They will agree not to seek a revocation of bail on the grounds that Robert tried to flee. Or try to raise it to five million."

"I didn't try to flee!"

She ignored me. "Or ask that he wear an ankle bracelet."

That stopped me. "An ankle bracelet? Can they really do that?"

"Sure they can," Oscar said. "They'd go in and tell the judge that in lieu of asking for greater bail, they'd like you braceleted. It's not such a big deal."

"I'd feel like Hester Prynne in *The Scarlet Letter*," I said.

Jenna smiled. "Robert, Hester Prynne wore the scarlet letter on her chest. You can't even see an ankle bracelet."

I didn't feel mollified.

She went right on. "But the most important thing is that if we agree to the early prelim, they assure us that they won't take the case to the death penalty committee."

"This isn't even close to a capital case," Oscar said. He actually rolled his eyes. "That stuff they fed Robert in the squad car about lying in wait as a special circumstance is horseshit. They *never* go for death on that ground."

I was having trouble being a balanced decision maker.

"Hey guys, whether the chance is remote or not, it sounds pretty damn good to me to be guaranteed that they won't try to kill me."

Jenna and Oscar both looked at me. I could see them thinking something like, "Oh shit, the client is sitting here listening to all this."

Jenna made the kind of decision good lawyers make when they don't want to go down a particular path right then. She found something else to talk about. "Oscar, could I get more coffee?"

"Sure, Jenna." Oscar got up to fetch the pot.

"How many cups have you had today, Jenna?" I asked.

"This is only my fourth."

"At 7:00 a.m."

"Yes. Are you now my mother?"

"No. Just asking." Jenna knew I was harking back to the days of "Senator James," when she was known not only for her all-business manner, but for consuming nine or ten cups of coffee a day. Her other nickname had been "Wired."

Oscar returned and refilled the QE2. Still standing, coffee pot in hand, he tried to reframe the issue. "Okay, on the one side, we have something the current DA—Horace Krandall—wants, and he's offering, really, not much in return. So if we didn't take the client's wishes into account, we'd tell him to forget it. Or something even stronger."

"But," and he waved the coffee pot in my direction, ". . . our client is a nervous Nellie and doesn't want to be sentenced to death." I thought I detected a ghost of a smile when he said that, but maybe not.

"I don't want to be sentenced to anything," I said. "But yes, it would comfort me to know that I'm definitely not going to an execution gurney." As I said those words, I realized that I had gone from thinking this whole thing was ludicrous to worrying seriously about being executed.

Jenna tore a piece of paper out of her legal pad and drew a line down the middle. She wrote "pros" at the top of one column and "cons" at the top of the other.

"Jenna," I said, "I know I taught you to do that, but you don't need to this time. I want to get rid of the capital crime threat. Even if it's weak. Let's take their deal."

Jenna picked up the coffee cup and downed maybe half of it. "Whatever you want, chief." She crumpled up the piece of paper and dropped it on the floor.

Oscar got up and started pacing. "Robert, my friend, I understand your decision. But before we make it final, we need to talk about exactly why the DA wants this deal." I recognized the technique. I was about to be handled.

"Okay. Enlighten me," I said.

Oscar continued pacing. He reminded me of an old professor I once had. One who never stood still.

"Enlightenment goes like this," he said. "Horace Krandall is unpopular. He's lost three high-profile cases in the last two years. People hate losers. The next election isn't that far away—people are already gearing up for it. He'll need 50% of the vote plus one to avoid a run-off. He's already got three potential challengers putting out feelers to campaign donors, two from his own office."

"So?"

"So he needs a big win in the courts right now to make himself look good. If your case takes the normal course of a complex case, the prelim could end up being after the election. So what he needs is to seem to win something big in your case right now. Very publicly."

"I still don't understand why you're so sure he'll win."

Oscar finally stopped moving. "Because they don't have to prove you actually did it. They don't even have to come close. Practically speaking, any two pieces of evidence that seem to link you to the crime will constitute sufficient evidence that you likely did it. Maybe just one piece."

"They could lose the prelim. They must have lost at least one," I said.

"Let me say it again. No one remembers the last time the DA's office lost a prelim in a major case that's in the public eye. Most judges have no balls in major felony prelims. They rarely kick them."

"Why not?" I asked.

"Because it might fuck up their chances for reelection," he said, "or lose them appointment to a seat on the Court of Appeals. So, bottom line, the DA not only knows he's going to win the prelim, he also expects to get lots of favorable publicity while he does it. The public will have no clue the fix was in."

Jenna was tapping her pen against her right ear. It was always a sign of Jenna thinking.

"Okay," she said, "if that's the case, and the DA desperately wants this, and Robert is going to insist we take the deal, we ought to be able to get more out of it."

"Yes!" Oscar said. "Exactly!"

Jenna held her cup out. "More coffee, please?"

"God, you're a regular addict," Oscar said.

"I know what I like," she said.

"I'll need to make some more, then." Oscar headed back toward the sink.

Jenna opened her legal pad again. "What do we want, then?"

"Ah," Oscar said, turning to talk over his shoulder. "I can think of many things."

Jenna tore out a new piece of paper and again prepared to write. "Okay, Oscar, list them."

"One," he said, "access to the courthouse for all hearings via the garage and a private elevator. That way we miss the media . . . Two, they agree not to mention anything about Robert trying to flee, either now or during the real trial."

"I didn't try to flee."

"I know," Oscar responded. "But they can paint a very nice picture that says you did, and there's that very nice jury instruction that tells the jury that attempted flight is a marker of guilt. So we want that shit out."

I had become an observer of the scene rather than a participant in it. Now I knew how clients really felt. Except most clients probably didn't get to see their lawyers doing strategy while one made coffee and the other gulped it.

Jenna was still making the list. "Is there a three?"

"Yeah, there is," Oscar said. "Three, they give us the names of all their witnesses. Ten days in advance, not the night before the prelim, like they usually do. And all their expert reports three business days before the hearing. Then let's add a number four."

Jenna's pen was poised. "Which is?"

"Four, we do the prelim the first week of the new year, not next week. That still gives them plenty of time to put on their prom dresses and gussy up for the election. One week is ridiculous. We can't get ready in a week."

Jenna closed her pad. "Okay. I take it that my assignment, should I choose to accept it, is to bargain hard for all four of those things?"

Oscar came back with more coffee and filled *QE2* once again. "Yeah," he said. "Call Benitez back and tell him those are our terms."

"Okay," she said.

"And there's one more thing, Jenna," Oscar said.

"Which is?"

"Tell him the terms are nonnegotiable."

Jenna looked pleased. She was, I knew, terrific at playing the unmovable rock.

She drank still more coffee. Then she started packing up to go. Which reminded me that I needed to get back home.

"Can I get a ride back to the house with you, Jenna?"

Oscar looked at me like I had lost my mind. "You can't just go ride in a car to get back there. The media swarm is probably five times the size it was when you left. We need to keep your picture out of the paper until the prelim starts. Pictures of your possessions, too. The late news last night showed a clip of them towing your car from airport parking."

I had completely forgotten about my car. "What do you suggest?"

Oscar grinned a big Cheshire Cat grin. I hadn't seen him grin that grin before. "Well, my friend, I have an old plumber's truck in the garage. Sign and all. It has no windows in the back and a nice privacy screen that completely blocks the back from the front."

"I have to sit on the floor of a truck?"

"No, it has a wooden bench back there. A bit hard, but no one can see who's sitting on it. So we could get you into your garage that way without the media noticing you. They'll think it's a repair guy. Or at least they won't be sure. I have a friend who'll drive you."

"You're kidding," I said.

"Nope. If you don't like that plan, Jenna can drive you out in the open." Oscar paused. "Jenna, that reminds me. Add a number five to the list: The police move the media back at Robert's house, starting tomorrow. They can say it's now a law office or something."

So that is how I got home. Sitting in the dark on a hard wooden bench in the back of a bouncing truck. I felt like Marie Antoinette going to the guillotine.

CHAPTER 31

I was back home by 9:00 a.m. So far as I know, the Blob never figured out that I was in the back of the truck. The young guy who drove— I later learned that he was a law student who sometimes clerked for Oscar—had actually donned coveralls to disguise himself. After we got into the garage, he came inside and waited around for an hour to make it look like he had stayed to do some work.

Perhaps the Blob actually thought my sink was clogged. On the other hand, it had to know that I wasn't in the house when the truck arrived, and it must, in its buzzing collectivity, have seen Jenna leave earlier that morning. So who knows what its little hive-brain really thought about the truck. Maybe it was just sporting us the fantasy that we had outsmarted it.

After the "plumber" left, it was quiet in the house. Jenna had not yet returned, and the murmur of the Blob, audible as we entered the garage, could no longer be heard. All of the drapes were drawn. I very carefully turned on only one light, a small one in an inside bathroom. Somehow, I thought that lights ablaze, glowing even dimly through the drapes, might give me away. Not that it would have mattered. The Blob had never tried to climb through the windows. But I wasn't in a particularly rational frame of mind.

I decided to give myself a time-out, so that I could stop thinking about my situation, enjoy the quiet of the morning, and get myself back to some semblance of peace of mind. First, I sat in my big leather chair and just stared at the blank slate of closed drapes. It didn't work. Then I tried sitting on the floor and quietly chanting a mantra I had learned in a meditation class twenty years before. That didn't work either. It never really had. I am not really mantra-amenable.

Eventually, I anesthetized myself by watching a DVD of *Casablanca*. Jenna walked in the front door just as Rick was giving Ingrid Bergman the letters of transit.

She glanced at the screen. "You think letters of transit could get you out of this, Robert?"

"God, don't I wish."

"It wouldn't work. Horace Krandall's such a stiff he's probably never even seen *Casablanca*. So he wouldn't honor them." And with that, she walked into the kitchen. I got up and followed her.

"What's next here in the real world, Jenna?"

She was rummaging in the refrigerator, with her head buried inside it. "Oscar is coming over this afternoon," she said. "We need a strategy meeting."

"Did you call Benitez about their proposed deal?"

"Yeah. I called him on my cell. They agreed to everything. I keep wondering what more we should have asked for. You know, what we left on the table."

"Ah, the table problem," I said.

Jenna and I had discussed the table problem a lot. If you settle lots of cases, as civil litigators inevitably do, you always end up wondering what you left on the table. How much more you could have taken off the table if you'd hung tougher, or how much less you would have had to put on the table if you'd been more of a recalcitrant asshole. Here was the same damn table, sitting in the criminal law parlor.

Jenna's head was still in the fridge. "Yeah, the table problem."

"What are you looking for in there?"

"Something for lunch. It's almost noon."

"Why don't I make lunch? I'm tired of my lawyers always cooking for me." It was the first lighthearted thing I'd said in days.

Jenna pulled her head out of the fridge. "You cook? This is new."

"I make a world-class tuna salad."

"With mayo or the competing product?"

"What's the difference?"

"The difference is that I've put on four pounds in one week because I've been mainlining pizza for stress relief. I'm going all protein and fat, no carbs. Mayo's got tons of fat, but no carbs. The competing product tastes better but has a couple of carbs."

I had not thought about the stress all of this was putting on Jenna. I had been too cooked in my own stew. "I think that diet theory is nonsense, but mayo it is."

While I started on the tuna salad—mayo only—Jenna extracted several piles of paper from her backpack and put them on the kitchen table. She riffled through the papers as I worked on the salad. Adapting to my role as a client, I didn't ask what the papers were.

I enjoyed making lunch. I turned the tuna salad into a sandwich on whole wheat for me. And since even I recognized that bread contains carbs, I put Jenna's tuna salad in a bowl. I located a couple of apples, carbs though they were, and cut them up. I felt enormously, fulfillingly competent.

The lunch became a debriefing. I told Jenna in detail what I had learned from the *Enquirer* reporter, from Serappo, and from the cops. Jenna took notes and, intermittently, bites of her tuna salad. She didn't touch the apple pieces.

"You learned a lot," she said, after I had finished both my report and my sandwich.

"In some ways, yeah. But I'm still no closer to knowing who did it, except that *I* didn't."

"*I* didn't either."

"Right."

"Oh shit," she said.

"What?"

"That's another thing I should have extracted from Benitez."

"What?"

"A promise not to try to disqualify me on the grounds that I could be a witness."

I had forgotten about that issue. Entirely. "Let's cross that bridge if we come to it," I said.

Which represented a big change of attitude on my part. As a lawyer, up to that point, I had always tried to imagine in advance *every* bridge I might come to and how to cross it safely. Or how to blow it up after I had made it across.

Jenna nailed me. "Well, that's a big change, Mr. Always-Be-Sure-to-Look-at-All-the-Options Tarza."

"You and Oscar can look at all the options."

"We will."

I changed the subject. "Jenna, what surprises you most about what I just told you?"

She was busy folding a piece of paper into ever-smaller rectangles. In her first year at the firm, during a particularly intense meeting, I'd seen her fold a dozen pieces of paper, one after the other. I had teased her about it one day, and she told me that the neurosis—my term, not hers—had started in grade school. After seven years of observation, I finally concluded that she did it when she was trying to think through a difficult problem, the way some people use worry beads.

Jenna didn't answer for a bit. She was completing the sixth and final fold. I noticed, to my distress, that I, too, had begun to fold a piece of paper. Just as I was contemplating whether such habits were communicable, Jenna stopped folding and answered my question.

"The business about there being many fakes, that's what surprises me," she said. "It sounds like someone was putting together a counterfeiting ring for the Ides."

"Which makes no sense," I said. "Because the Ides is too famous and too rare. If you tried to market even a couple of them, everyone in the coin world would be asking you where you got them."

"And if someone tried to market seven of them?"

"Everyone would instantly scream counterfeit, just like they did with the Black Sea Hoard."

"Suppose they were real," she said. "How much would a coin like that sell for if you went to sell all of them?"

"Well, Simon way overpaid me for mine. He just wanted to beat out the other bidders, or something. But if they were real—which they can't be, by the way—and they were sold one at a time, maybe the owner would get three hundred thousand each if they were in Extremely Fine condition."

Jenna put the new piece of paper she was folding aside, took a calculator out of her backpack, and punched in the numbers. I am always amazed at the simple math that Jenna's generation can't do in their heads.

"Well," she said, "that would be two million one hundred thousand dollars. A serious chunk of change."

"Yes, but the coins can't be real, so that isn't going to happen."

"What if they *were* real?"

I resisted rolling my eyes.

"Seven of them, all at once?"

"Yes."

"They can't be real. Think about it. Seven coins, hidden away for over two thousand years, suddenly pop up here in Los Angeles?"

"In your garden."

"Right. In my garden."

"Hey, you know, we haven't really gone out to look at your garden since the police dug it up," she said.

She was right. Without exchanging another word, we both headed for the kitchen door. Before going out into the backyard, I looked around to make sure I wasn't in the Blob's sightline. I wasn't, so I stepped outside.

"Yard" is kind of a misnomer. My yard is mostly a steep hillside, held back by a huge concrete retaining wall. But at the foot of the hill, nestled in the space between the house and the retaining wall, a prior owner had carved out a small garden, maybe ten feet by twelve, and surrounded it with a low, red brick wall pierced by a wrought iron gate. The perfect place for Peter Rabbit and his mother if they ever needed to get away from a damp English summer.

When my daughter was young, the garden had had a playhouse in it. It was long gone. In recent years, I'd done some desultory planting there in the summer, usually a few vegetables and some flowers. Now, in winter, it was mostly bare dirt, with a few weeds thrown in for good measure. Not at all Peter Rabbit-friendly.

We walked over to the wall and stood there, looking in at the garden.

"Alright, Sherlock," I said. "What do you deduce?"

"Well, for one thing, they must have been tipped off about where the box was buried."

"Because?"

She pointed to the dug up area. "Because they only dug up one corner in order to find it."

"Maybe they just got lucky."

"Maybe. But if they were digging at random and found a box, you'd think they'd go on digging to see what else they might find. So they were looking for something specific, knew where to look, found it, and left."

"Makes sense," I said.

"Who has access to your garden?"

I shrugged. "Pretty much anybody, really. All you'd have to do to get here is walk down the driveway between my house and the one next door. There's no fence or gate. So unless I was home or my neighbor was, nobody would see you."

"Maybe we should ask your neighbor."

"I'm embarrassed to say I don't even know her name. She's lived there about three years I think, but I've never even met her."

"Welcome to Los Angeles," Jenna said.

"Isn't it a little early to be planting spring flowers?" It was Oscar, who had come up behind us.

"What are you doing back here?" I asked.

"I was sneaking in. The media saw me arrive, and I felt like sticking it to them. So I walked around to the back, where they couldn't follow because someone has put up no trespassing signs all over your property."

Jenna beamed. "I did it yesterday."

"Smart work," Oscar said. "But unless you ace detectives have more to do out here, could we go inside? It's cold." Then he cast a knowing eye over the garden. "By the way, Robert, if you plan on growing anything there, you should be turning the soil during the winter."

"I'll keep that in mind, Oscar. If I'm still around to tend it."

He wasn't listening. He was instead staring at the dirt pile.

"What's that?" he asked.

"What's what?"

"That thing there."

He pointed at the dirt pile but didn't wait for me to respond. He opened the gate, walked into the garden, and reached into the pile of turned earth. Then he plucked out what appeared to be a coin, partially covered with dirt, and brought it back through the gate.

He handed it to me. "Is this an Ides?"

I brushed some of the dirt off and examined it as carefully as I could.

"Yes, it appears to be an eighth copy. Also fake, I assume."

"Let me see it," Jenna said.

I handed it to her. She turned it over a couple of times in her fingers. "I wonder how the hell it got here."

"Well," Oscar said, "I see only three possibilities. One, whoever buried the box dropped it. Two, the cops who dug up the box dropped it. Three, the cops planted it so we'd find it."

"There's a fourth," I said.

"What's that?" he asked.

"Brutus's army came this way on pay day, and one of his soldiers dropped it."

"Very funny," Oscar said. "Well, the good news is that now we've got one of the fakes. We can have it tested and maybe find out where it came from."

"Good luck," I said. "Counterfeiters don't usually put their initials on their fakes."

Oscar started to slip it into his jacket pocket.

"I wouldn't do that if I were you," I said.

"Why not?"

"If the police catch you with it, they'll change their minds and think *you're* the counterfeiter."

We all laughed, ruefully, and made our way back into the house.

CHAPTER 32

Oscar plunked himself down at the kitchen table, and Jenna and I followed.

"Okay," Oscar said, "I came over here for the meeting Jenna told me we absolutely *had* to have. I hope we're not going to have a lot of them. They're usually a total waste of time."

Despite the fact that we were already seated, I did *not* want to meet in the kitchen. It was too far down-market from the eighty-fifth floor.

"My study has a small conference table," I said. "Let's have the meeting there. It will be more comfortable."

"I'll have to move all my papers," Jenna said. She looked annoyed.

Oscar laughed. "Including those three there that you folded up?"

"One of them was folded by Robert." She said it deadpan.

"Oh, great," Oscar said. "*Two* people with obsessive compulsive disorder."

Jenna shrugged, gathered up her papers, and put them back in her backpack. She left the folded ones on the table. We headed for my study, toward the back of the house.

I love my study. All my books are there—almost a thousand of them—on ceiling-high shelves covering two adjoining walls. The other two walls are dark mahogany. The floor of the room is wide-plank dark wood, covered by an old oriental rug. One I bought during a trip to Turkey, after way too many glasses of something whose name I still can't pronounce.

In one of the corners there is a big chair, its red leather cracked from age and use, with a battered old ottoman in front of it. Next to the chair there's a small, marble-topped table on which I leave my coin magazines until I get around to reading them. In another corner, three black leather swivel chairs cluster around a round mahogany table.

I used to enjoy going into the study every night after dinner. I'd plop my body down in the leather chair, put my feet up on the ottoman, light up a cigar, and read my *Wall Street Journal*. A few months ago, Jenna, who'd seen me smoke cigars from time to time, started giving me a hard time about oral cancer. So I dropped the cigar part of the ritual. Which destroyed its magic, of course.

The cigars were still in the humidor though. And as the three of us walked into the study, I thought to myself that it might be time to light up again. I probably wouldn't last long enough in prison to get oral cancer.

We sat down at the round table.

"What's the agenda for this meeting?" Oscar asked.

"To outline the basic facts of the case," Jenna said. "To figure out what we've got."

"You know, that would make good sense in a *civil* case," Oscar said, in a tone that I took to be a not-too-guarded suggestion that civil litigators aren't real trial lawyers.

"In a civil case," he continued, "the plaintiff puts the defendant on the witness stand and proves the bad facts out of the defendant's very own mouth. In a criminal case, thanks to the Fifth Amendment, the defendant gets to sit there with his mouth shut. So, boys and girls, the first question in a criminal case is not, 'What are the facts?' It's always, 'What can the government prove?'"

"I get it," I said. "The government can't prove its case by asking me what Simon and I said to each other."

"Right. And they can't ask Simon either, because he's dead. So the government has to prove up its case some other way." He paused. "If they can."

Jenna sat for a few seconds, lost in thought. I could see the wheels turning. Then she returned from wherever it was she went when the wheels turned.

"Okay, I see it, too." she said. "So let's ask ourselves: what evidence does the government have that Robert's guilty?"

"That's what I want to talk about," Oscar said.

He pulled a dog-eared notebook from his back pocket. The kind with a tiny spiral binding at the top. He opened it and made an elaborate display of flipping slowly through the tattered pages until he came to the page he wanted. The one page I could see had messy jottings out to the margins in two different colors of ink. Not very professional.

"Here it is," he said. "My notes on motive. Let's start with that. My guess is that the DA is going to claim that you offed Simon to keep him from outing you as a counterfeiter and, as a side benefit, to avoid giving his 500K back."

"I guess," I said. I felt no enthusiasm for my supposed motives.

"So," Oscar said, "what's the best evidence the DA can put his hands on about that motive?"

"Well, there were a bunch of grumpy e-mails about the coin between me and Simon," I said.

"What did they say, exactly?"

"I don't really recall."

"I do," Jenna said. "I read them."

"And?"

"There were five of them. First, Simon writes and says the coin's a fake. Then Robert writes back and says it's not. Simon then demands his money back, politely. Robert doesn't respond, and Simon writes again and demands his money back again—or else. I actually have a copy of that one. I already showed it to Robert."

"Let's see it," Oscar said.

She rummaged in one of her piles of paper, pulled out the e-mail and set it on the table in front of Oscar, but positioned so that we could all see it.

Subject   Forged Coins
Date   11/25 4:03:37 PM Pacific Daylight Time
From   srafer@marmarflaw.com
To   rtarza@marmarflaw.com

Robert—

Quit pretending that your Ides is anything other than a clever Becker-like forgery. Take it back and return my money.

I'll be out of the office the rest of the day and the rest of this week and next. Your worthless fake will be in the top drawer of my desk. Pick it up while I'm gone. Don't bother to leave a check. Just wire the $500K to my off-shore bank account in Shanghai. Name on the account: Simon S. Rafer. The bank name, routing number and my account number are on a sticky on top of the coin.

This is my final offer. Accept it and I'll forget the whole thing. Stall any longer and it's going to get very public and very ugly. I think that at the very least you knew all along that it was a fake and I'm going to say so. Maybe you won't go to jail. But no one is ever going to buy a coin from you again and it won't exactly be good for your legal career. Here or anywhere else. Assuming you can find a job somewhere else.

The only reason I'm not going to the police right now is in deference to our long professional relationship.

Do the right thing, Robert.

Simon

Oscar read it and said, "It sounds, Robert, as if he was accusing you not only of selling him a fake coin, but of being the one who forged it."

"It doesn't say that," I said.

"I'm reading between the lines."

"I think Oscar's right," Jenna said. "Why else would it get ugly?"

"Have the police seen this piece of paper?" Oscar asked.

"No," Jenna said. "They've not served a subpoena, and the cops didn't find it in their search because it was in my office and they didn't search there."

"Okay," Oscar said. "Where did you get it?"

"I printed it out the morning of the murder, when I went over to Simon's place. Before the cops got there."

"But you didn't print out the others?"

"No."

"Okay, you said there was a fifth e-mail. What did it say?"

"Robert wrote back and told him to fuck off."

"I *never* said that."

"I'm paraphrasing." she said. "It was that hostile and maybe more."

"Perhaps the *sense* of it was that hostile," I said.

Oscar turned to one of the few blank pages left in his notebook, pen poised. "Robert, now that you've maybe had your memory jogged, do you remember more about what you said in the 'fuck off' one?"

"Please don't call it that."

He looked amused. I was once again behaving like a client.

"Okay. I'll rephrase the question," he said. "Do you remember what you said in that last e-mail?"

"Not exactly. Something along the lines of, 'My family always thought it was real. I still think it's real. You examined it carefully before you bought it. So if it's a fake, you had as good a shot at finding that out as I did. Stop pestering me.'"

"Is that what you remember, Jenna?"

"Yes, but it was profane, too," she said. "The a-word appeared, coupled with the name of God."

"Whatever," I said.

Oscar did not write any of that down. He just clicked the pen against his front teeth. "When did you send that last one, Robert?"

"Maybe eight or nine days before the murder. Not sure exactly."

"Did Simon give up after that?"

"No, over a day or two he called me maybe ten times and left screaming, profane messages on my voice mail."

"Any actual threats?"

"Yeah. In the last one, which was maybe the Tuesday before the murder, he said he was going to wipe me and my family off the face of the earth."

"He talked like that all the time," Jenna said.

"Yeah, he did," I said. "A lot of people even thought it was a sign of aggressive leadership based on some idiot business book they read. I never took it seriously."

"Did you keep any of the voice-mails?" Oscar asked.

"No. They've been taped over frequently since then. I get a zillion voice mails a day now."

Oscar looked over at Jenna, who had been studiously taking notes. "Jenna, did you hear any of those voice mails, either at Robert's end, on his machine, or when the calls were being made from Simon's end?"

"No."

"Robert, did anyone else hear them?"

"Not that I know of," I said.

"Well, the government isn't going to have those, then," Oscar said. As for the e-mails, they've probably already got all of them from the hard drives on the two computers. Yours and Simon's."

"No, they don't," Jenna said. "I deleted the e-mails from both computers—Simon's the morning I was there before the cops got there. Robert's while he was sleeping that first night. A couple of hours after the doctor put him out."

"All of them?" Oscar asked.

"Yep. All of them."

"Shit." He had the look of a man who was searching the floor for a convenient place to do push-ups. I probably had the look of a man who was merely stunned.

"I thought," I said, "that you only deleted the ones on Simon's computer."

"No, from yours too. I thought I told you that."

"I guess you forgot to," I said. "Because I'm certain you didn't tell me that."

"Why," Oscar asked, "did you do it?" He showed no signs yet of dropping to the floor to give us fifty.

"I was in a get-rid-of-this-stuff mode. Just to keep Robert from being hassled. Maybe it was a mistake, okay? If I had thought Robert was really going to be a target, I wouldn't have touched them. I'm not stupid, you know."

Oscar was clicking his pen against his teeth again and rocking a bit. "Jenna, you know that all those deletions can be undone, right?"

"I doubt it," she said. "I used ScrubBucket on both computers. It runs when you log off and deletes everything for serious ever. I set it to use the NSA standard, seven passes of random x's and o's over each file deleted."

"Did Robert already have ScrubBucket on his computer?" Oscar asked.

"No. I picked up the disk for it when I went home Monday evening to grab some clean clothes. While the doctor was still here with Robert."

"Well, alas," Oscar said, "the off-the-shelf delete programs aren't anywhere near as good as the cops' recovery programs. So the e-mails deleted from both computers are going to be recovered. Or they'll get them from the firm's servers, where ScrubBucket likely didn't delete them. Trust me."

"Okay, so they recover them," I said. "So what? Being angry at Simon doesn't mean I wanted to kill him. If that were true I'd have murdered dozens of people in the last thirty years."

Oscar looked at me. "Do you usually delete e-mails right after you read them?"

"No. I just let the system delete them automatically from my inbox after thirty days or something like that. My home and office computers are synched, so they get deleted from both."

"Well then," Oscar said, "In the hearing, Benitez is going to demonstrate from your very own computer that you don't normally delete e-mails. Then, also from your very own computer, he'll point to many e-mails intentionally deleted right after the murder."

"Okay," I said. "I get it."

"I'm not done. To top it all off, and as a kind of *by-the-way*, he'll point out that ScrubBucket wasn't loaded on your computer till the day *after* the murder. Once he unveils the contents of the e-mails, it won't take a computer scientist to conclude you tried to deep-six them because they showed your motive. It'll be a new marker of guilt—*guilty deletion*."

Jenna looked up from her note-taking, which had been assiduous.

"How will they explain that the e-mails got deleted from Simon's computer, too, when Robert wasn't anywhere near it?"

"They won't have to," Oscar said. "If they recover the e-mails from Robert's computer—home, office, or the firm's server—they don't ever need to mention what was or wasn't on Simon's. At least not in this preliminary hearing, where all they have to show is probable cause. It's a low burden, folks." He shrugged.

Jenna brightened, as if she were not herself the cause of the problem. "So, Mr. Quesana, what's the solution?"

"How about," he said, "we put you on the witness stand to admit you were the one who used ScrubBucket to delete all of them? That should solve it."

Jenna was silent.

Oscar started tossing his pen in the air and catching it. "Jenna, my friend, you've got a big hairy conflict. If you weren't a lawyer on this case, we'd just call you as a witness and be done with guilty deletion. But since you're one of Robert's lawyers, we can't really do that, can we?"

Jenna got up, too, leaned against one of the bookcases, and folded her arms across her chest. I was the only one left seated.

"Listen, Oscar," she said, "if you call me as a witness, you know I'll take the Fifth. It's a crime to tamper with evidence."

Oscar's pen was going ever higher with each toss. "If, if, if," he said. "If we had ham, we'd have ham and eggs if we had eggs. I suppose we should just cook with what we've got. What else do we have on motive, Jenna?"

"Lots, but first I need more coffee. Instantly if possible."

"Well I need a cigar," he said. "I can smell that they live here."

"Used to," I said.

"Let's dig them out."

"You big boys dig them out yourselves," Jenna said. "I'm going to the kitchen to make the coffee."

And she left.

CHAPTER 33

I reached into the humidor, took out two cigars, clipped the ends, and handed one to Oscar.

"Oscar, you take the armchair."

"No, you take it. I'm fine right here."

"Why, thank you. I will then."

I sat down in the big leather chair and felt its comfort swallow me up.

"Where's the cigar lighter?" Oscar asked.

"On the bookshelf to your left, right next to the big dictionary."

He walked over, found it, and began to light his cigar, turning it so the flame licked the end evenly. Then he handed the lighter to me, and I performed the same ritual. He went and sat back down in one of the swivel chairs at the table.

We both puffed for a few minutes. It felt good. It felt, well, manly.

After a while, he said, "It was nice of Jenna to do that."

"Do what?"

"Leave us here, just the two of us. She's giving us a chance to think again whether we really want her on the team."

"And?"

"It's close. Inside, she's a liability. Outside, she's a liability. But the decision is yours, my friend."

"I am bothered by the e-mail deletions. Among other things."

"Bothered enough to tell her 'thanks, but no thanks?'"

I paused a moment to consider. "No," I finally said. "Foolish as it may be, I want to keep her on the team, at least for now. If the conflicts get too bad, she'll go quietly if we ask her to. That's the way she is. And anyway, she really *is* a great lawyer." I laughed. "I ought to know. I trained her."

"Okay. She stays. Again."

He blew out a long stream of smoke. "Are these Cuban?"

"Of course. They're still the only decent cigars in the world."

He took another long drag, let the smoke linger in his mouth, then blew it out again.

"But they're illegal, eh?"

"You think I'll do even more time for that?"

"Do you really expect to do time, my friend?"

"I don't know. Maybe. Let's face it. I screwed up. The counterfeit coins in my pocket make me look guilty somehow."

"To say the least."

"On the other hand, I didn't do it."

He ignored my renewed protestation of innocence. "Truth is, Robert, you screwed up by playing detective on your own case. Period."

"I admit it. And I'm giving it up for Lent."

"Lent's not for another couple months."

"Okay, I'm giving it up now."

"Good."

We smoked again in silence for a while, savoring the cigars. With a good cigar in hand, you don't need to talk.

Finally, Oscar said, "Is there an ashtray around somewhere?"

"On the bottom shelf of the bookcase, the side next to the windows."

He walked over, found the big glass one, and brought it back to the table. He flicked his cigar ash into it.

"Well, Robert, I think we're at the point where maybe we ought to talk turkey here."

"Meaning what?"

"We ought to talk plea bargain."

I turned the cigar in my fingers and regarded the growing ash on the end. I'm a long-ash guy. After appropriate turning, and a pause I deemed worthy of Clint Eastwood in A *Fistful of Dollars*, I said, "I'm not pleading to goddamn anything. Because however it looks, I'm not goddamn guilty."

"Hear me out."

"Alright."

"They've nailed your motive. You look like a counterfeiter trying to off a fraud victim to shut him up."

"There's an explanation about how I came to have the two fake coins in my pockets."

"I've heard it already from Jenna. Candidly, no one's gonna believe it, because it's just your and Jenna's word about where you found them. And if you want a shot at someone believing you, one of you has gotta testify about it."

"Serappo could testify."

"That's only half the story, and it won't help. You brought him the coins to look at."

"I guess you're right."

He tapped more ash into the ashtray. "And they've nailed the physical evidence that links you to the crime. The crime lab report says the red stain on your office couch wasn't wine. It was Simon's blood."

"Somebody else put it there."

"Who?"

"I don't know."

"There's another problem."

I took another long drag on my cigar. The length of the ash was growing critical.

"Bottom line it for me, Oscar."

"You're beginning to resemble toast."

"Is that a technical legal term?"

"In a way, yes."

"What's comes next after toast?"

"Burnt toast."

"But I'm not that yet?"

"Not quite."

"Can I borrow that ashtray?" I asked.

"Sure." He flicked the ash from his own cigar into it again, got up, and brought the ashtray over to me. Then he went back to his swivel chair.

I looked again at the still growing ash on my cigar end. It could wait a tiny bit longer.

"So you think I should plead?"

"I don't think one way or another. I'm just presenting the option. If we plead now, you might do only ten years. It will be a hell of a lot longer if we wait until after we lose the prelim."

"Did you already talk to the DA about it?"

"Yeah."

"The rumors in the papers weren't wrong then."

"No, they were. The first time I talked to the DA about it was this morning. The DA leaked those rumors to send us a message: 'Come in and talk.'"

"You didn't get my consent to talk to him."

"Robert, did you ever think a civil case should be settled? And say to the lawyer on the other side, 'Hey, I don't have any authority from my client, and they might tell me to stuff it, but what would you think, just talking lawyer-to-lawyer, about settling this damn thing before it bankrupts everyone?'"

"Sure."

"This is no different. I told the DA you might tell me to stuff it."

I drew on the cigar and then blew out a long trail of smoke. I was finally going to have to flick the ash in the ashtray or risk it getting all over me. I flicked. As decisively as you can flick.

"Tell him I told you to stuff it."

"Why?"

"I'm sixty. In ten years I'll be seventy. Stuff happens to people in their sixties. I could die in prison. Screw the odds. I want to try to beat this."

"And we *can* beat it." It was Jenna. She had been standing in the doorway listening.

Oscar put down his cigar and sighed audibly. "Okay," he said, "let's get busy trying to beat it." Then he muttered, in a barely audible voice, "Against all odds."

CHAPTER 34

Jenna joined Oscar at the round table. I unlimbered myself from the leather chair and moved myself and my still-lit cigar over to the table, too.

"Could you guys please put those out?" she said. "It's one thing for you to give yourselves oral cancer. But *I* don't want to get lung cancer from the second-hand smoke."

"There's no persuasive evidence second-hand smoke causes lung cancer," I said.

"Put out the cigars!"

Oscar duly stubbed out his cigar. I reluctantly did the same. We have entered into that twilight of personal rights when guests can ask you to stop smoking in your own home and expect your compliance.

"You know," Oscar said, "there's something that doesn't compute about all of this."

"What's that?" Jenna asked.

"Well, if the last time Robert heard from Simon was the Tuesday before the murder, why did Simon stop bugging him after that? Did he just suddenly decide to blow off getting his money back? Or did he change his mind about the coin being a fake?"

"His e-mail says he was traveling," Jenna said.

"Yeah, but e-mails, cell phones and texts work from almost anywhere."

"What's your point, Oscar?" I asked.

"My point is that unless Simon was a give-up kind of guy, something happened six days before the murder."

"Hmm," Jenna said, "like maybe he decided that Robert wasn't the bad guy. Or at least not the only bad guy."

"Maybe," I said. "But to turn the tables on you Oscar, the only way we can get into evidence that Simon stopped hassling me about the coin is to put either me or Jenna on the witness stand."

"Or to hope the DA recovers the e-mails," Oscar said. "Which might actually help if they show that Simon stopped being interested in you returning his money. Then we can argue the inference that he stopped thinking you were the cause of his problems."

"There might be another problem with the e-mails," I said.

"Which is what?" Oscar asked.

"It stems from the old days when I was my own detective."

"Which," he said, "just ended a few minutes ago."

"Yeah. Well, back in the old days, and based on Jenna's advice, I told both Harry and Stewart that I had gone ahead and picked up the Ides from Simon's office desk drawer, like he invited me to do in the e-mail. And that I did it on Saturday."

"And the problem is?"

"Both of them went out of their way to mention they saw the Ides at Simon's condo on Sunday. So they may well think I'm lying."

"That could be a problem," Oscar said. "But only if Harry or Stewart told the cops that and end up testifying."

"I could testify and set the record straight on that, too," Jenna said. I thought I detected the ghost of a smile on her face.

"You could," Oscar responded, "but I don't even have to think about putting you on the stand right now, because we won't be putting on any witnesses in the prelim."

"Why not?" I asked. "That seems utterly wrongheaded."

"Because in a preliminary hearing, the prosecution puts on its case for publicity's sake, and we try to poke holes in their witnesses, also for publicity's sake. Plus maybe we learn how to bore better holes in their witnesses at trial."

"We do nothing with our own witnesses?"

"Nope. We save our own key witnesses—those whose testimony will help us— for the trial itself. That way, the DA doesn't get to find out in advance what they're going to say at trial."

"Oh," I said. Never having done a criminal case in my whole life, I was learning things. Things that were obvious if you thought about them, except that I had never thought about them.

"Well," Jenna said, "I don't think we can do much more with motive right now. The cops found the coins in Robert's pocket, and unless one of us testifies, it's going to be hard for us to show that they got there innocently. So let's move on to *opportunity* and *physical evidence.*"

I found to my surprise that I didn't want to participate in moving on to opportunity and physical evidence. I excused it in my own mind by saying that if Jenna and Oscar were going to be a team, they needed to bond, and they didn't need a lawyer-turned-client getting in the way. Perhaps, in truth, I just couldn't take discussing my own fate and prospects in a dispassionate way any longer. I was morphing into a true client.

"You know," I said, "Jenna knows all of this pretty well. You can always come and get me if you have questions. But if it's okay with you, I'm exhausted, and I think I'll take my leave for a while."

To my surprise, neither one of them made the slightest objection.

Awhile turned into more than three weeks. My study became a war room. Oscar taught Jenna about criminal law. Jenna taught Oscar how to use her notebook computer. Sometimes I thought they were going to get married. They consulted me as needed, and I was the tiebreaker on a few things, but for the most part I read books and magazines and watched TV. Daytime TV seemed especially well suited to anxiety relief. I also watched a lot of old movies I hadn't seen since they were first released. My favorite was *Night of the Living Dead.*

The only break in my routine occurred one day when some very official looking people brought a video camera setup into the living room. Oscar told me it was to be my arraignment, hi-tech style. I put on a set of headphones and listened to a judge ask how I wished to plead. I looked into the camera and pleaded "not guilty." Then I listened to the judge say a bunch of mumbo jumbo and set a date for the preliminary hearing.

Jenna later told me it was a first. That no one else had ever been arraigned remotely at home. That, in fact, it couldn't legally be done that way. But somehow, in her newfound relationship with Benitez, the two of them had arranged it with the judge. Frankly, I didn't care. The whole thing had interrupted *Treasure of the Sierra Madre* in the middle, and I wanted to get back to it.

Other than that brief transit of my image to the outside world, I never left the house the whole time. On some odd level I felt like I was away at camp.

Christmas came and went—I got many fewer cards than usual and didn't send any—until, one evening, Oscar and Jenna made me stop watching a rerun of *I Love Lucy* so they could present an outline of their final strategy plan for the prelim. The hearing was scheduled to start the next day. I approved the plan with a few tweaks. Then I went to bed to await the morning. Camp was over.

CHAPTER 35

On the day of the hearing, I found myself wide-awake at 5:00 a.m., unbidden by anything other than anticipation. Or maybe fear. Either way, it was hardly surprising.

I got up and took a long shower, then considered what to wear. For the prior two weeks I had been mostly in sweats and tennis shoes. There had seemed little point in getting dressed up. Especially since my days of going to my office had ended. At least for a while. Maybe forever. In between watching old movies, I had formally asked for and been granted an indefinite leave of absence from M&M. Caroline had graciously agreed that it would be a leave with pay. That was helpful, since my legal expenses were exploding. Jenna was a bargain, but Oscar had a high-floor hourly rate.

In exchange for getting paid during my leave, I had promised not to darken the eighty-fifth floor until and unless I was acquitted. I had also agreed that if I ended up being convicted I would immediately resign. No waiting around for an appeal. And resign on the spot if I pleaded to a felony. Which was a-belt-and-suspenders provision, because if I pleaded to any felony I'd promptly lose my bar card.

I assumed that the firm assumed they wouldn't have to pay me for very long. The one time I had looked at a newspaper when I was off at camp, it had featured still another front-page story about a potential plea bargain. There was nothing about Oscar telling the DA that I had said to stuff it.

The only question in my mind was whether M&M would wait for a conviction before taking me off the wall in Thomas Edison, the room where they had hung the portraits of all former managing partners of the firm. Thomas Edison, by the way, is the conference room on eighty-three near the firm's Patent Law Group, and the only conference room that included a first name. I believe that my patent colleagues had given the room that name as a kind of charm, to increase the chance that a twenty-first Century Thomas Edison might be lured through our doors.

In considering my clothing choices for my debut as the accused, sweats and tennis shoes were obviously not going to cut it. After thinking about it, I decided simply to resume my unvarying sartorial ritual from what seemed almost a past life: Crisp white shirt, blue pinstripe suit, red tie and polished black shoes. I put all of it on.

It felt good to be dressed up. Like I was somehow useful again. One of the hardest things about my forced inactivity was how unproductive I had felt. After almost forty years of productivity, if you count law school as productive, I felt utterly useless. Not to mention at loose ends. It is remarkably hard, at least for someone with a mind, to fill an entire workday if there is no work. Especially if you have to stay inside.

It was still dark outside when I walked into the kitchen. To my surprise, Jenna was already up, sitting at the kitchen table and working at her laptop. She was wearing her court clothes—starched white blouse, tailored blue-black suit, her red cloisonné dragon pin perched on the lapel, and two-inch black heels. She greeted me without looking up.

"Hi, Robert. Just finishing a few items. Ready for the day?" She was as cheery as a cheery lawyer can be.

"Yes. Anxious for it, in truth."

"Good, because it's going to be a long grind, this hearing. And you'll have to pass through the Blob every day just to get out of here."

"The new windows should help," I said.

The week before, Jenna had had the rear windows of her car replaced with glass of the darkest tint that the law allowed. Oscar had insisted to me that I'd be very hard to see if I sat in back. He also explained that the height of the Land Cruiser, together with the long interior distance from front to back, would make it difficult to photograph me clearly, even through the windshield. Especially, he had said, if I were to sit in the third row of seats. He then suggested we could also hang a blanket between the front and back to make it truly impossible to see me.

I told him I didn't know if I was willing to sit in the third row of seats behind a blanket. It was childlike of me, but I wanted to sit up front. I resisted threatening to get carsick if I had to sit in back. Finally, I told him I didn't really see why it mattered anymore if someone took my photo. He said it mattered. We reached no agreement. We still hadn't.

I put some cereal in a bowl, ate it, and chatted with Jenna about not much in particular. She had closed her laptop but did not eat. Either she had already eaten or was simply not eating that day. I used to find it hard to eat the first morning of a trial. I had no idea what Jenna's habits were in that regard. She had never lived in my house before.

There was a sudden knock at the kitchen door. I couldn't imagine who it might be, unless Oscar was arriving. Since we had agreed the night before that he would meet us at the courthouse, that seemed unlikely.

Jenna got up and opened the door. There was a guy in his fifties standing there. He was huge. About six-foot-seven and maybe 280 pounds. Not an ounce of fat. The thing that made him so distinctive, besides his size, was his impeccably tailored suit, his steel-grey hair, and his little rimless glasses. He could have been a super-sized version of Robert McNamara in his prime.

Jenna gave him a hug and then brought him over to the table. I stood to greet him. Politeness dies hard, even in your own house.

"Robert, this is Fredrick James."

"Uncle Freddie," I said. "My God."

He stuck out his hand. "I see that both my nickname and my reputation precede me," he said.

I reached out to meet his handshake and was pleased that he wasn't one of those giants who undertake to crush your hand on first meeting. Which would have been easy for him to do. His hands were both meaty and muscular at the same time. Mine are hardly small, but it would have been no contest.

"It's a pleasure to meet you," I said, just the way I was taught to greet people in third grade.

"And it is indeed a distinct pleasure to meet *you*," he responded.

"Jenna," Uncle Freddie went on, "has told me ever so much about you over these many years, and I do appreciate all you've been able to teach her. Among the many other qualities of mind you've been able to instill in her, she has a great deal more discipline now."

He paused. "Unlike during her formative years." He chuckled, and Jenna looked slightly uncomfortable. A lot uncomfortable, maybe.

I thought to myself that if I somehow got out of this a free man, I would have to take Uncle Freddie out for a martini and find out more about Jenna's formative years. He looked like a martini guy, but you never knew.

Jenna invited him to join us at the table. I sat back down myself, as did Jenna. Uncle Freddie declined Jenna's offer of coffee and asked for Earl Grey instead. I waited to find out exactly why he was in town.

Jenna explained. "About ten days ago," she said, "Oscar and I decided we needed a world-class investigator." She nodded at her uncle. "Uncle Freddie is the best of the best, and he's still got a California license."

I hadn't known that Uncle Freddie was a private investigator at all, licensed or unlicensed, and I said so.

"Well," Uncle Freddie said, "I haven't performed this function, really, for more than twenty years. But I inferred from Jenna's detailed account that you were being treated poorly by our vaunted justice system. I do so detest injustice." He stopped and looked at me, clearly waiting for a response of some kind.

"Well, yes, we all detest injustice," I said.

Uncle Freddie seemed satisfied with my bow to his thought and resumed.

"Thus," he said, "when Jenna called, I made an immediate reservation and winged my way here to see what small service I might render in order to be of assistance—to you and to justice."

Uncle Freddie's elaborate language was spectacularly not, I thought to myself, what you'd expect from an oversized private eye, and maybe former drug dealer, from Hawaii.

Jenna had in the meantime gotten up to look for the Earl Grey and put the kettle on. She seemed anxious to move the conversation along, though, and not to dwell on the exact hows and whys of her uncle's presence or provenance. "We don't have a lot of time," she said. "Tell him what you found, Uncle Freddie."

"What I found *so far*," he said. "I suspect there will be a great deal more of interest to uncover. But to commence, I investigated two people Jenna pointed out as obviously suspicious. *Messieurs* Harry Marfan and Stewart Broder."

I obviously knew why they were suspects, but I decided to ask anyway, more to hear Uncle Freddie talk some more than anything else.

"Why them?"

"Mr. Harry Marfan had some involvement," he said, "in that, according to Mr. Serappo Prodiglia, Mr. Marfan had participated, as a silent partner, in the undertaking of purchasing the Ides from you. Although his possible motive is at this point in time a matter of conjecture, he might well, by killing Mr. Simon Rafer, have been trying to conceal something compromising. Something of which Mr. Rafer might have been aware, but cannot now reveal to us given that he has passed into the other realm."

"Plus," I said, "Harry has been fingered by Stewart." I was pleased at my use of what I took to be detective language.

"Correct, indeed," Uncle Freddie said. "If Mr. Stewart Broder is to be believed, Mr. Marfan was quite seriously angry at Mr. Rafer about something and was present on the eighty-fifth floor only hours before the apparent time of Mr. Rafer's unfortunate death. If this is true, Mr. Marfan had opportunity."

"He also knew about the secret compartment," I added, "the one in which we found a counterfeit Ides and a scholarly coin book."

"Precisely," he said. "Although we do not know if he was cognizant of its recent contents."

"And Stewart?"

"He had opportunity, for one. By his own admission, he was present on the eighty-fifth floor not long before the murder, and his office is quite near to Mr. Rafer's. He also seems . . ." Uncle Freddie paused for a moment and then started again. "Let me phrase it this way. He seems to have intruded himself needlessly into this event by coming forward and volunteering information when he had no precise need to. In my profession, we are always prone to be suspicious of that behavior."

"'Equity abhors a volunteer' is the way we put it in my profession," I said.

"Beg pardon?"

"Oh, just an old legal adage that translates as 'volunteers get the shaft.'"

"Ah," he said.

Jenna had poured Freddie's tea and was now standing behind him.

"For God's sake, Uncle Freddie, skip the erudition and tell him what you found out!" In seven years I had never seen her so excited.

"Of course, Jenna, of course. But perhaps it would be best if I were to show the document to Mr. Tarza so that he might see it for himself." Whereupon he reached into his inner suit coat pocket and handed me an off-color, oily-to-the-touch piece of photo paper. It was clearly a printout from an archival microfiche.

I looked at it. As usual, it was so ill-copied and blurry that it was almost impossible to make out.

"I can't read it. What is it?"

"It is none other than a fifteen-year-old arrest record alleging possession of a pound of cocaine."

"Who was arrested?"

"May I suggest that you answer that question yourself by studying the faint, typewritten name set forth in the right-hand corner?"

I studied. And read the typed letters aloud, slowly, "H-A . . . can't read the next two, uh Y . . . then there's a space, maybe M-A- R . . . can't read the rest . . . Shit. Harry Marfan?"

"Precisely."

You could have knocked me over with a spoon. I started to connect the dots. Then I stopped myself. There are a lot of dots out there. If you automatically connect all the stray facts you hear to all the available dots, the next thing you know, the chaotic vagaries of the world will have you believing that the United Nations operates a fleet of black helicopters based in Wyoming and that that the World Trade Center was brought down by elves.

So I restrained myself and said only, "What happened to Harry after that?"

"Nothing at all it would appear. There is no further record of any court action in connection with the matter, and no mention of it in the press."

"I see," I said, still straining to be ho hum about it. "And what do you make of it?"

"In truth, I made little of it at the outset," he said. "I concluded that it should most likely be categorized as a mere oddity of fact. But then I had that difficult-to-read document blown up and examined more carefully, and I learned something else."

I glanced at Jenna. She looked like she was about to witness the cat coughing up the just eaten canary, alive and well. I waited for what was clearly going to be a revelation.

"I learned," Uncle Freddie said, "that the arresting officer at the time was Detective Spritz."

He and Jenna waited for me to react.

I was momentarily speechless. Finally, I said, "Really. And where has *that* led you?"

"Nowhere as yet," Uncle Freddie said. "We have just come into possession of that information. But the coincidences seem too stark to be a product of mere chance. I may have to place Detective Spritz himself on the truncated list of those to be scrutinized more carefully."

Truncated list? Did he mean short list? I could finally stand it no longer. Freddie had a flat, Midwestern accent, but his formal, polysyllabic way of speaking seemed almost a parody of an English don.

"Where did you go to school?" I just blurted it out.

He did not look put off by the question. "I went to a British-run private high school in Singapore. I acquired an excellent education, but was fortunate not to acquire the plummy accent along with it."

I felt horribly embarrassed. I had simply assumed that his use of language suggested academic origins at some erudite college or graduate school.

Uncle Freddie let me promptly off the hook. "Don't fear, my good man. People often mistake my use of language, so forcefully beaten into me by my British schoolmasters, as an *indicium* that I have an elaborate higher education. But in truth, Mr. Tarza . . . May I call you Robert?"

"Of course."

"In truth, Robert, I am just a simple former detective of uncertain talent who ventured into business for himself. It was my brother, the late Senator James, who went on to higher academic achievement."

"Okay." I had no idea what business he was talking about or what Senator James had achieved academically. Maybe I'd ask later. But I still felt embarrassed at having put the question to him. There seemed nothing left but to ask if he had learned anything interesting about Stewart.

"May I call you Freddie?" I asked.

"I prefer Frederick, actually. I permit Jenna to call me Uncle Freddie as a relic from her childhood."

"I understand perfectly," I said. "Frederick, did you find out anything of interest about Stewart?"

"Only a small thing."

"Which was?"

"Something I haven't as yet informed Jenna about, since it was only discovered in the early hours of this morning. To wit, inside what you and Jenna refer to as the secret compartment in Stewart's office, a dagger was concealed."

"I don't see how I could have missed that," Jenna said.

"The dagger was taped to the upper surface of the compartment. An amateur peering inside with a torch might well have missed it. Particularly if she were looking in with only a small torch rather than a large one."

I was curiously unflabbergasted. Who knew what was coming next. "Does it look like the dagger used to kill Simon?"

"It is not dissimilar," he said. "The photo taken of it is being digitally enhanced for better detail. You will be able to examine it later in the day. The dagger was also dusted for prints, but comparative results on that are not in our hands as yet."

Jenna was, apparently, flabbergasted. "Are you sure of all this, Uncle Freddie?"

"Yes, I most certainly am, since I examined the dagger myself before returning it to the place in which I had found it."

"You did it yourself?"

"Well, yes. I was perhaps a bit rusty, but it was certainly not the most difficult surreptitious entry to a building and office suite that I've performed."

Uncle Freddie had finished his tea. Jenna picked up the empty cup and moved it to the sink. Over her shoulder, she asked, "How did you get into the building?"

Uncle Freddie smiled, for the first time really. "The security in that building, to use the vernacular, sucks." He laughed uproariously. I remarked to myself that when we went out for that martini, I'd have to ask exactly how he got in and why he found it all so humorous.

Jenna was standing by the door to the garage. "We have to go," she said. "We don't want to be late and screw up the arrangements I've made to get you into the courthouse in a way that avoids the Blob."

I didn't know exactly what those arrangements were, but I certainly didn't want to screw them up. I got up to leave. Uncle Freddie was still sitting at the table. It was odd, leaving a near-stranger in my house. But a lot of things had been odd lately. As we reached the door that led to the garage, I realized I had another question. "Frederick, have you told any of this to Oscar?"

"Not as yet. We learned of Harry's peculiar *histoire* only late yesterday afternoon, and I undertook the surreptitious entry mere hours ago."

We left my garage in Jenna's Land Cruiser. I grumpily sat in the third row of seats, as requested. Humiliating as that was. I nixed the blanket idea, but it appeared that the tinted windows did an adequate job. I could see some of the Blob through the front windshield, but not much of it, and I doubted they could see much of me through the tinted side windows. I mainly knew the Blob was there from the bright television lights that went on as we drove out, plus the shouting of questions, apparently aimed at me even though no one could see me.

"Jenna," I asked as we cleared the bottom of the driveway, "did any of those idiots really think I was going to lower my window to answer their questions?"

"Probably not," she said. "The third row window doesn't even open."

I ignored her sarcasm. "Why hasn't the Blob been moved back? Wasn't that part of your deal with the DA?"

"I don't know," she said.

"I think you should do something about it."

"I have more important things to think about right now," she said.

"I think that's very important," I said. "Keeping deals is very important."

"Robert?"

"What?"

"Why don't you just relax and try to be less of an asshole?"

I shut up.

The rest of the drive to court was uneventful. No news vans followed us. Benitez had kept his promise and arranged with the Sheriff's Department that we be permitted to enter the Criminal Court Building through the underground garage. We didn't have to penetrate the thick Blob outside, and we were permitted to use a private elevator to reach the Seventh Floor.

CHAPTER 36

————

I walked into the courtroom with Jenna shortly before eight. I looked around and felt immediately uncomfortable. Maybe it was because every seat in the courtroom was filled, even the chairs in the jury box—filled by a combination of Blob members and the fifteen trial junkies who had won the daily lottery for the public seats.

Or maybe it was because I felt so out of control as a defendant. As a lawyer in courtrooms, I had always had a sense of control. Even if the judges liked to pretend that *they* were in control. But as we sat down at the defense table, I felt instead a sense of disorientation that approached vertigo.

Jenna put her hand on my shoulder. I recognized the gesture as the intuitive laying on of hands to soothe a nervous client. I took a deep breath.

I looked over to the prosecution table. At first, it was empty. Then Benitez arrived. He was slim, tall, good looking, and impeccably dressed in a well-tailored, blue pinstripe suit. Even nicer than Serappo's. I remarked to myself that if I survived all this, I'd have to ask him where he bought his suits. His jet black hair was almost down to his shoulders. He was at least in his late forties. If his hair wasn't dyed, I don't live in Los Angeles. He put a white cardboard file box on the table and took his seat.

Benitez had two assistants with him. Jenna was by herself. After much discussion, some of it heated, we had decided that in the prelim it would look better for me to have a lone defender, and that it should be Jenna. Oscar would do the trial.

Actually, it was Jenna and Oscar who had decided on that strategy, over my initial objection. First, they had pushed the baseball analogy—Oscar was like the pitcher, witnesses were like batters, the trial would be a new ballgame, and batters didn't do well against a good pitcher they'd never faced before. That hadn't persuaded me. I've always been deeply suspicious of baseball analogies. Too many improbable things happen in baseball games every day.

Then they had pointed out that Johnnie Cochran hadn't been the lead in the O. J. Simpson prelim. Just in the trial. And look how well that had worked out! Finally, I yielded. Or maybe just gave up. Jenna would start, and Oscar would come later in the morning and slip quietly into the back of the courtroom, where a seat had been reserved for him. That way, he could watch the press watching us.

So there I sat with just Jenna, waiting for the hearing to begin. Which is not to say that I was totally okay with the choice. I was still uneasy about it. Perhaps because, with the exception of her brief stint with the U.S. Attorney's Office, almost everything Jenna knew about trial lawyering she had learned from me. It was going to be a kind of self-test.

But it was what it was, and there we were.

The Honorable Tassy Gilmore entered the courtroom at 8:00 a.m. on the dot, and we all rose. I hadn't seen or spoken to Tassy in more than twenty-five years. Not since Marbury Marfan had failed to offer her a job when she graduated from law school. She had been at the very top of her law school class, but from a local school not then well regarded by my brothers at M&M—most of whom were indeed of the brotherly persuasion at the time.

I recalled my interview with her like it had been yesterday. We had sat in my office and discussed a hot copyright case the Supreme Court had just handed down. I was impressed with her. She was clearly smart and even good-looking, in that slim, almost bony, tallish-blonde kind of way. I also remembered her nail polish. Most women law students back then didn't go out of their way to emphasize their femininity. Tassy, by contrast, had long nails painted blood red. When the Hiring Committee had discussed her and decided to ding her, to use the language of the time, her nail polish occasioned almost as much comment as the generally low opinion of her law school. Had it been left to me, I would have hired her. But I hadn't felt strongly about it and elected to spend no marbles on her. Now Tassy Gilmore—*Judge* Gilmore to me—had all the marbles.

My brief reverie was interrupted by Judge Gilmore.

"We are here in the matter of People of the State of California versus Robert Tarza. Mr. Benitez, are the People ready to proceed?"

He remained seated. "Yes, Your Honor."

"Ms. James, is the defense ready to proceed?"

Jenna stood up. "Yes, Your Honor."

"Mr. Benitez, how long do you estimate your case is going to be?"

"Maybe two days, Your Honor."

"Ms. James?"

"It depends on what the People put on. I'm guessing an hour or two at most."

"Okay. We'll run till 10:00 each morning, with a fifteen minute break, then till 12:15. Lunch is an hour. So back here at 1:15, afternoon break at 3:00, then out of here at 4:30. And Counsel . . ."

Jenna and Benitez tipped their heads, waiting for whatever the judge was about to say.

"I run a very tight ship, and my schedule means something. If you're in the middle of a question when it's time for a break, I don't care. We break. There's no jury here. And don't be late coming back." She pointed a finger in their general direction. Her nail polish was as blood red as ever. "If you're late, I'll start without you."

"Yes, Your Honor." The two of them said it almost in unison.

"Mr. Benitez, do you have any preliminary matters you need to take up with the Court before we begin?"

Benitez finally stood up. "Only, Your Honor, that Ms. James and I have stipulated to the entry into evidence of a number of items. I'd like to present the Court with a set of copies."

"Let's get to each of those as we go along. That will be most efficient. Ms. James, do you have anything of a preliminary nature?"

"Thank you. No, I don't." Jenna sat back down.

"Let's get started then. Mr. Benitez, call your first witness."

Benitez moved to the lectern, speaking as he went. "The People call Henrietta Krepliak."

A woman who looked to be in her late fifties rose from the front row of seats, passed through the little swinging door that separates the onlookers from the court—the bar, as we lawyers call it—and took her seat on the witness stand. She looked quite harmless. As she was being sworn to tell the truth, she also looked quite nervous. I guessed that, unlike cops or other professional witnesses, she hadn't done this a hundred times before. Maybe never.

Benitez looked down at his notes, as we all waited. Then he began.

"Could you state your full name for the record?"

"Henrietta Morton Krepliak."

"What is your profession?"

"I'm a 911 operator employed by the County of Los Angeles."

"How long have you been so employed?"

"Fifteen years."

"On the morning of Monday, December 6, did you receive an emergency call concerning a murder?"

I nudged Jenna and whispered in her ear, *"He's leading her. Object!"* She whispered back, *"He's not and doesn't matter. We're here to learn."* She shot me a glance. *"Try to be a client."*

Henrietta Krepliak was meanwhile in the process of answering Benitez's question.

". . . the caller said that someone had been murdered."

"Did he identify himself?"

"Yes, he said his name was Robert Tarza."

"Did Mr. Tarza use the word 'murdered' or some other word?"

"He said, 'Someone has been *murdered.*'"

"Did he seem upset?"

I could see immediately where this was going. So could Jenna, who was on her feet with something to get in the way.

"Objection, Your Honor. Ms. Krepliak's testimony is not the best evidence of how my client *seemed.* The tape of the call is."

The objection was, in fact, enormously thin. While the tape might be the best evidence of what was actually said, someone who had participated in the conversation could certainly testify about her own impressions of that conversation and first present her recollection of the actual words said in order to do that.

"Mr. Benitez, what about that?"

I was surprised. Judge Gilmore wasn't going to overrule the objection out of hand? Perhaps Judge Gilmore knew we'd not gotten our hands on the tape, despite our repeated requests for it. Or so my lawyers had told me the night before.

Benitez looked down at the podium as if he were consulting his notes. Not exactly charismatic. "Your Honor, as counsel well knows. So Ms. Krepliak's testimony *is* currently the best evidence of what was said."

Judge Gilmore's eyebrows shot up. "Missing? What happened to it?"

"We don't know, Your Honor. It was checked into the police evidence locker and is now gone. We suspect someone checked it out but forgot to sign for it. We're investigating."

Jenna was still standing. "Mr. Benitez has indeed informed me that the tape is missing, Your Honor. Just yesterday, of course. But there should also be a digital copy of the call on the 911 computer."

Benitez was still looking at his notes. "Um, that's right. But it's missing, too."

Judge Gilmore was looking ever more interested. "Did someone check that out, too?"

"No, Your Honor, it was either never recorded or subsequently erased."

As I listened to this exchange, I thought to myself: How important can a recording of my 911 call be? I'm not denying that I called.

"Well," Judge Gilmore said, "this is certainly an inauspicious start to your case, Mr. Benitez. But it's a rather minor piece of evidence. Since this is just a preliminary hearing, which of course has no jury, I'll rule for now that Ms. Krepliak's recollections of the call are the best evidence. Please repeat your question."

Benitez finally looked up from his papers. "Ms. Krepliak, did the caller," and he nodded in my direction, "seem upset?"

"No."

"How many calls have you heard in your career where someone reported a death?"

She smiled. "Well, sometimes the people who get reported dead aren't dead."

Benitez looked surprised at the momentary bump in his no-doubt well-planned direct examination of his witness. "Yes, of course. But if we include those, too, how many?"

"Maybe a thousand."

"Of those thousand callers, how many sounded upset when they told you someone was dead?"

Jenna stood up. "Objection, Your Honor. No foundation has been laid for the expertise of this witness in assessing the psychological mindset of someone who calls 911. She has not been qualified as a psychologist, and . . ."

Benitez interrupted her. "I'm not asking Ms. Krepliak to assess the psychological significance of anything. I'm just asking her what she's used to hearing. A lay person can certainly testify if they think someone sounded upset or not." He looked annoyed. The objection was, in fact, something of a bullshit objection, at least at this point in Krepliak's testimony.

Now it was Jenna who looked upset, agitated even. "Maybe so, Your Honor, but I can see where this is going . . ."

Tassy Gilmore shrugged. "I can, too, Ms. James. But let's let it go there and stop wasting all of our time. I'm not your grandmother's pumpkin, you know. I'll weigh this evidence appropriately as it comes in."

Judge Gilmore looked at Benitez. "Go ahead, Mr. Benitez, but I hope you're ultimately going to have something more impressive than this."

"Oh, we will, Your Honor. We will." He looked back down at his notes. "Okay, Ms. Krepliak, I think the question was: Of the thousand callers who called someone in as dead, how many sounded upset?"

"Almost all of them."

"How did Mr. Tarza sound?"

"Calm as flat water. Like he was calling in a downed tree limb."

Jenna made her objection sitting down. "I renew my objection. No foundation."

"Overruled."

As the ruling came, I pushed a note toward Jenna: *Why give a shit?* She scribbled something on the note and pushed it back: *BLOB*!! I suddenly realized that all the action in the courtroom had come to a halt as everyone watched our exchange. Despite our best efforts to be invisible about it.

Benitez started up again. "Did you say anything to Mr. Tarza after he told you that he was reporting a murder?"

"Yes. I asked him if he was sure the victim was dead."

"What did he say?"

"He said, 'Very sure.'"

"Did you say anything else?"

"Yes, I asked him for the address, and he gave it to me." She paused. "Well, initially he gave me the wrong floor. But then he corrected himself."

"Did he say why he got it wrong to start with?"

"He said something about accidentally misspeaking."

I heard Jenna say "shit" under her breath.

"Did you say anything else to him?"

"I asked him if he himself had any weapons, and he said no. Then I told him not to touch anything and to remain there until the police arrived."

"What, if anything, did he say in response?"

"He said, 'Sure.'"

"Did you take any action with regard to the call?"

"Yes, I routed the information to the LAPD dispatch center with an urgent tag on it."

"Thank you. I have no further questions."

Jenna got up and moved to the podium. As I watched her, I wondered if she looked too young to be my lawyer. Then I put the thought out of my mind and concentrated on the fact that Jenna had no notes. Unlike the note-bound Benitez. It hardly mattered in this hearing, though. Jurors sometimes liked lawyers who worked without a lot of notes. But there weren't yet any jurors to impress.

"Good morning, Ms. Krepliak." That was something I had taught Jenna in our first trial together. Always greet the witness, even if they're hostile. Juries like polite lawyers.

"Good morning."

"Ms. Krepliak, how long after the events of Monday, December 6, were you first questioned by the police about Mr. Tarza's call?"

"Maybe four or five days later."

"How many calls do you usually handle a day?"

"Maybe seventy or eighty when it's busy."

"So between the time you handled Mr. Tarza's call and when the police interviewed you, you handled perhaps 300 other calls?"

"Yes."

"How many of those calls involved reports of a death?"

Krepliak looked thoughtful. "I'm not sure. Maybe ten or twenty."

"Sitting here today, do you remember the tone of voice of any particular one of those ten or twenty callers?"

Krepliak looked caught. I could see her struggling to find a way out of the trap if she answered yes. She decided to avoid that fate. "No, no I don't."

I realized that I was on the edge of my seat, waiting for Jenna to choose whether to go further and ask Krepliak whether she had any special reason to remember my call. Or just to let a good enough answer well enough alone. She decided on something in between.

"Ms. Krepliak, when you received Mr. Tarza's call, did you have any reason, from the outset, to think it would be an unusual call?"

"No."

Then Jenna apparently decided that Krepliak's answers in that area were now good enough, and took out her knife.

"Ms. Krepliak, if I remember an earlier answer correctly, you said that in your experience *almost* all the people who called in a death sounded upset."

"Yes."

"So 'almost' means some people didn't sound upset, isn't that right?"

"Right."

I could see it coming. I don't know if Krepliak herself could. I noticed Benitez squirming. He could see it. Judge Gilmore had a beatific smile on her face. She could see it, too.

"Did you ever learn whether *any* of those people, those people who you say didn't sound upset, had murdered somebody?"

Krepliak looked like a deer caught in the headlights. "Well . . . no."

Then Jenna twisted the knife. "So, Ms. Krepliak, you don't really have any basis at all, do you, for connecting up your *perception* of a caller's tone of voice with a guilty conscience, do you?"

"Objection. Irrelevant." The mostly silent Benitez was suddenly alive. "I didn't ask Ms. Krepliak to make that connection."

"Overruled."

Krepliak answered. "I'm not sure."

Unlike in a TV drama, Jenna didn't respond to the witness by saying, "Well, *I'm sure*," or ask that Krepliak be ordered to answer the question yes or no. Instead, she just let the non-answer hang there, looked over at me, and raised her eyebrows. That was our private signal, developed over six trials together. It asked, Shall I take a wild stab? The supposed rule in cross-examination is never to ask a question to which you don't already know the answer. But that rule can be violated, sometimes to spectacularly good effect. There was no downside here. I raised my eyebrows in response. Go for it.

"Ms. Krepliak, back on December 6, when you received Mr. Tarza's call, were you under any personal stress?"

Benitez was up again. "Objection. This surely goes beyond the scope of direct."

Judge Gilmore didn't wait for Jenna to respond to Benitez, and she looked annoyed. "Counsel, the mental state of a percipient witness when she perceived something, a 'something' that *you* brought out on direct, is right at the heart of proper cross-examination. Overruled." I had noticed long ago that when judges switch to calling lawyers whose names they know full well "Counsel," it was not a good thing.

Krepliak sat there without answering.

"There is a question before you, Ms. Krepliak," Jenna said.

"Sort of."

"Sort of?"

"That afternoon, I was scheduled to go to a custody hearing in my divorce."

"So you were under some stress?"

"You could say that."

"And you were trying to stay . . ." Jenna stretched out the pause before uttering the next word. . . "calm?"

"Yes."

"Thank you, I have nothing further."

I looked at the judge looking at Benitez. Normally, a lawyer with redirect to do would already be moving toward the podium. Benitez was just sitting there. Thinking about it.

"Any redirect Counsel?"

He sat for a second longer, staring at his papers. "No, Your Honor."

Benitez could have tried to repair the damage Jenna had done. There were a number of ways to attempt it. But he had clearly decided not to risk making it worse. Krepliak wasn't important to his case. All he had had to do with her, really, was put her on the stand for two minutes to start the timeline of his case. Get her to report receipt of the call, to identify the caller, to say what time he called, and what he said. Then out of there.

Gussying up her testimony with the "calm as flat water" stuff had been a gambit to hand a headline to the Blob. Something like, *Tarza Cold As Ice in 911 Call*. Now the gambit had, if it had not failed entirely, been at least blunted. So Benitez decided to cut his losses and move on. I could only hope the next witness would be as easy.

CHAPTER 37

There was a moment of silence in the courtroom as Judge Gilmore looked down and made some notes. I assumed she was making a note about something Krepliak had said. Then she looked back up.

"Mr. Benitez," Judge Gilmore said, "please call your next witness."

"The People call Detective Lionel Spritz."

Lionel? I had never heard Spritz's first name before, or bothered to ask if he even had one. Certainly I knew that *Detective* wasn't his first name, but somehow it had seemed to be. In any case, Detective Lionel Spritz did not promise to be easy.

Benitez did not go to the podium to start questioning Spritz or even stand up. He just continued to sit at the table and watched Spritz walk to the stand. You can do that if you want to in some courtrooms. With no jury present, it probably makes little difference whether you stand or sit. Spritz was sworn and Benitez, still sitting, began.

"Detective, what is your position?"

"I am a sworn officer in the Los Angeles Police Department, with the rank of Detective III."

"Do you have a particular specialty or assignment within the Police Department?"

"Yes, I am assigned to the Robbery-Homicide Division."

"How long have you been with the LAPD?"

"More than thirty years."

"Were you gainfully employed prior to joining the Police Department?"

"Yes. For two years prior to that I was a criminal investigator in the Los Angeles District Attorney's Office."

"And before that?"

"I was a first lieutenant in the United States Marine Corps. Three years."

"What was your specialty in the Marine Corps?"

"During my entire three years, I was in the Criminal Investigation Division working as a criminal investigator."

"Did you serve overseas?"

"Yes, I saw service in Vietnam."

"Could you describe in more detail your investigatory duties in Vietnam?"

"I investigated felony accusations against enlisted personnel."

"During that time did you receive any merit decorations for particular investigations that you conducted?"

Before Spritz could answer, Judge Gilmore interrupted.

"Counsel," Judge Gilmore said, "I'm sure Detective Spritz's career in the Marines is fascinating and very distinguished. But since there's no jury sitting over there in the jury box . . ." She paused and waved her hand toward the eighteen chairs to her right, all of them currently filled by the Blob's courtroom cousins, then continued, "I think you can move along."

I glanced over at the cousins and thought they looked uncomfortable at being pointed to, even in so collective a way. Because we all understood that Judge Gilmore's wave in their direction was intended to remind everyone of a key fact—the Blob's presence was the real reason Benitez was asking about Spritz's medals or whatever kudos he had received.

"Alright, Your Honor," Benitez said. "I can come back to Detective Spritz's deeper background experience if it becomes relevant."

"Yes," Judge Gilmore said. "*If* . . . it becomes relevant."

I was actually disappointed at the judge's intervention. Spritz had lately become a looming presence in my life, but he was still something of a stick figure. I had been fascinated to watch Benitez ink clothing on the stick.

I was also amused at the small hole that Benitez had dug for himself. In the face of such a small loss, he should just have said "Thank you, Your Honor," and moved on. Instead, he tried to cover his butt by carving out a reason to try again later. Which he could have done anyway. So all he had done in the end was to irritate the judge. If you do that kind of thing a lot, it can turn a judge against you. Fatally. Back when I taught trial practice, I used to warn young lawyers against it.

Benitez resumed. "Detective, did you investigate the murder of Simon Rafer?"

"Yes. I'm the lead detective on the investigation. Of course, we're still investigating that murder."

"When did you begin the investigation?"

"On the morning of the murder, shortly after 6:00 a.m. I received a call on my cell phone from an LAPD dispatcher informing me that a single homicide had taken place in a high-rise downtown office building. The dispatcher gave me the address, and I proceeded to the suspect building."

"What time did you arrive there?"

"Approximately 6:15 a.m."

"Did you have any difficulty gaining entrance to the building?"

"Not really. The lobby doors were already unlocked. A building receptionist had just arrived. After I showed him my badge, he told me the elevators were already unlocked and that I could go ahead and take Elevator 3 up to the eighty-fifth floor."

"Did anyone go up with you?"

"Yes. Officers Wong and Apple had been patrolling nearby and had responded to a backup call. I had called for backup on my way there. They arrived at almost the same time I did and accompanied me up the elevator."

"Did anyone else accompany you?"

"Well, Officer Hermann arrived just as we were about to enter the elevator. I told him the little I knew and instructed him to remain in the lobby to interview the building receptionist and monitor the perimeter while we went up."

"What did you find when you stepped off the elevator on the eighty-fifth floor?"

"We went up first to the eighty-fourth floor. I wanted to use an internal stairway to go up to eighty-five. I judged it to be tactically imprudent to elevator directly to the suspect floor."

It was the first time I'd ever heard *elevator* used as a verb. And rapt as I was on hearing these details for the first time, I was amused to hear first the building and then the floor referred to as suspects. Apparently I had not been the sole suspect.

"What happened when you arrived on the eighty-fourth floor?"

"We found the elevator lobby deserted. We then proceeded up a wide internal stairway that came out into the law firm's main reception area on the eighty-fifth floor."

"What did you observe there?"

"We observed a body, one that I later learned to be that of Mr. Simon Rafer."

"Please describe the body."

"The body was face-down in a large, carpeted reception area. It was lying halfway between a reception desk and a set of double doors that led from the reception area into the elevator lobby. A knife with an ornate handle was plunged up to the hilt in the victim's back. The knife was approximately in the middle of his back, about halfway down. The body was surrounded by a very large pool of blood, mostly brown and congealed."

"Did you also observe the defendant at that point?"

"Yes. He was standing between the body and the entry doors into the reception area, approximately three feet from the body. He was wearing a suit, had his arms folded, and appeared calm. He looked almost like he was guarding it."

"What did you do next?"

"I instructed Officer Apple to frisk the defendant and conduct a brief interview. I also instructed him to determine if the defendant knew of anyone on the floor or elsewhere who was armed or otherwise a threat or who should be detained. Then I knelt down and touched two fingers to the victim's neck to see if I could detect a pulse."

"What did you find?"

"There was no pulse. I also noted that the neck was cold to the touch. Well below normal body temperature. The victim was clearly dead. This did not surprise me. There was a large volume of blood on the carpet. He might well have exsanguinated."

Benitez was doing a nice job. Simple, direct questions. Letting the witness, not the questions, tell the story.

"What did you do next?"

"I spoke again with Officer Apple. He reported that the defendant told him that he had found the body when he arrived at work at about 6:00 a.m. and knew of no one nearby who was a threat."

I waited to see if Jenna would make the hearsay objection. Coming out of Spritz's mouth, what I told Apple, which Apple had in turn passed on to Spritz, seemed to me to be so-called totem pole hearsay—hearsay-on-hearsay—and inadmissible. Jenna could have objected.

As I expected, though, she sat silent. The hearsay didn't matter this time because Spritz was repeating accurately what I had said to Apple. He had to, because Apple's report of his interview with me was right there in the murder book. Also, Oscar had told me that there was an exception to the hearsay rule for police officers testifying at a preliminary hearing. Plus things I said, if related by a witness to whom I said them, would likely be subject to an exception to the hearsay rule. Maybe Jenna just didn't want to get into all that.

Spritz had left out one thing in his answer, though. I assumed Jenna would get to it on cross if Benitez didn't cover it on direct.

Benitez was continuing. "Where was Officer Wong at that time, Detective?"

"I had asked her to reconnaissance the floor to be sure there was no one else present. At the time Officer Apple reported to me, Officer Wong had not yet returned from that mission."

I wondered to myself exactly what Officer Wong had seen on her tour of the floor. It was a tour I had never been able to take that day. But Officer Wong's written report was silent on the matter, except to say that she had observed nothing significant. Apparently, she had not observed the blood stain on my office couch.

"What did you do next?"

"I ordered Officer Apple to immediately secure the crime scene with tape and to designate the entire floor as a crime scene. I also told him to ask the defendant to move into the elevator lobby and to remain there."

"What did you do after that?"

"I called the coroner's office and learned that a van had already been dispatched. Then I called my dispatcher to request a crime scene team. She told me it was already on its way."

"While you were there, did you observe anything else of interest to you?"

"Yes, I observed a large, longish depression in the carpeting, in the shape of a body. It was located toward the left-rear corner of the reception area, just behind a large plant, its length parallel with the reception desk."

"Did you observe anything else about the depression in the carpeting?"

"Yes. There were some blue-black fibers visible in it."

"Did you draw any conclusions from the nature of the depression?"

Jenna was on her feet. "Objection. Detective Spritz has not been qualified as an expert on anything, let alone carpet depressions, so he can't proffer an expert conclusion. And I smell an expert conclusion coming."

Judge Gilmore cocked her head. "Fe, fi, fo, fum," she said. The courtroom burst into laughter.

As we waited for the laughter to subside, I made a bet with myself that the judge was thinking the same thing I was thinking. That it would be a waste of time to argue about all this before we had heard the conclusion Spritz actually wanted to utter. But Jenna's objection was legitimate enough. Had there been a jury there, it would have been critical to make it. You can't un-ring the bell once a jury's heard it rung.

Judge Gilmore made her ruling. "Ms. James, you may be right. But since there's no jury here, let's hear the conclusion first. You can reserve your right to move to strike the answer if it's improper."

"Thank you, Your Honor," Jenna said.

Jenna had probably seen the ruling coming, too, but I understood her purpose. To remind the media that Spritz wasn't necessarily an expert on anything. To get in the way of the smooth flow of testimony. And maybe to show, as Brendan Sullivan, a prominent defense lawyer, once famously said, that she wasn't just a potted plant.

Benitez had not said anything in response. He could have nipped the whole thing in the bud by saying, "Let me rephrase," and laying a proper foundation for Spritz's expertise. But he no doubt knew the capabilities of his own witness, who had not exactly fallen off the turnip truck onto the witness stand. Spritz had probably been there a hundred times.

Judge Gilmore turned to Spritz. "You may answer."

"Well," Spritz said, "based on my many years of experience in the field, including literal fields in Vietnam, I have observed that murder crime scenes often feature body-shaped depressions which later turn out, when all the evidence is in, to be places where a perpetrator was lying in wait for a victim. In this case, I concluded that the depression in the plush carpet held a shape very similar to those which, *in my experience*, the bodies of perpetrators typically make when lying in wait on a soft surface." He smirked.

So Spritz had listened to Jenna's objection and fixed it himself by vouching in his answer for his own expertise. It was enough, at least to the level necessary for this kind of hearing. Spritz was indeed well down the road from the turnip truck.

Jenna could have renewed her objection on the grounds that Spritz had not testified to specific experience with depressions in carpeting. But, wisely in my view, she made no further objection.

"Was there anything else that led you to conclude that, Detective?" Benitez asked.

"Yes. The presence of some blue-black fibers in the depression. Based on my *experience*, they could have come from clothing."

I waited to see if Jenna would object that Spritz had not laid a foundation that he had any experience at all in distinguishing clothing fibers from drapery fibers. Or from anything else. But Jenna made no objection, so Benitez had no doubt nailed his intended headline: "Tarza Suit Fibers Match Fibers in Carpet Where Killer Hid." The additional "fact" that the fibers supposedly matched fibers from my suit would, of course, be attributed to an anonymous source, no doubt one inside the DA's office.

Benitez decided to go further and gild the media lily. "Detective, did you later learn whether any comparative fiber analysis had been done on those fibers?"

I could see Jenna tense on the edge of her seat.

"Yes, I did. The LAPD crime lab compared—"

Jenna shot into the air. "Objection, Your Honor! Detective Spritz is about to announce the written results of some unidentified crime lab test.

Not the best evidence, not to mention utterly without foundation, not to mention hearsay."

Benitez rose. "Your Honor, I have the fiber lab report right here, which I can use to lay a basis for the detective's testimony. It'll be admissible through him as a record which—"

The Judge cut him off in mid-sentence. "Maybe so, Counsel. But it's going to be achingly inefficient. Bring in the lab tech who actually did the analysis. Do it that way." As she said it, her clerk handed her a note, and I saw her glance down at it.

Benitez sat back down. "I have no further questions, Your Honor."

I was stunned. That was it? They weren't going to ask him about his interview with me? Or what I said to him at the meeting in my office? Or the blood on my cuff? I felt like a star whose best footage has been left on the cutting room floor.

Benitez was still speaking. ". . . but I'd like to reserve the right to recall Detective Spritz later in the hearing if I need to."

Judge Gilmore just looked at him. "That's quite an unusual request from the District Attorney's office concerning the lead detective on a case. I don't usually permit such witnesses to testify piecemeal. Too much like a movie shoot. One shot here, one shot there." She wagged her head back and forth as she said it. Her comment reminded me that Judge Gilmore was married to a movie director. Not a very good one, but a director nonetheless.

"I know Your Honor," Benitez said, "but this is an unusual circumstance."

Jenna had said nothing. She was applying a small but important rule of trial lawyering. If the judge is hanging someone, you don't need to help hold the rope.

I saw Judge Gilmore glance down again at the note.

"Okay, Mr. Benitez," she said. "Unless there's an objection, I'll let you do it this one time. Ms. James, is there an objection?" It was asked in a way that clearly said, 'I'm really busy right now, please don't object, I'll make it up to you.'

"No, Your Honor," Jenna said. "But if that actually happens, I want to reserve the right to inquire of Mr. Spritz *and* Mr. Benitez what caused the delay. I'd also like the right to split the testimony of one of my own witnesses if I need to." Jenna smiled slightly as she finished making the second request.

Judge Gilmore smiled back. It was a "nice try" smile, but the smile was a good sign I thought. "You've got your first request, Ms. James. We'll see about the second. Don't count on it."

Judge Gilmore had moved the note up, where we could see it more clearly. She was holding it in her right hand and conversing with her clerk while she shielded her mouth from view with the other hand. I saw her motion to the bailiff, an armed sheriff's deputy who sits at a little desk at the rear of the courtroom. He got up and moved toward the bench. Then she turned to speak.

"Ladies and gentleman, I apologize. There is an unexpected bit of official business I need to attend to. I don't expect it to take more than a minute or two. There is no need to leave the courtroom, and I expect to resume with Ms. James' cross-examination of Detective Spritz the moment I return to the bench."

With that, she got up and went through the door to her chambers, followed by the clerk and the bailiff.

I wondered what official business might require a man with a gun.

CHAPTER 38

Jenna turned to me instantly. The unexpected break was a Godsend. Lawyers love to have a minute or two, before starting cross-examination, to talk to co-counsel or the client. Jenna leaned in close and whispered to me.

"Suggestions?"

"Maybe we should just let him go, Jenna. He didn't hurt us much . . ."

"If this were a jury trial, maybe. But here we can go fishing for free."

"The Blob will get to smell any bad fish you pull up."

Jenna paused a second, considering my point.

"I'm going to fish, Robert. There's gotta be a reason Benitez only scratched the surface with Spritz . . ."

"Okay," I said.

We both straightened back up.

I looked down at my notes, where I had marked testimony that needed coming back to. It's my habit to write out the answers an opposing witness has given and circle a word for follow-up or make a check mark in the margin beside something unclear or suspect. I tore the pages out of my tablet and handed them to Jenna. She read through them and smiled when she got to the end, where I had written, in big block letters, "START WITH A LIE, END WITH A BANG."

It was a tactic I'd taught her. Try to start a cross by catching the witness in a small lie. In the middle, have the witness clarify some unimportant things. At the end, ask the witness about something important that you can't quite nail him on. If the witness gives an evasive or "can't remember" kind of answer, a juror will remember the small lie at the beginning and assume the witness is telling a big lie at the end.

Judge Gilmore and her clerk returned to the courtroom. The bailiff was not with them.

"Counsel," Judge Gilmore said, "please approach the bench."

I started to get up, and then sat back down. She didn't mean me.

Jenna got up and walked to the sidebar. Benitez went next. The court reporter followed with her steno machine. It was going to be an away from public ears transcribed session up there. A sidebar, despite what has happened in some highly publicized trials, is unusual. Judges don't like them, and with no jury present, there's usually little reason to shield what's being said. The conference took but a moment. I saw the judge talk, Jenna respond, and Benitez say something animated. Then the judge again.

Jenna headed to the lectern to start her cross of Spritz. She didn't have time to come by the table and tell me what had been said. As she reached the lectern, she just gave me a tiny shrug of the shoulders. I took it to mean the conference had been neither here nor there.

"Detective Spritz," Jenna said, "you testified that Detective Apple told you," she consulted her notes, "that, and I quote, 'Defendant told him he had found the body when he arrived at work at about 6:00 a.m. and knew of no one nearby who was a threat.' Is that correct, Detective?"

"Yes."

"Did Detective Apple tell you anything else that Mr. Tarza had told him?"

"Huh. Now that I think about it, I think maybe he did."

"What would that be, Detective?"

"He said the defendant told him he didn't do it."

"Thank you." Jenna cast a quick glance at me. I shook my head. I was confirming her instinct: *Don't ask Spritz why he forgot to mention it before. Don't touch it.*

Asking him would create a hole through which an experienced witness like Spritz would drive a truck. He'd say something like, "because I have been so overwhelmed since then with evidence of the defendant's guilt, it just drove his self-serving statement clean out of my mind."

Let Benitez try to fix the problem on redirect if he could, and if he dared.

Jenna simply moved on to something else.

"Detective, let me turn to the 'depression'"—she raised both hands and used her fingers to depict quote marks around the word—"in the rug. Do you know if a picture of it exists somewhere?"

I knew she was asking because, despite the death penalty threat Drady had made to me in the squad car, we had been unable to locate such a picture in the murder book or anywhere else, and the police had simply said they were still "looking." Indeed, Spritz was the only one who had mentioned anything about a carpet depression in a written report.

"No, I don't know if a picture of it exists somewhere." I noted that Spritz had carefully chosen to give an answer that mimicked the exact words of the question. Always an invitation to ask more questions. I could see Jenna thinking what to ask.

"Detective, does it surprise you that no picture exists, at least so far as you know?"

"Yes, it does."

"Why is that?"

"Because I asked that one be taken."

"Who did you ask to take it?"

"I asked Officer Wong to get it done when the crime scene team arrived."

"So she failed to do that?"

"No, I believe she did instruct the crime scene photographer to do so. But my understanding is that by then the crime scene and coroner's representatives had already obliterated the depression by walking on it."

I laughed quietly to myself. We had been had. Without a picture of the depression, there was no chance in hell of any jury buying a lying-in-wait special circumstance count. No matter how vehement Spritz was about having seen the depression himself and no matter what kind of fibers were in the carpet. They had bluffed us out. And used the bluff to scare me into this early prelim. At least I'd thrown up on them in the course of their duplicity. I waited to see if Jenna was just going to leave it, or go for more. I might have left it. She decided to see if she could hang the error on Spritz.

"You had delegated Officer Apple to tape off the crime scene, right?"

"Yes. Earlier."

"Did you tell him to tape off the supposed carpet depression as a special area?"

"It wasn't a supposed depression," he said.

She was getting to him.

"Whatever. Did you tell him or not, Detective?"

I had to suppress an actual giggle. I could never have gotten away with using the "w" word in open court. Jenna is of a generation that can. Although it wasn't very professional of her to use it. On the other hand, Jenna had learned to let her professional demeanor slip once in a while. Sometimes to wonderful effect. Here, it was a way of verbally rolling her eyes.

Spritz had still not answered Jenna's question. He was just sitting there. She asked him again.

"Did you tell him or not, Detective?"

"No, I didn't." There was no audible sigh, but I thought I saw the ghost of one in his breathing.

"Did you forget?"

"I did not forget."

"How did it happen, then?"

"I assumed he would *know* to do it, because I had pointed out the depression to him earlier and remarked on its importance. He is a trained professional."

Jenna walked back to our table and picked up a folder. She was intentionally in no hurry. She paged through it, pulled out three sheets of paper, and walked back to the podium.

"Your Honor," she said, "Mr. Benitez and I have pre-marked certain exhibits and stipulated that they can be admitted into evidence upon presentation. I now offer in evidence Defendant's pre-marked Exhibit 26, which is Officer Apple's written report of his activities on the day of the murder."

I looked over at Benitez. He was riffling through his own folders, apparently looking for his copy of Defendant's 26. Jenna looked over at him. "You have it, Charlie?"

"Yeah, I do, Jenna," Benitez said.

"May I approach the clerk to lodge the exhibit?" Jenna asked, directing her question to the judge.

"Yes," Judge Gilmore said. She didn't look particularly interested in any of this.

Jenna walked up to the clerk, sitting at a desk to the Judge's left, and handed her a copy of Defendant's 26. Then she passed a duplicate up to the judge and returned to the podium. "I move the admission of Defendant's 26."

Judge Gilmore looked at Benitez. "Any objection?"

Benitez did what I call the mini-rise of respect. He elevated himself ever so slightly from his seat. Maybe two inches off the chair. "No objection."

Judge Gilmore gave the document a cursory review. Two seconds, if that. "Defendant's 26 is admitted into evidence without objection," she said. I watched the clerk make a notation in the evidence log.

"May I approach the witness?" Jenna asked.

"You may," Judge Gilmore said.

I have always liked the formality of this ritual. In most courtrooms, you can't just waltz up to a witness like they do in TV shows. You have to ask permission. And you have to have a reason. Partly to avoid needless intimidation of the witness. But mostly because, to get to the witness, you have to cross the well of the Court. That's the area between the counsel tables and the bench. It is the Court's sacred ground, and you don't pass through it without begging the Court's leave.

Jenna walked up to Spritz, holding Defendant's Exhibit 26. Perhaps I imagined it, but Spritz appeared at least slightly apprehensive.

"Detective, let me show you Defendant's Exhibit 26. It's titled 'Officer John Apple's Report of Crime Scene Investigation, Homicide of Simon Rafer.'" She handed him the document. He held it without looking at it. A well-trained witness.

"Do you see there in the fourth paragraph where it says that he accompanied you up the elevator to the 84th Floor?"

Spritz looked at the document for the first time. He took a moment to study it. "Yes."

"Do you see there in the next paragraph where he describes the body and its position?"

Spritz looked at it again. "Yes."

"Do you see there, fourth paragraph from the bottom, where he describes the blood on the carpet?"

Spritz only glanced at it this time. "Yes."

"Do you see there, two paragraphs from the bottom, where it says 'Detective Spritz asked me to tape off the crime scene, and I did so?'"

Spritz looked again. "Yes."

"Please read the entire document carefully to yourself and then tell the Court whether you see, anywhere in it, any reference of any kind made by Detective Apple to a depression in the carpeting."

Spritz didn't bother to look at the document again. "I don't have to read it. It's not there."

I waited to see if Jenna would ask him *why* it wasn't there. She didn't. Smart move. Let Benitez fix it on redirect if he could. It was Spritz who claimed to have pointed it out to Apple. Benitez's list of fix-its seemed to be growing.

I could see that Spritz had been poised to explain. He looked slightly disappointed when Jenna moved on to a different topic.

"Detective, when you first entered the building, did you consider sealing it?"

"I did, but rejected the idea."

"Why?"

"First, didn't have the resources at that point. Second, sealing off an eighty-five story building creates an enormous inconvenience for thousands of people. Third, I'd have to deal with anyone who was already in the building. Fourth, I still didn't know if it was really a murder. For all I knew, some guy'd had a heart attack, huh?"

"The dispatcher did call it a murder, though, right? When you got the call?"

"Yes."

"Did you consider asking the building to block the elevators—up *and* down—to the six floors the law firm occupied—once you found a body on one floor, with a knife in its back?"

"Not right away. Three of the reasons not to do that remained."

"Wasn't the result that, by shortly after 7:00 a.m., a crowd of early-arriving workers had gathered in the eighty-fifth floor lobby?"

"You should know, Counsel. You were one of them."

Touché, I thought. I mean, really, I had to give one to Spritz for that. Judge Gilmore apparently thought otherwise. "All right, boys and girls," she said, "could we get on to something relevant?" I noticed that she had glanced at the door that led to her chambers as she said it.

Jenna got quickly to the point, ignoring his comment about who was there. "Detective, did you at least seal the eighty-fifth floor?"

"Yes, Detective Apple did that, with yellow tape, shortly after we arrived."

"Back when he was supposed to seal off the carpeted area with the supposed depression, too?"

I watched Benitez leap to his feet. His most animated move all morning. "Objection! Asked and answered, argumentative!"

Judge Gilmore looked more than annoyed. "Counsel, could we cut this out? You have already made the point. Sustained. Move on." It was not lost on me that she was now calling Jenna "Counsel," too.

"Detective," Jenna said, "did you let *anyone* past the tape that was blocking entry to the eighty-fifth floor?" We had not discussed that issue. It was a shot in the dark, I knew.

It drew a blinding light. "Yes, I did. Three people as I recall."

"Do you recall their names?"

He paused and thought a few seconds, as if searching his memory. "I believe they were Betty Menino, Susan Apacha, and Stewart Broder."

"Who are they, if you know?"

"Ms. Menino is the office manager of the Los Angeles office of Marbury Marfan. She arrived and offered to go to her office and send an all-hands e-mail advising employees of the firm not to come in until after lunch. At my request, she agreed not to specify the reason, but simply to say there had been a building malfunction."

I don't know why, but that really cracked me up. Internally, of course. I couldn't laugh out loud. Simon's murder was a building malfunction! What a wonderful euphemism.

In turning my head to shield my barely contained laughter from the judge, I noticed that Oscar had already slipped into his seat at the back of the courtroom. I also saw the bailiff they called the "Green Giant" come in. We'd heard of him even over at the civil courthouse. He wasn't so much tall as he was massively broad. A kind of horizontal giant, with hands the size of snowshoes. He was a free-floating bailiff who was dispatched to a courtroom when bad shit was going down. I looked around quickly for bad shit but didn't see any.

Meanwhile, Jenna was continuing.

"The others you let through, detective, who were they, exactly?"

"Susan Apacha is the building's security manager. She was informed of the situation by the building security guard and came to the eighty-fifth floor not long after 7:00 a.m."

"Were you the one who gave each of them permission to cross the tape?"

"Yes, but not until I returned from an, um, other mission on a different floor."

I noticed the awkwardness of his answer. I couldn't tell if anyone in the Blob had. Spritz was obviously trying hard not to open up the subject of his meeting with me on the "different floor." I couldn't quite see why. I also noticed that Benitez, who really had been imitating a potted plant, was suddenly attentive. Was all of this as much a surprise to him as to me?

"Why did you permit Ms. Apacha to go back?"

"She wanted to see if any of the security devices on the floor had been tripped. She said she could not check them remotely."

Security devices? I had never heard of those.

"What about Mr. Broder?"

I was keenly interested to hear the answer to this one.

"He said he was the deputy managing partner and urgently needed to send an e-mail to the firm's other offices because otherwise they would— I think his words were 'flip out'—when none of the firm's phones were answered after 8:00 a.m. and no e-mails were opened or returned. Because by the time I spoke with him, I had ordered all of the firm's floors sealed off. He explained that he was now in charge since the managing partner was the body on the floor."

I was dumbfounded. So was Jenna, from what I could tell. I could see that she had momentarily gone to wherever she goes. Stock still, thinking hard. I knew what was going through her mind. Should she follow up? Should she let it be? Who in the room knew what? Would the leverage be greater—if there was any here—in private or here in public? She came back from wherever it was and went for it.

"Detective, has anyone informed you that, at that time, Stewart Broder was not any kind of managing partner of the firm, deputy or otherwise?"

"Recently, yes."

"Who informed you of that?"

"The District Attorney."

"Mr. Benitez?"

"No, *the* District Attorney."

Jenna paused. "Did he . . ." I could see her change her mind and opt not to drill into the cover-up just yet. "Was Mr. Broder carrying a briefcase at the time he was permitted past the tape?"

Out of the corner of my eye, I saw several members of the Blob slip out the back door of the courtroom. I turned back to the action and noticed that Judge Gilmore was resting her head on a fisted hand, much like Rodin's The Thinker. But she wasn't staring at the ground. Just staring at Spritz.

Spritz paused, apparently considering Jenna's question, then reached out to take a sip from a glass of water. There is always a water pitcher and glass to the side of the witness box. To that moment, though, Spritz had not touched it. He sipped and then answered. "I don't recall one way or the other whether he was carrying a briefcase."

"Detective Spritz, in the police reports for that day, is there any mention of these three individuals being permitted past the tape?"

"Objection! No foundation, calls for speculation. The reports themselves are the best evidence of that. And, uh, calls for hearsay." Benitez was trying a shotgun spray of objections, most of them well taken. In other settings, they might have worked. But judges have a lot of discretion in applying the rules of evidence.

"Overruled." Judge Gilmore still held Spritz in an unblinking gaze. "You may answer."

"No, nothing in the police reports about that that I'm aware of," he said.

"Do you know why that might be?"

"I can only speak for my own report."

"And?"

"I didn't think it was important. Many things happen during the first hours of an investigation. You can't mention each and every one of them. I'd have to mention letting officers use the restroom."

He was trying to work himself up to be legitimately peeved at the question. I looked again at Judge Gilmore. Spritz's tactic didn't seem to be working. She hadn't budged, and she still had him locked in an unwavering gaze.

Jenna stood stock still again. Then abruptly changed the subject entirely.

"Detective, why were you downtown at 6:00 a.m. the morning you received the call about the murder?"

"I live downtown."

"Were you at your residence at the time?"

"No, I was having breakfast."

"Where?"

"At the DownUnder."

"Where is that, Detective?" Jenna, of course, knew damn well where it was.

"It's about four blocks from the suspect building."

"Do you eat there often?"

Benitez unpotted himself. "Objection. I don't see the relevance of Detective Spritz's breakfast routine."

"Overruled." There it was again. Discretion. For a lawyer, it could be the most beautiful thing in the courtroom if you were the beneficiary of it. Among the ugliest if you were instead its unwilling victim.

"No, I don't."

"Were you having breakfast by yourself that morning?" It was another shot in the dark.

". . . Yes, by myself."

I don't know if anyone else saw it. After decades of questioning witnesses, in both trial and deposition, you gain a sixth sense that automatically detects the slightest pause or hesitation in an answer. The tiny hesitation that says, "I'm trying to think how to answer that question literally, instead of fully."

Spritz's microsecond of hesitation had been there. I would have staked my life on it. He was having breakfast by himself? What about the others who might have been having breakfast at nearby tables? Or people who were at his table, but weren't there for breakfast but for something else? Or people who had been there earlier but had left? The possible number of tiny lies was endless. Why did he care?

Jenna was thinking, too. She walked to our table to take a sip of water. She needed the brief delay. She looked at me. I shrugged in the most minimal way I knew how. I had no guidance.

Judge Gilmore spoke. "Ms. James, I'm sorry to interrupt your cross-examination, but we've actually run past our morning break time. If we don't break now, I can see we'll be here till noon. That might work for a roomful of twenty-somethings." She smiled a crooked smile. "Why don't we take" . . . she looked at her watch . . . "thirty minutes, and then we'll push the whole day after that. You can step down for now, Detective."

I was pissed. There is nothing worse than having a good cross interrupted before it's over. The witness gets to relax and, worse, go talk to his lawyer. Who'll point out the problems and help the witness to find the solutions that lurk within him. Without being coached, of course. Spritz and Benitez would, I was sure, just take the elevator up to the DA's office. In fact, Spritz was already walking, almost loping, down the aisle toward the doors.

Judge Gilmore spoke again. "Detective Spritz?"

He turned, surprised. "Yes, Your Honor?"

"I'd appreciate it if you would not speak to anyone during our break. I think that would be fair, don't you?"

I'm sure Spritz thought it was anything but. "Of course, Your Honor, I'll just go downstairs and grab a cup of coffee."

"Thank you."

I had thought the judge was done, but she wasn't. "Counsel," she said, addressing Benitez and Jenna, who were sitting at their respective tables, gathering some things up, "I'd like to see both of you in chambers for a few minutes. With Mr. Tarza." She motioned with her head toward the court reporter. "You, too, Nancy."

We rose and followed the judge through the back door of the court-room, into the corridor that led to her chambers. The Green Giant came with us. So did Oscar.

CHAPTER 39

The corridor behind the courtroom looked to me pretty much like the back corridors in any courthouse. Nondescript dull beige carpeting, walls that were once white, anonymous wooden doors leading off the corridor here and there. In a word, utilitarian.

Judge Gilmore turned to all of us and said, "I need a few minutes to make some arrangements before we can meet in chambers. In the meantime, each group can wait in one of our small conference rooms." She pointed to one of the anonymous doors. "The defense can use this one here. Sorry there's no water or coffee. I can't spare staff to set it up right now. I'll come back and get you when I'm ready."

She turned and left with Benitez and his group, presumably leading them to a different conference room. We went into ours and looked around. The room was maybe twelve by twelve, with a very small metal conference table in the middle. There were four county-issue metal swivel chairs with cloth seats. Nothing else. No art, no sidetables, not even a pencil. We each took a seat.

Jenna began rocking back and forth in her chair, testing it to see if it would fall over backwards if she went too far. It didn't, but it squeaked every time it moved. I wondered if she had picked up rocking from Oscar.

"Imagine," Jenna said, "spending a whole day in this pit."

"Forget it, Jenna," Oscar said. "We have too much to talk about in the few minutes we've got before we go see the judge about whatever this is all about."

"It's about some kind of security breach," Jenna said. "That's what she told us at the bench conference. Were you already here when that happened?"

"I was just coming in. Did she say anything else?"

"Not really. She asked me if I'd be willing to delay crossing Spritz so she could deal with the problem right then, but I asked to at least begin the cross. I was feeling in the groove and felt like I might fall out of it if we took a break. Benitez, of course, was hot to stop on the spot. But Gilmore said okay, I could get started. You saw what happened next."

"Yeah, and I liked what I saw," Oscar said. "You're good. You'll make a great lawyer someday."

"She already is a great lawyer," I said.

They both looked at me. Up until then, I really hadn't been in the room as far as they were concerned.

"Let's leave the pointers I can give her till later," Oscar said.

"I'll enjoy getting them," Jenna said.

Oscar changed the subject.

"I imagine you two are feeling pretty good about what just happened," he said.

"I am," Jenna said.

"Me, too," I said. "She dismantled Spritz. Plus we learned some very interesting facts."

Oscar was trying to rock without squeaking. Without much success. He addressed Jenna. "You did start to take him apart. But the two of you are suffering from TDE."

"Which is what?" I asked.

"Transient Defense Euphoria," he said. "A tendency to think that just because you had a good moment or a good morning or a good day or whatever, you're on your way to winning."

"Well, aren't we?" I asked.

"No," Oscar said.

Jenna and I both began repeatedly squeaking our chairs. I'm not quite sure why. Maybe it was a kind of accompaniment to Oscar, who I sensed was about to commence a long soliloquy.

"Let's suppose," Oscar said, getting started, "that Jenna damaged Spritz so much they can't put him on the stand at trial. So what? All they need him for is to prove 'opportunity.' To say, 'Saw Tarza at the crime scene, standing over the body.' At trial, they can get Apple to say it instead. After all, he saw the same thing."

I heard Jenna sigh. Oscar was indeed launching into one of his "I know what I'm doing in criminal law and you two don't" lectures.

"Even," Oscar continued, "if Jenna does manage to eliminate Spritz this morning, the experts Benitez is gonna put on later today or tomorrow will kill us."

"We'll cream them, too," I said.

"Robert, you really don't get criminal law. For the DA to make probable cause in a prelim, his experts only have to be marginally credible. We'd have to destroy them completely to win, and we can't."

"I thought we had great counter-experts," I said.

"We've got only one really great one," Oscar said. "Our blood spatter guy, who's going to say their guy is full of it about the blood on your shirt cuff. But we can't put him on at the prelim. We need to guard his virginity for trial. Otherwise, we give the DA a dry run at discrediting him."

"Oh," I said. I was beginning to feel more downbeat.

Oscar continued to beat down. "And what the hell do you propose we do, Robert, about Benitez's computer recovery expert? He's gonna say that somebody deleted the e-mails between you and Simon about the coin. Then he's gonna read the recovered e-mails out loud to establish motive. Who's gonna say he's wrong?"

"Maybe they're fakes," Jenna said.

"You're not serious?" Oscar said.

"Well, no, I'm not," she said. "But I thought a hint of humor might help you, Oscar. You are so damn fucking serious all the time."

"Well," he said, "try this on for added humor, Jenna. The DA's elevator records expert will say the records prove that Robert was there at 4:30 a.m., which is one-and-a-half hours earlier than Robert told the police he arrived. So the DA's going to say that he either never left or he left and came back after the elevator was unlocked. But either way, they'll say, he lied about it. If that's not the kiss of guilt, it's sure as hell the kiss of probable cause." He paused. "And, oh yeah, there's Simon's blood on Robert's couch."

"Okay, Oscar," Jenna said. "We get it."

I interrupted Jenna's interruption. "Yeah, but I wasn't there at 4:30 a.m."

"Right," Oscar said. "I know. Unfortunately, the only evidence we've got of that right now is your own testimony. But you can't testify at a preliminary hearing. That's suicide." Then he took a breath and finished up. "So whatever our chances in front of a jury, our chances of actually winning this prelim are the same as finding a Christmas ham in your bathtub in August."

Jenna tried a different way to change the subject. "I've never heard that one before," she said. "It's cute."

"Something my third wife used to say," Oscar said.

Jenna cocked her head, got that flirty look she sometimes gets, and leveled the look at Oscar. "How many wives have you had, Oscar? In all the hours we've spent together the last few weeks, I don't think I've ever asked you that."

"Five. Would you like to be number six?"

"Dream on."

"Well," Oscar said, "it's a moot point. It would create a conflict for us to marry before this case is over. Especially with you still being a distant suspect. So we'll have to wait." Jenna and Oscar were by then actually holding a stare with each other.

I found it hard to believe that this was happening. Right in front of my eyes. But, then, it had happened with Simon, basically right in front of my office. That must have started, I had recently figured out, when Jenna second-chaired the Quintus libel trial with Simon.

I put that thought aside and said, "Can we get back to discussing my case before the judge comes back? Please?"

Oscar broke his stare with Jenna. "Okay," he said. "To sum up, Benitez will win this hearing, pretty much no matter what. But you're right, Robert, that his case might not be the world's strongest in front of a jury. That's why the DA—Horace Krandall himself—cornered me in the hall this morning and, once again, brought up a plea bargain. He offered to let you plead to second degree murder."

"Same answer as before," I said.

"I thought you'd say that."

"Oscar," Jenna said, "remind Robert about the difference in the penalty for first degree versus second degree. He needs to focus on it without emotion. He used to be good at doing that. He even used to insist that his own clients do it."

"With first degree," Oscar said, "you get twenty-five years to life. With second, you get twenty to life. Possibility of parole in both. So with a plea to second, and counting good behavior and brownie points for doing things like working in the prison library, you could be out in twelve, maybe even ten."

"And with first?" I asked.

"With first, you'll be in there for at least fifteen. Minimum, you'll be seventy-five when you get out. But the good news is that if they're offering second, I bet we can get them down to manslaughter. In and out in five or six years."

"Forget it," I said. "I'm not pleading to anything."

"Well, maybe," Jenna said. "Even so, we ought to go back to the DA and—"

She never finished her thought because, after a perfunctory knock, Judge Gilmore opened the door and stuck her head in. "If you'll follow me down to my chambers, we can talk." We duly followed.

CHAPTER 40

The term "judge's chambers" makes them sound fancy, and maybe in England or some courthouse I've never been in, it's true. But for state trial judges in the County of Los Angeles, it's not. For the most part, a judge's chambers in L.A. are just a group of carpeted offices, with the judge getting the biggest one, usually with a couple of windows.

Judge Gilmore's chambers, just down the hall from the conference room, were no different. Nicely done, but with furniture only a click up from the usual county issue. The main furnishings were a blonde oak desk in lieu of metal and four cloth-covered green chairs, arrayed in a semicircle in front of the desk. The desk itself was strewn with family photos—lots of kids, but no visible picture of the director husband. And unless the judge herself had taken up paint-by-numbers, the landscapes on the wall had been created by the kids in the photos.

Benitez and company were already there, sitting on a long, red-and-white striped couch that sat along the back wall facing the desk. It didn't surprise me that they'd taken the couch. Powerful lawyers tend to sit toward the back of such settings. It makes them look like people who don't really give a shit and makes the up-fronters look more like supplicants or suck-ups.

We took three of the suck-up chairs in front of the desk. I noticed myself scooting my chair back a bit. Old habits die hard.

Judge Gilmore sat down behind her desk. This was going to be formal. If she had wanted it to be informal, she'd have grabbed one of the leftover chairs, moved it a small distance away from the group and pretended to be more a friend than someone who wielded, at least temporarily, vast arbitrary power over us. In a criminal case, maybe not so temporarily over me.

I noticed that Nancy, the court reporter, had slipped into the room. This was going to be seriously formal.

"I thought I needed promptly to inform all of you, including the defendant," Judge Gilmore began, "about something that happened this morning. The vaunted security system that blocks access from the outer hallway to my chambers was breached while we were in trial. The gentleman who breached it then walked up to my secretary and said that he had been inside Marbury Marfan at the time of the murder and had 'excellent information' about who killed Mr. Rafer."

Benitez spoke up from the back. I was surprised that he had chosen to speak first. Maybe he already knew something about it.

"Do we know him?" he asked.

Judge Gilmore flashed him a smile and said, "I doubt it. According to my secretary, he was wearing an ill-fitting leather-fringed suede suit complete with coonskin cap and was carrying a child's popgun rifle. Fully loaded—with a red cork. He told her his name was Daniel Boone."

"Where is he now?" Jenna asked.

"In the special lockup in the basement," Judge Gilmore said. "I didn't personally see him or talk to him. He's at least in theory a potential witness, and it would be improper for me to do that."

I could see that she was thinking that the universe in which Boone was really a potential witness was a universe parallel to this one, in which live elephants danced on Broadway.

Benitez cleared his throat. "So why are we here?"

I thought it was rather cheeky to say that to a judge sitting on a hearing you were in the middle of, but then the DA's office does represent the sovereign. Yet Judge Gilmore didn't look the least offended at his lack of respect. Or courtesy.

"Well, Mr. Benitez," she said, "I could have asked to have him charged with a variety of crimes connected with how he broke through security. But I'm inclined instead to arrange for him to be sent for thirty days' involuntary observation at the loony bin. Since he'll be away, so to speak, I wanted to offer each side the opportunity to interview him before he goes . . . if you wish. I don't want to be accused of secretly sending potential evidence out of town."

"I don't think we want to bother, Your Honor," Benitez said. "He sounds like a total nutcase. It will be an utter waste of everyone's time and distract us from getting on with the People's justice." As Benitez said "everyone's", he looked directly at Jenna. Daring us to interview the guy and interrupt progress toward justice? I considered making a gagging sound, but then thought better of it.

"Your choice, Mr. Benitez," Judge Gilmore said. She turned to the court reporter. "This is off the record, Nancy." Nancy stopped moving her fingers, and Judge Gilmore resumed. "Mr. Benitez . . . I'm not sure I should say this. Your case could use some help. It's limping a bit at the moment."

Benitez had already started to get up from the couch. I could tell that her comment had startled him. But he recovered nicely.

"Your Honor," he said, "I can understand your feelings at the moment. But we don't need Detective Spritz to prove up our probable cause case. If Your Honor is doubtful about his testimony, we can put Officer Apple on for the same testimony. It's the experts we've got coming later who are the heart of our case. Especially the e-mail guy, the elevator records guy, and the blood guy."

Judge Gilmore cast a quick look at Nancy. "Back on the record, please. Okay, Mr. Benitez. Your call. But do stay a moment." She had turned toward Jenna, presumably looking for our answer, when Oscar spoke up.

"We'll see him, Your Honor," he said.

I could see Benitez hesitate. He had perhaps assumed we wouldn't want to bother either, especially since the judge had gone out of her way, without quite saying so, to depict the guy as a nut. Now Benitez had been put in a position where it would have been prudent to say, "Okay, in that case we'll tag along, too." He chose manliness over prudence, though, and said nothing.

Judge Gilmore focused on Oscar. "Mr. Quesana, it's so very nice to see you again." I couldn't tell if she was being sarcastic or not. "I saw your name on the court papers, and I'm delighted you're going to play a larger role. Not that Ms. James isn't doing a terrific job." She nodded at Jenna, who beamed. Benitez had in the meantime sat back down.

"The reason," Oscar began, "that we want to see him . . ."

Judge Gilmore held up a hand, in the universal language of "stop."

"Uh uh," she said. "I don't want to know your reasons, Mr. Quesana."

"Okay, Your Honor," Oscar said.

"One more thing," Judge Gilmore said. "I'm putting this matter under seal, and I'm gagging all of you about it until further notice. Totally. If one scrap of this leaks to the media—if I see it in one newspaper or on one sleazy cable channel, no matter how far up the numbers that channel is, I'm going to find out who leaked it and make it my lifetime goal to take that person's bar card. Is that clear?"

We all said, "Yes, Your Honor." In unison.

Judge Gilmore looked at the court reporter. "Please record each person as having individually agreed."

Then she seemed to realize, almost as an afterthought, that I was somehow different. She looked directly at me. "Mr. Tarza, that applies to you, too. Do you agree to it?"

"Yes, Your Honor," I said, and then added, "I'd like to go, too."

She cocked her head, considering. "Well, Mr. Tarza, that's really up to your lawyers. If they want you along, that's fine with me. If not, that's fine with me, too." She got up.

Her comment stunned me. It brought home how much my status had changed. The judge clearly regarded me, not as a Prince of the Legal Realm, which was certainly my former status, but as a piece of baggage that belonged to my lawyers. If they wanted to lug me along, fine. It made no difference to her one way or the other.

Judge Gilmore was already halfway out the door when she was clearly reminded of something she had forgotten.

"By the way," she said, ". . . still on the record, Nancy . . . Mr. Boone had in his possession a Kentucky driver's license showing his name as Daniel Boone, from Lexington, Kentucky. My secretary says the gentleman in the lockup matches perfectly the picture on the license. We checked with the Kentucky State Police, and the license is a valid Kentucky driver's license. The Kentucky file on Boone shows his profession as hunter, and the stats—height, weight, hair, and eye color—match this guy." There was silence in the room.

Oscar broke the silence. "We still want to see him, Your Honor."

"We still don't," Benitez said. "We have a solid case, and we don't need nutcases to bolster it." I thought the reverse implication of that statement a rather nice touch.

"Okay," Judge Gilmore said, "Mr. Benitez, we'll see you after lunch. I think you know how to get out of here. Ms. James and Mr. Quesana,"— she paused—"and Mr. Tarza, if you would wait in the small conference room you were using, I'll have someone escort you down to the special lockup."

Then she laughed and said, "Good hunting."

As she swept out of the room in her robes, I saw her shaking her head and thought I heard her mutter, although it may have been my imagination, "If I get that seat on the court of appeals, I can get out of this bin."

CHAPTER 41

———

So there we were, back in the small conference room. The chairs still squeaked.

"This is certainly unusual," Jenna said.

"Yeah," Oscar said. "It sure is. But I'm kind of surprised this Boone guy got in. They recently upgraded the security systems in this courthouse. Hired some big international outfit to install it. Cost over a million bucks."

Jenna looked interested. "Do you know its name?"

"International Security something or other. The last word is odd. Oh, 'Domain,' I think . . . International Security Domain. Do you know something about that world?"

"Kind of," Jenna said. "I was the associate representative on the M&M Security Committee last year. We dealt with, you know, access issues, stuff like that. We interviewed a few security contractors before we hired one."

"You deal with after hours elevator access on that committee?" Oscar asked.

There was an uncomfortable silence in the room. It didn't last long, but you could feel it.

"No. We did not," she said.

"Is that your final answer?" Oscar asked.

Jenna said nothing. Apparently it was her final answer.

I tried to change the topic to something more neutral.

"Shouldn't we be discussing what we're going to ask Daniel Boone?" I asked.

No one responded, so I tried to lighten things up with a different tactic. "Good thing," I said, "the guy's name isn't Peter Rabbit. It'd be harder to think what to ask him."

"Thank God," Oscar said, "you didn't lay that witticism on the judge."

"Oh, never," I said. "Saying something like that to a judge violates the local court rules."

Oscar looked puzzled. He even scrunched up his eyebrows. "Which rule?" he asked. I looked at Jenna. She was finally smiling, at least a little. She'd heard me cite the "rule" before.

"It's Rule H," I said, "'Initiation of humor shall be only and solely by the judge.'"

"Boy, ain't that the truth," Oscar said. "And then there's the rule two down the list from that one."

I bit. "Which one?"

"Rule J, 'Lawyers shall laugh immediately at all jokes told by the judge.'"

Jenna broke into a broad grin, apparently fully recovered from Oscar's momentary lapse into "maybe Jenna did it" territory.

The conversation did raise an issue, though, that I was curious about. I'd never heard of the firm having a security committee. As far as I could recall, it had never been mentioned in the Executive Committee. Did Simon have secret committees? I made a mental note to ask Jenna about it later.

Oscar brought the topic back to Mr. Boone. "Okay, first, as we all know, you can't really plan an interview like this one," he said. "We'll just have to see what Boone says and go with questions from there. Second, we should say very little *to* him. When this guy gets out of the bin he's gonna sell his story to the *Weekly World News* or something. So let's not give him anything to talk about."

Then he looked directly at me. "Third, it's a miserably bad idea to have you along, Robert."

"Why?" I asked. The day had begun to turn fun for me, and this promised to be the capstone outing. I wanted to go.

"For the obvious reason. This interview won't be privileged. So on the off chance you testify at the trial, the DA will be able to cross-examine you about what you heard from Boone. Frankly, the less you have in your head about the facts other than what you know personally, the better off we'll be. It's bad enough you already investigated the crime yourself."

"I'm going," I said.

"Fine," Oscar said. "You're supposedly a good lawyer, so you can see the risks. Any other client, I'd tell them, 'Stow it, you're not going.'"

"Thanks for the backhanded compliment," I said.

"You're welcome. But there's one other thing."

"Which is?"

"You have to keep your mouth shut," he added.

"I will," I said.

"Good," Oscar said. "So if you're going to come, that brings me to the fourth—"

He didn't get to say right then what the fourth thing on his mind was, because a knock on the door interrupted him. It was clearly not the judge, since the knock wasn't followed instantly by the door opening.

"Come in," I said. We all swiveled our heads to see who it might be.

The door opened, and there loomed the Green Giant, almost filling the doorway.

"Hi. I'm Deputy Green," he said. "Judge Gilmore asked me to take you down to the special lockup to see—" he paused, and you could see him thinking for a split second whether to make a joke out of it but deciding not to—"Daniel Boone."

Deputy Green led us to a non-public elevator and pushed the down button. The door opened almost immediately, and we got in. He inserted a key in the elevator panel, turned it, and then pushed a button marked B4. I don't know why, but I had assumed that an elevator heading for a basement jail cell would grind its way downward slowly. Instead, we went down like a rocket.

CHAPTER 42

———

We exited the elevator into a concrete block corridor painted institutional grey. As we walked along, Oscar said, rather emphatically, "Fourth, I'll do all the talking in this interview." I saw no reason to disagree, since I had already agreed to say nothing. Jenna didn't disagree, either.

We turned a corner and came upon three jail cells. Each one was about five feet wide, with bars for doors. Two built-in benches ran along the side walls, front to back, and there was a small sink and toilet. The bars of each cell were thickly padded, as were the floor, walls, benches, sink, and toilet. All in yellow padding. A temporary bin, or so it appeared.

Two of the cells were empty. Only the third had anyone in it. I assumed it was Daniel Boone. Before we could try to get a better look at him, Deputy Green addressed us as a group.

"Okay, guys, you have a choice. One option, I just leave him in there, and you talk to him through the bars. If you take that option, I'll leave the area, and I won't be able to hear you. If you want to interview him while he's not behind bars, I'll have to cuff him, and I'll have to be very nearby. Your choice."

"We'll talk to him through the bars," Oscar said. "But thanks for letting us know our options. We appreciate it."

"No biggie," Deputy Green said. "Let me introduce you."

He turned toward the occupied cell. The person in it was sitting on one of the benches, near the back of the cell, but gave no sign of having noticed us.

"Hey, Mr. Boone, you have visitors!" Deputy Green was clearly addressing Boone in the overly cheerful way I imagined you might address someone who's crazy. Boone looked up but didn't budge.

"Big deal," Boone said.

"Two of them are lawyers," Deputy Green said.

That got Boone's attention. He got up and came over toward the bars, but stopped a couple of feet back. He appeared to be in his fifties, about five-foot-ten, maybe one hundred eighty pounds, with dark, stringy hair that came almost down to his shoulders. He wore buckskin pants, red Nike tennis shoes, and a beige shirt of rough spun cloth, open almost to his waist. The shirt had small brass grommets where normally there'd be buttons and button holes. But the leather lace that would have passed through the grommets to hold the shirt closed was missing, as were his belt and shoelaces.

He also had mesmerizing eyes. Even at a distance of several feet, I could see their deep blue color. He could have been Paul Newman stepped out of *Butch Cassidy and the Sundance Kid*. I was certain I had seen those eyes before, but I couldn't quite put my finger on where.

Deputy Green introduced us. "Mr. Boone, this is attorney Ms. Jenna James." He motioned toward Jenna with his head. "And her colleague—" he took a small three-by-five card out of his breast pocket and looked at it, clearly reading Oscar's name from it, "Mr. Oscar Quesana." He nodded toward Oscar.

Then he turned to me. "And this is, uh, the defendant in the Rafer murder, Mr. Tarza." I could tell from his brief hesitation that Deputy Green had never before brought a defendant to interview someone in a jail cell. Clearly, he was used to the defendant being the one in the cell.

"Hi," Oscar said. "Nice to meet you, Mr. Boone."

"What do you want?" Boone asked. "I thought I was doing the court a favor here, and now I'm in jail." He seemed really pissed off. His voice was familiar, too, but I couldn't quite place it.

Deputy Green interrupted. "I'll leave you guys now. When you're done, I'll be in my office right around that corner down there." He pointed to a bend in the corridor. "I'll leave the door open just a crack, but please knock anyway. Or yell loudly, and I'll come running. I can hear a yell easily from there." He headed off down the corridor.

He had not gone far, when Oscar yelled, "Deputy Green?"

Green turned. "Yeah?"

"Is this area miked or bugged or surveilled in any way?"

Deputy Green smiled the smile of those who recognize a fellow professional at work. "Yes. Sorry. Forgot that. I'll turn it off. Give me a minute." He turned and continued away.

"Forgot, my ass," Oscar said, more to himself than out loud.

We all stood there, silently, awkwardly waiting. Suddenly, a speaker hidden somewhere inside the cell blared, too loudly, "Okay, I've shut it off now."

Oscar turned to face the truculent Mr. Boone. He started by ignoring Boone's opening anger.

"Mr. Boone," Oscar said, "could you tell us how you were going to help the court? That would be enormously helpful to us, and we'd be deeply appreciative."

I had never seen Oscar so courtly.

"First, get me out of here," Boone said.

"Well," Oscar said, "we're not in a position to do that, but I can promise you that as soon as we get back upstairs, I'll call a lawyer friend who knows the sheriff. He'll contact you right away, and I assume he'll do whatever he can to speed up getting you out of here. We criminal-lawyer types don't like places like this. They treat people like dirt."

It was clever. Oscar was being sympathetic to Boone, almost empathetic. Like he'd been unfairly slapped in jail himself once. Maybe he had.

Boone considered it. He actually stroked his chin. "All right. Maybe that's the best you can do right now. I'll trust you to contact your friend."

"Well," Oscar said, turning almost jolly, "you must have scared the bejesus out of those folks in the judge's chambers when you walked in. They think they've got the world's best security."

"Yeah, I guess they were startled all right," he said.

"How'd you get past all that security stuff, if I might ask?" Oscar said.

"Truth? I had some help."

I could see Oscar thinking where to go with it. He chose the camaraderie of people who know something others don't.

"Some help?" Oscar said. "I won't ask you who or exactly how, then. We all have our little secrets."

"Thanks for that," Boone said.

"Hey," Oscar said, "is your name really Daniel Boone?"

"Yes, it is. Attention getting, isn't it?"

"It certainly is. Is it your legal name?" Oscar asked.

"Yep."

I kept staring at Boone, trying to see him better. I knew that somehow, somewhere, I had met Boone before. It was driving me crazy.

"Mr. Boone," Oscar asked, "is Boone your original name? The one on your birth certificate?"

"Oh, goodness no. That was Ezekiel Smith. I always hated it. Ezekiel was too weird, and Smith was too common. I changed it as soon as I got to be 18, to Jedediah Smith. Pissed off my family, though. Ezekiel was an old family first name. I was actually Ezekiel Smith IV or something. And I had six or seven cousins named Ezekiel. Can you imagine being at a party with three or four other Ezekiel Smith's?"

Oscar responded casually, clearly trying to encourage Boone's chattiness. "It would be an odd party, for sure. But I'm curious. Is Daniel Boone the only name you've had since you changed it from Ezekiel?"

"Oh, no," Boone said. "I've had maybe six or seven of them since I turned eighteen. Maybe more. I kind of forget them all, in truth. Got 'em in different states, too. So nobody'd get too nosey."

"Hey," Oscar said, "sometimes I wish I had the courage to pick a new name. Oscar Quesana ain't so great. Quesana's hard for a lot of people to spell, and Oscar is, well, not all that common here. But I'm real curious, what was the last name you chose right before this one? Something just as creative?"

"Not really. I picked Alexander Hamilton. Used it for only one year, though. Most people, believe it or not, have never heard of him. So it didn't cause the kind of stir I like."

As he said it, Boone smiled in a goofy, lopsided kind of way, and then moved closer to the cell door, where I could get a better look at him. And then it came back to me. Boone was the client who'd put Stewart's head on the chopping block by not paying his legal bills. Except then he had called himself Top Quark and had a buzz cut and preppy clothes.

Quark is a physicist. Back when he was an M&M client, he had been the founder and president of Physical Science Concepts, one of the hottest of the hot composite materials companies. He had the reputation in the firm of being brilliant—a Nobel Prize winner in waiting, some said—and seriously daffy at the same time. When a couple of his company's projects crashed and burned, he'd been forced to put his company into bankruptcy. And then he had vanished, leaving behind a huge bill for legal fees and leaving Stewart deep inside a million dollar billing hole.

I had never spent real face time with Quark, but I knew about him. I'd seen him once in reception, though, waiting for Stewart, where I chatted him up for a minute or two. I considered whether to alert Oscar and Jenna about who I thought Boone really was but decided to wait. I wanted to be sure he was Quark.

"Well," Oscar was saying, "I'm admiring, truly, of your sense of innovation and adventure, Mr. Boone. But the deputy will probably be back shortly, and the longer we spend with you, the more time it will be before I can call my friend and see if he can get you out of here. So let me ask you . . . what can you tell us about the day Simon Rafer was murdered?"

"It's easy," Boone said. "I was right there on the eighty-fifth floor when it happened."

"You were?" Jenna said. She seemed both dumbfounded and unable to contain herself.

"I'm conducting this interview," Oscar said, and glared at her.

"I'd rather talk to her," Boone said. "She's prettier than you are—um—Oscar? That is your name isn't it?"

I glanced over and saw Oscar considering. I guess he decided not to blow the whole thing over who was prettier, because he just said, "Okay, Jenna can do it if you prefer. I'll just listen and maybe chime in once in a while."

Jenna looked not the least bit displeased at the turn of events. She picked up the questioning without missing a beat.

"So, Mr. Boone, Judge Gilmore told us that you were in the offices of M&M the night of the murder. But I had no idea you were on the eighty-fifth floor."

"I never talked to Judge Gilmore," Boone replied.

"I'm sorry," Jenna said, "I meant to say that Judge Gilmore's secretary told her, and then Judge Gilmore told us."

"I'm a scientist, you see," he said, "so I like precision."

"Okay," Jenna said. "I'll try to be more precise. But you were actually there?"

"Yes."

"Well, speaking of precision, do you remember what day that was and what exact time it was?"

"Not by date," he said. "But it was last month in the early hours of the day that guy Rafer was murdered. I was on the eighty-fifth floor the morning it happened. I'm not sure of the exact time. It was still dark while I was there. I had planned it that way. It didn't start to get light till I was leaving."

"Do you mind, Mr. Boone, if I take some notes?" Jenna asked.

She held up a pad of lined paper she had brought with her and showed it to Boone at eye level, as if revealing the notepad in that way would help to generate his consent.

Notes, of course, were an excellent idea. If we ended up using Quark as a witness and he later changed his tune, his testimony could be impeached by reference back to Jenna's notes. But Benitez might have a hard time getting his hands on them in advance since they'd be attorney work product, and he had passed on his own chance to interview the witness.

In response to Jenna's request, Boone craned his neck back and looked at the ceiling for maybe fifteen seconds.

Finally, he lowered his head and gave Jenna one of his goofy smiles. Then he said, "Sure go ahead with the notes. I'm an open book. Take a look!" He spread his arms wide, which made his shirt gap open, and began to do an odd little tap dance. Which, with no laces in his tennis shoes, looked even odder.

Jenna ignored the performance and said, "I'm glad to hear that, Mr. Boone. We like honest witnesses."

Boone stopped dancing and said, "Well, you've got one, so lay the questions on me."

"Let's cut to the chase, then," Jenna said. "What the hell were you doing there?"

"It's easy," he said. "I went there to scare the shit out of Stewart Broder."

"Why?" Jenna asked.

"Because his bad tax advice ruined me. If it hadn't been for that weirdo creep, I'd be a wealthy man today."

Now I was sure that Boone was Quark.

"He gave you excellent tax advice, Mr. Quark," I said, interrupting. "And, in any case, your problems weren't caused by taxes." On both points I was certain from the many discussions we'd had in the Executive Committee of the overdue Quark bill.

I suddenly felt, as much as saw, both Jenna and Oscar glaring at me. I had stepped out of role. The suitcase had become a lawyer again.

"Ah," Boone said, "I see you have finally recognized me, Mr. Tarza."

"Perhaps," Oscar said, "the two of you could enlighten us about what you're talking about."

"Sure," I said. "Mr. Boone used to call himself Top Quark. The company he founded, Physical Science Concepts, was an M&M client starting about six years ago. In fact, a client that Stewart Broder brought into the firm. Mr. Quark is a physicist."

"Short-listed," Boone said, smiling his goofy smile again.

"Short-listed for what?" Oscar asked.

"The Nobel Prize in Physics," Boone said.

"Oh, I see," Oscar said.

Ignoring Oscar's incredulity, I picked up on Jenna's questioning. "You sneaked into the firm that morning?"

"Yes," Boone said.

"Why?" I asked.

"Like I just said," he responded, "I wanted to scare the shit out of Stewart. I was going to strip him, tie him, gag him, and leave him under his desk. Then close the door to his office and hang a sign on it that said, 'Do Not Disturb, Lawyer at Work.' Call it an in-office kidnapping."

"All for what you call bad tax advice? I guess it's getting more and more risky to be a lawyer trying to do a job," I said.

Boone ignored my sarcasm. "I would have been far better off," he said, "getting tax advice from my local pharmacist."

"Your company crashed four years ago," I said. "Why did you wait four years to get even?"

"My anger was there the whole time," Boone said. "It finally boiled over last month. When my shitty little used car broke down. I used to drive a new Mercedes. But for Stewart's advice, I'd be driving a Rolls now."

"Enough about tax advice," Jenna said. "What did you see that morning, Mr. Boone?"

"Very good, Ms. James," Boone said. "I like lawyers who can stay on target. I'm sorry you weren't working on my matter."

"Thank you," Jenna said. "And the answer to my question?"

"Around 5:00 a.m.," Boone said, "I saw Stewart, some guy named Harry, and two women having a big argument right outside Stewart's office. They were mostly talking in very low voices. I was hiding under the desk in the secretarial cubicle, so I couldn't hear what they were saying very well. Just caught a few words here and there, but only if they were loud words. That's how I know one guy's name was Harry. Stewart kept repeating it in a loud voice."

Jenna was holding her notepad in the crook of her arm, writing notes on it as she went, looking up frequently to keep eye contact with Boone.

"You weren't able to see any of it, then?" she said.

"Well, at one point, I peeked over the edge of the desk, for just a few seconds. To see what was going down. Stewart and the Harry guy were facing me. They were gesticulating, like they were arguing about something. The two women were just standing there. So I can only tell you what they looked like from the back."

"Okay," Jenna said. "What did they look like from the back?"

"One of them was a bleached blonde," he said. "You know, with that greenish tint it gets when it's been bleached too much. The other had black hair." Boone peered out of the cell at Jenna. "Hair color and length a lot like yours. Just over the collar I guess you'd call it."

Oscar made a harrumph-like noise in his throat, and Jenna turned her head to look at him. "Okay, fine!" she said and turned her back to Boone. Then she raised her voice so she could still be heard while facing away from him. "Did the woman with black hair," she asked, "or the bleached blonde, for that matter, look at all like me from the back?"

"Not really," Boone said. "You're pretty slender, and both of them, at least up top, looked pretty wide."

Jenna spun back around. "Happy, Oscar?"

"Maybe," Oscar said. "Were they wearing coats, Mr. Boone?"

"No," Boone said.

"Okay, I'm mostly happy now," Oscar said.

Boone's eyes were darting back and forth between Oscar and Jenna. He was laughing. "Are you a suspect, Ms. James?"

"No, I'm not. These two male pig lawyers are just having some fun with me. They enjoy having me turn around for them."

Jenna's answer was excellent, in the circumstance. Although I couldn't recall ever having asked her to turn around for me.

Jenna was consulting her notepad, looking to pick up at the exact place she had left off. She found it and said, "Mr. Boone, I'd like to go on with what you were saying, because I think it's going to help a lot. But maybe you're getting tired. You don't have to stand. It's okay if you want to sit on the bench and talk from there. Or maybe we could get you some water or coffee."

"They've refused to give me any coffee," he said. "Too dangerous if it's hot or something like that."

"Okay," Jenna said, "but if you want some water, just let me know."

"I will," he said.

"When you peeked out, could you see or hear anything else?" she asked.

"Only saw what I already told you. They went on talking, and I could hear slightly better, but, again, only fragments. They kept saying 'Hello.' Said it maybe four or five times."

"Are you sure that they weren't saying 'Hilo'?"

"Could be. Those two words sound pretty much alike."

"Anything else?" Jenna asked.

"Yeah, the thing that caused me to try to see the judge today. One of the men said, 'Simon, that nosey fucker.' I couldn't really tell whose voice it was, but it was a man's voice."

Boone paused a second, as if gathering his recollections, then resumed. "I ducked back under the desk. A few minutes later, I heard people leaving.

After that, it was quiet for a bit. So I poked my head up above the desk again to see if the coast was clear and saw Stewart walk through the doorway into reception. I ducked back under the desk again."

"Then what?" she asked.

"Maybe thirty seconds later, I heard the elevator bell ping, like the elevator was arriving. Then I heard footsteps running into the reception area. Then right after that, the elevator bell pinged again, and I heard a scuffle. And grunting sounds. Then I heard a shout."

"Could you make it out?" she asked.

"Yes. Someone whose voice I didn't know—a man—shouted, 'It's fake!' Or maybe he said, 'They're fake.' I'm not sure. It was hard to make out."

"Anything else you remember?" she asked.

"Yeah," Boone said, "there was more. There were some more sounds. But I could sure use that cup of coffee now. Any chance one of you lawyers could scare one up?"

Both Jenna and Oscar turned their heads and looked at me. I got the message. I had turned from a suitcase into a coffee cart.

"Okay," I said. "I'll go see if I can scare one up from Deputy Green."

CHAPTER 43

———

When I got to Green's tiny office, he did have coffee but was reluctant to give it to me for Boone because it was hot. At my suggestion, he watered it down, but insisted on filling almost half the cup with water before he poured in the coffee.

"I hope," he said as he handed it to me, "that he doesn't throw it at you."

"I hope not too. Did he throw something at you?"

"No, but he seems like he could. When I gave him a cup of water earlier, he poured it on the floor. Said it was obviously tap water, and he only drank Evian."

"Oh," I said.

"In any case, you don't have a lot of time left with him," Green said. "Gotta risk giving him lunch shortly. It's been ordered early for some reason."

"Okay," I said. "Thanks for the coffee."

When I got back, I was both surprised and pleased to see that Oscar and Jenna were just chatting with Boone about this and that. They apparently had had the decency to wait for me to come back to hit the substance again.

I went up to the cell bars and held the coffee cup up. "Here's your coffee, Quark. I'm sorry it's only lukewarm. Deputy Green insisted."

Quark reached through the bars and took the paper cup from me.

"They think I'm crazy, don't they?" he said.

"Why on earth would they think that?" I said.

"Am I going to get any lunch?" he asked.

"The deputy told me they'd bring it shortly," I said.

"Okay, thanks."

"Can we," Jenna said, "get back to what happened, Mr. Boone?"

"Sure."

"What did you hear next?" she asked.

"Then I heard a . . . I don't know how to describe it. A sharp thwacking sound? Maybe two? Then a really big thud. It scared me, so I waited under the desk until it had been quiet for a while. Then I crawled down the hallway on my hands and knees to where I could see into reception. I couldn't see much because the lights were out. So I just got up and bolted through, heading for the elevators. And, then . . ."

Boone stopped and took a long swallow of his coffee, as if he needed the jolt to relate the rest. "Then I saw a . . . a body on the floor as I ran by. It was a man, but I couldn't see him very well. I thought maybe there was a knife in his back. I was only in there a few seconds."

"You went down the elevator?"

"Yeah. I remembered that there was a security guard in the lobby, so I pushed the button for the first parking level and walked out that way, up the ramp. I was worried the garage gate would still be down, but it wasn't. I guess they open it really early."

"Did you notice what time it was when you walked out of the garage?"

"No. The best I could tell you was that it started to get light out well after I left. But it was December. It stays dark late."

"Where did you go after you left there?"

"I took a bus home. I live in a small apartment in Santa Monica."

He was at the end of his story. The three of us just stood there for a moment, and I could tell we were all thinking the exact same thing. Was there any way to prove that his story was true? Because if he told it uncorroborated, it would not be believed.

I posed the first question along that line.

"Do you have any way to prove you were actually in the building?" I asked. "And it's not that I doubt you. It's just that the DA is going to say you made it all up."

"Nothing that I can think of," Boone said. "I mean, no one saw me. That was the whole idea."

"Anybody or anything else that would tend to show you were there?" Jenna asked.

"Not that I can think of. But if I do, I'll let you know."

"You know," I said, "I think one of the most important things in terms of the credibility of your story is how you got past security and into the building at 5:00 a.m. Monday morning? How did you?"

"It was easy," Boone said. "I was already there. I had been a client, so I knew the drill—that the elevators locked at 7:00 p.m. and that the firm's receptionist went home at 7:00 sharp. I took a guess it hadn't changed much, even with 9/11. So I went into the building on Friday evening, about two minutes before 7:00. I got asked to show ID to go up, of course. I used a fake one. I've got a bunch. But the elevators weren't locked yet."

"Okay. Then what?" I asked. I kept to myself my thought that having a witness with lots of weird name changes, who keeps a drawer full of fake IDs, would not be helpful to his credibility.

"I went up the elevator," he said, "and walked into the reception area about one minute before 7:00 on Friday. The receptionist was just packing up to leave, same timing as when I'd been a client. I told her I had an appointment with Jack."

"Did you actually know Jack Strachan?" I asked.

"No, I just picked his name up off the directory in the lobby. But like I said, I told the receptionist that I had an appointment with him. An appointment with Jack. That's what I called him. Jack. Like I really knew him. I only gave her a last name when she asked for it because I knew that M&M has that system where the receptionist sends an e-mail to the lawyer, telling him he's got a guest."

"You took a risk. He could have been in his office. Or on vacation or something, with the receptionist aware he was gone."

"Yeah, I took a risk. I took all kinds of risks that weekend. And, hey, now that I think about it, maybe the receptionist would remember me."

"Yeah, maybe," I said. "But if she did, she'd remember you from Friday evening, more than two days before the murder, not the morning of."

"True, that could be a problem."

I glanced at Jenna, a former member of the apparently secret Security Committee, and I could see that she was both believing it and not believing it, all at the same time.

"Then," Boone said, "I told the receptionist I was desperate to use the john. So she gave me the key card, and I told her I might be awhile. Something I ate for lunch. So please e-mail Jack to come get me in about ten, if you will. If he doesn't respond I'll call him on his cell. I'll drop the key card back. She bought it, because when I got back from the john, she was long gone."

"And then?" I asked.

"I stayed in a stall in the men's room till almost midnight. Nobody ever knocks on a stall door to ask who's home, you know. Especially if, when they look underneath, the pant legs they see near the floor are pin-striped. I stayed in there and read *The New York Times* I'd brought with me till I thought the coast was clear."

"That's rather clever," I said. "Then what did you do?"

"I waited to come out of the men's room until I heard the cleaning people show up. When I came back, they had all the doors open. I walked into reception and then down the internal stairs to the eighty-fourth floor, like I knew what I was doing. And then into reception on eighty-four, where there were more cleaning people. Cleaning people don't challenge a guy carrying a Gucci briefcase and wearing a thousand-dollar suit."

"Okay," I said. "That was Friday night. Where'd you hide out till early Monday morning?"

"In a lawyer's office. When I walked in, I just looked around for an empty office. One that still had the desk and phone and stuff, but was obviously vacant. When I found one, I sat down, took my laptop, pads, pens, and so forth out of my briefcase and set up shop. Then I did some work I'd brought with me."

He paused, looking quite pleased with himself, then continued.

"In the end, hardly anybody came by," he said, "and no one asked who I was. Had they asked, I was going to say I was a client working with Stewart to close a tax-driven deal before year's end, that our closing was on Monday, and he'd lent me the office for the weekend. I was prepared to say that Stewart was over at the underwriters. I spent the whole weekend there, and slept there, too."

It all made sense to me. I had always said, "If you want to rob a law firm, wear a suit and carry a briefcase. You can go wherever you want." In a place as big as M&M, most people didn't even know all of the other lawyers by sight.

Oscar chimed in. "What about food?"

"I brought some food in the briefcase," he said. "Plus you can get a lot from the vending machines these days. And I didn't even have to risk the public bathroom again. There are a couple offices on that floor with private ones. No one uses them much on weekends."

"Well," Jenna said, "as someone who's been involved in office security, I'm impressed. How long did you spend under the desk, waiting for Stewart?"

"Not very long. I knew that Stewart liked to get in super early on Mondays, so about 5:00 a.m. Monday morning, I went out to reception to wait for him so I could surprise him and really scare the shit out of him when I nabbed him. I was lying on the floor next to the big plant. But then I heard a bunch of people coming, not just him, and I ran and got under the desk."

"Were you in court this morning?" I asked.

"Yeah," Boone said, "I was. And yes, I saw that police detective testify about the depression in the carpet. It was there. It just wasn't you who put it there."

Oscar stopped and tapped his chin. "Another question, sir. One you'll be hammered on if you take the stand."

"What's that?" Boone asked.

"Why'd you wait so long to try to tell anyone about this?"

"Well, after I saw the body, I was so freaked out I went down to Mexico for three weeks. So I didn't know who or what was being investigated for it. When I got back, I read the papers and saw they were investigating Mr. Tarza." He nodded his head at me.

"Go on," Oscar said.

"I had met Mr. Tarza only once when I was a client, and only briefly. But as a result I knew what he looked like, and I'm quite sure I never saw him in the firm that weekend or that morning. So I thought he was being framed. But to prove it, I would have had to admit I'd committed a bunch of crimes getting into that building. Finally, I just couldn't stand it. I loathe injustice, so I called my local police station to tell them I knew something about it."

"You did?" Oscar seemed genuinely surprised.

"Yeah, but they blew me off. No one would make an appointment to meet with me, nobody ever returned my call. And I called three times."

"Did you use your real name when you called?" Oscar asked.

"Well, no, of course not."

"What name did you use?"

"I was sloppy. I used Top Quark. That was a mistake, because I was kind of famous under that one."

"Famous where?" Oscar asked.

"Well, with other physicists. I mean, the top quark particle was the holy grail of physics before it was finally discovered. So pre-discovery, the name attracted attention." He paused. "Okay, maybe it wasn't always favorable attention."

"I bet," Oscar said. "Do you think the person who answered the phone at the police station knew about top quarks?"

"Oh, good point," Boone said. And then he clapped his hands. "Very good point!"

Deputy Green appeared suddenly, carrying a lunch tray. The food was on a paper plate, with a soft rubber spoon next to it.

"I'm sorry folks," he said, "it's lunch time for Boone here, and anyway, the judge called and wants you all upstairs post haste. I'm going to feed Dan Boone here. You guys can just go up yourselves. I'm sure you can find the elevator again, and I unlocked it electronically so that you can go up without a key. Just punch 7."

And so we were dismissed, just like that.

As we left, Oscar said, "Mr. Boone, as soon as we walk out of here, I'm going to call that lawyer friend I mentioned—his name is Christian Ogalu—and see what he can do to get you out of here. He is a good man, I guarantee it."

"Okay. Thank you, Oscar." Boone said. "In exchange, I'll be sure that you have a front row seat in Stockholm."

"Stockholm?"

"At the Nobel ceremony. I'm guessing it will be next year."

"Why, thank you," Oscar said. "I'd be truly honored. And thank *you*, Deputy, for arranging this."

"No problem, Counsel."

We got in the elevator, and Jenna pushed '7' as instructed. The elevator started up.

"Do you think," I asked, "that he's telling the truth?"

"Only if pigs can fly," Oscar said.

CHAPTER 44

———

When we emerged from the elevator, Judge Gilmore herself was waiting for us. Along with Benitez and his two assistants.

"Welcome back," she said. "Mr. Benitez has changed his mind. He's going to interview Mr. Boone after all." As she said that, Benitez and company, without so much as acknowledging our existence, brushed past us into the elevator. I heard the elevator door slide shut behind us.

"I thought Boone needed time to eat his lunch," Oscar said.

"Well," Judge Gilmore responded, "They'll just have to chat with him while he eats. And speaking of food, we've set up that conference room and ordered some sandwiches for you. You can go out if you'd prefer. But I'd like to start the hearing again by 3:00, and there's not a lot of time."

I looked at my watch. It was only 1:15. There was still plenty of time to go out and get a decent lunch at a decent place.

"We'll use the conference room, Your Honor," Oscar said, without consulting either me or Jenna. "Thank you for arranging the food and drink."

"You're very welcome. I'll see you at 3:00." She turned and left.

When we got inside the conference room, the middle of the tiny table held, as promised, two pots of coffee, three cups, three glasses, a carafe of water, and six sodas, three diet, three regular. We squeaked ourselves into the chairs and helped ourselves to the drinks. Oscar grabbed a regular Coke, Jenna took a diet root beer, and I poured myself a cup of coffee, caffeinated.

"What," Jenna asked, looking at Oscar, "do you think Boone is going to tell Benitez?"

"Same bullshit he told us," Oscar said.

"Why are you so sure it's bullshit? It sounded right down the alley to me."

"And to me too," I said. "I may not have any criminal experience, but a witness is a witness, and that guy feels like he's telling the truth."

Oscar looked slowly from one of us to the other, as if he were looking at children in a nursery school who had just reported to him that the milk on the floor had been spilled by Martians.

"Listen my friends, Boone fits exactly the M.O. of a jailhouse snitch. You know, the playwrights of the cellblock. The guys who learn the details of a cellmate's crimes from TV or newspapers and then make up a story that their cellmate confessed, complete with convincing detail. Which they then trade to the DA in exchange for a better deal for themselves. The only difference here is that Boone got the facts for his made-up story just by sitting on his butt in court all morning."

"That makes no sense," I said. "Even if Boone wants to trade, he's got nothing of value to trade to the DA because his story exonerates me."

"Exonerates you, my ass," Oscar said. "He didn't say he saw somebody else kill Simon Rafer. All he said was that he saw people on the eighty-fifth floor early in the morning, heard them argue, and heard them leave. And then he heard the elevator bell ding, and then he heard a struggle. Know what the DA will say if he hears that story?"

"No. What?"

"That the ding was you, Robert, arriving on the elevator. And that the sound of a struggle was also you, Robert, struggling with Simon right before you killed him. And that you killed him because he yelled at you that the coin was a fake. The DA will be delighted to trade Boone a lot for that story."

"But, Oscar," I said, "what Boone actually said was that the voice he heard might have said *they're* fake, or might have said *it's* fake. He wasn't sure."

"What possible difference does that make, Robert?"

"I don't know, exactly."

"Well, I'll tell you," he said. "It makes no damn difference. None. Whichever it was, his story kills you."

No one said anything for maybe thirty seconds. All I could hear was the squeaking of the stupid chairs.

Finally, Jenna spoke. "You know, Oscar, I think you've been at this too long. All you see is the downside. This guy's story helps Robert, if only by putting a lot more people in the picture the morning of the murder. I want to put Boone on the witness stand as our first defense witness."

"Sorry to sound like a broken record," Oscar said, "but to remind you—again—this is a preliminary hearing. This judge ain't gonna let Robert walk based on the testimony of some nut who waltzed into her chambers carrying a pop gun."

"See," Jenna said. "You're a defeatist. You've given up. I want to win. Right now. At this hearing. And Boone is somehow the key to doing that."

"I admire your spunk, Jenna," Oscar said. "But for now, we should just investigate Boone's story. If by some miracle it checks out, we'll be much better off doing something with him at trial."

"Stop being so fucking condescending, Oscar. Spunk is the kind of word people reserve for cute little girls who aren't expected to get their socks dirty."

Oscar looked genuinely taken aback. "I'm sorry, I didn't mean it that way. Really."

"Okay," Jenna said. "Apology accepted. And I'll think some more about your point. But whether we use Boone in a couple of days or in a couple of months, there's one more big problem."

"Which is?" Oscar asked.

"That guy is going to disappear into some other pseudonym."

"Not gonna happen," Oscar said. "I'll call Christian Ogalu like I said I would, and he'll get Boone out. But out doesn't mean gone. The DA will want him around while they sort out the security breach. Christian will make sure he stays put. Where the DA can find him, and so can we."

That reminded me of something I'd been meaning to ask. "Does Ogalu actually know the sheriff? Like you said he did?"

Oscar laughed. "Well, only in a manner of speaking. Christian has sued the Sheriff's Department maybe thirty times for excessive use of force. I think he's taken Sheriff Hansen's deposition a couple of times in those suits."

"And that helps how?" Jenna asked.

"They're afraid of him. They won't want to incur his wrath by making a big deal out of a pissant case like this one. They'll do him a favor and expect one in return later."

There was a knock on the door. It was a guy with the sandwiches. He came in and put three Styrofoam boxes on the table. One was marked beef, one turkey, and one vegan.

"I'll take the turkey," Jenna said.

"The vegan one is for me," Oscar said, as he reached for it.

Jenna looked thunderstruck. "You're a vegan?"

"Yeah. I want to be able to do just as many pushups when I'm seventy as I can now."

"I thought you already were seventy, sir," Jenna said.

"Not yet, my twenty-something friend."

I ignored the banter and took the leftover beef. But I had a different question. "How did the judge know you'd want a vegan meal?"

"Let's say we know each other."

"How well?" I asked.

"Not so well as you're imagining. But well enough. What is it they say these days? Let's not travel there?"

"It's let's not *go* there," Jenna said.

"Well," Oscar said, "whatever it might be, let us not arrive there."

So we did not travel to the land of how Judge Gilmore knew that Oscar was a vegan and instead turned to eating our respective sandwiches, vegan and otherwise. Between bites, we tried to outline our strategy for the afternoon. It boiled down to: Keep what Boone said in mind, but forget about him as a witness for now and concentrate on the next scheduled witnesses.

Jenna needed to finish Spritz's cross-examination, of course. We agreed that she was going to push him about who else was at the DownUnder the morning of the murder, whether they were personally having breakfast with him or not. She was also going to ream him, if she could, about why he apparently hadn't even bothered to investigate anyone else.

The deputy coroner was scheduled to be the next witness after Spritz. The one who'd done the autopsy on Simon. Jenna had brought a copy of the autopsy report with her, and she paged through it.

"First thing I want to do is mess with time of death," Jenna said. "The deputy coroner estimates it at between 4:00 a.m. and 5:00 a.m. I want to push it toward 6:00 a.m. if I can. Your elevator card record supposedly shows you, Robert, coming up at 4:30. So their current theory is you killed him around 4:30 and then came back later, mimicking your regular arrival time at 6:00, to discovery the body."

"Okay," I said, "but what's to keep them from arguing I came up at 4:30 and then killed him and just hung around till 6:00, when I called it in?"

"Nothing," she said. "But it's not their current theory."

"How does that help?"

"Well, if we show that the death was closer to 6:00, they'll have to revise their theory and explain, among other things, what you were doing during that hour and a half."

"I'll bet," I said, "that a person could find a way to busy himself for an hour and a half while waiting to kill somebody."

"Robert, the real point is that if I do it right, their expert pathologist will have to change his testimony substantially about the time of death. And, as you know, an expert who changes his mind on the stand is . . ."

Oscar completed her thought, ". . . a dead expert."

"Okay," I said. "Maybe that will help. But how are you going to get him to change his mind?"

"While you were watching *Casablanca* for the fifth time last week, I did some research on time of death. It's a very inexact science, it turns out. But we don't have a lot of time right now, so wait and see, okay?"

"Okay," I said. "What else?"

"Just a minute," Oscar said. "Maybe it's not such a great idea for you to take on the coroner, Jenna."

"Why not?" she asked. "I'm the one who's done all the work on this issue."

"Yeah, I know," Oscar said. "And we agreed to that breakdown of work. But now that I'm hearing it, it sounds weird for you to be cross-examining the guy who cut up your boyfriend on the autopsy table."

"Maybe you'd feel weird about it," Jenna said. "But I don't. So let's move on."

"It's not about how you feel about it," Oscar said. "It's about how it will look. Spritz knows about you and Simon, so presumably Benitez and his friends know too. Sooner or later, the press is going to know. And then you grilling the coroner about cutting up your boyfriend's body is going to turn you into Little Miss Tabloid Cover Story. They'll say you got off on it."

"I just don't care," Jenna said.

"Maybe the case should care."

There was obviously no way to decide the issue rationally. I had long ago learned that some decisions in litigation just have to be made, one way or the other, for better or for worse. So I decided to make the decision myself. I was the client, after all. "Jenna should just go ahead and do it," I said.

Oscar looked at me as if he were seeing a ghost. And it was true that I had more or less withdrawn from a decisional mode. But he accepted it.

"All right," he said. "Let's move on."

Jenna was looking at some notes she had made on the autopsy report.

"There were some weird bruises on Simon, according to the report," she said.

"So?" I asked.

"I have a couple theories about those that I want to explore with the witness. The theories come from, well, something I know about Simon that I had forgotten about until I listened to Daniel Boone just now."

Oscar grimaced. "Shit. Like what?"

"Why don't you wait and see, too, okay? I promise you it has nothing to do with *my* having killed him. And nothing to do with my getting off on all this."

"Okay, okay," Oscar said. "Explore what you want to explore. I'm just your co-counsel."

I waited a second to see if Jenna was going to respond to that. When she didn't, I said, "I have one more issue."

"Which is what?" Jenna asked.

"The angle of the knife in his back. I swear it was in sideways—horizontally across his back—instead of vertically up and down. It's just not how someone would stab someone. Although I don't know if that's an autopsy issue."

"Actually," Jenna said, "I don't think you're right about that. The pictures of the Holbein dagger show it with a round handle. So you could stab somebody holding it either way. Blade straight up or blade sideways. But I've been thinking about it, and *where* the blade went into Simon's back is something else again. I think I can mess with them about that, too. But again, wait and see."

I could feel Oscar grumbling, although he didn't actually grumble out loud. Instead he just said, "Who's the witness they've scheduled after the coroner?"

"It's Susan Apacha," I said. "The building security manager. The one Spritz let onto the eighty-fifth floor. But I'm not sure how we can exploit that."

Jenna had finished her sandwich and was beginning to fold and refold her napkin. "You know," she said, "talking about Susan Apacha reminds me of something."

"Are you going to share it with us this time?" Oscar asked.

"Yes. I am. Before the murder, Susan Apacha had bleached blonde hair, with a greenish tint. But the day I cleaned my office out, I saw her at a distance, and her hair had become dark brown."

"Aha," I said. "One of the women Boone saw from the back had bleached blonde hair."

Oscar was not impressed. "The woman Boone *says* he saw *supposedly* had bleached blonde hair. Besides, there are a hell of a lot of women in Los Angeles with bleached blonde hair. And probably even more women who look like that in Beverly Hills."

I was about to ask what Beverly Hills had to do with it, since M&M's offices were downtown, but I never got the chance because there was a knock on the door followed by its almost immediate opening. A herald of the judge.

Judge Gilmore stuck her head in. "Sorry to interrupt, but there's been a change. We're going to go again in ten minutes, at 2:00."

"Benitez is already finished with Boone?" Oscar said.

"Well," Judge Gilmore said, "it seems Boone refused to talk to him."

"Why?" Oscar asked.

She actually rolled her eyes. "According to Benitez, Boone refused to talk to him because, and I quote, 'You haven't gotten me out yet, Mr. Benitez.'"

None of us said a thing in response.

"See you in the courtroom," Judge Gilmore said, and left.

"Can I borrow your cell phone, Jenna?" Oscar asked. "I need to call Christian so *we* don't fail to get Boone out. On the off chance you guys are right and we need him. I'll make the call from here and see you in a couple minutes."

Jenna dug her cell phone out of her briefcase. "I have to turn it back on." I watched her push a button and then stare at the little screen, waiting for the phone to confirm its return to cellular life.

The phone gave out a message-waiting beep. Jenna pushed a button and looked at the screen. "It's just another text message. Nothing to do with the case."

Then she handed Oscar the phone. "Here's the phone, Oscar. Call Chris Ogalu."

"Christian," Oscar said.

"Whatever. We'll see you back in court in a few minutes."

As the two of us made our way back to the courtroom, Jenna said, "I think you're right. There's a big difference between Boone overhearing 'they're fake' or 'it's fake.'"

"I agree," I said. "But I can't quite figure out what."

"I can," she said. "So far as we know, Simon thought *you* made only *one* fake."

CHAPTER 45

————

When we walked back into the courtroom, Benitez and crew were already seated at their table. I thought they looked pissed off, but maybe I just imagined it. The court reporter was already set up, and the clerk was in place. Deputy Green had also returned. The clock on the courtroom wall said 1:57.

I looked for Detective Spritz but didn't see him. Perhaps he was one of those people who liked to make an entrance. I did spot Uncle Freddie sitting in the back row. He spotted us at the same instant, got up, and headed toward us. Jenna walked over to meet him. He handed her a large book and an inch-thick orange folder. Then he turned and walked out of the courtroom.

Jenna made her way back to our table, sat down, and began to study the contents of the folder.

I was about to ask her what was in it when, at 2:00 p.m. sharp, Judge Gilmore entered and began to speak, even before she had finished sitting down.

"We are here for the afternoon session in the matter of People of the State of California versus Robert Tarza, Number CR 29856. Mr. Benitez, are the People ready to proceed?"

"Yes, Your Honor."

"Ms. James?"

"Yes, Your Honor."

"All right, let's have Detective Spritz resume the stand then," Judge Gilmore said.

"Well, Your Honor," Benitez said, "I'm afraid Detective Spritz is not immediately available this afternoon."

Judge Gilmore actually raised her eyebrows. "I thought you said the People were ready to go forward, Mr. Benitez."

"We're ready to go forward with a substitute witness."

"What happened to Detective Spritz? Weren't we in the middle of his cross-examination, Counsel?"

Benitez had started out the afternoon with the regained status of "Mr. Benitez" from the judge, but seemed once again to have been demoted to "Counsel."

"Unfortunately, Your Honor, Mr. Spritz was called away on an urgent police matter."

"To do with this case?" the judge asked.

"Well, yes, to do with this case."

"Would you like to share with the court what that might be, exactly?"

"I don't think that would be appropriate, Your Honor, at least not in open court."

It was a challenge. The judge could take up his offer and find out what was going on, but only if she was willing to call everyone up to the bench and delay things even more. With the clock ticking steadily toward midafternoon.

Judge Gilmore turned to Jenna.

"I assume you object, Ms. James?"

"I certainly do. Detective Spritz is just trying to squirm out of finishing his cross-examination."

"I agree with you," Judge Gilmore said. "But do we want to waste time *right now* with the explanation or just get on with it? I leave the choice up to you, Ms. James."

Now Jenna was in something of a pickle. The judge had just told Jenna, in judge-speak, "I don't want to find out about this right now. Do *me* a favor and I'll do you one later."

Jenna accepted. "I'm willing to go with a new witness now, Your Honor. But I request that Mr. Benitez and his team agree that they won't talk to Detective Spritz about his testimony until after he's back on the stand. Whenever that might be."

"Agreed," Benitez said. It was almost too quick. Maybe he didn't want to speak to Spritz. Something odd was going on.

Judge Gilmore had on her face a look that judges get when the orderly flow of courtroom life has been disrupted. "Call your next witness, Counsel."

"The People call Stefan Eliopolous."

A gentleman arose from the front row, went through the swinging door in the bar, and headed for the witness stand. He was not tall, or even broad, yet somehow imposing nonetheless. His head was as bald as a cue ball, and his face was crinkled, as if from a life spent at the beach without benefit of sunscreen. His most striking feature was a walrus mustache, jet black with a sprinkling of grey.

He was wearing a beautiful pearl grey wool suit of supple fit and a silk maroon tie. I remarked to myself that at some point I'd need to learn who made his suits, too. My life of late seemed to be full of guys with great tailors.

He took his seat on the witness stand as if he lived there and was sworn in as Stefan C. Eliopolous, M.D.

"Dr. Eliopolous," Benitez began, "what is your profession?"

"I'm a deputy medical examiner for the Los Angeles County Office of the Coroner."

"Could you tell the court, briefly, your professional background."

"I received an MD degree from the Yale School of Medicine in 1980. I subsequently did a five-year residency in anatomical and clinical pathology at Massachusetts General Hospital. I'm currently board certified in both of those specialties as well as in forensic pathology."

"Where did you do your initial training in forensic pathology?"

"I did a one year fellowship at the University of Texas Southwestern Medical Center. The training included performing or assisting at well over two hundred suspicious death or homicide-related autopsies."

"Are you involved in any professional associations?"

"Yes. I'm the current president of the International Forum of Forensic Pathologists."

I wondered why the hell someone with those credentials was working for the county in a junior position. I also wondered how a county salary paid for suits like that.

"How long have you been employed as a medical examiner for the County?"

"Since I completed my fellowship in 1985."

"What are your duties as a deputy medical examiner?"

"I supervise other deputy medical examiners, I teach in our office's residency program in forensic pathology, and I conduct autopsies."

"How many autopsies have you personally conducted in your career?"

"More than three thousand."

"How many of those have involved homicides or suspected homicides?"

"Perhaps half of them."

"And of those, how many involved knife wounds?"

"At least a couple of hundred, although we would have to define what you mean by knife—"

Judge Gilmore interrupted. "Counsel, I'm already persuaded of Dr. Eliopolous' expertise in forensic pathology. Can we just get to the core of the matter, which is the autopsy in *this* homicide? Please?"

"Of course, Your Honor," Benitez said. "Doctor, when did you become aware of the death of Simon Rafer?"

"On the morning of December 6, I was in the office very early, trying to catch up on paperwork, when we received a call from the LAPD of a possible homicide. Since we were short on staff that early in the morning, I decided to go to the scene myself. I left immediately and took two forensic technicians with me."

"What time did you arrive on the scene?"

"At 6:40 a.m."

"What did you observe when you arrived?"

"There were a number of police officers at the scene, as well as the defendant." He nodded in my direction. "There was a body face down on the floor with a large, ornate knife protruding from its back. The body was surrounded by partially congealed blood to a distance of approximately three feet on the torso's left and approximately one foot to its right."

"What did you do at that point?"

"I asked Detective Spritz, whom I knew from prior homicide scenes, if it would be destructive of the crime scene for me to touch the body and move it slightly to help determine time of death. He said that photographs and prints had already been taken and that I could do so."

"What did you do to determine time of death?"

"First, I touched the victim's neck to be sure there was no pulse, although it was obvious that the victim was dead. Then I pulled the victim's shirt up so that I could see the skin and determine the extent to which there was already postmortem lividity—discoloration of the skin as the blood settles. That is one approximate indicator of time of death."

"Did you take any other steps to determine approximate time of death?"

"Yes. I moved the victim's jaw, fingers, elbows, and head. Full rigor mortis—stiffening of the entire body—doesn't set in until approximately eight hours have passed. But stiffening of smaller muscles, particularly the jaw, occurs sooner."

"Did you take any other steps?"

"Yes. I asked one of the techs to take the temperature of the victim's liver, which she did with a pointed thermometer inserted through a small incision under the rib cage. Liver temperature can give you an approximate time of death because it drops by approximately 1.5 degrees Fahrenheit per hour after death until it reaches the temperature of the surroundings."

"What were the results of that measurement?"

"At 7:00 a.m., the temperature of the victim's liver was 95.8 degrees Fahrenheit, 3.8 degrees below normal liver temperature, which is on average 99.6 degrees."

"Different from what most of us call 'normal?'"

"Yes. The liver's average temperature is usually about one degree higher than the average of 98.6 degrees you get when temperature is taken by mouth."

"From all of that information, do you have an opinion, to a reasonable degree of medical certainty, as to the time of death?"

"Yes, from the state of the body's mild livor mortis—the reddish blue discoloration of the lower portions of the body—the temperature of the liver, and the small degree of rigor mortis of the jaw, the time of death, to a reasonable degree of medical certainty, was somewhere between 4:00 and 5:00 a.m. that day. Approximately two to three hours before I got there."

"Doctor, did you later perform an autopsy on Mr. Rafer?"

"Yes, I did."

"Were you able to determine the cause of death to a reasonable degree of medical certainty?"

"Yes. The cause of death was a knife wound. The knife entered through the victim's back, well below the heart and to the left of the spine. On the way through, it transected the descending aorta—sliced it horizontally. The immediate cause of death was thus heart failure caused by rapid exsanguination."

"Can you estimate how long the victim lived after the knife wound was inflicted?"

"The size of the cut through the artery—it was almost severed—was such that death was very quick. Unconscious in seconds. Surely dead in minutes."

"Did you prepare a written report of that autopsy?"

"Yes, I did."

"Your Honor, the autopsy report has been pre-marked for identification as People's Exhibit No. 4. The People will move the admission of the exhibit into evidence at the conclusion of the hearing."

"Do I have a copy?" the judge asked.

The judge's clerk spoke up. "It's to your left on the bench, Judge."

"I have no further questions," Benitez said.

CHAPTER 46

———

Jenna moved to the podium, the large textbook Uncle Freddie had given her in hand. "Dr. Eliopolous, have you ever personally conducted any studies related to determining time of death?"

"No."

"So all of your information is from studies outlined in textbooks?"

"From textbooks and other published studies. Although that is true of a lot of inferences drawn on the clinical side of forensic pathology."

It was a polished answer from a polished expert.

"So you've never personally, for example, measured the liver temperature of someone whose time of death you knew exactly?"

"No. But many others have done so and recorded their observations."

"Or personally studied the stiffness of a jaw muscle of someone whose time of death you knew with precision?"

Eliopolous thought about it. You could almost see him reviewing in his mind all the jaw muscles of the dead he'd ever moved. He was not an expert to be rushed. "No."

"Would you call your determination of time of death an estimate, then?"

"I'd call it a very good estimate."

"Well, in those textbooks and studies you've seen"—Jenna looked at the thick book she had placed on the podium, but did not open it—"have you ever read that the rate at which the temperature of the liver falls after death is in part dependent on the ambient air temperature around the body?"

"Objection!" It was Benitez coming to life. "The question calls for speculation and is without foundation, since it assumes such books and studies say what Ms. James says they say. But she hasn't produced them so that we can see if they do."

It was an utter bullshit objection with an expert, particularly because Eliopolous had already acknowledged that the studies and textbooks existed. But the objection certainly sent a nice message to the witness if he wanted to take it up—ask her exactly what damn books she's talking about.

Judge Gilmore had looked to be reading something on the bench and paying attention out of only one ear. But one ear was clearly enough, since she didn't even wait for Jenna to respond before ruling. "Overruled," she said. "You may answer, Doctor."

"Yes, I have read that kind of thing," Eliopolous said.

"Did you determine the ambient air temperature of the reception area at Marbury & Marfan between 4:00 and 5:00 a.m. that morning?"

"No, I didn't."

"If the ambient temperature at the time of death was, say, sixty degrees, the drop in liver temperature would have been faster than if it were seventy-two degrees, isn't that right?"

"Yes . . . somewhat."

"Making the time of death later rather than earlier?"

"Yes . . . slightly. Which is why I estimated time of death as a range."

"Have you also read, Doctor, that the rapidity with which liver temperature drops after death is affected by the amount of blood loss?"

"Yes."

"Is the drop faster or slower if there was a lot of blood loss?"

"Faster . . . again, somewhat."

"Was there, in your opinion, a major loss of blood by the victim here?"

"Yes, he had lost perhaps half his volume of blood."

"So that situation, too, might have pushed the time of death later rather than earlier?"

"Yes, I suppose. By a small amount."

"And Doctor, have you ever read that the rate of decrease in liver temperature is impacted by how much body fat the victim has?"

"Yes, fat is an insulator, so the less body fat, the faster the temperature drops."

"In your opinion, did the victim here have an average amount of body fat?"

"No, he was very lean. He had the body of an athlete."

"So his liver temperature after death might have dropped faster than 1.5 degrees per hour?"

"Yes, that's again *possible*."

"Again, pushing the time of death toward a later time?"

"It could, somewhat."

"Doctor," Jenna said, "are you familiar with the fact that some people have lower body temperatures than other people? That not everyone is at 98.6 degrees?"

Up to the moment of that question, Eliopolous had displayed the usual demeanor of an expert being questioned by someone he clearly regarded as a technical inferior. The attitude of "Yes, there are those little quibbles, but nothing of importance, unknowledgeable worm." With Jenna's last question, though, I thought I detected a slight stiffening of *his* body.

"Um, yes. I am. There is a range."

"Did you make any effort to determine Mr. Rafer's average body temperature when he was alive?"

There was a very long pause, as, I had no doubt, Dr. Eliopolous' very agile brain searched for a way out but failed to find one. "No, I didn't."

"If it were the case that Mr. Rafer's average body temperature, measured by mouth, was only 96.9 degrees instead of 98.6, would that make a difference in your estimate of time of death?"

Benitez was up and animated. "Objection! There is no evidence in the record that Mr. Rafer had a below-average body temperature."

"I'm presenting it as a hypothetical, Your Honor," Jenna said.

"It's unethical, Your Honor, to pose a hypothetical unless Counsel has a good-faith basis to support the facts she's put in the hypothetical."

Judge Gilmore peered down at Jenna. "Miss James, do you have a good-faith basis for that particular hypothetical fact?"

"I do, Your Honor."

"The objection is overruled, then." She turned to the witness. "You may answer the question."

I waited to see what Dr. Eliopolous would do. Experts are funny witnesses. On the one hand, they are owned by the side that brought them, and they understand that their job is to help their owners. On the other hand, professionals, even the slimier ones, have some sense of fealty to truth.

He chose to tell the truth. But with a lot of backing and filling.

"Well, Ms. James," he said, "if Mr. Rafer *truly* had an average body temperature, measured by mouth, of 96.9—which would be unusual, perhaps even rare—and assuming that his average liver temperature was also correspondingly lower, and assuming that the rate of fall of temperature in his liver after death was the standard 1.5 degrees per hour, your hypothetical fact could push my estimate of time of death one hour later, to a range of 5:00 a.m. to 6:00 a.m."

That seemed to me like a pretty good answer, despite the hedging. But, then, after a very slight pause, Dr. Eliopolous showed himself to be an experienced expert by adding something to his answer.

"However, Counsel," he said, "the rigidity of the victim's jaw, based on my personal experience, suggests an earlier time of death to me. And I have no information about what his average body temperature actually was, so I have to assume it was like most people's rather than subnormal."

Jenna could have reminded him that he had just admitted that his own experience didn't include measuring actual, known time of death against jaw stiffness. Instead, she chose to ignore his wiggle and to try to pull the noose of the hypothetical a bit tighter.

"Doctor," she asked, "if, hypothetically, the ambient air temperature at the time of death was sixty degrees, and given that you found Mr. Rafer to have lower-than-average body fat, and given that you yourself observed that he had lost a great deal of blood quickly, and assuming hypothetically that his average body temperature was 96.9, isn't it possible that within a revised range of 5:00 a.m. to 6:00 a.m., the time of death was actually closer to 6:00 a.m. than to 5:00 a.m.?"

"It's possible, yes. But I still don't regard it as likely, and by the way, I haven't bought into your revised range, even hypothetically."

"But it would be within the realm of reasonable medical possibility?"

"Yes, I suppose it would. Assuming your key hypothetical fact is true."

And then Eliopolous did something that experienced witnesses aren't supposed to do. He stepped out of role. "Ms. James," he asked, "do you actually have Mr. Rafer's medical records showing a lower than average body temperature?"

Judge Gilmore was suddenly fully awake. In our odd system of law, witnesses don't get to ask questions, only answer them. So Jenna was not required to answer Eliopolous' question. But the judge could have left her to twist in the wind of having to decide whether or not to answer the question anyway, with the press watching. Or the judge herself could have asked exactly what records Jenna was referring to. Instead, Judge Gilmore returned the earlier favor.

"Dr. Eliopolous, you're enough of an experienced expert to know that that's not a proper question for a witness to put to a lawyer. Ms. James has represented to the court that she has a good-faith basis for her hypothetical, and, particularly with no jury present, that's all we need. Ms. James, do you have further questions of this witness?"

"Yes, I do, Your Honor."

"Then please proceed."

At that moment, Oscar slipped into the chair beside mine at the counsel table. I hadn't noticed him come into the courtroom. He pushed a note at me: *Called Ogalu. He'll get Boone out.* Meanwhile, Jenna was moving forward.

"Dr. Eliopolous," Jenna asked, "do you have a copy of People's Exhibit 4 there?"

"Yes, I do."

"Let me call your attention to page six. Do you see there where you refer to a large bruise on the heel of the victim's right palm? On the fleshy area directly below the thumb?"

"Yes."

"Doctor, in your opinion, was that more likely a premortem or post-mortem bruise?"

"It appeared to be premortem. Before death. Although, from the looks of it, it was very fresh. So it might have come just before death."

"Do you have any theory as to what caused that bruise?"

"Likely, after Mr. Rafer was stabbed, he fell forward and, and in his last seconds of consciousness, instinctively tried to break his fall with his hand."

"Wouldn't a fall like that also have caused trauma to the bones or ligaments of the hand, wrist, or forearm?"

"It could have."

"Did you observe any such collateral damage?"

"No."

"Wouldn't someone breaking his fall in that way normally bruise the other side of the palm as well?"

"He could, but the biomechanics of falls are funny. They can go a lot of different ways."

"Doctor, wouldn't a person, falling in that circumstance, normally try to block his fall with both hands?"

"Perhaps. I think that's also hard to say for sure."

"Did you observe any bruising on the victim's left hand?"

"No."

Oscar pushed another note at me: *So what? How's this help?* In truth, I had no clue. I wrote *Beats me* on the note and pushed it back to him. Meanwhile, Jenna continued on about bruises.

"Doctor Eliopolous, on page eight of your report, I notice that you observed a bruise on the front of the victim's right ankle."

"Yes, I did. And anticipating your question, it appeared to be a pre-mortem bruise, again rather new. It was the type of bruise likely caused by a trauma—hitting something—rather than being twisted or sprained."

So now, Eliopolous had turned to volunteering helpful things during cross. Sometimes that meant an expert had started to go native. Maybe he'd been intimidated by Jenna's clever trap on the liver temperature stuff.

"Do you have any suppositions as to what caused that bruise?" Jenna asked.

"Maybe something about his fall, although a bruise in that area caused by a fall would more likely be on the shin or knee. But, again, falls are rather unpredictable in their biomechanics."

"So you really don't know?"

"No, I don't."

Eliopolous was now looking bored by the questioning. I looked over at Team Benitez, and they also seemed rather uninterested. Benitez himself was studying a file of some sort, and his assistants were whispering to each other about something. I didn't want to turn around, but I could almost feel the courtroom Blob pulsing with the thought: "For God's sake! Will you please give us something we can write home about?"

Jenna switched to a new topic. One that held more interest for me.

"Dr. Eliopolous, did you remove the knife that was in the victim's back?"

"Yes, during the autopsy."

"Did it appear to you that the knife had been dislodged in any way when the victim was moved from the scene of the crime to the autopsy room?"

"No, I instructed that he be placed face down on the transport gurney so that the knife would not be disturbed. I also instructed that his back was to be only loosely covered with a drape so that the knife would not be moved by the drape."

"Did you do anything else to assure it had not been dislodged prior to the autopsy?"

"Yes, I took pictures of the knife at the scene, before the victim was moved, and compared those pictures to the appearance and placement of the knife in the autopsy room. It had not budged."

Clearly, Dr. Eliopolous thought that Jenna was questioning whether he had competently made sure that the knife wouldn't budge during transport of the body. I suspected she was going somewhere else.

"Dr. Eliopolous, did you make note of the exact placement of the blade in Mr. Rafer's back?"

Eliopolous cocked his head to the side, clearly thinking about it. "Yes. Is there something about it you want to point out to me?"

"There is. Could you look at the photo that is attached as Exhibit A to your report?"

Exhibit A was sitting in a folder, just to my left, marked Filed Under Seal. Unlike the body of the autopsy report, the photos had not been released to the press. The judge had promised the Blob that if they became a topic of testimony in the preliminary hearing, she would permit them to view the photos in private but would not release them for publication. I could hear whispering behind me. From the Blob's point of view, it was the first really interesting thing that had happened since court reconvened.

For myself, I had not been able to bring myself to look at the photos, despite the fact that we had had them for weeks. But if I was not to be a complete vegetable, totally at the mercy of my gardeners, I needed to look at them. I reached over to the folder, slid it in front of me, opened it, and looked. Exhibit A was a photo of Simon taken from above. He was lying face down, still wearing his blood-soaked suit jacket, with the beautiful Holbein dagger sunk to its hilt in his back.

But it wasn't as I remembered it. The blade was not exactly halfway between Simon's shoulder blades. It was much lower down and slightly to the left. As a lawyer, of course, I learned the first year I practiced law that eyewitness recollection usually sucks on the details. But somehow I had not expected that rule to apply to me.

Eliopolous had been studying the picture, too. "Okay, Counsel, I've looked at it. What about it?"

"Do you see where the knife is relative to the horizontal midline of the victim's back?"

"Yes."

"It's below the midline, isn't it?"

"Yes."

"In fact, it's below the rib cage, isn't it?"

"Yes."

"Well, if the killer and the victim were approximately the same height, and the killer stabbed the victim from the rear, swinging his arm down with force, wouldn't you expect the blade to go in somewhere farther up the back?"

Eliopolous clearly had to think about it. "I suppose so." He hesitated, and then did something experts really shouldn't do. He proffered an unstudied explanation. "Maybe it was plunged in underhand."

"Like a girl throwing a softball underhand, Doctor?"

There was a burst of laughter from the Blob.

Judge Gilmore glared. "If there is one more outburst like that, I will clear the courtroom. And I will also discover that the viewing of this autopsy photo by the press won't be convenient until late next week. Or maybe even the week after that." There was instant silence.

"Well," Eliopolous said, "underhanding a knife into someone's back might be unusual, but I think it could be done. I've seen lower-back stab wounds before."

"The knife penetrated the muscle below the rib cage, didn't it?"

"Yes."

"And that muscle tissue is pretty tough, isn't it?"

"I suppose you could say that, although I don't know that it's really any tougher than well-worked-out abs."

"How long was the knife, Doctor?"

"I don't recall exactly."

"Your Honor, may we put a picture of the knife up on the ELMO? I think it's Exhibit R to the report."

"Yes, you may."

"I'll need a second to get it out."

While Jenna looked for the photo, I thought about the ELMO. It's an oddly named device used in courtrooms to project magnified images of exhibits onto a big screen. When I first encountered the name, I imagined it to have been invented by a court clerk named Elmo. When I finally looked it up, though, it turned out to be a mere acronym for the pedestrian phrase Electricity, Light, Machine, Organization.

Jenna found Exhibit R, and it flashed up on the big screen in the back corner of the courtroom. There it was, the Holbein dagger that I'd last seen buried in Simon's back. Its elegant painted handle looked pristine, but its broad blade was covered in what was clearly dried blood. A twenty-four inch ruler was displayed to the side.

"Dr. Eliopolous, does this refresh your recollection as to how long the blade was?"

"Yes, it was almost thirteen inches long."

"Did the knife make an exit wound in the abdominal area?"

"Yes, it did."

"Let me direct your attention to Exhibit F of your report."

Eliopolous reached for his report and paged through it until he came to the exhibit. "Okay, I have it here."

"Do you see the sketch you made of the path of the knife through the victim, from entry wound to exit wound?"

"Yes."

"It shows a downward slant, doesn't it?"

"Yes, it does."

"So, Doctor, do you really think that someone thrusting the knife *underhand* at a downward angle could develop enough force to drive a thirteen-inch blade through the muscle of the victim's back, through his internal organs, and out the muscle in his abdominal wall, on the other side?"

"Objection!" It was Benitez. "Doctor Eliopolous is not an expert in biomechanics, and we haven't presented him as such."

Judge Gilmore peered down at him, bemusement spread across her face. "Mr. Benitez, wasn't your witness just telling us a moment ago about the biomechanics of how bruises might be acquired?"

"Well, yes, Your Honor, but that's different."

"I'm not persuaded it's so different. Overruled. You may answer the question, Doctor."

A really talented expert witness would simply have responded to the question by saying that he didn't know whether it could be put in underhand with enough thrust, and leave the answer to some other, better-qualified expert. But I sensed that Dr. Eliopolous was not a guy who liked to say he didn't know the answer to a question.

"I don't think that would be so difficult," Eliopolous answered.

"Your Honor," Jenna said, "may I be permitted a demonstration?"

"Yes, you may," Judge Gilmore said.

"I'll need my co-counsel to help me." Jenna turned toward us. "Mr. Quesana, could you join me, please?" Oscar got up and moved toward the witness stand.

"Your Honor, may the witness step down from the witness stand?"

"Yes."

I had no clue what Jenna had in mind. But since she was proposing to do a demonstration with the *other* side's expert, it promised to be good. If it worked.

CHAPTER 47

———

Eliopolous stepped down off the stand, looking as if he wished that he had said he didn't know the answer to the question. Oscar was standing beside Jenna. He didn't look nervous, but he did look puzzled. Like me, he clearly had no clue what Jenna had in mind.

"Mr. Quesana, would you just stand here, please?" She pointed to a spot in front of the witness stand. "And Dr. Eliopolous, would you just stand right behind him?" Eliopolous positioned himself behind Oscar.

Jenna handed Eliopolous a piece of chalk. She must have had it in her pocket. "Doctor, could you mark, right there on the back of Mr. Quesana's suit jacket, the approximate spot where the knife went in?"

"Objection," Benitez said. "Improper hypothetical. There's been no showing that the witness and Mr. Quesana are the same heights as the victim and the defendant."

"Overruled," the judge said. "You can bring that out on redirect. And unless I'm going blind, the defendant and Mr. Quesana clearly are about the same height."

Eliopolous took the chalk and made an "x" on Oscar's back, just below the rib cage and slightly to the left of his spine.

"Thank you, Doctor," Jenna said.

Then from somewhere, and to this day I don't know where she had hidden it, Jenna produced a rubber knife of about the same size and shape as the Holbein dagger that had killed Simon. She held it out to Eliopolous.

"Doctor, would you show us how—in your expert opinion—you would use a knife like this to stab Mr. Quesana underhand, with a slight downward angle of the blade?"

"Objection!" It was Benitez again. "I renew my objection to this entire line of questioning. Doctor Eliopolous is not an expert in *this type* of biomechanics. This is the kind of thing a police officer, like Detective Spritz, might be able to shed light on."

Judge Gilmore looked more than a little annoyed. "Well, Counsel, if you ever locate Detective Spritz, maybe you can ask him about it. But for the moment, I want to hear from Dr. Eliopolous on this topic. Overruled . . . again."

Benitez then risked the judge's ire by piling a second objection on top of his first. "Thank you, Your Honor. But then I want to make a second objection. This demonstration is an improper hypothetical demonstration because the *rubber* knife is not the exact size—and certainly not the same material—as the original."

Judge Gilmore looked over at the screen, on which the image of the dagger was still projected. "It looks close enough to me, Counsel, at least for a demonstration in a preliminary hearing. Your objection is overruled. Go ahead and see if you can do it, Doctor."

Eliopolous took the knife from Jenna, hefted it, and made the attempt. The blade bent as it hit Oscar's back. There was a single titter from one of the spectators. The judge glared quickly out at them, but apparently decided not to punish the group for the sins of one.

It was apparent why the titter had come. In order to thrust the knife at a downward angle, Eliopolous had had to raise his elbow up and out. That had made the thrust puny at best, and it was clear to everyone that a thrust like that wouldn't have had enough force to push a thirteen inch knife through an entire body.

It was even clear to Eliopolous, who muttered, in a just barely audible voice, "Okay, doesn't work." Then he just stood there, looking at a loss for what to do next.

Jenna helped him out. "You can take your seat on the witness stand again, Dr. Eliopolous."

He took his cue and went back to the stand, although he no longer looked like he lived there. Oscar came back to our table.

"Doctor," Jenna said, "do you have any theories as to how an assailant might have managed to put the knife in overhand, so low on the back, with a downward thrust?"

"Same objection," Benitez said. "Not this witness's area of expertise."

"Same overruled," Judge Gilmore said. "You may answer."

Jenna's question was, in fact, a risky one. She was giving an adverse witness an open-ended question in an important area. That's something you're not supposed to do, but every once in a while, you take the risk.

Eliopolous had learned the hard way not to go out on a limb. "No, I don't," he said.

"How about if the victim was falling when he was stabbed?" Jenna asked.

"Your Honor," Benitez said, "can I just have a continuing objection to this line of questioning?" It was the right thing for a lawyer to say at that point, because judges have a lot of discretion in such rulings, and it must have become clear to Benitez that he was simply being punished—tortured really—for letting Spritz go wherever he had gone.

"Yes, you may," Judge Gilmore said.

During this exchange, Eliopolous had been pondering Jenna's question.

"I suppose he could have been stabbed when falling, but I'm really not sure. I'm not an expert on the biomechanics of that."

"How about if he was stabbed when he was already lying down?"

"Seems more logical. But again, I don't really know."

"Doctor, was the point of the dagger embedded in the carpet and floor beneath the body?"

"I'm not sure because the body could have been moved or raised slightly before I got there. You'd have to ask . . ." You could see him hesitate as he realized what he was about to say, then just went ahead and said it. "You'd have to ask Detective Spritz."

"Doctor," Jenna said, "is the bruise on the victim's ankle, the one we were discussing earlier, consistent with his having been tripped by being kicked in the ankle?"

Eliopolous looked happy to be asked something that he might actually have some expertise about. "Yes, it was a contusion, and it could have been caused by a kick. Or by many other things, of course."

"Doctor, have you ever done an autopsy on someone who was seriously into martial arts?"

Now there was a question that truly came from left field. I could see Eliopolous trying to figure out where it was going. He had clearly come to respect Jenna. Even fear her.

He answered with caution. "Um, yes, a few times."

"Did you notice bruises on those bodies?"

"Yes. Each of them had bruises of varying ages in many places—on the torso and on the hands, arms, and legs."

"Including on the palms?"

"Yes."

"Is it possible then, Doctor, that the bruise on the heel of the victim's right palm was caused by some sort of martial arts move made by the victim when he hit somebody?"

"Objection," Benitez said. "Calls for speculation."

"Overruled."

Eliopolous answered. "It's possible, yes. But . . . well, yes, it's possible."

The "but" in the answer hung there, waiting to be plucked. Jenna chose not to pluck it.

"I have no further questions," she said, and walked back to our table. Oscar was sitting beside me and flashed her a none-too-subtle thumbs up. Jenna acknowledged his thumb with a small nod of her head. I hoped the Blob had caught the exchange.

Judge Gilmore looked over at Benitez. "Redirect, Counsel?"

Benitez was now in full possession of what old John Jordan, the very same one who had taken me to dinner at the Yorkshire Grill so long ago, had called a BHP. Big hairy problem. Benitez's BHP was that he had probably not anticipated several things Jenna had brought up on cross. Most especially the below average body temperature thing. And so he had no idea what his witness was going to say if he tried to get him to clean it up. He desperately needed to talk to him first.

He tried to create the opening, and I was impressed at the audacity of the try.

"Your Honor," Benitez said, still sitting at his table, "I'm afraid I drank an awful lot of coffee during the lunch break. Would it be a problem if we took a really short break—maybe five minutes—so I could go deal with that?"

"Well," Judge Gilmore said, "I could say to that what my third grade teacher would have said. But instead I'm just going to say that it's getting toward midafternoon, and I'd like to get finished with this witness so we can all go home. Unfortunately, five-minute breaks don't exist. It seems the smallest human break-unit for humans is inevitably fifteen minutes. So just push through. And if it's more urgent than that, ask one of your co-counsel, who've been sitting so patiently there beside you, to do the redirect." She smiled a beatific smile.

My choice, in his shoes, would have been to say, "No questions." For the simple reason that Benitez could call Eliopolous again at the trial and try to clean up the problems Jenna had created. And if Oscar was right, what holes Jenna had managed to punch in the prosecution's case weren't going to sink the prosecutorial boat in a preliminary hearing. On the other hand, whatever Eliopolous said here, under oath, Benitez would be stuck with at the trial. Fatally, if the answers turned out to be bad.

Benitez got up and moved to the podium. He started by plucking the "but" that Jenna had left hanging.

"Doctor Eliopolous, I noticed that in answering Counsel's last question, you said, 'But . . . well, yes, it's possible.' Was there a but?"

"Yes," Eliopolous replied. "I was going to say, 'But it still seems more likely to me it was caused by a fall.' And then I was going to add that in any case, if the bruise on the victim's palm was caused by the victim's martial arts move against his killer, you would expect to see a very nasty bruise on that killer." As he said it, he looked directly at bruiseless me.

"Thank you." Benitez had brought his legal pad with him to the podium, and he began paging through it. Taking his time. Clearly, he was reviewing his notes of Jenna's cross to see what else he ought to try to fix. There wasn't a lot that could be reliably fixed. But some lawyers find it hard to leave a damaged witness well enough alone.

Benitez was apparently one of them, because he went for the one thing he should have left completely alone.

"Doctor, do you have any information about what percentage of the population has below average body temperature?"

"Yes. I think it's about ten percent. Although I'm not certain of the exact percentage."

I was looking directly at Eliopolous as he answered, and I could read the message to Benitez in his eyes: stop asking me about this. But Benitez didn't receive the message because he was still looking down at his notes. He barged right on.

"And," he asked without looking up, "on average, do people with below-average body temperature have any particular physical characteristics?"

Eliopolous did his best to try to soften the answer. "Yes. Well, I'm not really an expert on this subject, but I understand they are often people with low heart rates who are also lean and in excellent health."

That answer caused Benitez to snap his head up and look at his witness. As if coming out of some trance. I don't know what answer he had been expecting, but it clearly wasn't that one. I suppose he had expected Eliopolous to pull a helpful answer out of his expert hat. In any case, Benitez had apparently had enough. Finally.

"I have no further questions," he said.

Judge Gilmore looked at Jenna. "Re-cross, Ms. James?"

"One question, Your Honor."

Jenna asked it without getting up. "Doctor, when you conducted the autopsy, did the victim here appear to you to have been lean and in excellent health prior to his murder?"

"Yes."

"I have no further questions."

Judge Gilmore looked at Benitez. "Any re-redirect, Counsel?"

"No Your Honor."

The Judge turned and looked up at the clock on the wall behind the bench. It was a few minutes past 3:00. "You know," she said, "it's been an unusual day. Why don't we call it a day. Mr. Benitez, will Detective Spritz be with us in the morning?"

"I hope so, Your Honor," he said.

"You *hope* so?"

"Yes."

Judge Gilmore just sat there, looking at him. I'm not sure what was going through her head. The efficacy of a threat? Get him here or else? Most judges hate to make threats because if they don't get compliance, they have to carry out the threats or lose all credibility. And trying to hold a senior homicide detective in contempt would be messy. She chose instead to utter a veiled threat. "Well," she said, "let us hope your hope is fulfilled. And please communicate to the detective that I hope your hope is fulfilled."

She got up, turned, and started to leave the bench, but then appeared to remember something. Still standing, she turned back around and asked, "Counsel, who will be your next witness tomorrow after Detective Spritz?"

"It was going to be Susan Apacha, Your Honor, but there's been a slight change of plan, and it will now be two really quick witnesses. Sergeant Drady and Maria Hernandez."

"Who," the judge asked, "is Maria Hernandez?"

"The mailroom supervisor at Marbury Marfan."

"All right. And after the two short ones?"

"Stewart Broder. But he shouldn't take long either, and then we have the blood analysts."

"Okay, fine," the judge said, and headed out of the courtroom.

Precise witness order is normally not of much interest to a judge, and her lack of concern did not surprise me. One name that Benitez uttered did concern and surprise *me.* And Jenna, too, because she gave me a quizzical look.

Stewart was on the prosecution's witness list of course. Their witness list held almost a hundred names, as did ours. The normal practice is to list everyone under the sun, even if you intended to call only five of them. You just never knew who you might need. But I don't think anyone on my team had ever seriously considered that the prosecution might call Stewart.

I didn't have long to think about it because Jenna and Oscar were quickly packing up. "Come on," Jenna said. "The sheriff is still being cooperative about getting us out of here *sans* Blob, so we've got to hustle."

I turned around and saw Stewart himself sitting in the last row of spectator seats. He didn't look happy. Maybe he'd had a major acne outbreak, because his makeup looked thicker than ever. I waved to him, expecting that he'd wave back, but he didn't. Instead, he bolted out of his seat and practically zoomed out the double doors. Doors that were enmeshed in a milling Blob presence, clearly waiting to accost us.

Several sheriff's deputies suddenly appeared, formed a flying wedge, and pushed the Blob away from the doors. We followed the wedge out.

There were a lot of shouted questions as we went by, which we ignored. The coarsest of them asked if I would please take off my shirt.

The wedge protected us all the way to the elevators, where we were permitted to enter the "judges only" elevator for the trip to the parking garage. It was only as we got in that I realized Uncle Freddie had joined us.

CHAPTER 48

———

O scar pushed the button marked "G," and we headed down.
        "Why the hell are they going to call Stewart?" I asked.

"Probably," Oscar said, "because Spritz testified he let Stewart onto the eighty-fifth floor. Best guess, they want him to testify that he didn't disturb evidence while he was there. Probably on and off in five minutes."

"Maybe I'll keep him there a bit longer," Jenna said. "I might have a few questions for him myself."

"He didn't wave back at me," I said.

"Perhaps," Uncle Freddie said, "he wished to avoid bringing upon himself undue attention from members of the Fourth Estate."

"Yeah," I said. "Could be."

The elevator doors opened, and we all walked over to Jenna's Land Cruiser, which was parked nearby. Oscar got in front with Jenna. Uncle Freddie climbed into the back with me.

Oscar spoke first. "Good job, Miss James. You took their case down a peg. Maybe even a peg-and-a-half."

Jenna put the car into first gear and headed toward the exit ramp. "Enough to win, Mr. Quesana?" she asked.

"No," Oscar laughed. "Not hardly. Not yet, anyway."

I thought the "not yet" was a big concession.

"Can I ask a question?" Oscar said.

"Sure," Jenna said.

"What was your good-faith basis for your hypothetical fact that Simon had a below average body temperature?"

Jenna actually giggled. "Oh. When he had the flu, I took his temperature and told him it was normal. Ninety-eight point six. And he told me that that meant he had a fever, because his normal temperature was 96.9."

"That was it?" Oscar asked.

"I thought it was enough."

"Well, I sure as hell hope his medical records or something else supports that somehow. Other than you as Nurse Jenna. Because if we end up needing to prove it, it's gonna be kinda awkward to put you on the stand."

"Oh, something will turn up," Jenna said.

We had by then started to move up the exit ramp. To my delight, there was no Blob presence at the top, and we were soon on city streets, headed toward the blessed anonymity of the freeway. Slowly, though, because rush hour had begun and the traffic had already started to congeal.

Jenna changed the subject. "So, Uncle Freddie, what'd you learn today?"

"Not a great deal, alas," he said. "The prints on the other dagger came back, most unfortunately, as a 'no match.' My colleagues report that those prints are not on the national fingerprint database."

"Interesting," Jenna said. "All lawyers have their prints on file with the state. So that means Stewart didn't handle that dagger, and Harry didn't either. It was somebody else."

"Or they wiped it clean," Uncle Freddie said.

"What other dagger are you talking about?" Oscar asked.

"Oh, I forgot," Jenna said. "You missed Uncle Freddie's morning briefing. Uncle Freddie found another dagger hidden in Stewart's office. I'll fill you in later." In response, Oscar simply grunted.

"I should also wish to report," Uncle Freddie said, "that one of my colleagues used some connections we have to check on recent travel itineraries of various individuals of interest to us."

"Which ones?" I asked.

"Detective Spritz and Mr. Stewart Broder."

"What about Harry?"

"We weren't able to locate anything about Mr. Marfan."

"All right. Then what did you find out about Spritz and Stewart?"

"Nothing much. Mostly holidays. Last October, Detective Spritz went to China on a trip organized by the International Society of Homicide Detectives. And Stewart Broder took a holiday in Greece last summer."

"Where in Greece?" I asked.

"Skopje."

"That's the capital of Macedonia," I said.

"Right you are. It was in Greece only in classical times. Which were the best of times, wouldn't you agree?"

I had no interest in comparing historical epochs. I responded simply by saying what was on my mind. "It's not far from Philippi, where Brutus began to coin the Ides to pay his armies. Not long before he was defeated by Mark Antony and committed suicide."

"You find that significant?" Oscar asked.

"I find it a seriously odd coincidence," I said.

"Perhaps so," Uncle Freddie said. "But, on the other hand, Macedonia is also an increasingly popular tourist destination for those who wish to remain in Europe, but nevertheless seek to find something that lies on the less well-trodden path. And in any case, Mr. Broder journeyed there on a archaeology trip planned by a Yale Law School alumni group."

"Okay," I said. "But on the *other* other hand, Stewart is the kind of person who beats a very well-trodden path to five-star hotels and three-star restaurants. And I'm guessing there aren't a lot of either in Skopje."

Before I could pursue that line of thought further, Jenna's cell phone rang. She answered it and then handed it to Oscar. "It's your friend Chris Ogalu."

Oscar did not immediately take the phone from her. "It's *Christian*," he said.

Jenna continued to hold the phone out and, finally, Oscar took it. He listened for a minute as we all sat silent, listening to him listen. Then he said, "Okay, thanks," and handed the phone back to Jenna.

"What did Christian say?" Jenna asked.

"He said he got Boone out already, and Boone's headed back to wherever he lives in Santa Monica. He promises Boone will stay put for now. If we want to interview him further or call him as a witness, we should get in touch with Christian first."

"That was quick work," I said.

"Yeah," Oscar said. "He does good work. The only fly in the ointment is that Boone apparently insists that he's going to call Stewart."

"What for?" I asked.

"To complain."

"Well," Jenna said, "I don't suppose there's much we can do about that. Let's hope Stewart refuses to talk to him."

"So," Uncle Freddie said, "I gather then that you have all made the acquaintance of the unusual Mr. Boone?"

Oscar twisted fully around in the front seat and stared at him. "You know Boone?"

"I do not, but one of my colleagues has made his acquaintance. Four days ago, I placed an ad in the classified section of the *L.A. Times* requesting that anyone with pertinent information about the unfortunate demise of Mr. Rafer communicate that information to a tip line. In exchange for a monetary reward of course. It's remarkable what an advertisement like that will sometimes yield. Indeed, I was hoping that the killer himself might even call. Killers are oft voyeurs of their own killings, you know.

"I gather the killer didn't exactly call," I said.

"Correct. Indeed, most calls proved of little worth. But then, early yesterday, Mr. Boone rang us up. His information sounded a trifle more interesting, so I requested that one of my colleagues interview him in person."

"You have a lot of colleagues," Oscar said.

"Yes, I do. Trusted colleagues."

I found it all hard to fathom. "Why the hell would Boone be reading the classifieds?"

"A great many neurotics peruse the classifieds, Robert," Uncle Freddie said.

"Forget about why he was reading them," Jenna said. "How did he get into Judge Gilmore's chambers?"

"Oh, quite explicable," Uncle Freddie said. "I was of the view that the District Attorney would not be inclined to give him a serious listen were he to ring them up directly, and especially not if we presented him. So I suggested—through my colleague, of course—that Mr. Boone might visit Judge Gilmore herself to relate his story."

Oscar was still turned around in the seat. "That's *why* he went to see Judge Gilmore. Did your colleague also tell him *how* to get in to see Judge Gilmore?"

"Well," Uncle Freddie said, "I do own an interest in the security company that supplies the software for the courthouse security system, and I am aware of certain codes that might be used to override the system, but I would certainly never supply those codes to someone as unstable as Mr. Boone. And I'd be deeply shocked if any of my colleagues had disclosed them. Shocked to my toes. I cannot even imagine it. So I have no idea how he got in."

No one said anything. Oscar turned back around and faced the front. Jenna drove, saying nothing. Uncle Freddie and I just sat there.

To distract myself from the awkward silence, I looked out the side window. We were at that moment totally stopped in downtown traffic, and I could hear the honking of horns—quite rare in Los Angeles, but increasingly common as New Yorkers have moved in—that seemed to announce that we weren't going anywhere for a while. I looked at the real people on the streets, going about their business, not on trial for anything. I remembered when I was able to do that.

The car had started to creep forward again. "Stop the car," I said. "I'm going to get out and take a little walk." I unbuckled my seat belt.

"Are you carsick again?" Oscar asked.

"No, I'm just tired of being cooped up like a bird in a cage. It's been weeks since I've been anywhere other than my house, this car, or the courtroom."

I had expected Oscar to protest. Instead, he simply said, deadpan, "You're the client."

That's code, of course. When a lawyer says that, particularly in that tone of voice, it translates as, "You're a serious moron, but you're over the age of eighteen, I've done everything I can for you, and there's apparently nothing I can do to stop you, so good luck."

Jenna simply said, "I don't think it's wise." But she pulled to the curb and stopped the car.

"I know," I said. "But I'm going anyway." I started to open the door.

"Where shall we pick you up?" Oscar asked. "Do you want us to follow you?"

"No, I'll just grab a cab at the Biltmore. There are always cabs there. It will be a new adventure for me. Taking a cab in L.A."

"Promise me," Jenna said, "that you won't talk to anyone, especially not the cab driver."

"I never talk to anyone about the case."

"Like," Oscar said, "you didn't talk to the *National Enquirer* reporter on the plane."

"That was different."

"Or that kid who asked you for your autograph."

"Okay, okay. I get it. I'm just going for a walk. No talking to anyone."

Uncle Freddie grabbed my arm. I thought he was going to try to keep me from getting out. Instead, he reached into his inner suit coat pocket and pulled out a mechanical pencil. "Here you go, old man, you might want to take some notes."

"Take notes of what?"

"Oh dear me," Uncle Freddie said. "I forgot you are not in my business. It is also a digital recording device. If anyone accosts you in a threatening fashion or tries to trick you into confessing, press the eraser gently, and it will record what they say on the chip embedded in the pencil body. Up to five hours. The microphone is in the metal clip."

"Isn't that a crime in California? To record a conversation with someone without telling them?"

"Not if they're threatening you with a crime."

"Well, I don't think I'll need it, but thanks." I took it from him, slipped it in my shirt pocket, and got out. A light rain had begun to fall. I felt truly alive for the first time in weeks.

CHAPTER 49

I walked a few blocks, enjoying my freedom. A couple of people stared, but nobody approached me. After a while, the rain began to intensify. I was soon going to be seriously wet if I didn't find shelter. I realized that I was only a block from the DownUnder, and that I could probably stop by and borrow an umbrella from the owner, Tommy Flannery. A good stiff drink sounded great, too. After all, I wasn't driving. I promised myself that I would exchange only pleasantries with Tommy. And since it was not yet four o'clock, the place wasn't likely to be crowded with other people. I quickened my pace, got to the DownUnder, and headed down the steps. Carefully, because they were slippery from the rain.

Upon entering, I was stunned to see Detective Spritz sitting at the bar. He was the only customer. I pivoted and started to head back out, but he had apparently seen me.

"Wanna join me for a drink, Tarza?" he yelled.

"I don't think so," I said, without turning to face him.

"Big bad lawyer is afraid?"

In my newfound state of euphoria, I reasoned this way to myself: I wouldn't need to say anything to him, but maybe I'd learn something useful from him. I pushed the "record" eraser on the mechanical pencil, turned back around, and went and sat down next to him. He was obviously drunk.

"Where's your girlfriend, huh?" he asked, not bothering to turn his head.

"She's not my girlfriend."

He turned and looked at me. "If you say so. But whatever, she won't like it, you talkin' to me. Not supposed to, you know. Might tell me some deep dark secret or somethin."

"I'm an adult," I said. "I can talk to anyone I want. And right now I'm happy to have a drink and talk to you."

Just then, Tommy Flannery, who had been drying glasses down at the other end of the bar, sauntered over. I'd known him for more than thirty years. He had once been a very large Irishman with flaming red hair. Thirty years had removed most of the hair and all of the color from the residual fringe. He now looked like a very large, mostly bald leprechaun.

Flannery displayed not even a raised eyebrow at seeing the accused felon-of-the- moment sitting at his bar, right beside his chief accuser. "The usual, Roberto?" he asked. Flannery had years ago fallen into the habit of Latinizing everyone's name. Not unlike the food on his breakfast menu. At least Spritz wasn't eating Huevos Pancho Villa.

"No, I'll have a Bloody Mary," I said.

"No martini? Never seen you drink anything else."

"Times change," I said. Flannery shrugged and went to look for the Bloody Mary mix.

Spritz was still staring directly at me. "When you drink do you throw up?"

"No."

"Okay, then. Whadya wanna talk about, huh?"

"Not a thing. I just want to have a drink."

"You wouldna come over here if ya didn't want to ask something."

I did have a couple questions. And I had a recorder. Maybe it was a crime to record it, but I was already charged with a much bigger crime. Information is power.

"Who was having breakfast with you here that day, Detective?"

"Like I said in court, nobody."

"Who else was here who you knew?"

"Buncha people. Didn't know any of 'em."

Spritz turned back to staring down his drink. It was a scotch and soda, and it was almost empty. Flannery came back and plunked my bloody Mary down in front of me. I picked it up, took a sip, and stole a glance at Spritz. The DownUnder is fairly dark, and the bar area is even darker. When I first sat down, my eyes hadn't fully dark adapted, so I hadn't been able to see Spritz very well. Now I could. He had large, dark circles under his eyes and his skin looked pasty. I looked at the drink in front of him and wondered how many he'd had.

"Okay," I said, after more than a minute of drink-sipping silence had gone by, "Let me ask you a different question. Where were you this afternoon?"

"None of your business."

"It is my business. You're trying to send me to jail for twenty years, remember?"

"Twenty-*five.*"

"Whichever. You owe me an explanation."

"I don' owe you shit, Tarza. But you know what, huh? It's gonna come out in court tomorrow anyway, so maybe I should jus' fucking tell you."

I was immediately suspicious. This was too easy. I looked down the bar at Flannery and mouthed the words "How many?" He held up four fingers and then spread his thumb and forefinger wide apart. If Spritz had already had four big ones, he was seriously gone. So maybe he was going to tell me the straight scoop with no devious motive.

"Go ahead," I said.

"I was staking out Harry Marfan's house in Manhattan Beach."

"Why?"

"Witnessing the heroin drop. Hardly news to you, I'm sure, huh."

"I seriously have no clue what you're talking about."

"Sure you don't. You were a part of it, remember?" He drained what was left of his scotch. "Tommy, gimme another okay? A double this time."

"Part of what?" I asked.

"Part of a clever deal to import heroin from South America into L.A. via Hawaii."

"You're out of your mind. Not to mention drunk."

"The Honolulu office was opened when you were the managing partner, wasn't it, huh?"

"Yes."

"There aren't any other major L.A. firms with a Honolulu office, are there?"

"We have a big client there. Simon did, anyway. And it's the gateway to Asia, where we have a lot of clients."

"We?"

"M&M," I said. "The law firm."

Flannery put the double down in front of Spritz. "Okay, Spritzo," he said. "Four plus two makes six. No more after this one, Detective."

By way of reply, Spritz picked up the glass and tossed down a big swallow.

Then he turned back to me. "It's clever. No one's ever used a big-deal law firm to move drugs before, huh?"

"I know zero about any of it," I said. "But if Harry's involved in drug smuggling, so was Simon."

"How do you know that?" Spritz asked.

"They were like father and son."

"Well, look," Spritz said. "You say what you want, huh. We've got it nailed. The whole thing. First you guys move the stuff from Rio, where you also conveniently have an office, to Hawaii. Use unsuspecting associates goin' on business. First give 'em firm-issued brief cases with sniff-proof false bottoms. Clean-cut guys in suits. Or even girls. What narc is gonna suspect snotty skirts like that as mules, huh?"

It was true that we gave each new associate a leather M&M briefcase. The big kind that come with their own wheels. It had been Simon's idea. A welcome-to-the-firm gift.

Spritz wasn't done. "Then someone in your Honolulu office moves the stuff to LAX. They don't check incoming domestic flights for drugs much. Then someone takes it to your big-deal firm in L.A. Gets repackaged right there in your office, huh? Shove those pretty fake coins aside and cut it up, right there on the coffee table."

He took another long drink. "And then down to Manhattan Beach, so Marfan can give it to the mules to move it out in small boats."

"What on earth makes you think I was involved in that?"

"Makes sense, huh? Marfan dreams it all up when he's managing partner. You're the next chief guy, so you do it. With a little help from that building security manager, huh? Whatever the hell her name is. That way you guys can come and go at night with no elevator records. And then Rafer takes over as head honcho and he runs it."

"I'm astounded," I said. I picked up my still almost full glass and drank it down in two swallows.

"Yeah, sure you're astounded," Spritz said. He took another big swig of his scotch and plowed on. "As astounded as when Rafer tried to back out and you drew the short straw and hadda kill him, huh?"

Up until that moment, I had actually liked his story, implausible as it seemed. They were all involved in drugs and fell out; Stewart had mentioned something similar. But since I was not involved in drugs, it meant that someone else had killed Simon over drugs. Now it seemed I was part of it, at least in Spritz's mind.

"You've had way too many scotches," I said.

"You're right," Spritz said, and started to get up from the barstool. "I should go home, huh."

"Wait," I said. "Why did Simon try to back out?"

"The usual reason."

"Which is?"

"Fell in love with your lady lawyer. Wanted out so they could have kiddies and live happily ever after."

I felt like I had been punched in the stomach. He had a lot of facts, but he had put them together wrong. If all these interlinked theories were going to be brought out in court, I was in even deeper likely conviction shit than I had thought. If that was possible.

"Hey," Spritz said, "I have a question for you, huh. Fair's fair."

"All right, what?"

"That coin shit? Using those things to wash money? What the hell was that all about? Better ways to put drug money in the wash, huh? Amateurs. Jesus. And all those fake e-mails back and forth about you cheating him? Why bother?"

"The coin I sold him wasn't fake. And I, at least, wasn't washing anything."

Spritz was by now on his feet, if unsteadily. "Sure, sure," he said, and started stumbling toward the door. I watched him go and then turned back to my empty glass, thinking whether to order another one. Flannery was behind the bar, right in front of me. I supposed he had heard most of it. Maybe all of it.

"He's going to kill himself," I said. "Not to mention the other driver."

"Nah," Flannery said. "I ordered him a cab about ten minutes ago. It's sitting out front. The cabbie will take him home . . . huh?" And he laughed.

"Why do you think he got so drunk? What's eating at him?"

"Truth? He goes on binges. This one started yesterday evening."

"Really? That's not something I'd have guessed about him."

"He has his demons, like the rest of us."

"I used to think I didn't have any. What are his?"

"Can't say. Bartender-customer privilege."

I laughed. "You think it's still raining out?"

"No reason to think it's not. They were predicting a storm."

"Maybe I'll have another, then," I said.

Flannery was wiping the bar with a red cloth, making large circles, then smaller ones inside them. "You're not drunk, but you don't need another drink."

"You're right," I said.

"Know something?"

"What?"

"He told you the truth about that morning. There were four or five other people here, I think, but I doubt Spritzo knew any of them."

"So I was going up a blind alley."

"Not quite. I think *you* know one of them."

"Who?"

"Guy from your firm who comes here a lot. Stewart Broder."

"Stewart was here with three or four other people?"

"No, he was alone. Sitting in a booth. But he didn't eat anything. Just drank coffee. Maybe four cups. And then he asked me for a tea bag."

"He drank tea after four cups of coffee?"

"No. I saw him put the tea bag in his pocket. That's all. But he's a weird guy, you know."

"Yeah, he is," I said. An absolutely crazy plan was beginning to form in my head. "Tomasito"—that's what he truly likes to be called—"is there still a Hertz place across the street?"

"There was this morning."

"Thanks." I paid the bill and left.

CHAPTER 50

A s I crossed the street, the rain was coming down more heavily than it had when I arrived. By the time I got to Hertz, my suit was more than damp. I had forgotten to borrow an umbrella. All Hertz had left was a single green Honda Accord, so I grabbed it. My credit card even worked. Jenna had, at some point, gotten it restored.

It took me almost two hours of driving in steady rain to make the forty-five minute drive to Manhattan Beach. Harry was down there, and my gut told me that he knew what I needed to know. It wasn't going to be like the last time. If he wouldn't tell me all of it, I was going to beat the shit out of him until he did. I'd never even hit anyone before, but I felt angrier than I had ever felt before.

I parked several blocks away, where my car wouldn't be seen. My Chicago trip had taught me a lot. When I got out, the rain was coming down in buckets. By the time I made it to Harry's front door, I was soaked.

The door was wide open, and I stepped inside, mostly to get out of the rain. The lights were on, but there was no sound. I walked cautiously into the living room.

Harry was face down on the floor, with a small dagger plunged into his back.

He wasn't moving, and there was a lot of blood. This time I noted where the dagger was. Low down and slightly to the left of the spine. To the right of the dagger, there was a dime-sized dark spot, partially covered in blood. I bent down to look at it more closely. It was another Ides.

This time I didn't touch the body. I just turned and ran.

By the time I got back to my car, I was shivering badly. Maybe from my soaked clothes. More likely from shock. If I'd had a cell phone with me, I might well have called someone. But I hadn't been taking it to the courthouse. My hand shook so much that I had trouble unlocking the car. I finally got the door open, then took my dripping jacket off and tossed it on the back seat. I got back in the car, turned on the engine, and turned up the heat. After maybe ten minutes, my shaking finally stopped. I put the car in gear and headed home.

The traffic was worse going back than it had been coming, so it took me well over two hours to get home. Which unfortunately gave me a lot of time to think. One of the things I dwelled on was the dagger in Harry's back. I had recognized it instantly. It had a unique miniature painting on the handle—Richard the Lionheart with his foot on a slain stag. A dagger with an identical image had been the pride of my collection.

As I neared my house, I considered whether to continue my criminal ways by parking a few blocks away and then trying to sneak in through the back door. Or to pull boldly into the driveway and let the Blob have its way with me. I opted for the driveway. If they hassled me, I would give them all the finger. The photo would look nice in the paper, probably above the fold.

But when I pulled into my driveway, the Blob was nowhere to be seen. There were a few leavings—a couple of discarded Styrofoam cups and a short length of coaxial cable—but that was it. No people, no equipment. I got out of the car and noticed that it had finally stopped raining. I hadn't been carrying my keys—I had minders who had keys—since the preliminary hearing started, so I walked up the path to the front door and rang my own doorbell.

I stood there, waiting, shivering a bit as the chill made its way again into my still wet clothes. After what seemed an interminable time, Jenna opened the door.

"Well," she said, looking me up and down, "Detective Tarza returns."

"Where's the Blob?" I asked.

"We don't know. About an hour ago, it just picked up and left. Like locusts leaving a picked-over wheat field. Probably found something more urgent to Blob up."

Jenna was still standing in the doorway, blocking it. "Are you going to invite me in?" I asked.

She laughed and stepped aside. "Well, it is your house."

"I've got to get out of these wet clothes," I said, and headed for my bedroom. Out of the corner of my eye, I noticed Uncle Freddie and Oscar sitting on the semicircle of couches in the conversation pit, talking. They seemed relaxed. I stood in the hot shower for a very long time, then put on jeans, a sweatshirt, and dry shoes, and headed back out to the living room.

No one was talking. Instead, Jenna, Uncle Freddie, and Oscar were all rapt at whatever was on the TV, although they had muted the sound. I walked over, much warmed up, and plunked myself down on the couch next to Jenna.

"That's where they went," Jenna said, pointing at the TV. I looked. There was the Blob, gathered in front of Harry's condo, which was cordoned off with yellow tape. The flashing lights of several squad cars lit the scene.

"Harry was murdered," Jenna said.

"Yeah, I know," I said. "I was there."

The other two heads snapped around to look at me.

"What do you mean you were there?" Oscar asked.

"Just that. I stopped in at the DownUnder on my walk and learned some things there that I thought Harry needed to explain, so I went to see him. When I got there, he was dead. He was lying on the floor, with a dagger in his back. In exactly the same spot as the dagger in Simon's back, by the way." I said it all in a matter-of-fact tone, like I might have reported seeing a dead bird on the sidewalk.

There was a long silence. Finally, Oscar asked, "What size shoes do you wear?"

"Size twelve," I said. "I'm five-foot-ten, but have really big feet for my height. Why?"

"One of the reporters just said that the killer left footprints from wet shoes, and that whoever it was had really big feet."

"That would make sense," I said. "It was raining, and the soles of my shoes were no doubt quite wet."

Uncle Freddie looked directly at me. "So, my good man, did *you* kill him?"

"No, I didn't."

"Sorry," he said, "I thought that I should cut to the chase. No offense meant."

"No offense taken," I said.

"You know," Oscar said, "you're a horse's ass, Robert."

"Why?" I asked.

"For playing at detective again," he said. "First time, you did some damage, but not damage that can't be repaired. Now you've fucked up all the good work Jenna's done for you in the hearing by going and putting yourself in the middle of a murder scene . . . again."

"Not to mention," Jenna said, "the unfortunate fact that the victim was on the prosecution's witness list."

"There are a hundred people on that list," I said. "They weren't really going to call Harry."

"Tell it to the Blob," Jenna said. She pointed the remote at the TV and unmuted it. A reporter was looking into the camera and saying ". . . this murder by dagger of a prosecution witness throws another odd twist into what was already an odd day in court at the trial of alleged murderer Robert Tarza . . ." Jenna hit the mute button again.

"That detail rather piques my interest," Uncle Freddie said. "Robert, were you able to determine the type of dagger utilized by the dastardly person who did the deed?"

"You bet," I said. "It was exactly like a dagger in the collection that was stolen from me ten years ago. The prize piece, really. Had a miniature painting of Richard the Lionheart on the handle. Very rare. There are only maybe a dozen of them around."

Uncle Freddie reached into a briefcase that had been sitting beside him on the floor and pulled out a manila folder. He removed a photo and handed it to me. "Was it like this one?"

I held it under a lamp so I could see it better. "Looks like the very one," I said.

"That's a photo of the small dagger that was hidden in the secret compartment in Stewart's office," he said. "One of my colleagues just handed me the print a bit ago."

Jenna got up and came and looked at the photo over my shoulder. "Robert, when was your collection stolen, exactly?"

"About ten years ago," I said. "I went to look for it one night in late September and found it gone. The last time I'd seen it before that was at the annual summer party at my house. In early August. Some new associates who were into collecting had wanted to see it. So it was stolen sometime between early August and late September."

"Was Stewart at the party?" Jenna asked.

"I'm sure he was," I said. "He was a regular at those things. But so were a lot of other people. Harry, for example."

"So one possible inference we might draw," Uncle Freddie said, "is that it was Stewart who spotted the collection at the party and later stole it. Then used one of the daggers from the collection to kill Simon and another to kill Harry."

"It doesn't really compute," Oscar said. "It would mean that Stewart left the courtroom, after being seen by the Blob and publicly identified as the next witness, drove straight down to Manhattan Beach, probably followed by a reporter, and killed Harry. He'd have to be as dumb as our friend Detective Tarza here."

"He's not really very smart," I said.

Oscar went silent. Uncle Freddie was looking thoughtful. "Robert," he said, "we've not yet talked in detail about your fine adventure at the DownUnder. What precisely did you learn there that persuaded you to drive to Manhattan Beach on such a lovely, rainy evening?"

"Well," I said, "Spritz was there. He told me Harry, Simon, and Susan Apacha were running a heroin smuggling ring, Brazil to Hawaii to Los Angeles, using unsuspecting M&M associates as mules."

"Righto," Uncle Freddie said. "Taking advantage of the distinct possibility that drug searches of passengers arriving in Hawaii from Brazil would be light, and searches of those going from Hawaii to LAX would be light as well. Domestic flight. Clever. Very clever . . . if true."

"You talked to Spritz?" Oscar asked, his eyebrows distinctly raised. "He was there?"

"Yeah," I said. "He was drunk as a skunk and felt like talking. He even told me their motive. They killed Simon because he was trying to back out of the whole thing."

"Why was he trying to back out?" Jenna asked.

"Supposedly because Simon had fallen in love with you and, to quote Spritz, 'wanted to have kiddies and live happily ever after.'"

"Spritz was just jerking your chain," Jenna said. "I told you before, we weren't in love. Simon least of all."

"Maybe there was more between you than you want to know," I said.

Before Jenna had a chance to respond, the phone rang in the other room, and she leaped up to go and answer it. While she was gone, I filled Oscar and Uncle Freddie in on more of the details from my conversation with Spritz, including the fact that Stewart was at the DownUnder the morning of the murder and had asked for a tea bag to take with him. They seemed only mildly interested. I had the sense that their brains had moved on to the latest murder in which I was apparently about to be falsely accused.

Jenna came back into the room. "That was Spritz," she said. "He wanted to know where the green Honda was. I told him I didn't know what green Honda he was talking about. What green Honda was he talking about, Robert?"

"The one parked out front in the driveway," I said. "I rented it at Hertz. I needed a car to get to Manhattan Beach, and mine was here. I didn't want to be followed."

"Jesus," Oscar said. "You drove a rental car to get there? That you rented in your own name?"

"Yeah," I said. "I did."

Jenna interrupted Oscar's incredulity. "Spritz wanted to know one more thing."

"What?" I asked.

"What size shoes you wear."

"Did you provide him that information?" Uncle Freddie asked.

"No, of course I didn't. I told him I didn't go around asking men their shoe size."

"Good," I said.

Jenna looked at me like I was an idiot. "Good? It won't make any difference. You can expect a search warrant for your shoes first thing in the morning."

Uncle Freddie was staring at my feet. I was wearing loafers. "I don't suppose," he said, "that is the footwear with which you were shod when you went to visit the late Harry, is it?"

"No," I said. "I was wearing my black wingtips. Church."

"English," he said. Then he added, "I dare say there are not all that many citizens of this metropolis who wear Church wingtips."

"No," I said. "I suppose not. But I couldn't care less. Bring 'em on. I'll tell them exactly what I did and exactly what I found. If Spritz is right about the drug ring, it's going to be pretty clear, once all the evidence comes out, that I didn't kill Harry. It's just one more killing among drug lords, and there's no evidence of any kind that I've ever had anything to do with drugs."

Oscar got up and started pacing. "That's not how prosecutors think, Robert. Let me guess. Spritz suggested you were in on the deal, right?"

"Right," I said.

"So," Oscar said, "they'll call this your second murder. To silence someone who was going to rat you out on the first. Did Spritz suggest you had to kill Simon because you drew the low card?"

"No, he said I drew the short straw. Of course, I didn't draw anything, and I didn't kill him."

"Right," Oscar said. "But I'll give fifty-fifty odds they arrest you tomorrow in open court for Harry's murder. Right after Spritz testifies and reveals their new theory. The press splash will make the DA's heart sing."

"Well," I said, "the press splash will be even bigger if the cops leak it right. Because the real killer, whoever it was, left an Ides on the body, right beside the dagger."

"Jesus," Oscar said, "now I'll give eighty-twenty odds they arrest you tomorrow."

"I'll give odds they won't," Jenna said. "They'll wait until they have an absolutely airtight case against Robert. If they can make one out. For now, they'll just live with the murder they've got."

"Hey, look guys," I said, "like I said before, I couldn't care less what they do. One murder, two murders, whatever. I'm paying you all good money to figure this out. I didn't kill Simon. I didn't kill Harry. And I got you some damn good information tonight about what was really going down at M&M. Not to mention that it sounds like Daniel Boone was telling the truth about who he saw. So figure it out. I'm going to bed.

By the way, I recorded my conversation with Spritz and the bartender on the mechanical pencil Frederick gave me. Here it is." I tossed it to Jenna and left.

When I reached my bedroom and sat down on the bed, the adrenaline pump that had been sustaining me shut down with a bang. I barely managed to get my clothes off and climb under the covers before sleep hit me.

CHAPTER 51

———

When I awakened, I felt refreshed. I must have dreamed, but I had no recollection of what I had dreamed about. I stretched, got out of bed, took a long shower, and got dressed. As I finished knotting my tie, I glanced down at my watch. It was already 7:00 a.m., and court started at 8:00. Which meant no time for breakfast. And, indeed, when I got to the kitchen, Jenna had already finished eating and was standing by the door, ready to go. There was no sign of either Oscar or Uncle Freddie.

She handed me a banana. "Here, Robert, eat this. You're going to need something. We can dig up some food for you at the courthouse if we get there in time. Maybe the traffic will be light today and we'll be early." I took the banana, and we headed for the garage and Jenna's Land Cruiser. She opened the back door for me.

"Forget it," I said. "I'm sitting up front."

"Well, you certainly are Mr. I'm-in-Charge-Today," she said. "Do you want to drive, too?"

"No. You drive." I got in the front seat.

When the garage door opened, I could see that sometime in the dark of night, the Blob had re-formed, larger than ever, and had now oozed over into the neighbor's yard. Jenna noticed it, too. "The police must have tipped them off that you're a suspect in Harry's murder," she said. "That would explain it."

"They'll leave when they hear about Daniel Boone," I said. "I hope his neighbors in Santa Monica won't be too annoyed when they Blob-up wherever it is that he lives."

We drove slowly down the driveway, gently pushing the expanded Blob out of the way. I didn't bother to give them the thumbs up. Instead, I turned my head and stared directly at them. As if they were the hunted ones. I conjured up my fantasy of the night before, about giving them the finger. And then I did it. For a long and rather joyful ten seconds. So they would be sure to get it on film. I thought I saw shock on their collective blobby faces.

"That wasn't very smart," Jenna said.

"I'm tired of being smart."

"That was pretty obvious when you got out of the car last night at the DownUnder."

"Well," I said, "I got you a lot of good stuff last night. And I have utter confidence about your ability to use it to knock this whole case right out of the ballpark."

"I'm glad you have confidence," she said. "Because I have none. I have no idea what I'm going to do today. With Spritz or anybody else. For example, I don't know whether to use what you learned last night or ignore it. Frankly, I think it's likely bullshit. A diversion to throw us off."

"Why don't you use it to find out what Spritz knows about Harry's murder? Oscar keeps saying a prelim is free discovery for the defense. So if I'm going to be charged with killing Harry, too, we might as well find out what Spritz knows."

"Good point," Jenna said. "I'll do it."

"I'm starving," I said. "I haven't eaten anything since yesterday afternoon."

"Eat the banana."

"Oh right." I had put it on the console between the seats. I picked it up, peeled it, and began to eat. By the time I finished, we were merging onto the freeway, heading downtown.

"Jenna, what did you make of Stewart wanting a tea bag?" I asked.

"What are you talking about?" she said.

"Oh, I forgot. You were on the phone with Spritz when I was telling Oscar and Uncle Freddie about it. After Spritz left last night, Tommy Flannery, the guy who owns the DownUnder, told me that Spritz and Stewart were both there on the morning of the murder. Dining separately. Perhaps the pen, which I assume you listened to, didn't capture that conversation."

"Yes, I did listen to it," she said. "And you're right. I had trouble making out your conversation with the bartender. Maybe he wasn't as close to you as Spritz when he was talking. But what's that information prove, exactly? Stewart eats there all the time. It's even where he invited you to breakfast so he could feed you the line that Harry did it, remember?"

"Well, maybe so. But here's the deal on the tea bag, according to Tommy Flannery. Right before Stewart left the DownUnder on the morning of the murder, he asked Tommy for a tea bag. Then just stuck it in his pocket and took it with him."

"Maybe he used it to hide drugs," Jenna said.

"Could be," I said. "But it's not all that hard to get your own tea bags. Why would he need to get one from Tommy Flannery at breakfast?"

"I don't know," she said. "Stewart is one strange dude. Has no friends, collects butterflies, always wears heavy makeup, for God's sake. So maybe the tea bag's just another weird fetish."

"Stewart wears makeup because he has bad skin. And I collect ancient coins," I said. "Do you think that's a weird fetish?"

"I'm beginning to think so," she said.

It broke the tension. We both laughed.

I was still hungry. "Do you have any more food in the car?" I turned around to search in the back seat. Maybe there was a day-old pizza or something else that Jenna hadn't finished.

"Look in the glove compartment," Jenna said. "There's like a whole bag of jelly beans left. Not that you need more carbs after that banana."

I opened the glove compartment. Sure enough, there was an almost full bag of jelly beans stuffed in there amidst God knows what else. I ate all of them. They tasted great.

"Robert, do you think you're losing it?"

"No, why?"

"Well, you just ate an entire bag of jelly beans. Which is not exactly your usual style. Not to mention the sugar rush it's going to give you. On top of whatever other rush you've got going."

I ignored her comment. "By the way," I said, "what makes you think Stewart's telling me Harry did it was a line? Harry is a prime suspect. After all, Boone said he was there that night, and Harry was the guy who had the secret compartment built, among other things."

"Well, Mr. Smarty Pants, if Harry killed Simon, then who killed Harry?"

She had a good point. I had no idea who had killed Harry. I tried to think it through, but it made my head spin. I didn't have long to think about it, though, because the traffic was light, and we were soon heading into the underground parking garage at the courthouse.

Jenna pulled into a parking space, turned off the ignition, and pulled up the emergency brake. "I very seriously think Stewart killed both of them," she said.

"Stewart?" Even though technically he'd been a suspect, I really couldn't imagine it.

"Yeah, Stewart."

"What's your evidence?"

"Okay," she said. "First, Stewart was at the DownUnder the morning of the murder. So he was in the vicinity. Second, he was hanging around, waiting to take you home a couple hours later."

"I don't know that he was hanging around. I had the impression he was there by happenstance."

"Maybe," she said. "Third, he saw the dagger collection at the party and probably stole it. Because the dagger used to kill Harry was in Stewart's office."

"Harry and a lot of other people were at the party. Plus there's no proof Stewart stole the dagger, and it was Harry who had the secret compartment built," I said.

Jenna wasn't really listening to my points. "Fourth, Stewart had also stashed a fake Ides in the secret compartment, along with that coin book."

"Harry could have put that stuff there," I said. "Including the dagger. And we don't even know if Stewart knows about the compartment."

"Fifth," she said, "Harry's killer left a souvenir. Another Ides. If Stewart had one in his possession—the one we found in his office—he probably had others."

"Yeah," I said. "But those clues could point just as much to Harry."

"Robert, the clue that points away from Harry is that someone killed him, too." She looked at her watch. "Shit, we've got to get going or we'll be late." She grabbed her briefcase from the back seat, opened her door, and started to get out. Then she turned around again and grabbed a large purse.

"A purse?" I said. "That's something I don't usually see."

"I thought I might need it today to hold some stuff Uncle Freddie is looking for. Anyway, I do own them, you know."

I proceeded to get out on my side and walked beside her, heading for the elevators.

When we reached the elevator lobby, I pushed the button, and we waited in silence for an elevator to arrive. When it came, we found it empty, so we were able to talk freely as it ground its way slowly upward.

"There was one more thing," Jenna said, "that makes me think it was Stewart."

"What's that?"

"Something one of my friends at KZDD told me."

"Which was what?"

"It was info from a reporter who's been doing interviews about the case. She was the one who texted me yesterday."

"You said that wasn't about the case."

"I didn't know then that it was. Anyway, she told me that lots of people had agreed to be interviewed. That all of them had been eager to talk to her about their history with you but utterly unwilling to talk about the crime. Except for Stewart."

"He talked about the crime?"

"No, but he kept trolling for details of what she knew about the crime. Like he was trying to put a story together. I thought about it, and that's exactly what the killer would do."

"You could be right. You know, that day he drove me home, he did ask what the murder scene looked like."

"He did? You never told me that before," she said.

"I never thought it was important. Anyway, all that stuff is circumstantial, and there's no motive unless you want to buy into the drug thing. So even if you're right, how are you going to prove it?"

"I don't know."

"Great," I said, as the elevator doors opened.

CHAPTER 52

———

When we walked into the courtroom, the clock showed 7:59 a.m. We had made it with only one minute to spare. Benitez and crew were already at their table, and Oscar was already at ours. I didn't see Spritz, but I did see Stewart, who was again sitting in the back row. I resisted the temptation to wave this time.

I was about to ask Jenna what he was doing there, but didn't get the chance because at 8:00 a.m. sharp, Judge Gilmore took the bench. She looked expectantly at Benitez. "Well, Mr. Benitez, is Detective Spritz going to be with us this morning?"

Benitez rose, looking a bit nervous. "Well, Your Honor, I expect him momentarily."

"Is he a late riser?" the judge asked.

"Um, no," Benitez said. "He was just finishing something up. He will be here momentarily. In the meantime, I have two very quick witnesses to put on. So as to save the court's time . . ."

Judge Gilmore cut him off. "Which Detective Spritz has been wasting."

"Um, yes Your Honor."

"All right," she said, "go ahead with your two quick witnesses. But if Detective Spritz isn't here after that, I'm going to strike all of his direct testimony."

"Yes, thank you, Your Honor," Benitez said. It is odd how often lawyers, in their search for deference, can be heard thanking judges for threatening them. "The People call Sergeant Von Drady."

Drady, who had apparently been sitting in the back of the courtroom, walked to the witness stand and was sworn. Benitez chose to question him from the table.

"Sergeant, did you arrest the defendant in this case?"

"Yeah, at LAX. Well, actually on his plane when it landed."

"Did you conduct any kind of search?"

"I frisked him. And, uh, so then, you know, I searched his suit jacket. On the seat next to him. Needed to make sure it didn't have weapons in it."

"Did you discover anything during the search of his jacket?"

"Yeah, in the pockets. Two silver coins. I learned later they're called the Ides denarius of Brutus."

So, I thought to myself, they *are* going to try to put the coin motive together in this hearing. This was the first piece. I wondered when they would get to the drug part.

"I have no further questions, Your Honor."

"Any cross, Ms. James?"

"Yes, Your Honor. Briefly."

Jenna, too, stayed seated.

"Good morning, Sergeant Drady," she said.

"Good morning."

"Sergeant, in your search, did you find any drugs or drug paraphernalia on Mr. Tarza's person, in his suit jacket, or anywhere else?"

"No."

"When you arrested Mr. Tarza, was Detective Spritz also present?"

"Yes, he was."

"Are you Detective Spritz's superior?"

"Objection," Benitez said. "Beyond the scope of direct."

"Overruled."

"No, I'm not."

"Have you supervised him at all in this investigation?"

"No, I don't have that responsibility."

"Who does supervise Detective Spritz?"

"Well, Detective Spritz has been with the Department so long at such a high level that he can really pretty much supervise himself. You know what I mean?"

"So you were just along for the ride?"

"No, I had been specially assigned to assist in what was expected to be a high profile case. And I was present for the arrest, I'd point out."

If Drady had understood Jenna's dig, he certainly didn't react to it.

"Is there someone in charge of the Robbery-Homicide Division?"

"Your Honor," Benitez said, "I renew my objection to this line of questioning. It's gone well beyond the scope of direct."

"Overruled. But why don't you finish it up quickly, Ms. James?"

"Thank you, Your Honor. Do you recall the question, Sergeant?"

"Yeah, sure. And the answer is, yeah, and the officer in charge is Captain Fernandez."

"Does he actively supervise Detective Spritz?"

"You'd have to ask him."

"I have no further questions, Your Honor."

"Nothing further, Your Honor," Benitez said, without waiting to be asked. "The People call Maria Hernandez."

Maria, who is M&M's communications supervisor, walked to the stand. She's an attractive woman in her early forties, dark haired and stylishly dressed. During the time she reported to me, I used to think that she looked more like a lawyer than most of the lawyers. She sat down in the witness box and was sworn.

"Ms. Hernandez," Benitez began, "could you tell the court your job title?"

"Yes, I'm the Communications Department Supervisor at Marbury Marfan."

"Thank you. And what are your duties in that position?"

"I supervise all of the firm's personnel in the areas of communications. That includes mail services, overnight mail services, fax services, messengers, and copying services. Sometimes we also do travel arrangements for lawyers, although mostly these days, with the Internet, they or their secretaries do it themselves. I also serve on the Liaison Committee on M&M's e-mail policy. I report to the managing partner."

"So do you pretty much know what goes into and out of the firm?"

It was an overly broad, dumb question. Maria answered it as such.

"Not in a detailed way, obviously. I supervise and set policy for the general process."

"Okay. But are you familiar with the firm's business records in regard to communications?"

"Yes."

What Benitez was trying to do, albeit in a slightly clunky way, was to lay the foundation that Maria was familiar with the firm's business records, so that he could get one of those records admitted into evidence as an exception to the hearsay rule—a business record kept in the ordinary course of business, with the basis for admission laid by someone familiar with the records.

"Does the firm keep a log of overnight packages that it sends out?"

"Yes, we do."

Judge Gilmore, who had been sitting in her usual chin-on-left-hand pose, interrupted.

"Mr. Benitez, I can see that this is all going toward laying the foundation for admitting a business record of the firm. Isn't this a document to whose admissibility you and Ms. James can stipulate to so that we can save time and get on to Detective Spritz?"

She looked at Jenna, who was the one, obviously, with the power to stipulate in this situation.

"Your Honor," Jenna said, "this is one of those documents where we have offered to stipulate that it was found in the firm's records and says what it says. But not that it's authentic, or was kept in the regular course of business, nor to the truth of the statements written down on it—all of which Mr. Benitez insists we stipulate to."

"I see," the judge said. "Okay, please proceed Mr. Benitez."

Benitez resumed. "I'd like to have marked, for identification as People's 89, a document consisting of one page of lined paper, dated November 7 of last year at the top, and filled with 30 rows of data, divided into six columns marked Requestor, Recipient, Destination, Date, Method, and Charge. I'm handing two copies to the clerk, including one for Your Honor. Ms. James already has a copy."

The clerk marked the document as People's 89, handed one to the judge and one to the witness.

As we waited for the routine to play itself out, Maria smiled at me, and I smiled back. We had always gotten along well. I didn't imagine she was there by choice.

"Ms. Hernandez," Benitez said, "do you recognize this document?"

"Yes, it's a page from a paper log the firm keeps of overnight mail sent."

"What do the columns mean?"

"The first column is the name of the sender, the second the recipient, the third the recipient's city, the fourth the date it leaves the firm, and the fifth the carrier being used, Fedex, DHL, UPS or whoever, and we always put the tracking number there, as well. The sixth is the charge code. Client, in-house charge, personal, or whatever."

"Do you supervise those who prepare this sheet?"

"Yes."

"All right, could I draw your attention to line 27?"

"Sure."

"What does that say?"

"That on November 7 last year, Mr. Tarza sent a package to a Mr. Chen in Shanghai, via DHL, and it was to be charged to him personally."

"No further questions, Your Honor."

So, bam! Just like that, the DA had dropped in another piece of incriminating evidence. Or maybe it was just a plink meant largely for the Blob. Because it was easy to see how even a first-year lawyer could render the testimony almost useless, at least without a couple more witnesses.

"Ms. James?"

Jenna walked to the podium.

"Good morning, Ms. Hernandez. I have just a few quick questions."

"Okay."

"Did you personally enter the information on Line 27?"

"No."

"I notice there are lots of different handwritings on the document. Do you know why that is?"

"Yes. Many different people in the department can enter the data, plus the secretaries of the various lawyers. The goal is to capture the charge and be able to know the document is out there, not to determine who wrote in the entry." She sighed slightly. "It's not a great system, since, particularly at night, people can come in and take an overnight envelope without entering any information, or only limited information, on the charge sheet. I've been trying to get the firm to change the system for years." She sighed again. "Without success."

Benitez looked a bit perplexed at the complex answer Jenna had just received with no prompting. One no doubt helpful to where Jenna wanted to go. Mary smiled at me again. I wondered if she was helping me out because she liked me or because of her feelings about Simon. She had loathed him. Maybe she didn't care who had killed him. Hell, maybe she did it herself.

Jenna followed up.

"Do you know who filled in that entry?"

"No."

"To your knowledge, has anyone claimed to have seen Mr. Tarza or his secretary fill out that entry?"

"Not that I know of."

"Do you recognize the handwriting on Line 27?"

"No."

"Do you recognize it as the handwriting of anyone on your regular staff?"

"It is not."

"Have you made an effort to determine whose handwriting it is?"

"Yes, we were asked to do so by the LAPD. But we've had no success, despite substantial effort. And that particular entry is in blocky print, which makes it especially hard to match to someone."

"So anybody could have written the entries on Line 27?"

"Yes."

"Thank you. I have no further questions."

"Redirect, Mr. Benitez?"

"A few."

Jenna and Benitez changed places at the podium.

"Ms. Hernandez, were you able to find a receipt for the shipment in the firm's records?"

"No."

"Did you follow up on the DHL tracking number to learn from DHL to whom the referenced package was sent?"

"Yes."

"Who did it actually get delivered to?"

"Objection! Hearsay."

"It is," Benitez started to say, "a business record of . . ."

"Counsel," Judge Gilmore said, "the DHL tracking number and the listed recipient may be business records of Marbury Marfan, but seems to me the information linked to the tracking number—like where the package, whatever was in it, actually went—is a business record of DHL, not the law firm. So I'm going to rule anything further along that line from this witness inadmissible hearsay."

"With all due respect, Your Honor . . ."

"Oh, respect me later, Mr. Benitez. You can get this information in some other way if it's really critical to this probable cause hearing. Call someone from DHL as a witness if you must. And why don't you wait until the end of the hearing to move the admission of this exhibit into evidence, when I have more context for it."

"Thank you, Your Honor," he said. "No further questions."

Of course, as soon as the next break came, the cops would tell the Blob where the DHL records said the package went. To a Mr. Chen in care of a tea shop in Shanghai. Where the coin would be copied and used as a model for counterfeits. Jenna had protected the formal record in court, but not, no fault of hers, the public record that really mattered in terms of biasing the jury pool. Despite some of Jenna's small victories, I could feel the noose tightening. My ridiculously ill-placed euphoria of the morning was fading, and I was beginning to contemplate my upcoming trial.

While I was lost in these thoughts, Jenna had said she had no re-cross, the judge had said she needed a very quick break, and most people began heading for the doors. After wallowing for a while in more self-pitying thoughts, I realized that Maria Hernandez was standing silently beside me, waiting. I looked up.

"Hi, Robert," she said. "Hey, I'm sorry I had to come here today. They subpoenaed me."

"It's okay, Maria. You were just doing your civic duty."

"Well, it still feels awful."

"Tell me about it." Then I had a thought. "Hey, do you guys still do travel arrangements for Harry Marfan? I recall you used to do all that stuff for him."

"Well, we *did*," she said, correcting my verb. "As a courtesy for a former senior partner."

"Do you remember if he went anywhere outside the country last month?"

She looked around briefly to see if anyone was watching us. No one was. "Not out of the country, but he went to Hawaii."

"Do you remember where?"

"He was taking a vacation on the Big Island and asked to fly directly into Hilo."

"Okay, thanks. Um, if I asked you where he stayed, could you get it for me?"

She paused for a second. "Well, since he's dead, I don't suppose it invades his privacy. So sure. And Robert?"

"Yes?"

"I know you didn't do it. I wish I knew who did. Take care of yourself."

She turned and left. Sometimes it's nice to have people you treated well return the favor, even if it's only a small one.

Jenna and Oscar had gone out into the hall. I got up and went to look for them.

CHAPTER 53

―――

The long, marble hallway was, as in most courthouses, crowded with knots of people. Clients sitting on wooden benches, waiting for their lawyers. Witnesses looking at their watches, waiting to be called to testify. People on cell phones, some trying to shield what they were saying, others not. Lawyers from courtrooms down the hall, huddled with their clients, not quite whispering. Jenna and Oscar were halfway down the hall, locked into an intense, not-quite-whispered conversation.

"Hello," I said, walking up to them. "They're really going after the coin stuff. It's my fault, I know. Going to Chicago, leaving the coins in my pocket, all that."

Jenna looked at me with a half-smile. "Robert, you look like a sad little kid with his lip stuck out. Buck up. Those were unimportant witnesses. They didn't say anything we didn't already know."

"Maybe. But they're zeroing in on this crazy theory that I killed him to keep from revealing I was counterfeiting the Ides. It's not true, but it's gonna sound like a real motive."

"Be positive, Robert," Jenna said. "Help us figure out what to do with Spritz. He's the one who knows something."

"I don't have any ideas," I said.

"Your ideas are always pretty good," Oscar said. "Think with us."

"You're being kind, Oscar. Usually my ideas on this case suck. And you know it. Don't coddle me."

"I'm not coddling you."

Over his shoulder, I noticed the sign above one of the wooden benches. I had never noticed it before. It said DO NOT PUT FEET ON WALL.

I pointed at it. "Is that sign a joke?"

Oscar and Jenna both turned to look where I was pointing.

"No," Oscar said. "People do that here. The judges tend not to like it. They're fussy."

"My God," I said. "We're in a criminal courthouse. With criminals."

"I think you'd better go back to the courtroom," Jenna said. "You're kind of losing it."

"Yeah, you're right. I'll see you back there." I turned to go, then turned back around. "Jenna, ask Spritz about the drug stuff!"

"Okay, Robert," Jenna responded. "We'll put it on the list."

I went back to my seat in the courtroom. The courtroom was still empty. I sat there, waiting for everyone to return, thinking dark thoughts.

CHAPTER 54

———

fter a while, everyone else filtered back into the courtroom and took
their seats. I noticed Stewart come in and sit yet again in the back
row. It seemed to have become his favorite place. Finally, Judge Gilmore
appeared on the bench and posed the now familiar question to Benitez.

"Well, Counsel, is the famous Detective Spritz with us again as yet?"

A voice from the back of the courtroom responded. "I'm here, Your
Honor." It was Spritz, who had apparently just walked through the
courtroom doors. He strode to the front of the spectator section and stood
expectantly just behind the bar, waiting.

"Welcome back, Detective," Judge Gilmore said. "I hope you had a
pleasant afternoon yesterday."

"More productive than pleasant, Your Honor," Spritz said.

"In either case, Detective, why don't you take the stand again so we
can resume your cross-examination?"

"You got it, Your Honor," he said. And then he walked—ambled,
really—over to the witness stand and took a seat, looking quite chipper.
For my part, I was astonished that he was able to look so repaired after his
encounter of the night before with six scotch and sodas.

The Judge reminded Spritz that he was still under oath, and then
Jenna stood up.

"Your Honor," she said, "before I continue the cross-examination, I
request that Mr. Stewart Broder, who is sitting in the back of the courtroom, be excluded from these proceedings until after he has testified. Mr.
Benitez said yesterday that he will be a witness."

"Any objection, Mr. Benitez?" Judge Gilmore said. Not that there
was any real objection that he could have made, since you can almost
always get a potential witness who is not a party excluded from the courtroom.

Benitez looked momentarily pensive. If he wanted Stewart to stay, his
only viable option was to decide on the spot not to call him as a witness.

"I have no objection," he said.

I turned and looked as Stewart, seeming a bit taken aback at being pointed out, rose and exited. A couple of the more junior members of the Blob followed him out the door.

As Jenna moved toward the podium, legal pad in hand, Judge Gilmore herself aimed a question at Spritz. "Detective, between our lunch break yesterday, and right now, have you discussed your testimony or this case with Mr. Benitez or anyone else associated with the District Attorney's office?"

Spritz paused, clearly thinking. "Not *this* case, Your Honor."

"Which case, then?" she asked.

"I don't know if you want me to mention it," Spritz said.

"I think I do," she said.

"Okay, then. As you may know from news reports, a Mr. Harry Marfan was murdered last night in Manhattan Beach. I am cooperating with the Manhattan Beach police in the investigation of his murder. That was what I discussed last night with Mr. Benitez."

"Was Mr. Marfan somehow connected to this case?" Judge Gilmore asked.

"He was on the witness list."

Judge Gilmore smiled. "Looking at that list, Detective, it appears the entire County of Los Angeles is on it." She looked over at Benitez. "Mr. Benitez, was Mr. Marfan someone you had actually planned to call?"

"Maybe, Your Honor. But I really think his murder is . . ." He paused. I could see him searching for words that would be not quite a lie, but not the full truth either.

Then he got it together and tried again. "Mr. Marfan's murder is only, um, tangentially related to this case. And we don't, we don't plan to raise those issues at this preliminary hearing. And, uh, I don't think my conversation with Detective Spritz about the Marfan murder would shed any immediate light on this case."

Judge Gilmore sat with her chin on her left hand and just stared at him for a few seconds. "Okay, Mr. Benitez, I'm not sure whether 'shedding immediate light' is the legal standard to be applied in deciding the question. But I suppose this hearing will be long enough without my intruding some other murder into it by pressing Detective Spritz about it . . . at least for now. Ms. James, you can resume your cross of this witness."

Jenna apparently decided that Spritz didn't deserve the usual polite "good morning" and went straight at it.

"Detective Spritz," she said, "what did you discuss with Mr. Benitez about the Marfan murder?"

It was cheeky, of course, since the judge had basically just suggested that the subject of the Marfan murder was, if not technically irrelevant, likely a waste of time. But Judge Gilmore smiled as Jenna posed the question, which I took to mean that she admired the cheek.

"Objection, Your Honor. Irrelevant," Benitez said.

"What *is* the relevance, Ms. James?" Judge Gilmore asked.

"This witness mysteriously disappeared yesterday afternoon. Since then he has, by his own admission, spoken to Mr. Benitez about something at least tangential to this case. I'm entitled to find out if their discussions really were tangential."

"You have a point," Judge Gilmore said. "But on the other hand, this evidence seems likely to be more time-wasting than probative. I'll permit you to ask the witness if he discussed either Mr. Tarza or the murder of Mr. Rafer with anyone since he left us yesterday. If he says yes, go for it. If he says no, please go on to other things."

"Detective," Jenna said, "Between the time you left here yesterday and right now, have you discussed either Mr. Tarza or the murder of Mr. Rafer with anyone, including Mr. Benitez?"

Spritz smirked. "No."

That was a lie, of course. Spritz had discussed the murder at least with me. But I didn't suppose Jenna wanted to impeach him with *that* conversation.

"Fine," Jenna said. "Let's move on. Detective, the morning of the murder, you had breakfast at the DownUnder, correct?"

"Which murder, Counsel?"

A lot of lawyers would have taken the bait. Jenna ignored the sarcasm and moved right on.

"The one we're here about today, Detective Spritz, the murder of Simon Rafer."

"Oh, that one," Spritz said. "Yes, I was there that morning."

"And I believe you testified earlier that you didn't have breakfast with anyone."

"Correct."

"Did you meet anyone there, even if they didn't dine with you?" she asked.

"No."

"Were any other people there besides you and the people who work at the DownUnder?"

"Yes," he said. "There were. Maybe four, five other people, huh?"

"Did you know any of them?"

"No."

"Have you subsequently made the acquaintance of anyone who was there that morning?" Jenna asked.

"Not to my knowledge," Spritz said.

"Do you know Stewart Broder?"

"Yes, but I didn't know him before the murder."

"Well, now that you know him, can you say if he was at the DownUnder that morning?"

Spritz cocked his head and seemed to think a moment. "I can't say. Might have been, but since I didn't know him at the time I wouldn't have noticed him being there. And right now, I don't have an image in my head of him being there."

Jenna looked down at her legal pad. She was clearly searching for a note she had made during Spritz's earlier testimony. She circled something with her pen and looked up.

"Detective didn't you tell me yesterday that Stewart Broder was one of only three people you let go by the yellow tape on the eighty-fifth floor?"

"Yes," he said, "I did testify to that."

"And you also testified, didn't you, that Mr. Broder's excuse was that he was supposedly the deputy managing partner and needed to notify the firm's other offices why the telephones were down so that they wouldn't, and I quote, 'flip out'"?

"Yeah, I testified to that, too."

"Well, didn't you then say to yourself, 'Hey! This important guy is someone I just saw an hour ago at the DownUnder!'"

Judge Gilmore interrupted. "Ms. James, can you represent to this court that you have credible evidence that Mr. Broder was in fact at the DownUnder that morning? Because if you don't, this is rather a waste of time."

It was a pointed interruption. Usually, judges waited for the lawyers to make the objections. Especially if there is a sharp question like that one pending. It meant Judge Gilmore was growing impatient. On the other hand, one of the problems of trial work is that you usually can't tell the whole story through one witness. Each witness provides a small piece that you have to weave together with the other pieces later, in closing argument. So you have to beg the judge's patience as you go along.

"I do have such evidence," Jenna said. "I promise this is going somewhere."

"Okay, continue, then." The patience had been temporarily extended. "Please answer the question, Detective. If you recall it."

Spritz had not forgotten it. "Well, Counsel, if Mr. Broder was there, maybe I should have said that to myself, huh? But I didn't. I was kind of busy at the time with other tasks."

"I thought detectives were trained to be observant, Detective Spritz."

"Objection," Benitez said. "Argumentative."

"Sustained."

"I'll do it a different way, then," Jenna said. "Detective, do you believe you are more or less observant than the average detective on the LAPD?"

"Objection," Benitez said again. "There is no foundation that the witness knows, one way or the other, how observant other detectives on the LAPD are. So he has no basis of comparison."

"Overruled," Judge Gilmore said. "He's an experienced witness. If he doesn't have the basis to answer it, he'll say so, I'm sure."

Jenna had put Spritz in a box. Without knowing where it was all leading—and I didn't really know myself—he couldn't easily figure out if he'd be better off answering that he was more observant or less observant.

Spritz pondered a second. Perhaps he was considering taking the judge's lead and simply saying he didn't know. But then his ego apparently got the better of him and he said, "More observant, probably."

"Thank you, Detective," Jenna said. "Did you observe anything out of the ordinary about Mr. Broder that morning you let him past the tape?"

"Not in particular. Did you have something in mind?" Spritz asked.

"Was he," Jenna said, "wearing makeup?"

"Come to think of it," Spritz said, "he was. And I remember thinking it was weird, a guy wearing that much obvious makeup. But then, we live in Los Angles."

That brought a laugh from the Blob, a glare from the judge, and puzzlement to me. Stewart had indeed been wearing makeup for a year or more, and had seemed to be wearing even more of it than usual on the day he drove me back home. I had mentioned that to Jenna in passing, weeks before, but I had no clue why she was asking about it now. Nor was I to be enlightened right then, because Jenna dropped the subject and moved on to something else.

"Detective, you met with Mr. Tarza the morning of the murder, didn't you?"

"Yes."

"In fact, you questioned him, right?"

"Yes."

"Questioned him less than an hour after you arrived at the murder scene, right?"

"Right."

"Did he seem nervous to you?"

"Not really, no."

"Did you notice any bruises on him?"

"No, although I didn't look closely."

"You saw his face and hands, right?"

"Yes."

"Any bruises there?"

"Not that I noticed."

"And you asked him to take off his dress shirt, so you saw his arms, right?"

"Yes, I did."

"No bruises there, either, right?"

"Not that I noticed."

"Detective, did you already suspect Mr. Tarza at that time?"

"'Suspect' is a word out of detective novels, Counsel. What I'd say is that I felt he was a person of interest. Someone we should investigate further."

"Excuse me a moment," Jenna said. She walked back to the counsel table and picked up her water glass. She stood sipping for a few seconds. Either she was genuinely thirsty or she was borrowing time to consider what she wanted to do next. I pushed a note at her: Ask *about drugs*! She glanced at it and pushed it back. Then she walked back to the podium.

"Detective, why did you feel you should investigate Mr. Tarza further?"

Even without looking at him, I could feel Oscar stiffen beside me at the open-endedness of the question Jenna had just asked a hostile witness.

"Because he found the body. And because one of my officers had immediately examined the building's after-hours elevator access records, which cast suspicion on the defendant."

Jenna had made a mistake. Now she faced the choice of whether to ask him to explain his suspicions further or to drop the subject. She chose to drop it.

"And yet, Detective, despite the fact that you were suspicious of him, you didn't ask him to take off his undershirt to see if he had any bruises on him, did you?"

"No. There was no indication at that time that there had been any kind of struggle."

"But there was no indication that there *hadn't* been a struggle, was there?"

"Objection," Benitez said. "This whole line of questioning is irrelevant and speculative. There's nothing in the record to suggest, one way or the other, that the killer sustained bruises or that there was a struggle."

Benitez had to that point been pretty quiet. His objection seemed kind of silly. Particularly since it was the chief detective on the case who was being cross-examined. I assumed that he had objected just to show that he was still alive.

"There *is* evidence of a struggle, Your Honor," Jenna said. "I established with the medical examiner that the victim had premortem bruises on both his right palm and left ankle."

"It's only speculation," Benitez said, "that they were caused by a struggle instead of a fall."

"Overruled," Judge Gilmore said. "This is cross-examination. You may answer, Detective."

"Put it this way," Spritz said. "I had no indication at the time of a struggle—one way or the other."

Oscar pushed a note at me: *Where is this going?* Without turning toward him, I shrugged. I had no idea. It was a small piece, apparently, of something larger that Jenna was trying to construct. But I couldn't yet make out what it was.

"Detective," Jenna said, "did you investigate anyone else for this murder?"

"It depends what you mean by investigate, Counsel."

"You used the term earlier yourself, Detective. So let's say investigate means exactly what it meant when you said you thought you should investigate Mr. Tarza."

It was a classic technique. Stuff the witness's own words back in his mouth. It usually works like a charm.

Spritz had no ready answer. He sat silent for an uncomfortably long time. Long enough that Judge Gilmore looked over at him to see if he was actually going to answer. Finally, he did.

"Well, no, we didn't investigate anyone else that way. But we did interview everyone else who'd had recent contact with the victim, everyone else who had a potential motive."

"Did you interview me?"

"No."

"Wasn't I the victim's secret girlfriend? Didn't that give me a motive?"

There was a stir behind me. To my right, I heard Oscar say "Ah, shit" under his breath. And then say it again. When I glanced at him, his eyes were closed while his lips continued to move. I didn't turn around, but I heard rapid footsteps and then the door slamming open and closed as a few members of the Blob sprinted for a cell phone-usable area.

Spritz had a lopsided grin on his face as he waited for the murmur to die down. Then he said, "Yeah, well, being his girlfriend isn't a motive unless you had some reason to kill him. Did you?"

Jenna actually laughed. "Maybe you'll interview me and find out, Detective."

Judge Gilmore, who had to that point been impassive, raised her hand off the bench, as if to punctuate something she was about to say. Then she apparently thought better of saying anything, put her hand down, and sank back into her large leather chair. Waiting, I guess, to see where this bizarre scene might go. As it was, it went nowhere else.

"So Detective Spritz," Jenna said, "did you investigate Harry Marfan?"

"No."

"Or Susan Apacha?"

"No."

"Or Stewart Broder?"

"No."

"Or . . . anyone else."

"Not seriously, no."

"I have no further questions, Your Honor," Jenna said, and headed back to our table.

CHAPTER 55

J udge Gilmore looked expectantly at Benitez. "Any redirect, Mr. Benitez?"

"Just a few questions, Your Honor." Benitez got up, walked unhurriedly back to the podium, and peered down at his notes. As we waited for him to find what he was looking for, Oscar passed me a note and whispered to me to give it to Jenna. I read it as I passed it on. It said: *That was fucking stupid.* Jenna looked at it for a microsecond, crumpled it up, and dumped it in her large purse, which was beside her on the table.

"Detective Spritz," Benitez said, "what led you to consider Mr. Tarza to be particularly worthy of further investigation?"

"He discovered the body, and he had no alibi. Also, the elevator records showed he came up very early in the morning, around the estimated time of the murder. Also, the crime lab later detected Mr. Rafer's blood on the cuffs of the defendant's shirt and more of Mr. Rafer's blood on a couch in the defendant's office."

"Objection," Jenna said. "The testimony about the elevator records and the crime lab report are hearsay, and I move that the answer, after the word 'alibi,' be struck."

A sly smile of superiority attached itself to Benitez's face. "Pursuant to the Penal Code, a law enforcement officer is permitted to testify on the basis of hearsay at a preliminary hearing."

"That's all correct," Judge Gilmore said. "Overruled."

Jenna looked pissed. Lawyers hate to be shown up on small things like that. Oscar shoved a note in front of me: *Told you, forgot to tell her.* Meanwhile, Benitez went on mining hearsay from his witness.

"Were there any other reasons to investigate Mr. Tarza?"

"Yeah. After we looked at the elevator records, we examined Mr. Tarza's computer files. We found he had tried to delete certain files. But we recovered them. When we read them, we found that the victim and Mr. Tarza were having a dispute over a rare ancient coin—the Roman Ides—

that Mr. Tarza sold the victim for five hundred thousand dollars. The victim claimed that the coin was a fake."

"Same objection," Jenna said.

"Same ruling," the judge responded.

"Anything else?" Benitez asked.

"We found two more counterfeited Ides in the pocket of the defendant's suit coat when he was arrested and several more buried in a box in his garden."

"Objection," Jenna said. "There is no evidence in the record that the coins allegedly found are in fact counterfeits."

"Sustained," the judge said. "I will not consider the statement that they were counterfeit in ruling on probable cause."

Jenna had won a small point. Very small, given the evidence being stacked up against me. Of course, Jenna had opened the door to all of this by asking why he had investigated me. Perhaps she had thought that whatever new information the open-ended question might turn up was worth the risk. It wasn't turning out that way.

Benitez continued. "Did you know that Ms. James was the victim's girlfriend?"

"Yes."

"How did you know that?"

"Susan Apacha told us when we interviewed her."

"Why didn't you investigate Ms. James further?"

"We did a preinvestigation, and although she might have had opportunity, we couldn't find any plausible motive. Or any physical evidence connecting her to the crime."

Preinvestigation? It was a nice way to cover his earlier answer that there had been no investigation of Jenna.

"I have nothing further," Benitez said.

"Any re-cross Ms. James?" Judge Gilmore asked.

Jenna sat for a few seconds, thinking. I pushed my note at her again, to which I had added a line. *Ask about drugs! Harry went to Hilo last month!* She glanced at it but didn't even bother to push it back.

"Only two quick questions, Your Honor," she said. She rose from her chair but didn't return to the podium.

"Detective, did you have an expert evaluate the coins you found as to whether they are in fact fake?"

"Based on an interview with an expert, we believe that the two recovered from the defendant's pocket are. We are in the process of evaluating the others, the ones from his garden."

Had they talked to Serappo?

Jenna went on to her second question.

"Did you know, Detective, that there is a secret compartment in a bookcase in Mr. Broder's office and that there was an Ides coin in there? Plus a dagger?"

Spritz actually blinked. It was quick, and it was subtle, but it was there. Benitez had started to get up, presumably to object that the question was not only compound but that the second part of the question was without foundation because the second part assumed a 'yes' answer to the first part. Spritz saved him the trouble.

"No," Spritz answered, "I didn't and don't know that."

"I have no further questions," Jenna said.

"Any re-redirect Mr. Benitez?" Judge Gilmore asked. She said it in a tone that suggested that she wanted the answer to be 'no.'

"Your Honor," Benitez said, "could I have a minute to consult with my co-counsel?"

"Of course."

While Benitez put his head together with his two assistants, Oscar put his hand over his mouth and leaned across me so that he could whisper to Jenna.

"*You should have kept your mouth shut about being his girlfriend.*"

"*I had my reasons.*"

"*Why didn't you ask about drugs?*"

"*I think it's bullshit.*"

"*Why?*"

"*Boone never said he heard anything about drugs.*"

Before I could respond, Benitez spoke up and said, "I have no further questions for this witness, Your Honor."

"Please call your next witness then."

Benitez headed back to the podium. "The people call Stewart Broder."

CHAPTER 56

Iturned and watched as someone in the back row, apparently in Benitez's employ, went out into the hall to fetch Stewart. I was startled to see Daniel Boone sitting quietly in that very same back row. He was wearing his trademark leather jacket, but it had a crisp, clean look. If you told me he'd bought it at Brooks Brothers, I wouldn't have doubted it.

Stewart must have been lurking nearby, because he came in through the doors only a few seconds later and walked quickly up to the witness box. He looked nervous as he took his seat, stated his name, and was sworn.

"Mr. Broder," Benitez began, "are you acquainted with the defendant, Robert Tarza?"

"Yes, I *am*," Stewart said.

I had almost forgotten about Stewart's strange way of speaking, but there it was, front and center.

"How are you acquainted with him?"

"We have worked at the same *law* firm for more than thirty *years*. We started there together, within *weeks* of each other."

"How would you describe the nature of your relationship, then?" Benitez asked.

"Good friends."

I would not have used anything close to that term to describe my relationship with Stewart. I had a sudden sense of foreboding. Maybe this wasn't going to be the quick on-and-off the stand Oscar had predicted.

"Could you explain what you mean by that?"

"Sure. We've gone to *parties* at each other's homes, we've *gone* to dinners together, we've gone to breakfasts *together*, we've gone on outings together, we've attended each other's important *family* events. You know, weddings, birthdays, *stuff* like that."

What he said was, of course, literally true. But all those dinners, breakfasts, and events are the kinds of things you always do with your law partners, even if you loathe them. A close friendship they are not.

"Did you see the defendant on the morning of Mr. Rafer's murder?" Benitez asked.

"Yes, I *did*. I ran into him in the *parking* garage and gave him a ride home. Because his own car was taped *off*."

Stewart, I noticed, was avoiding looking at me. But I also noticed that Judge Gilmore was looking at him rather intensely. Probably trying to figure out his weird speech pattern. I wished her luck. There was no rhyme or reason to it.

"How did he seem to you?" Benitez asked.

"Objection," Oscar said. "Vague and ambiguous."

"Overruled," the judge said.

It had surprised me that Oscar, not Jenna, had made the objection. I looked over at her, quizzically. She scribbled a note and pushed it at me: *Oscar's doing it. Short witness. I needed a rest.* Meanwhile, Stewart was answering the question.

"He *seemed* really nervous," Stewart said.

"Did you ask him about the murder?"

"Yes. He didn't *want* to *talk* about it."

"Not at all?" Benitez asked.

"Not *at* all."

That was not true, of course. I had talked to him about it some and then clammed up because I was in such a state of shock.

"Did you ever talk to him again about the murder?"

"*Yes*, I did," Stewart said.

"When was that?"

"Well," Stewart said, "two days after the murder, Robert called me up and asked me to have breakfast with him at the DownUnder."

I felt ice go down my spine. He had invited *me*. Jenna, who had been quietly taking notes, jerked her head up. Oscar growled something, although I couldn't make it out.

"Did you have breakfast with him?" Benitez asked.

"*Yes*, I did."

"Please relate the conversation at breakfast to us."

"Objection!" Oscar said. "Calls for a narrative."

Judge Gilmore cocked her head, which I had learned meant she was thinking it over. She brought her head back to the vertical and ruled. "Technically, you're right Mr. Quesana. But there's no jury here, and it will be more efficient just to let him tell the story. You can probe the narrative on cross. Overruled. You may answer, sir."

"There's not a lot to tell, really," Stewart said. "We engaged in chit-chat for a while. Then he just blurted out that he had killed Simon. And his eyes began to tear up."

For a few seconds, I was in a state of shock. I was being framed. I needed to pay attention, though, and I managed to pull myself out of it. Then I thought about something. Stewart had lost his odd inflection. Just like he had at our real breakfast at the DownUnder. I suddenly put it together. Stewart lost the inflection when he was under great stress. Like when he was lying. Like when he was trying to put me in a prison cell.

"Did you ask him why he had done it?"

"Yes. He talked about the Ides. You see, Robert *owned* a rare Roman coin. The Ides of Brutus. He and Simon both collected Roman *coins*. Anyway, he *sold* the Ides to Simon for a lot of money. There were a lot of collectors in the *firm* and everybody knew about it. It *caused* a big buzz. Then Simon discovered Robert had sold him a *fake* coin and demanded his money back."

"Did the defendant say," Benitez asked, "that that was why he killed him?"

"Objection. Leading."

"Sustained."

I laughed inwardly, despite the painful knot in my stomach. Benitez was having a classic problem with his witness on direct. Stewart hadn't managed to say flat out that I told him I had killed Simon because of the counterfeiting dispute, and Benitez wasn't permitted to lead him to the right answer. So Benitez would have to fish for it, probably dangling the "was there anything else" lure in front of Stewart to try to reel it in.

"Well," Benitez asked, "did the defendant say anything else about the killing?"

"Oh, yes, yes he did." Stewart reached out and took a sip from the water glass next to the witness stand. His hand shook slightly. "Robert said he killed Simon because Simon had discovered that Robert had had many counterfeits made in China, not just one, like Simon originally thought. So Simon stopped just demanding his own money back and was going to go to the police on Monday. That's why Robert said he had to kill him early Monday morning. To keep him from revealing the counterfeiting."

The fish had bitten. Of course, the fish was lying.

"Did he say why he was telling you this?"

"Yes. He said he felt guilty, and needed to tell someone. He said he was making me his priest. And he asked me to promise not to tell anyone."

"Are you Catholic?"

"Well, I was."

"Did you promise?"

"Yes, I did."

"Why?"

"Shock, I guess. Friendship, I really don't know."

Oscar had been writing a note, and now he shoved it in front of me. WE'RE FUCKED. Jenna was rummaging for something in her giant purse, but I wasn't sure what. I was feeling cold and starting to shake slightly, but I knew that if I started visibly shivering, some people might take it as a sign of guilt. I tried saying my old mantra, quietly, to myself. It seemed to work. I stopped shaking. Then I took Oscar's note and wrote on it and shoved it back to him: *Loses weird accent when he lies.*

"Did Mr. Tarza say anything else to you about the murder?" Benitez asked.

"No . . . Well, yes. A little. He said he felt guilty about killing someone but wasn't sorry it had been Simon. That Simon was a shit who deserved to die."

"Did you learn anything else?"

"No, I should have asked for more details, I know. But I was upset, and I just wanted to get out of there."

"Did you go to the police with the information?"

"No."

Benitez paused, put both hands firmly on the podium, and leaned forward slightly, as if the question to come was going to be a big piece of drama.

"Why not?"

The drama, of course, was that Benitez had just, as we lawyers say, pulled the sting on his own witness. Brought out the bad thing on direct, so that the cross-examiner wouldn't be the first one to bring it up.

Stewart was silent for a second or two as he considered the question, then shrugged. "I really can't explain it. The promise I had made to Robert to keep it secret, maybe. Misplaced friendship. I'm not sure."

"I have no further questions," Benitez said. As he said it, I heard noises behind me as part of the Blob thumped through the courtroom doors.

Oscar got up and moved toward the podium. I thought I heard him sigh as he walked behind me. In truth, I would rather have had Jenna. But I wasn't apparently going to get a choice.

CHAPTER 57

"Mr. Broder," Oscar began, "you're lying, aren't you?"

"Objection!" Benitez had stood up and raised his voice.

"What's your objection, Mr. Benitez?" Judge Gilmore said.

"Argumentative," Benitez said.

"Overruled."

"No," Stewart said, "I'm not lying."

"When did you first go to the police, sir?"

"Yesterday morning. I called the DA's office and *spoke* to a deputy DA Then I went down *there* and was interviewed."

"What time was that?"

"About 11:00 a.m."

"Your Honor," Oscar said, "the prosecution should have notified us immediately of this witnesss's changed testimony. There's nothing at all about this in their earlier interview of Mr. Broder that was turned over to us. I move that his testimony be struck, in its entirety. And that the District Attorney's office be sanctioned."

Benitez was on his feet, and started to reply, but Judge Gilmore cut him off. "I agree that the circumstances here are peculiar at best. But I want to postpone dealing with your sanctions motion, Mr. Quesana, until the cross-examination is completed. Please proceed."

"Mr. Broder," Oscar said, "didn't you already lie once before to the police in this case?"

"No," Stewart said.

"Didn't you tell Detective Spritz, the morning of the murder, that you were the deputy managing partner of the firm?"

"I don't remember saying that."

"So if Detective Spritz were to say you did say that, he'd be lying?"

"I, uh, don't know how to answer that." He shifted in his seat. "All I can say is that I don't remember saying that to him."

"Well, in any case, you weren't the deputy managing partner that morning, were you?"

"No."

"But you did talk to Detective Spritz the morning of the murder, didn't you?"

"Yes."

"What did you say to him?"

"I just told him I needed to *call* the other offices about the phone situation, and that since I *was* there early, *I thought* I should do it, especially with the *managing* partner dead."

"Did you go into Mr. Tarza's office while you were at the firm that morning?"

"No."

"Sir, is there a secret compartment in a bookcase in your office?"

"Not that I know of."

"Are you sure?"

"Pretty sure."

"Where did you get the bookcase that's in your office?"

"Objection," Benitez said. "Relevance."

"What is the relevance of this, Mr. Quesana?" the judge asked.

"I'll link it up shortly, or drop it, depending on the witness's answer."

"Okay. Overruled. You may answer, sir."

"*When* Harry Marfan *left* the firm, I inherited it."

"So if it turned out to have a secret compartment, you'd be shocked?"

"Yes."

I could see what Oscar was trying to do. Cast doubt on a lot of little things about Stewart's testimony, so that at the trial the shadows cast by all those little doubts might dim the bright sun of his big lie about our meeting. It was a good tactic. The problem with the tactic was that a meeting between me and Stewart at the DownUnder had actually taken place, and there were lots of witnesses to it. Unfortunately, only Stewart and I knew what had really been said there.

And now I finally understood that e-mail Stewart had sent me two days after the murder. The one that "confirmed" our meeting at the DownUnder, even though the e-mail had arrived *before* Stewart actually called me to request the meeting. The e-mail would be read, in retrospect, to suggest that I had asked for the breakfast meeting, not him. Oscar's note was right. I was fucked.

"Mr. Broder," Oscar said, "you testified that you protected Mr. Tarza out of friendship, right?"

"Yes."

"Have you protected any other friends from the police?"

I thought I saw Stewart blink. "No."

"What about Harry Marfan?"

"Pardon?"

"Harry Marfan. You knew he was dealing drugs through the firm's offices, didn't you?"

"No, I didn't *know* that."

A few more Blob elements hit the doors and exited.

"Didn't you go down to Manhattan Beach and kill him last night, to silence him?"

"Objection!" Benitez said. "Unless there's some good-faith basis for these questions, this is outrageous conduct."

"It's outrageous all right," Oscar said. "Outrageous that this witness is being put forward by the People as a truth-teller, when, by his own admission, he hid this supposed key fact from everyone for weeks."

Judge Gilmore leaned forward, looked over at the witness, then looked at me, then looked at Benitez, and finally fixed her gaze on Oscar.

"Osc . . . Mr. Quesana, what is your basis for asking these questions?"

"I'd prefer not to say in open court, Your Honor."

"I can understand that," Judge Gilmore said, "but why don't you at least give me a little hint, okay?"

"Okay," Oscar said. "Daniel Boone."

"Oh," Judge Gilmore said. "I see."

"I don't see at all," Benitez said.

"That's because you were too lazy to interview him when you first got the chance, Charlie," Oscar said.

"Mr. Quesana! That's enough. You will address the Court, not Mr. Benitez. I will not have counsel arguing with one another in my courtroom."

"Sorry, Your Honor," Oscar said. The word was there, but in fact he sounded not the least bit contrite.

I could not restrain myself. I wanted to see what the Blob was making of all this, so I turned fully around to look. For the most part, those who remained were stock still, staring at what was going on in front of them. A few were scribbling madly in their notebooks. What really caught my eye, though, was Daniel Boone. He was grinning his loopy grin, staring straight at Stewart. I wondered if Stewart had noticed him.

"I'm satisfied, for the moment, with the good-faith basis of the questions," Judge Gilmore said. "You may proceed, Mr. Quesana. But before Mr. Benitez does the redirect of this witness, I'm going to order you to turn over to him your notes of your interview with Mr. Boone."

"I will," Oscar said, "although under protest."

"Noted," Judge Gilmore said. "Now let's get on with it."

"I'll ask the court reporter to read back the pending question," Oscar said.

It was a nice touch. He could just as easily have put the question again himself. But it is somehow more dramatic to have the court reporter read the question back, in that oh-so-neutral tone court reporters employ. In the old days, the court reporter would have had to pick up the white tape coming out of her steno machine and search methodically for the passage. Instead, she just scrolled quickly back through the pages displayed on the small computer monitor that was hooked to her steno machine, found the passage and read it out loud: "Didn't you go down to Manhattan Beach and kill him last night, to silence him?"

"No," Stewart said. "I didn't."

"Well," Oscar said, "did you go down to Manhattan Beach last night for any reason?"

Stewart paused. "No."

"You were in the courtroom yesterday afternoon when court ended, weren't you?"

"Yes, I *was*."

"Where did you go when you left the court?"

"I went home and spent the evening there, watching TV."

"What did you watch?"

"A couple of movies."

"Which ones?"

"I don't recall right now. They were bad ones, and I didn't see either of them from the start. I don't even know if I ever learned their names since my screen guide wasn't working. One was a war movie of some kind, and the other was a mystery. That's all I recall."

Now there was a clever answer. On any given night on TV, there are always war movies and mysteries playing on some channel, somewhere. Stewart looked increasingly nervous though. He was beginning to sweat, and the sweat was beading on his face.

"Do you," Oscar asked, "have any witnesses who saw you enter your house or can prove you were at home last night?"

"Objection," Benitez said. "Again. To this whole line of questioning. Mr. Broder isn't on trial, so he doesn't need an alibi. And I don't know what any of this has to do with Boone. What he told Mr. Quesana couldn't have had anything to do with the murder of Harry Marfan. The interview with Boone was in early afternoon. Marfan wasn't murdered until last night."

"It has everything to do with it," Oscar said.

"Mr. Benitez has a point," Judge Gilmore said. "These questions are quite far afield. I'll let the witness answer the pending question, but then, Mr. Quesana, I think you should move on to a new topic."

She turned to Stewart. "The question, sir, is whether you know of anyone who saw you enter your house or can prove you were home last night."

"Not off the top of my head," Stewart said. "Maybe some neighbors saw me come home. I'd have to check."

Oscar resumed. "Mr. Broder, do you know someone named Daniel Boone?"

"I don't think *so*."

"How about someone named Top Quark?"

I heard someone in the Blob giggle at the name.

"Yes, I did *know* someone by that name," Stewart said.

"Did he call you yesterday?"

Stewart paused, started to speak, then stopped and paused again. Oscar's question was a brilliant shot in the dark. Because if Boone had in fact called Stewart as he had threatened to do, then Boone could put the lie to Stewart if he denied the call. I glanced over my shoulder again at Boone. He was still grinning. I looked back at Stewart and saw that his eyes were now fixed on the back row. He had seen him.

Stewart answered. "Uh, *yes* he did."

"What did he say?"

"That he needed to *talk* to *me*."

"What did you tell him?"

"I told him I was busy and to *call* me back in a couple days. He said *he* would." I saw Stewart's eyes flick toward Boone.

"If Mr. Quark were to come in here and testify under oath that he saw you, Harry Marfan, Susan Apacha, and a fourth person in the law firm, on the eighty-fifth floor, shortly before Simon Rafer was murdered, would it be a lie?"

"Objection," Benitez said. "Compound, no foundation, improper hypothetical."

"Overruled."

Stewart flicked his eyes again at Boone. Then he said, firmly, "Yes, it would be a lie."

Oscar looked down at his notes. I knew exactly what his problem was. He had roughed the witness up a bit, but he hadn't proved him a liar. If it could be done, it would have to await the trial. Maybe Boone could testify and put the lie to Stewart, but who knew if Boone would be believed. Doubtful. Now there was no doubt that what Oscar had said to me earlier was true. I was fucked.

Oscar tried a new tack. "Sir, do you make it a habit to cover up serious crimes?"

"Objection! Argumentative. There is no evidence Mr. Broder covered up a crime. He just didn't report it. It's hardly the same."

"Mr. Quesana," the judge said, "why don't you rephrase that?"

"Okay," Oscar said. "Sir, do you make it a habit not to report serious crimes you stumble on?"

"No," Stewart said.

"You were aware, weren't you, that there was drug dealing going on in the firm? Why didn't you report that?"

"Objection!" Benitez said. "There is no good-faith basis to support that question, not to mention that it assumes facts not in evidence and is compound."

Judge Gilmore was staring, quite openly, at Stewart, with a frown on her face. I hoped she was thinking he was a lying shit. She turned to Oscar.

"Mr. Benitez is certainly correct that you've posed two questions, Mr. Quesana, not one. But before I deal with that objection, what's your good-faith basis for asking the first part of the question?"

"Detective Spritz is the basis. He has represented that there was drug dealing going on on the eighty-fifth floor of Marbury Marfan."

I heard the sound of more Blob hurrying out. Then I noticed that the judge had locked her gaze on the back row of the courtroom. When I turned to see at whom she might be gazing, there was Boone, sitting in the back row, not far from Spritz. His face was impassive. He was casually dressed now—khakis and a sport shirt. Like he was at a sporting event. Maybe he had gone and changed out of his frontier outfit in the restroom to try to look more normal. Just then, as if on cue, Uncle Freddie walked through the courtroom doors, carrying a manila folder.

Judge Gilmore took her eyes off the rear of the courtroom and looked back down at Oscar.

"I do think that question is a bridge too far, Mr. Quesana. At least for the moment. I'm going to sustain the objection. After Mr. Benitez finishes his redirect, we're going to have a conference in chambers, and you can explain your good-faith basis for these questions. I hope it's good. Do you have anything else?"

As the judge was talking, Uncle Freddie came up to the bar. As if expecting him, Jenna got up, went over, and took the manila folder from him. She was studying the top page inside it as she made her way back to our table. Then she walked over to the podium and handed the open folder to Oscar, pointing to something.

Oscar looked at it and said, "I do have something further, Your Honor."

"Go ahead then."

"Mr. Broder, did you ever take karate lessons?" As he asked it, he was looking down at the contents of the folder. It was an old trick, of course. It suggested to the witness that he might have papers to back up his question. Or it might just be the daily racing sheet.

Stewart focused on Oscar's manila folder for a few seconds. Then he looked up and said, "*Yes*, I did. A *few* years ago. Everybody in the firm *was* doing it."

"Did you get pretty good at it?" Oscar was running his finger down one of the pieces of paper in the folder as he asked the question.

"*Look* at me, Mr. Quesana." He gestured to his fat body with the open fingers of both hands. "Do *you* think I was good at it?"

It was disarming enough that it brought a small group chuckle from the Blob. Oscar laughed, too, of course. He had to. Then he asked, "Well, how much proficiency *did* you achieve?"

"I *was* only okay at it. That's how I'd *put* it."

"Did you learn how to bring somebody down by kicking them in the front of the ankle?"

Stewart's eyes moved again to the folder. He hesitated. Then he said, "Yes."

"Did Simon Rafer take karate lessons with you?"

"Yes."

"So as far as you know, he could have struck back at an attacker with, say, a palm strike, right?"

"Objection!" Benitez said. "That question calls for rank speculation. There's no basis whatever for this witness to know what the victim was capable or not capable of doing."

"The question I asked him was 'as far as he knew,'" Oscar said. "If he doesn't know enough to answer, he can say so. He's a smart cookie, you know."

"Overruled," Judge Gilmore said. "Go ahead and answer, Mr. Broder."

Stewart chose a very careful answer. "He might *have* been able *to*."

Oscar gripped the sides of the podium with both hands, leaned forward, and said, very slowly, "Do you have any bruises on *your* body, Mr. Broder?"

"Ob—" Benitez started to say. But Stewart was too quick with his answer, which cut off Benitez's objection.

"No," Stewart said.

Benitez was apparently satisfied with Stewart's answer, because he didn't move to strike the answer. For my part, I was annoyed that Stewart had answered in only one word. I couldn't detect if he was lying in one-word answers.

"Your Honor," Oscar said, "I request that the court conduct an in-chambers proceeding in which Mr. Broder is required to remove his shirt."

Benitez got up, presumably ready to launch some furious objection. The judge made it unnecessary. "I think not, Mr. Quesana," she said. "We'll just add that request to our list for our chambers discussion. Do you have anything else?"

"Let me look at my notes a moment, Your Honor."

As Oscar paged through his notes, taking his time, I was overcome with a feeling of utter hopelessness. Oscar had done a great job. He had opened up a lot of things. It would all make great press. But by the standards of evidence, it had gone nowhere persuasive. When Benitez got around to putting into evidence the e-mails between me and Simon about the coin, the elevator access records, and the blood analysis, I was going to be bound over to be tried for first degree murder.

I assumed Jenna had been thinking the same thing, because she'd been very quiet. Suddenly, I heard her say, under her breath, "Tea bag. Bruises. Shit." I turned toward her and watched her begin to rummage in her giant purse again.

After a moment of rummaging, Jenna pulled out the coin book we had found in the secret compartment in Stewart's office. Jenna put the book down on the table, went back into her purse, and appeared to manipulate something that was hidden inside. Then she pulled her hands back out and stuffed a lump of some kind into her jacket pocket. I couldn't see what it was.

Jenna stood up, walked over to the podium, and whispered something in Oscar's ear.

"Your Honor," Oscar said, "there is one more thing, possibly. But I need to consult with Ms. James about it. If I could be permitted just a moment to do that, I think it would save us a lot of time."

"Okay," Judge Gilmore said.

Oscar and Jenna walked back to our table, stood there, and whispered to each other. I couldn't hear what they said, although Oscar seemed to shake his head in the negative a lot. Finally, he shrugged in what seemed a gesture of acquiescence and walked back to the podium.

"Your Honor, there is one more thing. It's very brief, but it's something Ms. James is much more familiar with than I am. I would appreciate it if the court would permit Ms. James to question the witness about this one small area. It will save time."

"Any objection, Mr. Benitez?" the judge asked.

"No, not at all," Benitez said, with the cheery air of someone deigning to grant a last request by the condemned for an extra scoop of ice cream.

CHAPTER 58

Jenna picked the book up and made her way to the podium.

"Your Honor, I would like to have marked as Defendant's next exhibit in order—I think it's number 99—a book titled *Coins of the Roman Republic in the British Museum, Volume III.*, by H.A. Grueber."

"Can you spell the proper name?" the court reporter asked.

"Of course," Jenna said, "it's G-R-U-E-B-E-R." She walked over to the prosecution table and, as is customary, handed the book to Benitez, who looked at it without much curiosity and handed it back to her.

"Your Honor, may I approach the clerk to have it marked?"

"Yes, you may," the judge said.

Jenna walked up to the clerk's desk, where the clerk duly marked it and handed it up to the judge to look at, saying, "It will be Defendant's 99." Judge Gilmore looked at it briefly, then handed it back down to the clerk, who handed it back to Jenna.

"Your Honor, if I might stay here to question the witness? It will be easier, since I have some things in the book to point out to him. I apologize for not having made advance copies of the page I'm going to refer to. We'll make copies of the relevant page for distribution after the hearing."

"That will be fine," the judge said.

"If Mr. Benitez wants to," Jenna said, "he can come and look over my shoulder at the page while I question the witness about it."

"That's okay," Benitez said. "I'll see it later." He put his hands behind his head and stretched and yawned, like a baseball team manager waiting for the last strike of the last out at the bottom of the ninth, with his team ahead twenty to two.

Jenna walked over, stood directly beside the witness stand, and handed the book to Stewart. "The record should reflect that I have handed the witness a copy of Defendant's Exhibit 99. Mr. Broder, are you familiar with that book?"

"Yes," Stewart said, "I *am*."

"How did you become familiar with it?"

"I collect *ancient* coins, and it's a *standard* work in the field."

"Is this your personal copy?"

"I don't *think* so."

"After Simon Rafer bought the Ides from Mr. Tarza, did you go over to Mr. Rafer's condo to look at it?"

"Yes."

"Okay, then. Let me point out a particular coin entry in this book to you, Mr. Broder," Jenna said, and moved to the side of the witness stand. She leafed through some pages until she got to the one she wanted. "I've now opened the book to a page in the back labeled Plate 72 and placed it in front of the witness. Do you see entry Number 21 there, Mr. Broder?"

"Yes."

"Does that appear to be a photo of the exact same coin you examined at Mr. Rafer's condo?"

Stewart bent over the book to get a better look at the postage stamp-sized image on the page. Then he turned toward her, head still bent, with a quizzical look on his face. "It doesn't look anything like it."

"Are you still sure you don't have any bruises on you?" Jenna said.

"Objection!" Benitez dropped his arms from behind his head and was on his feet.

"Ms. James! I ruled this out of bounds!" Judge Gilmore said it almost simultaneously with Benitez.

As they were objecting, Jenna pulled the lump from her jacket pocket, which I could finally see was a wad of tissue soaked with some kind of lotion. She grabbed the back of Stewart's head with her left hand, and with her right, wiped the tissue hard across his left eye socket and cheek. Then did it again.

Stewart clamped his hand over the left side of his face. I heard a distinct click in the back of the courtroom and turned to see Deputy Green, standing, gun drawn. The click I had heard was the safety coming off.

"What is the meaning of this, Counsel?" Judge Gilmore asked.

"Your Honor, I request that Mr. Broder be instructed to take his hand away from his face. Then the meaning will be clear. If it's not, you can jail me for contempt."

I waited for an objection from Benitez, but it never came. When I looked over to his table, he seemed as riveted on the drama as everyone else. He was still standing.

Judge Gilmore smiled the broadest smile I'd ever seen her smile. "You've got it, Counsel. Deputy Green, you can stand down. Mr. Broder, please take your hand away."

Stewart had by then straightened back up, his hand still pressed tightly against the left side of his face. He looked slowly around the courtroom, one-eyed, as if seeking some escape from his predicament. Finally, he took his hand away.

"Voila!" Jenna said.

And there it was. A large bruise, now in the late yellowing stage, long faded from its no doubt original black and blue.

"How did you get that bruise, Stewart?" Jenna asked.

As the question hung there, momentarily unanswered, the remaining Blob began to buzz and stir. More members got up, no doubt headed for the door, their chair bottoms banging as they rose.

Judge Gilmore looked out at the courtroom. "Ladies and Gentlemen, this is a court of law, not a sporting event where you can go out to buy peanuts and come back whenever you feel like it. The Court requires both decorum and silence. If you need to leave, leave now. But you will not be permitted back in until after our next break."

There was a moment of quiet as the members of the Blob made their choices. I turned around to look. Every one of them sat back down, trading the phoned-in scoop for what might come next. Silence returned to the room.

"Deputy Green," the judge said, "seal the courtroom. Absolutely no one is to leave or enter until I say so. No one."

Green moved to the right side of the courtroom doors and stood next to them, gun holstered, but with the holster rather plainly unbuckled. He folded his arms over his chest.

"Now, Mr. Broder," the judge said, "I think the question was, 'How did you get that bruise?'"

"I don't really remember," Stewart said. "I think maybe I ran into a door or something last month."

Jenna was still standing next to the witness box. She bent in closer to Stewart. "Come off it, Stewart. Didn't you get that bruise when Simon Rafer hit you in the eye socket with a palm strike as you were about to stab him? And didn't you then trip him with an ankle blow, stand over him, and stab him in the back when he was down? Holding the blade in both hands and driving it in with the tip angled towards his feet?"

I waited for an objection from Benitez, but it didn't come.

Stewart didn't answer at first. Then his eyes began to fill with tears, washing away more layers of makeup, exposing even more of the bruise, which covered much of the left side of his face. He finally turned to Jenna.

"It wasn't just *me*." He raised his hand and pointed towards the very back.

As I started to rotate my body to follow his pointing finger I heard a sudden scuffling noise at the back of the courtroom, followed almost instantly by the crack of a gunshot. I finished turning just in time to see Spritz slide slowly down the courtroom doors, coming to rest in a sitting position, clutching his right shoulder. Deputy Green towered over him, smoking gun literally in hand.

"You asshole," Spritz said through a groan, "You didn't have to do that."

I would have expected Judge Gilmore to look at least startled. Instead, she just raised her eyebrows and said, "Deputy Green, was that absolutely required?"

Green frowned. And then looked around the crowd for possible support. Finding only blank faces, he said, "You told me nobody was to leave, Your Honor. You said it twice." He gestured toward Spritz. "He tried to."

Judge Gilmore seemed to be pondering Deputy Green's literalist logic when Daniel Boone suddenly jumped up from his seat, shouted, "I'm a doctor! Let me through!" and rushed toward Spritz as the people in his row of seats rose to let him pass.

As Boone reached Spritz, Deputy Green just stood there. Perhaps he had learned something about Boone down in the lockup that we had missed. Or perhaps he felt a newfound need to think carefully before shooting again.

Boone bent down and, using two hands, ripped open Spritz's now blood-soaked sport shirt, popping the buttons. Spritz wasn't wearing an undershirt, and I could immediately see a gaping exit wound on the front of his right shoulder. The bullet had apparently entered from behind, the force of the impact spinning him around to face us.

I could also see a large, yellowing bruise on the left side of his chest, just above the nipple. Which was odd, because Boone hadn't said anything about Spritz even being there. Maybe he had been lurking in the reception area, unseen by Boone as he rushed out. In any case, it must have hurt like hell when whoever it was—Simon probably—landed that blow on Spritz's chest.

Boone tore off a piece of Spritz's shirt and pushed it into the wound to staunch the bleeding. Deputy Green stood beside him, gun still raised, alert.

Judge Gilmore looked around, surveying her courtroom with remarkable aplomb. She turned to her clerk. "Call 911 and get an ambulance for Detective Spritz. Deputy Green, you can holster your weapon."

I saw Deputy Green frisking Spritz as Boone worked on him, then handcuffing him despite his wound, painful as that must have been.

Then she turned to Stewart. "Mr. Broder, it appears you lied, at the very least, about not having any bruises."

She looked out at Spritz. "And it appears that you, too, Detective Spritz, have some explaining to do."

"I'm not saying anything until I have a lawyer," Spritz said, still propped up with his back against the doors, "Doctor" Boone still working on him.

"No problem, Detective," Judge Gilmore said. "Deputy, before they take the detective off to the hospital, read him his rights. After he's treated and booked into the jail ward, he can use his phone call to get himself a lawyer."

Green was already reading Spritz his rights as the judge spoke.

She turned again to Stewart. "Mr. Broder, I think you'll be wanting a lawyer, too. You're under arrest for perjury." She gestured to Green, who, having finished with Spritz, was heading towards Stewart, holding another pair of handcuffs ready.

She stood up. "We're adjourned." Then she looked out at the Blob. "You're free to go now. Please try not to bump Detective Spritz on your way out." She turned to leave the bench, and her clerk and court reporter quickly followed. Some members of the Blob rushed out, stepping around Spritz, who by then had slid to a prone position on the floor.

A few minutes later, a paramedic crew showed up, hooked Spritz up to an IV, and placed him on a gurney. Boone hovered around him, giving orders to the paramedics, while the part of the Blob that had stayed surged around them, shouting questions. Stewart continued to sit awkwardly on the witness stand, his hands cuffed behind him, frozen in place.

Jenna was packing up her stuff. None of us had said anything at all. I think we were all in shock. Finally, Jenna spoke.

"Looks like there was a Christmas ham in the bathtub after all," she said.

"Yeah," Oscar said, "I guess so. Congratulations."

"Thanks, Oscar."

"Want to join my law firm?" he asked her.

"We can talk about it," Jenna said. "But maybe you should join *mine*."

I was not up to banter. All I could manage was, "Let's get out of here."

We got up and headed out. At the back of the courtroom, I had to sidestep Spritz's gurney to get through the doors. As I stepped around the gurney, I heard Spritz mutter something to me. I couldn't make out what he said. I didn't ask him to repeat it, and I didn't look back.

EPILOGUE

———

I had the distinct pleasure, months later, of watching the murder trials of both Spritz and Stewart. As a spectator.

First I watched the trial of Spritz. Jenna did a brilliant job of defending him. That trial ended halfway through, though, when Jenna persuaded Spritz to turn state's evidence against Stewart. Which earned him a plea deal for first-degree manslaughter—six years with good behavior.

Then I watched Stewart's trials. There were two. One for killing Simon and one for killing Harry.

I learned a lot from listening to Spritz rat him out. I learned that it was Stewart and Harry who had cooked up the idea to make copies of my original Ides and then sell them. Not so much for profit, I was given to understand, as for the sheer fun of screwing people.

It seems that after Simon got my Ides, he entrusted Harry to take it to the photographer to be photographed for his catalogue. Harry had it photographed all right, but then arranged to send it to Shanghai to be copied by an expert forger who worked with Chen. To cover their butts in case they were caught, they used the firm's DHL number, charged to me personally, to send it. And they used Spritz, Harry's old friend from the days of Harry's covered-up drug arrest, as the courier to bring back the copies. In exchange for handling that and other logistics, he was going to get a cut and retire. For helping later with the cover-up and the framing of me, he had apparently asked for a still larger share.

When the copies of the Ides came back, Harry and Stewart had an idea that turned out to be too smart by half. They persuaded Simon he ought to get an appraisal of the Ides from Serappo. Harry and Stewart then sent Serappo one of their copies to appraise instead of the original. They figured if the copy could pass muster with him, their fakes were going to sail through any challenges to their authenticity. Unfortunately, the copy didn't pass Serappo's muster, and that's when it all began to fall apart.

At that point, the original was still in Shanghai, and it was too late to hide Serappo's appraisal of the fake from Simon. Initially, Simon believed it was me who had cheated him. Then, a week before the murder, he somehow figured out what had really happened and was threatening to turn them all over to the police. So it turned out that Stewart had testified truthfully about the reason Simon was killed. It's just that he and Harry did it instead of me. With Spritz looking on in order to, in his words, "make sure those amateurs planted the evidence"—against me—"properly."

In his trials, Stewart didn't make out as well as Spritz had. Stewart was tried for Harry's murder as a special circumstance. Killing a witness. He's now on death row. The DA's theory of the case was that Stewart got worried they were going to be caught and so killed Harry as the first step in a plan to get rid of all the witnesses to Simon's murder, one by one.

My conversation with Spritz at the DownUnder, where he had tried to rat out Harry, would probably have nailed Spritz as a co-conspirator in a plot to murder Harry. But no one ever called me as a witness.

As for the other conspirators, Harry was dead, and Susan Apacha, who had had only a small role in the thing, had turned state's evidence, too. She got off with only two years. A real plus was the discovery, during a "routine" federal tax audit of the firm and certain of its senior partners, that Caroline Thorpe—the interim managing partner who had tried to get me fired—had filed falsified personal tax returns. She was charged with tax evasion, got two years, and was disbarred. Which made it a tad difficult for her to continue as the firm's managing partner.

As for me, I took a long vacation in France, visited an old girlfriend there, and then returned to the firm. I even got my old office back. And since there weren't any other grey hairs around who could do it, I agreed to be the managing partner again. But only for a year. Or so I have told them. My first task had been to stop the exodus of lawyers who thought the firm's reputation was going to suffer from the whole thing. With the help of a good P.R. firm, we managed to turn it into a plus to get the firm more national name recognition, and the hemorrhage of lawyers stopped.

Today was a special day, though. After the trials were over, Jenna had been invited to rejoin the firm. As a partner. We had just had a small, late-afternoon firm party to celebrate her return, and the two of us were in my office for a private celebration. It was really the first time we'd had any serious one-on-one time together since the trials began.

It was almost five o'clock. Jenna was standing by the window, watching the sun splash its glow on the mountains as it set. She turned to face me.

"Robert, did you ever ask Oscar if he would come to M&M and join us in opening our criminal defense department?"

"Yes, I did."

"What did he say?"

"He said it was too high up."

We both laughed.

"Even without him, it's time for a toast," I said. I poured two glasses of *Cristal*, handed one to Jenna and raised my glass.

"To a great career for you," I said.

"And to a great managing partnership for you, Robert. Second time around."

We clinked glasses and drank down the contents.

Jenna put her glass down on the small coffee table, next to the silver *tetradrachm of Athens* in its Lucite cube. She picked up the cube and turned it in her hand. "This is such a nice way to display things," she said. She put the cube back down.

"Jenna," I said, "there are some things I've been wanting to ask you."

"Such as?"

"Was there ever any drug dealing in the firm?"

"Nope."

"None at all?"

"None at all."

"Well, why did Harry go to the Big Island then?"

"He went there every year in December. Had an interest in a time share there. Something he started when he retired."

"Oh. So they were just scamming me about the drugs, trying to throw me off?"

"Something like that. But don't feel bad about it. Your meeting with Spritz in the bar is what led to our learning about the tea bag and got me to thinking about the alternate uses of tea bags."

"Okay. Another question then. Did you ever learn from Spritz what Harry and Stewart were really planning to do with the fake Ides?"

"Just sell them, so far as I know."

"That's never made any sense to me," I said.

"Why not?"

"You couldn't move seven or eight newly discovered Ides. Everyone would want to know where they came from, and there's no logical explanation."

"So what's your theory, Robert?"

"Remember that Stewart went to Macedonia on an archaeological tour?"

"Sure," she said. "But I never made anything of it."

"I think they were planning some kind of fake discovery of a hoard of Ides. Just like the Black Sea Hoard."

She shrugged. "Could be. I wouldn't put it past those guys. But what would that get them? I thought you couldn't move discoveries like that out of the country, that they'd belong to the Macedonian government."

"If they could believably fake finding the hoard, it would get them on the cover of *Coin World.* They'd be famous in certain circles."

Just then, Gwen popped her head in. "Your visitor is here, Mr. Tarza."

"Send him in," I said.

"Who is it?" Jenna asked.

"You'll see."

And then Serappo Prodiglia walked through the door.

"Good afternoon, Robert," He reached out and shook my hand, then turned to Jenna. "Ah, the courier," he said. "I don't believe I ever learned your name, Miss . . ." He cocked his head, as if waiting to learn her identity.

Jenna smiled, almost shyly, and extended her hand. "Jenna James. Nice to see you again."

Serappo picked up her hand and kissed it in the European manner. "The pleasure is mine," he said.

"Well," I said, "I assume you came for something."

"Indeed, I did," Serappo said.

I went to my desk drawer, opened it, and took out the real Ides, which I had placed in a small glassine envelope. Simon's estate had retrieved the original from China, and I had bought it back from the estate for the same $500,000 Simon had paid me for it. I handed it to Serappo. "Here it is," I said.

He took it from me, removed it gently from its envelope, and, holding it carefully between thumb and forefinger, lifted it up to the light. He gazed at it for a long time with what can only be called a beatific smile.

"I really own it," he said. "Finally. Thank you, Robert, for honoring your contract. And for fulfilling an old man's wish. I know you could have sold it for much more to someone else. It's doubly infamous now, and that adds value."

"You're welcome," I said.

"I trust that the money I wired to your bank account was received."

"Yes, it was."

"May I ask," Jenna said, "what you are going to do with the Ides?"

"Well, Miss James, in the manner of coin collectors everywhere, I will look at it a lot at first. Then I will no doubt place it in a long, red cardboard box, and put the box on a shelf. I doubt I shall ever sell it, though. When I pass on, the Ides will move to other hands, continuing on its own journey."

"That's quite romantic," Jenna said.

"Yes, I suppose in a way it is," he said.

"Serappo, will you join us for some champagne?" I asked.

"Thank you, Robert, but I'm afraid I must decline. I came only to pick up the coin, and my flight back leaves shortly."

"All right," I said. "Have a safe flight."

He shook each of our hands, said, "Adieu, my young friends," and left.

"An intriguing man," Jenna said.

"Yes, he is. But I'm glad he has gone and taken the Ides with him. I needed to be rid of it. It ends it."

"I can see that," she said.

"And now that it's over-over, Jenna," I said, "I have a little end-of-the-case thank-you present for you. A souvenir of a puzzle you solved."

I went back to my desk, opened the large bottom drawer, and pulled out a small box wrapped in red paper. I handed it to her.

"Oh, I love presents!" she said.

She unwrapped it and held it up. "Oh my God, a tea bag in a Lucite cube. How perfect! Thank you!" She walked over and gave me a kiss on the cheek. "Didn't work to fix Stewart's shiner, but I'll keep it nearby in case I ever get one myself."

"Good. You never know what can happen to you in a law firm. But you know, Jenna, there was one other puzzle I never did solve."

"Which one was that, Robert?"

"Who the second woman was in the firm that night, the one that Boone saw."

Jenna shrugged. "I don't think there was one, Robert. At least Spritz and Susan Apacha swore there wasn't. And Boone, well, you know, he has a screw loose a bit."

"I guess we'll never know for sure, then," I said.

She leveled a gaze at me—half way between 'oh, brother, here we go again' and 'I am so sad.'

"You think it was me, don't you?"

"The thought has crossed my mind. I admit it. But I figure if it had been you, Stewart would have ratted you out while trying to trade it for something."

"Right. Like life in prison instead of death by injection."

"Makes sense to me. What say we forget about it and have some more champagne?"

"I'd love some, Robert."

I refilled her glass, and then mine.

Eventually, we finished the bottle.

THE END

Acknowledgments

———

Many friends, acquaintances and colleagues have been kind enough to read and comment on the manuscript as it progressed, and I am enormously grateful to each of them. A particular note of thanks is due those who read and critiqued earlier drafts. Without their comments, suggestions, encouragement and support, *Death on a High Floor* would still lie unfinished on my desk. They include my son, Joe Rosenberg, and Holly D'Lane Miller, Melanie and Doug Chancellor, Roland Miller, Deanna Wilcox, Lauren Gwin, Amy Huggins, Alyssa Heisten, Jill and John Bauman, Lindsay Pedder, Pamela Pedder, Lou Pedder, Dale Franklin, Nicole Gregory, Julie Dermansky, Roger Chittum, Linda Brown, Annye Camara, Patricia and Ned Wright, Kelly Guzman, Helen Brandt, Maxine Nunes, Abigail Rose Solomon, Ira Zuckerman, Joyce Mendlin, Janey Place, Tom and Juanita Ringer, Nancy Boyarsky, Becky Novelli, Harold Lee, Maureen Gustafson, Michael Asimow, Hannah Lee Morhman, Tara Palty, Berry Silverman, Wendy Perkins, Sally Daily, Tom Stromberg, Estelle Rogers, Jack Walker, Susan Futterman, Julia Chen, Marilyn Katz, William Wright, Diana Wright, Doreen Weisenhaus, Dana Finkey Barbeau, Kelty Logan, Jerry Seelig, Mary Lane Leslie, Carol Lucas, Anne Kenney, Arvin Brown, Ellen Fulton, Fred Golan, Elaine Jarvik, Tyson Butler, Liz Seltzer-Lang, Christina Rea, Susan Goodrich, Chris Sorgi, Nancy Cohen, Christine Ong, Elaine Katz, Brinton Rowdybush, Beth Greenberg, Zdravka Tzankova, Claire Abrams, and Marty Beech. I want in addition to thank my terrific publishing consultant, April Hamilton, whose advice has been invaluable, as well as my excellent proof reader, Annie Kim. Any errors that may remain in the text, however, are mine alone, and not Annie's.

15498491R00241

Made in the USA
Charleston, SC
06 November 2012